Survival

By

Summer Paige

Important Notice

As with any darker romance book, this novel comes with some heavy content warnings. Please ensure you are in the right headspace to engage with this content before entering into Luca and Isabella's story.

Child abuse, domestic abuse, mentions of past suicidal ideations and attempts, PTSD nightmares and related traits, abuse recovery, on page sexual assault, off page rape, acts of modern day slavery, scars, kidnapping, strangulation, torture in various methods, murder, mentions of starvation, bodily fluids, graphic violence and gore, on page graphic murders, bleeding out, grieving parents, siblings and friends, burning as a form of torture and murder, confinement, controlling behaviour, mental health representation including but not limited to grief, anxiety, shame, shock and depression. Mafia themes, brief mentions of miscarriage, guns and knives, alcohol consumption, explicit sexual situations, strong language and crabs. The sea kind, not sexual.

Whilst the situations written in this book are purely fictional, some of these topics are not. If you are experiencing anything similar to Isabella's story or struggling with your mental health, please seek help.

You are wanted.

You are loved.

You are important.

Dedication.

To those who lose themselves in books when reality is too tough.

You are not alone.

Brighter days are coming.

Playlist

Game of Survival - Ruelle

Keep Holding On - Avril Lavigne

Troubled Waters - Alex Warren

Darkest Hour - Andrea Russett

Man! I Feel Like A Woman! - Shania Twain

WONDERLAND - Neoni

deserve - Jake Clark

Follow You Anywhere - fawlin, Bangers Only

Greener - Taylor Acorn

Praying - Kesha

She - Jake Scott

BLOSSOM - RØRY

Right - Morgan St. Jean

Bad - Royal Deluxe

Goddess - Xana

I Did Something Bad - Taylor Swift

It's Always Been You - Caleb Hearn

Part One.

Chapter One

What. The. Fuck.

LUCA

The very second Lorenzo closed the door behind him, I could hear Penelope pulling herself free of his grip and running down the hallway. I'm more than a little insulted that she'd snarled at my attempt to distract her. Sometimes I fear she gets the lack of humour from her father, which sets her up for a pretty boring life, really.

The past four years have both gone by in a flash and yet dragged so slowly. It's like we all blinked and we've gone from Tori telling us she's pregnant whilst covered in her father's blood, to having a walking, talking, spoiled rotten, pile of attitude. I'm so glad I've been here for every step of the way, though pregnant Astoria is something I wish to avoid for the rest of eternity.

I sit up slowly after tying the laces of the fancy pants shoes Lorenzo had demanded I wear today. My suggestion of wearing something that didn't make my toes look like they were six inches longer than was realistic had been met by a more than unimpressed glare. Tori just rolled her eyes and said I could wear these or clown shoes and honestly, it was a pretty tight choice. At least the clown shoes would have been entertaining.

But, there wasn't a chance I was going to take away any attention from those two today. They'd been through a lot to get here. Astoria specifically. I can't say I'm not glad I let her go the first night we met. It sent Lorenzo into a spiral that led to him becoming obsessed with her, and even now, some things don't change. What has changed though, is Lorenzo's entire personality.

Long gone is the miserable ass that sits in the shadows and glares at everyone. Now he sits at the table and glares at everyone except his girls. Pops being my little 'bestie', as Tori calls it, means I am entirely immune to his shit, though. She just stomps her little feet up to him and demands he be nice whilst we both wear matching tiaras and sip 'tea' from her tiny china set.

Three quick knocks at the door have me looking over my shoulder while I make a fourth attempt to tie my tie, before giving up and leaving it hanging around my neck. Astoria can sort it out before I walk her down the aisle, because I cannot for the life of me remember how she showed me to do it, despite her trying no less than thirty times over the past month.

It only takes eight steps for me to pull the door open, and I can only surmise that the girl standing in a navy blue dress before me is a figment of my imagination.

She drops her hands from where she's picking at her nails, eyes wide, the corner of her painted pink bottom lip tugged between her teeth.

"Is Enzo here?" I blink, tipping my head at her voice. "Luca? Hello?" Bella steps forward, waves her hand at me. "Come on, it's urgent."

I'm either going insane or someone who is supposed to have been dead for the past fourteen years has suddenly materialized from thin air. If it is the latter, there's a hell of a lot of crap that needs to be worked out right now, and her standing in the hallway isn't going to make matters any better. Wrapping my hand around her wrist, I pull her into the room before anyone else sees her.

The door slams shut behind us as I kick it closed, causing the walls of the freshly renovated hotel to shake.

"Isabella?"

"Yeah?" She looks around the room then back to me, standing halfway across the room and still staring at her in complete shock with a slightly slack jaw. "Oh. Supposed to be dead. Right. Um. We can cover that later. I need to find Enzo."

"He's a little preoc- what the fuck are you doing here?! You're- you. Dead. You're supposed to be dead. There was a funeral. You have a headstone. A grave."

"Luca, come on, I really need you to focus here." Bella runs a hand through her hair, letting out a heavy sigh as she does. "Petrovich is planning to ambush this whole thing. We're kind of on a time limit to stop this right now. I know this is a lot to process but-"

"Wait. How do you know that-" My question doesn't need finishing. The look she gives me might as well write the answer out in black and white. It's a mixture of sadness and anger and a whole tonne of other emotions, but it's exactly what I need to know. That asshole has something to do with her being gone for all this time. Lorenzo's not going to end up getting married today if he knows that. He'll hunt down every member of that family and tear them all limb from limb. "Okay. Shit. Okay. Um. Details."

Bella word vomits all the information she has as I pull my phone out of my pocket and call Nicky and Carlos. The four of us take a matter of minutes to form a plan that feels so perfectly organized and yet chaotic.

The intention is for Tori and Lorenzo to not find out about this. To not know about the danger that's trying to destroy a day they have both put their heart and soul into. This day has to be perfect for them. It has to go to plan. They deserve to have the big wedding they want, to have a celebration that isn't soaked in blood and death, and decay. Both of their lives are coated in the stuff, and if I can give them anything that shows them how much I appreciate them, today is the one day I can give them.

No, today is going to go perfectly for them both, I simply won't allow fucking Petrovich to ruin it for them.

The phone call lasts all of five minutes, and all I can do is pray that the boys can get on with what they need to. As I put my phone away, Bella is standing a few feet away, pulling gently at her lips nervously as she watches me. We stare at each other for a handful of seconds, and I use the time to soak it in.

She's so much older. We both are. I mean, obviously. It's been fourteen years. She was a kid when I last saw her. Running around the farm back home in a pastel yellow summer dress. If I'd known that her going home later that week would end how it did, I wouldn't have let them. Any of them. But especially Bella.

She looks good. I mean, a little thin. A touch on the grey side but not worryingly so, considering she's just turned up to save her brother's wedding day and family from being destroyed. She's short, which maybe I'll be taking the piss out of her for when this is a little less weird. Her hair is a little curly right now. Not how it used to be. It's smooth, like she's done it herself, rather than her natural crazy curls that used to be all over the place. Her eyes are still the same bright baby blue, though.

"Luca?"

"Si, Amore?" Bella blinks, eyes narrowing for a second like I was talking nonsense. She swallows, rolling her lips together. Finally, her arms drop from being crossed around her waist, only for her to wipe her palms carefully down the smooth fabric of her dress.

"Where is Enzo?"

"Oh! He went to take Pops to see Tori. We should go find them before he spots you in the crowd and freaks out. You are staying, right? For the wedding?" Taking off towards the door, I'm suddenly very aware that Isabella isn't here to stay in a room. She is here to see her brother get married, and I am harbouring her in a room, to myself.

"Uh - I - yeah, I can stay for the ceremony."

"Got somewhere else to be, Bella?" She doesn't answer. Just steps out of the room and into the hall, allowing me to close and lock the door behind her. It's a solid few uncomfortable seconds of silence before I open my mouth again, eager to make her feel as comfortable as possible. "You are going to love Tori. She's hilarious."

"I've met her before."

"You know her?" My head snaps in her direction as we turn another corner. Bella just nods and the closer we get, the more I can see the anxiety beginning to write itself across her face.

"I used to work for her dad." I almost stop walking. Almost turn around to face her to work out what the hell that means. Worked for her dad? How-

"Daddy! I found Uncle Luca! He looks mad." Lorenzo appears in the doorway as I try to work out a reason as to why Bella is here that isn't because someone is going to try to destroy his day. I watch as he urges Penelope back behind him and closer to the door and Astoria appears in the doorway with her hands protectively on her daughter's shoulders, still left with no reasonable explanation that won't ruin their day.

"Lorenzo. I uh-" What do I even say? Hey, so I know we've spent fourteen years thinking your entire family is dead, but surprise, your sister is here to stop you being killed? Sure. Great start to a wedding day and a top-grade A way of traumatising Pops.

"Spit it out, Luca." With a short sigh and no solid excuse as to why Bella is here, I step to the side and let him set eyes on his little sister for the first time in almost a decade and half.

He stares and a beat passes before he practically whispers, "Isabella?"

"What, you didn't think I would miss my big brother's wedding, did you?" He stares at her harder, searches her face before his glare softens and he wraps her in a heartbreaking hug. He lets her go a few seconds later, sets her feet on the floor and proceeds to check her over. "I'm fine, Enzo."

"I-" he starts, but just shakes his head and wraps her up again.

"Mummy? Who's that?" Penelope's voice seems to be the one thing that breaks Lorenzo out of his shock, and out of all the years I've known this man, this is the first time I have ever seen his eyes filled with tears.

"Uh, Bella, this- these are-" Enzo clears his throat, straightens his back and tries again. "My daughter Penelope, and my wife-to-be, Astoria."

"Pleased to meet you." Tori smiles and extends her hand, but I can see it. The glint in her eye that says she doesn't trust Bella.

It's not until me and her are completely alone half an hour later, her in her wedding gown just a few feet away from her officially becoming family, that she can openly admit it to me.

"I know her," Tori says, "her name's Anastasia. Not Isabella."

"It's Bella, Tor. Trust me."

"She worked-"

"For your dad. I know. Look, there's a reason she's here, and I don't want to freak you out right now because it is completely under control, plus I haven't had the chance to get much info myself yet. What I do know is that she turned up looking for Lorenzo, and Petrovich has had her this whole time. I wouldn't put it past that pile of shit to have forced her to work for your dad under an alias. I grew up with Isabella, Tori, I'd recognise her anywhere, and that is Bella."

"Wait. Petrovich?" Tori tightens her grip on my arm, turning to look up at me as the music begins to play out, signalling that we're seconds away from walking down the aisle.

"Not now, Tor. I've got it under control. You trust me, right?"

"If anything happens-"

"You'll redecorate the room with my intestines? Or is this more a ruin my life irrevocably situation?"

"Oh, this is so much worse than those threats. If this goes wrong, Luca, if anyone I love gets harmed because I trusted you, I won't second guess watching you burn alive. Got it?"

"Message received, Menace. Now, let's get you married, huh?"

Chapter Two

Surrounded by familiar strangers.
ISABELLA

With only a matter of hours to get my head around the fact that Enzo wasn't dead, never mind the reality that he was marrying fucking Russell Bardot's daughter, I'd not thought this through enough to have a plan; I barely had a '*P*. Astoria had always been super nice to everyone, so I didn't have a single bad word to say about the woman. Her father was a whole other matter. He's not here today though, so I guess that's a plus. I'd be totally screwed if he was.

Sitting here at a cluttered dinner table in the corner of the room, I can't help hoping that maybe if I think about it hard enough, I'll suddenly develop the ability to disappear into the walls. Fade into the background and not be stared at. I've managed to spend the past three hours avoiding everyone's questions. Lied through my teeth to familiar strangers. People whose faces and names I remember, but their relationship to me and the reality is too fuzzy. I'm unsure if digging that far back into my brain is a good idea. I've been telling people I'm someone Tori used to work with and not that I'm *me*.

Luca's been talking to the men standing on all the exits and entrances, clearly handing out instructions before taking calls. He said that he's got guys on this and Nicky (I think that was his name) seemed like he knew what he was doing with the information I gave them, but if this doesn't go to plan, one of two things can happen.

The first is that Feliks and whoever else turn up here, and the past fourteen years I've spent believing everyone is dead will finally no longer be a made-up fantasy; it'll be real life.

The second is that Feliks notices something has gone wrong, heads home early, and realises I'm not where I'm supposed to be. Then I might as well be dead, because there is absolutely no chance I won't be shipped halfway across the world and back into Tomas' grimy hands.

To be able to get in unnoticed, I had to play dress up. Act the part of a wedding guest at a wedding, and no one bats an eyelid when you walk into the huge hotel. Staying for the wedding wasn't planned out. It was supposed to be a get in, get out thing. Disappear again. It's better for everyone here that way. Me too.

It feels weird. Watching Enzo smiling as he dances with Penelope on the dance floor. Spending your whole life being told your entire family were slaughtered, only to find out on the off chance they are not is bewildering.

If I hadn't woken up early yesterday morning. If I'd decided to work in my room or to have a long bath or read instead of going down to the gym, I'd have never overheard Feliks talking to Anton. I'd have never heard him saying '*Lorenzo Santoni is getting married and now's our chance to make sure she's the last of their bloodline*'.

I used to dream of moments like this. Of finding out he was alive too and him finding me and bringing me home. But with each passing year it became less likely, and by the time I hit fourteen, I gave up fighting it. Handed myself over to the Petrovichs entirely, and decided that survival was my only option. That hoping someone else could get me out of this was stupid. Anastasia has been playing the perfect Petrovich daughter ever since.

"You should be careful, Bella. Thinking too hard might burn your brain out." I lift my head up as Luca slowly pulls the chair out beside me and sinks himself down into it. All I can offer him is a tight smile before going back to watching my brother from across the busy room. "How are you?"

"Hm?" I snap my head back to Luca, who looks a mixture of amused and concerned. "Oh. I'm fine. Good. Yeah. You?"

"I'm not gonna lie, Bella, I've been better, but I've also been a hell of a lot worse." He shuffles in his seat. "Where have you been? What happened?"

"I don't think this is the place for this conversation."

"Amore, you've been gone fourteen years and then just randomly show up out of the blue. We could be actively bleeding out in the middle of the Mediterranean, in a leaky boat, and it would still be a good time to talk about this. If you want to talk about this tomorrow, that's fine. I've got someone clearing a room back at-"

"No." Luca blinks as I try to straighten myself out. "I- um- I'm fine where I am. I only came to tell you about Feliks and whatever. I'm not here to intrude or anything."

"Intrude? Bella, you're not intruding. You're family. If you don't want to come home, fine. But tell me where you are so we can-"

"Uncle Luca?" Penelope tugs on Luca's arm. "Dance with me?"

"You were dancing with your dad, Pops."

"Daddy's boring. I want to dance with you. You're better."

"I'm just talking to Bella right now. Why don't you-"

"Auntie Isabella." My heart stammers as she looks up at me with a gentle smile. "That's what Daddy said I have to call you."

"You can call me Bella, if you want to."

"Bella means pretty in Italian." Penelope tips her head sideways. "You're very pretty."

"So are you. Very clever too, if you know Italian."

"Thanks. Daddy teaches me. He says when we go to Italy for our holidays that I have to speak Italian and no English, so we've been practising hard. I'm good at it." She turns back to Luca and scowls. "Dance."

"Not right now Pop-"

"No, Luca, it's all right. Go dance." He looks at me, shoulders relaxing a little. "I'm fine, we can catch up later."

"If I go, you'll still be here when I come back, right?" I smile brightly and nod, adding another line to my seemingly endless tally of lies. "Promise?"

"Cross my heart." Luca accepts our childhood guarantee of truth and rises from his spot beside me, taking the hand of an excited four-year-old before she drags him down to the dance floor.

Eventually, he looks relaxed enough for his attention to be completely on Penelope and it's only then that I stand up, gather anything that belongs to me and try to keep calm as I head out of one of the guarded side doors.

I don't want to go back. If staying with Enzo would be fine, if I knew that it wouldn't cause catastrophic bloodshed, I'd stay. I'd take Luca up on the offer to move in with my brother, and I'd live with the knowledge that Rurik Petrovich tried and failed to keep me from my family.

But the god's honest truth is that not going home would cause chaos. An entire collapse of the world as anyone knows it. Petrovich would seek me and Enzo out and slaughter any remaining family I have left. There's not a single drop of doubt in my brain that the punishment for betraying my 'family' would be a thousand times worse than anything they have ever done before this point, and that is not something I can risk.

So, until I have another option, my focus is on survival. And this time, not just my own. Everyone else's lives are in the palms of my hands now and I pray to every god, deity and natural power that has ever and will ever exist that I can continue to act as though I am a Petrovich, even when I hold the knowledge that I am no longer alone in the world.

Chapter Three

I promise, Papa.
ANASTASIA

Two hours of sweat and burning muscles that I've learned to ignore. My personal trainer down here changes so often that I don't even bother trying to remember their names any more. Today it was a new guy again. He spent the first five minutes shaking his head as he looked across my frail body, prodded at my bloating with the tip of his pen and scoffed when I told him I'd had a slice of wholemeal toast for breakfast.

Every new guy Rurik sends in here limits my food intake further and still pushes for more. At this point, I'm digesting less than half of a healthy number of calories per day, and I am downright sick to death of whatever concoctions continue to be put in bowls and served to me, whilst everyone else in this goddamn house eats like kings.

When I moved here after spending so long under Tomas' control back in Moscow, I realised the regulations Rurik had on me were better. That I was better off here than I had ever been with his enforcer back in Russia. That was five years ago now, and I can look in the mirror and see the ghost of myself that I am becoming. A skeleton with no ability or will to fight back.

I woke up in the middle of the night and caught myself in the mirror. The shadows hit all the sharp edges, and I think that was the realisation I needed to know this was all about the Petrovich family's aggressive control over every aspect of me.

They'd murdered my family, erased my existence from Earth and rebuilt me as their passive doll, Anastasia Petrovich. Any rebellion is met with brutal punishments. The remnants of which still cover my skin and infect my nightmares, as I fear they will until the day I die.

Today, I've been pushed exceptionally hard in the gym. Something about getting me ready for a husband I have to be 'prepared for'. Whatever the fuck that means.

"Anastasia," My blood cools to an icy minus sixty. Solidifies in my veins as an all too familiar voice demands my attention. I just want to vanish. To shower and sit in my room with my head in a book and forget that anything exists outside of it.

Feliks' dark eyes meet mine when I slowly turn around in the bright hallway. He's pissed. All tense muscles and furrowed brow as his eyes drag up my body slowly. Behind him, stands Anton. If it was me and him alone in this house, I'd kill myself. It'd be a better outcome than anything he'd try.

"You know Ana, we're not technically blood-related. Are we?"

"What do you mean?" I ask innocently, not buying into his sly way of trying to get me to slip up. All he needs is an excuse. He stalks forwards, quickly caging me in with my back against the door to my room.

"Well, I could do with a little, how do you say it? Relaxation." I could do it now. Bring my knee up to his balls with enough power to cripple him for a few minutes. Lock myself in my room and hide, try to break the locks on the windows. It'd be useless, even if I got away. He'd find me.

"You're my brother, Feliks."

"Am I really, though?" Feliks drops one hand off the wall, tugging at the hem of my tight-fitting gym tee. "I heard through rumours that you're pretty good on your knees, Ana. I'd love to stuff that dirty little mouth with-"

"Feliks." Another demand; this one makes him freeze, stand up straight and turn to face the deep echo. "What do you think you're doing?"

"Nothing, Father." He looks back at me, eyes me up and down and snarls before taking a step back. "Not with this whore, anyway, wouldn't want to catch whatever she's riddled with." He finishes his lovely compliment by spitting at me before walking off. Anton chuckles and I can see the way he smiles, so fucking proud of the shit they both pull on a day-to-day basis.

I exhale, close my eyes for a second before swiping my hand across my face to remove the droplets he's left there.

"Anastasia, my office." Uh-oh. If I had to choose between Feliks spewing his shit-for-brains insults or this, I'd choose death. My eyes tear through the hallway to Rurik standing at the corner leading to the rest of the house.

"I was just about to shower after my workout, Papa. Do you want to see me now?"

"Yes." He says, turns and disappears. Wonderful.

Won-der-ful.

The house is horrifyingly silent as I follow him down the maze of marble floor hallways and it doesn't end when I'm in Rurik's walnut wood-clad office. Everything is polished to a high shine. There, the greying man sits in his oversized leather chair, squiggles a few lines on some paper and then points at the chair I'm expected to sit in. Knowing better than arguing with the beast, I do as I'm told.

He's quiet for a few minutes, the papers on his desk taking all of his attention. When he eventually does look up at me, I have to remind myself that he is keeping me alive for a reason, and whatever that reason is, in his mind, it is valid. As long as I don't pose a threat to any of his plans, I will be fine.

"How was your night last night?"

"It was fine, Papa." He purses his lips and sits up straighter in the chair.

"I'm going to ask again, and this time I will remind you of the consequences for betraying me, Anastasia. Something I didn't think I needed to do any more." Rurik steeples his fingers. "How was your evening, Anastasia?"

"I went to the bookstore." He gives me a solid nod, and I know right off the bat, that was the answer he was expecting. The one he wanted me to give him.

"Why didn't you say that you went to the bookstore?"

"Because everyone was busy. It was the last time to pick up the book you bought me online, and I needed it to finish the series. I knew you would be upset about me going alone, but I was really careful and it wasn't long." He stares at me, so I stutter. "I'm- I'm sorry, Papa. I just really wanted that book. I parked in front of the store, put my hood up, got the book and came right back. I promise, Papa."

"I will send you back to Tomas if you're lying to me, Anastasia. All it would take is one call." I freeze, fear flooding my veins, and I can feel the way the colour drains from my face. "Do you want that? To go back to our home country for your punishment?"

"No, Papa." He nods once. "I'm sorry."

"Very well." He straightens. "But I will not allow your deceit to go unnoticed, Anastasia. I believe you have scared yourself, but I will not allow you to think you can do this again. I see everything in this house. Do you understand?"

"Yes, Papa."

"Good. You will go without food for the next four days as punishment for sneaking out. It is not safe for you out there. You will learn this the hard way. Go to your room and stay there until you are instructed to come down for dinner this evening. You can watch the rest of us eat whilst you think about your behaviour."

"Yes, Papa." I nod and slowly stand up, leaving the room in otherwise silence.

He likes to keep me teetering on the edge of life and death; it's a power trip. I'm thankful though, that this punishment is the best outcome after sneaking out to Enzo's wedding last night. Lord knows I've handled longer and worse conditions than four days of starvation. I'll just keep myself busy.

Chapter Four

I've got this. I can do this.
LUCA

If looks could kill, I'd be buried in pieces. Scattered across miles and miles of land after being brutally murdered and fed to the pigs. Too many broken bones to count, probably a brain injury, minimal blood left in my body.

"Liliana, can you take Pops upstairs, please?" Tori keeps her voice calm as they both glare at me from across the kitchen counter. Liliana doesn't question her. Just moves across the room from the sink, scoops Penelope off my lap and walks out of the room.

Up until now, I'd been glad Pops was up with her parents. I knew they wouldn't blow up about this if she was here. They did once, and it made her sob uncontrollably and refuse to go near her dad for two days. It broke his heart more than I think I've ever seen. From that day onwards they have both remained brutally silent in moments like this. I'm not sure which I prefer, honestly.

Lorenzo is frozen with his death glare aimed directly into my soul. Jaw tensed so hard I'm worried about his teeth cracking under the pressure, and I swear that the vein on his forehead is going to burst if he doesn't ease off soon.

"What do you mean, '*Isabella isn't here*?'" He grinds the words out of his mouth like stone on stone. He's trying his damned best to remain calm and I guess I'm grateful all the guns are locked away; that he's not currently armed.

"She left the wedding last night. Poppy dragged me to the dance floor; she promised me she'd be there when we were done, but I searched everywhere and she wasn't in the building. I checked the cameras, and she just walked out. Got in a cab and left. Tracked the cab, but it just went into town and dropped her off on a random street without any cameras." The glass in his hand cracks under the force he's squeezing it with. "I'm as pissed off about it as you are, Lorenzo."

"Oh, I can assure you, you are not." He slams the glass onto the counter with a force that makes the crack spread up to the rim, but not shatter. "Why the fuck do I even trust you with important shit, Luca? Time and time again you prove you can't do the fucking job you're told to and this time, you just what? Just let my sister walk out of my wedding? She's been fucking DEAD for fourteen years, and you let her just disappear again?" Tori steps closer to Lorenzo, trying to soothe him and bring him back down to a calmer level. It wasn't going to work. I completely understood why Lorenzo was continuing to rant at me about 'losing' Isabella.

I don't think he remembers how close Bella and I were before. Isabella was the closest person to my age that I was allowed to spend time with when she was visiting. From the moment she first visited when she was three and I was five, me and her were inseparable. She was the one that sat with me after my parents died. My life went on because of the support Bella gave me in those passing weeks.

When she 'died' a part of me did too, and knowing she's alive, out there somewhere, under Petrovich's grasp? From the second I realised she was gone I haven't stopped looking for her, and I don't intend on stopping until she's in my sights permanently.

"Are you even listening, Luca?" Lorenzo slams his fist down on the countertop, rattling my fourth cup of coffee that was starting to go cold.

"I'm going to find her, Lorenzo." He stares at me blankly. "I want her back here, safe, probably more than you do, so stop making out like I don't give a damn about it. You love your sister and I get that. But just because she's your blood does not mean you're the only one who cares about her wellbeing. This is under control. I've got a whole bunch of people tracking her down. Just go on your honeymoon; I've got this."

"Oh, there is not a chance in hell I'm going anywhere and leaving you in control of this."

"You need a break, Lorenzo."

"This is my SISTER."

"I'm aware of that." Hoping she'll take my side on this, I pull a classic 'sad puppy dog' look at Tori. Without the dramatic pout. That might be a little bit over the top. It'd piss Lorenzo off more, too. Not exactly what we need right now. She holds my eye for a moment, doing what she does best. Tori knows me. She knows I can handle this if I'm given the space. The only sound she makes is a slightly exaggerated sigh when I mouth the word 'please' at her.

"Enz? He's right." Lorenzo blinks and looks between Tori and I before settling on her, looking a lot less frustrated than he had with me. "He is more than capable of finding Isabella. We've had this trip planned for months, Pops is excited to go, we all need some time away from work, just the three of us. Marco is here, Carlos is here. So is Nicky. If things go south they can take over until we get back, and we will handle it all together. But if she is with Petrovich, it isn't going to end easily, and before we start a full-blown war, can we at least make sure Penelope has some good memories first? Just in case."

"Nothing's going to happen," Lorenzo confirms with absolute certainty and then turns to me. "If you fuck this up and Bella gets hurt, you better hope you get killed in the process, because if I get my hands on you–"

"Inexplicable pain and suffering? Yeah, that's usually your go-to." I half roll my eyes at him before pushing myself out of the chair and turning to go and handle everything I need to do. "Go on your little loved-up family holiday, make a dozen more little shits like Poppy, because I know for a fact Bella is gonna want to be around for that whole thing this time. I have got this under control."

"Luca?" It's Tori's voice that makes me spin around dramatically. "Fuck this up and I'll make sure you never see Penelope again. Got it?" She's worse than her husband sometimes, I swear.

"I've got it, Menace. Cross my heart."

Chapter Five

You're insane.

LUCA

It's too quiet in this house without Poppy causing chaos. The only real noise is the occasional sigh from Carlos or myself as we look over everything we possibly can in an effort to track Bella down.

Petrovich has a total of six houses on this side of the country alone. Working out where Isabella is and how to get to her safely is a whole ordeal. This is more delicate than hand-carving glass. If one thing goes wrong, it could end in complete annihilation of not only Bella, but every single person who is now looking at me to make sure I bring her home safely.

I'm used to having the world on my shoulders. Used to having everyone needing me to be stronger, faster, harder, more than what I am. But this is exhausting.

High-definition live CCTV footage inside one of the houses plays out on the screen I've been staring at for – fuck – fifty eight hours now, but there's been no movement for three hours on any of the little views. I'm sure it being four am has nothing to do with that. Most sane people are asleep right now. Or at least doing something more productive than watching what might as well be a Van Gogh painting. Seriously. All it's missing is the bright colours. And life. And paint. Okay, so it's not exactly a painting, but you get the point.

This room is suffocating. My eyes are beginning to sting as they blink back to fight the blur, yet still become unfocused again almost instantly. Everything is illuminated with the blue-white light from various computer screens. Sheets of paper covered in scribbled notes or things we've seen or heard are spread across the slightly worn table that takes up most of the room. It's dark, depressing and practically hopeless and I can't handle it for another second.

"I'm going for a walk," It's an announcement that just earns a short, unimpressed, grunt from Carlos, who is half asleep with his chin pressed into the palm of his hand.

We've barely left this room in the past three days since Lorenzo and Tori left. First it was a matter of hacking into all of the security cameras. This isn't something we usually waste our time with. As much as Petrovich is a looming presence, he hasn't recently dared to actively harm us or our plans. We've not had a reason until now to amp up our surveillance on him.

Petrovich's family is spread across the world. Whereas we are small in number and mighty in power, they are strong in both. They're flimsy though. Distrust runs deep in their family and if we had the right angle, tearing them apart could be pretty easy. If Lorenzo allowed it.

After we had access to all of the visuals, it was a matter of finding out where Bella was. That meant no sleep until one of us set eyes on her and there is yet to be a single glance.

I tug the back door open, opting for a bit of fresh air in the hope it will help to wake me up, or I will see some kind of epiphany. Maybe if I stare at the stars hard enough, the answer will be written in them. They'll start to dance across the sky until I'm provided with a step-by-step process on how to bring Isabella back home, where she should have been all along.

My heart burns in my stomach as more nightmarish thoughts take over my train of thought. Everything that she could have been subjected to over the past fourteen years seems to play reel for reel like the trailer for this year's best-selling horror film. Thoughts I haven't been able to turn off from the moment I saw her standing in the doorway.

She was just a kid.

When I close my eyes, it's her that flashes in my mind. At first it's the Isabella I knew. Feisty and pure. Spinning in the sun, giggling as she runs around picking flowers from my parents' flowerbeds. Then in a heartbeat it changes. The sky grows dark and the memory turns imaginary. I can't make out exactly what is going on, but I can see the agony in her eyes. Bloodshot from tears she's forced to keep trapped. Hair a matted mess. That carefree smile is long gone.

Seeing her like that, even if it's my imagination, is enough to shake me out of the sleep deprived exhaustion and push me straight back into determined hyper-focus.

I need to get her out of there. And if I can't get her out of there, I need to get in and make sure that she knows we're not leaving her alone any more.

The freezing early morning air slams into my chest.

That's it.

Getting Bella out of Petrovich's hands might be almost impossible, but getting in would be a lot easier. And that way I would be able to keep an eye on Bella and Petrovich whilst we come up with an iron clad plan to get her out and potentially bring Petrovich down with ease.

I don't remember when my feet started moving back towards the back room, I was too busy planning out details in my brain.

"I found her." Carlos is sitting up straight when I step into the room. I'd be lying if I said it didn't catch me off guard. "She's in the main house. Right at the back of the building. I don't know where she's been for the past few days but-"

"I'm going undercover." I pull my laptop across the table, sinking down into the chair as I start ironing out my plan.

"Funny joke, Luca. Now seriously-"

"I'm not joking." When I lift my eyes over the top of the laptop screen, he's watching me as though he's assessing my mental ability. I can physically see the guy tallying up how much I've slept over the past three days, if I could have taken something whilst I was out of the room, was I stupid enough to dip into our own supply when Lorenzo already wants my head on a fucking chopping block?

"Think about it. Getting Bella out of there is going to start a whole war that's gonna end in most of us getting hurt or killed. We can't spare that many people. I can go in, have my eyes on Bella whilst we work out how to get not only her out of there, but bring his whole network down with it. There's no way Lorenzo is going to let him get away with whatever they all had to do with Isabella, and either way it's gonna be a long few months of hacking and everything. It'll be so much easier if one of us is on the inside."

"Did you fucking take something out there?" *Told you that's what he'd think.*

"Oh yeah, because I'm that fucking insane."

"Luca. You are fucking mad if you think he's gonna allow this."

"I don't need his permission."

"There isn't a chance this is going to work. You're gonna get both of you killed." He hasn't even fully finished his sentence before I'm staring him down and trying to phrase the words in the right way so he understands. He needs to understand just how much I have invested in this. In her. I owe Bella too much to not take the only option I have right now.

"Isabella saved my life on more than one occasion, Carlos. She might be Lorenzo's sister, but that girl gave me a reason to keep going after my parents died. She's the only reason I didn't take myself and Mia off and just end both of our fucking pain after the crash. She is the only reason I am here. And I'll be damned if I'm going to leave her for more than another second to feel like she's alone out there. I'm going to bring her home safe and sound. If that means I die in the process, then so fucking be it."

Chapter Six

Perfectly normal.
ANASTASIA

I'm starting to think that the wedding was all some kind of cruel nightmare. For three weeks I've been reliving that entire day on constant repeat, and the longer I think about it, the more I'm convinced it never happened.

Things in the Petrovich house are as they always are. Loud. Violent. Terrifying. I don't remember a time when I wasn't chronically exhausted from years of not sleeping for longer than a handful of hours at a time. If I'm not woken by someone trying to sneak into my room unseen, it's the nightmares.

It's like I'm numb to it all now, though. I don't feel it as much as I used to. They say if you tell yourself something enough that you eventually begin to believe it, and I guess I'm choosing to believe that nothing has changed.

I know in my bones that every other blood relation to me is dead. They have to be. I wouldn't still be here if they weren't. They'd have found me years ago. Enzo wouldn't have let any of this slip past him. He'd have known something didn't feel right and he'd have worked it out. He'd have torn the universe apart and found me locked up in that fucking basement and brought me home and everything would have been okay.

But he didn't.

And he didn't because he's dead.

Corpse fully rotted somewhere undisclosed.

It's the only answer I allow myself to accept. Any other reality is fictional. Made up by my subconscious to torture me further. Losing them all once hurt more than enough for the next twenty lifetimes, and I was simply not going to do it again.

I refuse.

So life is continuing as normal.

I am still taking Feliks' shit. Still being worked within an inch of my life. Clinging to the fact that I am still breathing and that is a positive.

There is still blood running in my veins, I still have a roof over my head, some kind of food right now, water, clothes. No matter how bad everything is, there is still a positive somewhere, and I will hold onto that slither for the sake of my own sanity.

Today is a brighter day than many in the past few weeks. As heavy as the world feels on my shoulders, the house has been relatively quiet, and there hasn't been anything eventful to make the atmosphere feel excessively dark.

When I come out of the kitchen, it's almost shocking to hear Feliks and Anton bickering about how much they could trust someone. Conversations like this are normal around here. They're usually kept behind closed doors, but this one seems to be following them around whilst they go on with their days. Meaning it was stealing up a lot of focus and had to be important.

"He can't be trusted, Anton."

"I know you think that, but if he proves he's not trying to double-cross us, he could be useful."

"If. *If.* You say that as though it is a doubt. He will. It is almost a guarantee."

"Is it, though? He's already fucked them over three times trying to prove to you he doesn't want to-" Anton abruptly finishes his sentence as they both round the corner and come face to face with me. "Anastasia."

"Don't you have a date to be getting ready for?" Feliks scowls, his eyes trailing down me slowly. I feel so unbelievably sorry for whoever ends up with this mouldy carrot of a man in the future. The lack of respect he has for women is downright disgusting.

"I was just grabbing some water." I gesture at my glass, knowing better than to try and get around the pair.

"Well, what are you doing here, then? Standing looking at me like a fucking bitch needing to be put down. Move." I nod, knowing I'll have no other choice but to squeeze between them in order to get to where I need to go. As I do, Anton pulls a classic move, wrapping his hand around my ponytail and pulling me back slightly.

Feliks is seemingly pissed off as he rolls his eyes and heads off into the kitchen; his father has clearly reminded him again that we are supposedly related.

Me and Anton however, are not. Meaning that when he stares at me with a bitter grin, no one in this house is going to stop him from squeezing my breast hard enough that I let out a choked whimper.

"Better keep your door unlocked tonight." He snarls. "God help you if it's locked."

"I'm bleeding." My response is a little rushed, knowing it is the one way I can get away with him not coming into my room tonight.

When they pull shit like this regularly, you work out ways to avoid it from certain people. Anton hates the idea of the menstrual cycle. Something I'd learned six months ago when he tried something and ended up beating the living daylight out of me when I hadn't told him before he put his hands down my pants.

Anton immediately takes his hands off me, pushing me forcefully against the wall once more.

"Of fucking course, you are." He grimaces, spitting at my chest before he turns and follows Feliks into the kitchen. Pain ripples across the expanse of my back, but I pull myself together, heading slowly back up to my room.

I jump in the shower, turning the heat up in the hope it will ease the muscles that Anton has injured in his minor outburst. I don't think about what he might have had planned for tonight if I hadn't faked a period. There are too many other things I need to focus on.

Tonight, I need to pull on the mask and act like I am living a dream. I have to pay my way in this family, and how else does Anastasia do that than by finding out information?

Rurik doesn't expect a lot of me. Most of the time I'm seen as this bimbo sitting in the corner without enough brain cells to rub together. The only reason he keeps me around is because of the expectation I'll eventually need to be married off to someone. Rurik is a big, influential member of upper class society, and having me as a marriage candidate is the perfect way to get all of the insider secrets he wants, so he can make the most money possible. And boy is he making use out of me whilst he can.

If my time wasn't as otherwise empty as it was, I'd likely lose track of the ridiculous rotation of men Rurik has me dating. Each guy takes me out to dinner where we talk, he gets tipsy and I am expected to find out certain nuggets of information. By any means necessary. That part was made extensively clear. No matter what, I had to come home with that information.

I've found most men hand it over pretty easily considering I play the dumb card. They don't realise they are giving me vital intel, then I come home and tell Rurik everything.

These dates are some of the very few times I am able to get a break from whatever cruel punishment is going on. In the days leading up to the date, the abuse tends to get worse and if I am still able to deliver, it stops. No one lays a finger on me. No one talks to me. No one sneaks into my room. Everything feels like a normal life - I have solid meals and I am no longer punished or treated as a burden.

All because I am proving myself worthy of keeping around in some fucked up respect.

It makes me keep going. I keep agreeing to the dates they set, and I do everything I can to get just the right amount of information that keeps Rurik happy, but allows me to get further dates because he needs more.

It's a fine line I'm walking, and it took me months to find the perfect balance. But I have it now.

I make sure all of my scars are fully covered with make-up. Checking multiple times under the different lighting I have available to ensure nothing is visible around the hem of my tight-fitting dress. The last thing I need right now is Rurik's target seeing the scars this family has covered me in and raising any suspicions that everything isn't perfectly normal.

Chapter Seven

Good to have you on board.
LUCA

Don't get me wrong, I know pain. I'm constantly being riddled with it, especially when my usual sparring partner is downright violent. No matter how petite she may be, Astoria packs a solid punch. But this is extreme. I didn't think getting into Petrovich's family would be easy, and I knew from the second the idea spiralled in my head that it was going to be hell on Earth. I'd expected the three weeks of pure torture just as much as I'd expected to be bleeding out for days on end.

I didn't, however, expect to spend six hours in a fucking dilapidated warehouse, taking down his guys one by one without a single thing to make the fight fair.

These guys have very clearly been training for moments like this and have been living it up. Me, however, I've been given bare minimum food and drink over the past three weeks, I'm weaker than normal and Petrovich's men are still coming at me like I'm in a goddamn warzone.

I'm pretty fucking lucky that it's just fist fighting right now. I don't think I can handle dodging weapons in my state. As much fun as it sounds, I'm not down for another night of sewing my own wounds up with a needle and thread, thanks.

I know exactly why this is being amped up, though; why they are trying to push me past my limit. It's only because I'm doing better than they were expecting. Every single form of torture they've put me under, wanting me to crack and admit this was Lorenzo's way of getting someone inside, so they could kill me and go for everyone else, that's all it's been; a loyalty test. To see how far I'd be willing to go for them and how much I was willing to protect Lorenzo and the Santoni name. I'd already willingly 'given up' information that led to some huge Petrovich wins.

The idiots were too impressed to notice it was all a set up. They needed to trust me and they could do that if they thought I was worth keeping around. Because of me, they'd successfully taken over control of the farm, costing Lorenzo a huge loss of product, and then I'd given out information about a delivery down at the ports that essentially handed them over a tonne of weapons.

It's safe to say Lorenzo was less than impressed by my plan and outright called me a fucking imbecile about eighty times. And no, that isn't an exaggeration. On a good few of them I agreed with him, because it is, admittedly, an insane idea. I just can't stand the idea of Isabella being alone with them any longer than necessary. The quicker I get these guys onside, the better.

I throw another punch into some six-foot-six Russian guy who looks like he belongs in some '80s spy film. It's hard enough that he immediately collapses to the floor. Pain ripples through my knuckles, but it's nothing compared to what I have no doubt is already my poor broken nose and a concussion. Both of which Lorenzo will be very happy to hear I've received. At least it might put a teeny tiny little smile on his face.

"Enough." *There he is.* The piece of shit himself. I've had very little contact with Feliks since this whole thing started. He isn't one to get his hands bloody unless he thinks it's worth it. He'd stood on the edge of the warehouse when I was tied to the chair. Smiling viciously whilst I screamed out in agony. I'd say that the electrocution was the worst I'd experienced during this whole thing, but honestly, the food is pretty shit.

"You look a little worse for wear today, Luca." Suppressing the urge to kill this guy right here is a damn lot harder than it looks. All I can do is swipe the blood from my face and stand as tall as I can manage. Astoria showed me years ago how to kill someone by snapping their neck with one solid twist, so I reckon I could do it like a pro. It seemed simple enough back then and I bet if the need presents itself, I'd remember exactly where she said she put her hands. Only issue is, I just don't think it'd be as painful as he deserves for keeping Bella from me.

"Not as bad as some of your guys, though, I must admit." I nod my head down to the hunk of muscle that's slumped up against the wall, cradling his shattered nose as crimson red slides down the length of his arm, eventually dripping into the puddle beginning to form on the floor.

"Yeah. That's what I came to talk to you about. You are holding up a lot better than I was expecting. Lorenzo trained you well." I scoff.

"Lorenzo did fuck all other than ruin my life. I've told you this."

"Yes, but I still do not understand why a cousin would turn on his family so easily." Feliks slowly removes his suit jacket, passing it back to who I now know as Anton, otherwise known as his top goon. Goon would be the right word. The guy is an absolute idiot. "It's almost as though you are hiding something, and I don't appreciate being double-crossed."

Feliks lunges at me. Fist narrowly missing my face as I dodge it. Hitting him back right now would be a mistake. Him feeling threatened by me right now is the last thing I want and I desperately need Feliks to believe I am here to bow to him and his father's demands. Knocking him out would do the exact opposite of that.

"Okay, first of all. He's not my cousin, I am not related to that piece of shit. Secondly, I'm not double-crossing you, Feliks. That family has done nothing but cause me trouble. The Santonis are the reason my family is dead. The second I can get my sister out of their hold, the better."

"Ah, so this is for your sister." I scrunch my face up. "Mia, correct?" Feliks tries to punch me again and this time, I let him land one on my stomach. I clench my teeth to stop myself from moaning out. "Can't say I've seen much of her."

"Blame them for that." I dodge again, swiping my feet under his. He doesn't fall, instead, just stumbles and quickly regains control of himself. "Look, Feliks, I've given you every bit of information you wanted. I've suffered your fucking torture for almost four weeks now. How much longer is this gonna go on? Because if you can't help me, I know for a fact there are other people out there who will happily take over–"

"Oh no. You're not getting out of this. You know too much."

"And so do you." I raise an eyebrow at him, but this time he doesn't respond. Just pulls out a block from his pocket. At the press of a button, a knife pops out and my stomach churns with pure anxiety.

What fucking psychopath brings a knife to a fist fight?!

How the hell is that fair?

Fuck.

Keep it together, Luca.

Think about Bella.

This is for Bella.

A fucking knife?! IS HE SERIOUS?!

Somehow, despite the chaos racking around in my head as he toys with the blade, I manage to keep up the façade of complete nonchalance. "I know your dad is responsible for his parents." Feliks tips his head to the left a mere inch as his scowl deepens. "I'm not fucking stupid. I don't believe for a second it was the

Bakers. Those idiots couldn't manage a fire in a match factory."

"Does Santoni know?"

"Santoni thinks everyone responsible is dead." They aren't, though. They will be. Lorenzo will make sure this whole family is wiped out for everything they've done to him and Isabella. And if he can't follow through on it, I for sure fucking will be doing.

"Do you know what happened that night?"

"Why would I care?" Feliks narrows his eyes. "Everyone but him is dead. I'm just hoping you'll give me the pleasure of ending that bloodline. To make sure it's done completely this time. You guys kind of left one and it's fucked up a lot of shit. I need to make sure it's done right this time." That's the final straw before Feliks attacks me again, this time with a lot more power and a lot more anger than he had before.

My life is on the line now that he's armed himself. Maybe I was a saint in my past life and I'm being rewarded for my bravery and good karma, because miraculously, I am able to dodge most of his unhinged attacks and the few times I am caught by the blade, it's never deep enough to cause any concerning damage. I'm able to get a few punches into him and this time when I swipe at his feet, he is too focused on trying to sink the damn knife into me to be able to stop himself from slamming down on the floor.

In a heartbeat, I have the knife out of his hand and pressed to his throat, proving to him that I could kill him if I wanted to. That I have the chance, and even in my weakened state, I can take him.

But I don't. I just keep him pinned to the ground, staring down into his black eyes with my hardest glare. Making my demand for his respect something he can't refuse.

"I want them dead, Feliks." I state simply, hating the way the words taste in my mouth and that I have to say these things to make them believe it. Having to act like Lorenzo, Astoria and Pops aren't the best things to happen to me, while knowing Isabella is locked up in that fucking house with men who are known for beating and raping their wives makes me sick to my stomach. "So, are you going to trust me, so we can cut this shit and focus on taking them down, or are you going to keep treating me like a traitor whilst they plan to kill you off?"

"If you cross us, Luca, I will make sure your sister has a worse fate than you."

"I wouldn't expect any less. But if a single finger is laid on her I will tear this family apart with my own hands." Feliks stares at me for a beat before he nods once in silent agreement.

As I climb off him, I toss the knife in the air and catch it by the blade, holding it out to him with a slightly cocky smile. He takes it, and I extend my hand for him to shake. There is no hesitation when he does, and an honest smile creeps up on his face.

"It's good to have you on board, Luca. Let's get you patched up and in to see my father."

Chapter Eight

Yes, Papa.
ANASTASIA

"You're new to Alamea, right?" Louis sips his wine slowly as he watches me from across the candlelit table. Months of planning and preparations have come down to tonight. I have a whole list of information that Rurik wants, and I'm sure as hell going to go back to that house with it all.

Part of getting this information means wrapping Louis around my finger. He doesn't deserve this. Being pulled into something that has nothing to do with him. But Rurik has set his sights on Louis' father's company and that means I have a job to do. Louis' innocence can't be something that enters my mind.

"Mhm." I nod and carefully set my own glass down. "Originally from Russia."

"You don't have the accent, though."

"Well, you're from France and you don't have a strictly French accent." He smiles. That kind of smirk you give when someone lays you out. From the information I'd been given about the girls Louis is known to have dated, he likes the innocence. He likes a woman who can speak up but doesn't feel the need to harbour attention. He likes playing the gentleman, but is so used to women throwing themselves at him that it's the slightly reserved women that tend to catch his attention. The ones who don't seem like they give a damn about who he is, the ones that treat him like anyone else. So that is the plan.

Tonight isn't a smile, nod and do as I'm told kind of night. Tonight is a 'raised eyebrow, unimpressed with his advances because he's punching above his weight class with me' kind of night.

"You're correct." He relaxes slightly. "It comes out more when I am around family or back there, though. I guess I haven't been home in a while."

"How long have you lived in Alamea?"

"I was seventeen, so about fifteen years now." I nod politely. "And you?"

"Not that long, really. I moved over here at eighteen so-"

"Four years?"

"About that." I offer him a simple smile.

"Do you miss it? Being back home? I imagine you had a lot of friends, boyfriends maybe?" Louis smirks as I raise my eyebrow and try to not visibly cringe at the thought of dating a single person in that hell hole.

"I don't think my dating history is suitable first date material."

"I think it's perfect material."

"Yeah, okay, let's talk about your relationships then shall we, Louis? How is Annabelle?" He laughs. Loud enough that the guard Rurik sent to watch me tonight stares over with an intense glare.

"You are funny, Anastasia. How did it take me this long to talk you into letting me take you out?"

"Well, you've been a busy man as much as I am a busy woman. Tell me about work."

"I try to not mix work and pleasure."

"Well, if this is going to work, I need to know what I'm setting myself up for." Louis shifts in his seat, and tugs slightly on his navy suit jacket. Normally, I wouldn't be so out there with my questions, but I know Louis isn't a fan of being tiptoed around. "I'm not here to waste my time. If we're not compatible I would rather realise that now."

He stares at me for a long while, but I don't allow it to make me feel on edge. There are very few moments in my life where I feel like I am in control. Spending most of my days under Rurik's thumb and in his eyeline, everything from the food I eat, to the room temperature, to the time I wake up is his to demand. But here, right now, this is mine. This conversation, this 'date', this man. All of it is mine to control and I will revel in that for the limited amount of time I have.

"I knew I liked you for a reason." Louis smiles. "What exactly do you want to know, Princess?"

"How much does your father's business make in profit each year?" I expect him to pull back. To scowl and say that it's a terrible question. He doesn't, though. No. Instead Louis' eyes flash with an emotion I can't pinpoint, and I feel a little guilty about all of this being a lie. It's a feeling I'm often riddled with and by now, I've learned how to live with it, even if it burns my lungs each time I inhale.

"Enough for me to give you the world and more."

"I'm an expensive woman to please."

"It wouldn't matter."

"I highly doubt that."

"Are you underestimating my income? As though taking you to the most expensive restaurant in the country, driving you here in one of the most luxurious cars in existence, gifting you high end jewellery and flowers dusted in gold, all on our first date isn't the perfect example?" Louis just shakes his head in disbelief before chuckling when I sit back and give him my most unimpressed look. "We're turning over a billion in profits annually. It increases every year."

I give him a single nod, as if it is an acceptable answer.

"And when exactly is your father set to retire?"

★★★

The rest of dinner passes in very much the same way as the first half. Gathering the answers to my questions whilst handing out very limited details about myself is almost as easy as breathing after doing it for so long.

I like Louis. He is a sweet man with a soft heart that has clearly been trampled on a couple of times. He very obviously wants to have someone pretty on his arm that he can show off. A woman who will be spoiled beyond her wildest dreams.

Rurik has always been money motivated, and as much as I know he only wants me to date Louis for the insights into the business he plans on investing in, part of me hopes he'll finally settle on someone to marry me off to.

Louis is harmless. During all my weeks of research that is one thing that came up time and time again.

He is a kind, charitable person, and has this calming energy around him. It's almost revitalising to spend time with him. If Rurik so chose that it is Louis I am to spend my future with, I might actually have a shot at real happiness.

But I don't dare to think about that too much. About a future with Louis. Or anyone for that fact. I am terrified of what Rurik would do if he found out I had someone I loved. It would just be another vicious tool he could use against me. A knife forever dangling over their head, and I've already lost too many people for that to be on my shoulders every day.

Louis rounds his fancy car and pulls on the door handle, extending his hand for me to take so I can climb out. The uneven pebbles make it easy for me to fake a stumble when I plant my heels on the drive, just so he can feel good about helping me to keep standing.

"Careful there, Princess. Last thing we want to end our first date with is a broken ankle."

"Yeah, that's much more of a fifth or sixth date thing. Besides, the boot wouldn't work with any of my shoes."

"I'd buy you some more."

"I'm afraid no shoes in existence would work with those boots."

"Then I'd have a pair made specifically for you." Louis smiles as he walks me up to the front door, like the perfect gentleman he is. "I had a lot of fun with you tonight, Anastasia."

"Me too."

"We should do this again. Maybe next time we take my jet to France? Dinner at the top of the Eiffel Tower?"

"Perhaps. I might be busy though."

"I haven't given you a date yet."

"Well, I'm a very busy woman." Louis smirks, leaning down to drop a soft kiss on my cheek. His perfectly trimmed moustache tickles against my skin before he stands back up a few seconds later.

"I will be in touch later this week. When I'm in the office and can see my schedule. Will you make time for me?" All I can offer him is a carefree shrug. "Please?"

"I'll have to see what else I have going on. See if I have a better offer."

"A better offer than dinner at the top of the Eiffel Tower?" I carefully pull his suit jacket from my shoulders, hand it back to him and take a step back towards the front door, pushing it open slowly whilst maintaining eye contact with my date.

I can smell Rurik from here. Whiskey and cigar smoke just lingering behind the door as he waits for me to finish up and come inside for my 'post date interrogation'.

"I told you, Louis. I'm a busy woman with a dozen men begging for time in my calendar." He looks concerned. Suddenly connecting the realisation that obviously he isn't the only guy fighting for my time or attention. I'd place bets on having a delivery of four dozen roses first thing tomorrow morning as he begins trying to 'one up' anyone else taking my time from him.

"Okay. I will look." I nod at him.

"Good night."

"Goodnight, Louis." Finally ending the night, I turn, heading back into the house and closing the heavy wooden door behind me as gently as I can manage. I was right to think Rurik was standing in the hallway. Dark eyes glaring at me as he waits for me to show any form of emotional response, but I don't give him the benefit. "Hi, Papa."

"Anastasia." He brings the cigar up to his mouth, takes a long drag before slowly releasing the smoke into the atmosphere. "How was your evening?"

"It was fine. I got all the answers to everything you asked me to get."

"All of it?"

"All of them, Papa." Rurik slowly smiles as I nod in confirmation. It's a grin that stretches across his dull face, and I feel like I can exhale for just a few moments. He turns then, heading down the hall towards his favourite room in the house.

"Good. Come sit and tell me about it. I may need you to see him continuously, so I know when to pull out. He was well behaved, I trust?"

"Yes, Papa."

"He didn't touch you?"

"Just a kiss on the cheek on the doorstep." Rurik's head bobs as he confirms it was an acceptable form of affection from the man he's using me to scam.

"Good." He sits down in his oversized leather chair, and pours an amber liquid into his glass that is already sitting out; the ice already slightly melted from his first glass. The fire roars a few feet away, providing the only light in the room. Not exactly bright but enough for me to see the gun he's likely been polishing whilst waiting for me to come home. "Now, tell me. The company turnover. Is it as high as the papers say?"

Chapter Nine

Act natural.
ANASTASIA

Life has been somewhat easier the past few months. I have been handing Rurik so much information from my numerous dates that I now look like I'm paying my keep. Every day, without fail, I have something to give him, so I'm no longer that pain in his neck, sitting around waiting for him to give me some instructions or demands. No matter how small it may seem, between the eight men he has me dating currently, I am able to give him a slither of something. It is exhausting mentally, but at least I have a break from the abuse and punishments.

Feliks has been busy too. In fact, it's been months since I last saw him wandering down these halls with enough time on his hands to stop and torment me. There always seems to be a rush on something he's doing, somewhere he needs to be, someone getting shot in some factory that needs handling. I'm counting my lucky stars. It won't last forever and I am going to enjoy breathing clearly whilst I can.

Today is a rest day, in some respects. For once, I don't have a date, thanks to an awards evening at city hall that most of them are heading to. It isn't a secret that I'm dating multiple people. They all know there are others, just not precisely who. Of the eight men, four had asked me to go tonight and each one had received the same answer. Unless there is a ring on my finger and a wedding date in the church diary, I'm not doing something so public. Rurik had written it down exactly as he wanted it stating, and considering he has access to my phone and messages on his computer, I don't dare to break a single one of his rules.

I am happy for the break that Rurik and his men being out of the house gives me. Other than my mandatory gym session, I can hide away in my room and read in peace without the fear of someone barging in and demanding I get to my knees.

After finishing my workout, I desperately need a snack and a fresh bottle of water that is cold enough for my head to stop spinning so hard. The house isn't exactly empty but it isn't busy either. Rurik, Feliks and a few other guys are getting ready upstairs, so I know people are hanging around. What I hadn't been expecting, was that I'd walk into the oversized kitchen to find Luca standing at the back exit doorway like some fucking bodyguard.

I blink a few times, not entirely sure if I am seeing things or not because, I mean, I have to be, right? There isn't a chance in hell that Luca is actually standing in the kitchen in an all-black suit that doesn't look right on him. When I'm about to open my mouth and say something, he gives the smallest shake of his head and continues glaring at me.

"Cameras." His mouth doesn't move but I know his voice. Luca's thick accent isn't something I can make up, and it is so undeniably clear there's no chance in hell that I am making this up as part of some insane malnourished hallucination. "Act natural. I'm not me." I swallow, turning back to the fridge and grabbing a bottle of water. I stay there, staring at the contents on the shelves and clinging to the plastic bottle as I try to settle my palpitating heart and connect my brain back to reality.

I'll turn around and it'll be someone else. After six months of not seeing a single glimpse of anyone from the wedding, there isn't a chance they're just now showing up.

Maybe the new trainer pushed me too hard in the gym and I passed out from dehydration and this is some hyper realistic nightmare like the ones I have sometimes. It wouldn't surprise me, honestly. They're pretty common. And they have cut down my food again over the past few days.

Knowing I can't have been stood here this long without having an excuse, I grab an apple and turn around, staring at him before just walking out. I need to drink the water, have a shower and clearly sleep because my imagination is running wild. Maybe I am going insane.

Anton suddenly appears before I can completely clear the stairs, almost making me slam into him. Luckily, I manage to stop before I do and save my future self from a severe beating.

"Anastasia. You look flushed." He smirks. A smirk that I know inside out at this point. My stomach instantly churns, filling with a toxic poison that makes me feel violently ill. I fucking hate that goddamn smirk. I daydream sometimes of the things I could do to rid him of it permanently. Today though, my mind is already in overdrive, and I am not in the mood to play along with whatever he's planning.

"A long gym session." I turn my shoulders and manage to get past him, desperate to get behind the safety of my bedroom door as quickly as possible.

"Where are you going? I wasn't done talking to you." I almost make it. Almost, but not quite. I am all but two steps away from my door. If I reach my hand out I can probably open it from here. There's not a chance I'm going to attempt it though, because moving even an inch from where Anton has me pinned to the wall by my throat would be a very, very bad idea. "You know better than to walk away from people when they're talking to you, Anastasia. Especially a man. Don't you?" I nod, not even bothering to try and talk. "So why are you in a rush to get out of my eyeline? Hm? In these skimpy little shorts."

Anton runs his finger under the bottom hem of my running shorts. The snarl on his face turns into a wicked smirk when he feels the panicked pulse that I can't even hide pounding in my neck, under his palm.

"Do you need to be taught another lesson on how to respect men, Anastasia? Have you forgotten this quickly?" He pushes his feet between mine, kicking my legs to separate them before cupping an area I certainly don't want his grimy hands on. My chest burns as I struggle to breathe in, and I have to hold onto my instinct to respond with violence.

I could fight back. Dig my nails into him until he's bleeding. But the scars across his hands and the memory of the first time he did this, practically rewires my brain until I become completely limp.

He tightens his grip on my throat, his other hand squeezing until I have to bite my tongue to avoid whimpering in pain.

"It'd be fun to teach you that lesson again, Anastasia, but I'm sure Tomas will do a better job of reminding you exactly where you stand next week when he gets here." And just like that, the peace I've had for the past few months doesn't just crumble, it disintegrates.

It turns into a dark smoke that my body knows all too well is it's only warning sign of something horrific coming over the horizon.

In an instant, I feel myself begin to pull away from my body.

It was idiotic of me to think things were going to stay as easy as they have been recently. That I had gained some form of control over my life now, and that all of this was finally manageable to some degree. I should have known it wouldn't last forever. I should have known I'm not that fucking lucky.

Anton drops his hold on me, steps back and looks disgusted. He does so too quickly for me to stabilise my footing, and I fall to the floor with a thud, catching my arm on the sharp edge of the cabinet beside us as I do. I feel the impact but the pain I'm expecting never comes.

"You're lucky he's flying over, you know. You need teaching a lesson. I'm starting to think every fucker else in this house isn't doing it right and I need to take over for him again. I must admit, the idea of tying you to your bed and watching the fear on your face again as I slide my blade over your skin is a memory I relive every morning in the shower."

"Anton! You were supposed to be grabbing bottles of water not fucking about with that waste of oxygen. We don't have time for this today. Move your ass." Anton quickly looks over his shoulder towards my so-called brother before looking back at me with contempt. He kicks me in the thigh, adding another tally onto today's injuries that I need to fix, but as he walks back to the stairs and I pull myself up to my feet; my physical pain is the very least of my worries.

Because if Tomas is coming over, then I'm fucked. And there isn't a doubt in my mind that there is a hell of a lot more physical torment in store for me during his trip.

Chapter Ten

Get rid of him.
LUCA

I know for a fact they're keeping an eye on me. Watching the cameras whenever Isabella is wandering around the house. They check in after. Feliks acts all chummy, he keeps asking me how close I'd been with Lorenzo's family before they died. I lie and say they were just kind of there, that I only really had any important contact with them after I was orphaned and dragged into their family and even then I tended to keep to myself and focus on Mia.

It really is bewildering how little this family look into stories. Especially from someone like me.

How this family has got this far without being torn apart I have no idea. In reality it hasn't been that difficult for me to get in here. A hell of a lot of will power and internal strength, but I have something, someone, to do it for.

Every time it gets so hard that I want to pull out, I think about Bella sitting alone in a room here. I think about how thin and grey she looked at the wedding. How easily she disappeared and how much she must have gone through. I have the power to stop it. To stand in her eyeline so she knows she isn't alone, and I'm not about to let her down.

The past week has been a lot of me standing around the house without anyone watching. Directly, anyway. They are testing me, to see whether I'll follow the instructions of 'stay put and guard the door', so I have. I have stayed put. And I've guarded the door that no one ever uses.

That first day when Bella walked in, from the look on her face, I could see the way she wanted to question it. I had to tell her not to, because just her saying my name would ruin it all. If someone realised that she knows who I am, we'd both be screwed. So, using every technique I've used with Pops whilst trying to get her to say things she shouldn't without anyone seeing, I told her not to say a word.

I've seen her since. Multiple times a day. Each time looking more and more depressed. She's thinner. The bags under her eyes are darker, and I'd been right here when she came down for water at three am with slightly puffy eyes and swollen lips, and her head hung low.

Isabella had always been the centre of attention. Big, boisterous and loud. Her laugh was the kind that just made you turn and stare for a few moments. She was effervescent. But this Bella levitates around this house like some ghost desperately searching for the thing that would help it cross over. She has this cloud hovering over her, and the longer I'm in its presence, the more I'm filled with a desperate need to fix it.

"Luca," I don't react. Just stay standing in the same doorway, in the same stance I've had for the past week. "I want to introduce you to Tomas. He's going to be around for a few weeks to help us with some jobs. He has unlimited access to anywhere in this house. Any locked door he wants in, he gets access to." I nod once, staring at the man now standing in the doorway. He isn't smiling, or scowling. It's more of a nonchalant, yet sinister look. There's a presence that followed him into the room, too. This house is filled with negative energy that threatens to tear you down if you're not strong enough. But him, he's different. With him, it's pure evil encased in human skin.

"Santoni, right?"

"Bottaro." I scoff, and he smirks. Clearly I've given him the right answer.

"You're free to take a break, Luca. Now Tomas is here we can step down security a little. You have free roam of the house. Just stay out the rooms with locked doors, and eyes off Anastasia."

"Ah. Yes. Anastasia. Where is my Ptitsa?" Tomas' smile takes on a vicious twist as he turns to Feliks.

"In her room. Where she should be. I'll take you to her now. Luca, make yourself useful. Don't stand there like a tree." I wait until they leave to wander outside, lighting up a cigarette that I have no intention of smoking for any reason other than keeping up appearances.

I know of a few areas that are out of camera view, simply from looking for Isabella months ago. There were always points where people walked but went out of sight on one corner. I have them imprinted in my mind for moments like this, so I can use my burner phone to call Lorenzo and Astoria and give them updates.

"Luca. What do you have for me?"

"Oh hi, Lorenzo. How nice to speak to you. I'm very well thanks, and yourself? How's the family?"

"Aren't you supposed to be telling me how my family is? Isn't that the whole point you've got your stupid ass in the fucking Russian's house?"

"You're cranky. You should lay down with Pops for her nap. Maybe I can try to call you back when you're not stroppier than the four-year-old." There's some rustling on the other end of the line followed by muffled conversation and then a sigh.

"Lu, it's Tor. Look, he's gonna have an aneurysm. Can you be nicer?"

"I am being nice, Menace. He's the one who didn't even bother asking if I was okay. He went straight to being rude. I could be dying from the flu and he wouldn't even care." Astoria goes quiet and I can picture her look of amusement mixed with slight annoyance. "How are you guys?"

"We're fine, Lu."

"Pops?"

"She wants her uncle back. She's not quite sure why he's not reading her to sleep every night or playing tea parties. So how about we focus on trying to get you and Bella home rather than bullying my husband?"

"Fine."

"Good. What's going on?"

"Tomas is here." I turn slowly, looking up at the huge building to where I know Isabella's bedroom is. Her curtains are open, giving me a full view of Tomas and her talking. She's looking at him but he looks pissed off at whatever they're talking about. "What do we know about him?"

"Uhh... Not a lot. Just that he's high up, based over in Moscow. Pretty elusive. Why?"

"He has access to every locked door in the house and right now I'm watching him shout at Bella."

"What's he saying?"

"Well there's two floors, a window and a whole bunch of space between us so I —" I am halfway through my smug remark when I watch Tomas slap the back of his hand across Isabella's face and she recoils in a way I know means it came from an intense force. Unable to speak, I'm just cemented to my spot as it escalates.

He wraps a hand around her throat and pushes her until she slams into the window, the tie he'd been wearing now securing her wrists behind her back. There is a bang and I realise it's him forcing her back again, even though she doesn't have any further to go. The glass shakes behind her as he starts to go red in the face, mouth moving too fast for me to pull out a single word.

"Lu? Luca? Hello?"

"Who guards her normally? When she goes on these date- things?" My words leave my mouth too quickly as my brain tries to catch back up with itself. I need to get her out of there. Or him. Anything. I need a… a distraction. That's exactly what I need. Just until I can work out how to stop whatever the fuck is happening permanently.

"Uhh, that'd be Alek."

"Get rid of him."

"What?"

"Before her next date. Whatever we need to do to make her main guy gone, make it happen. I need to get closer to her. Urgently."

"Luca, what's hap-" I have to turn around when Tomas pushes Bella to her knees in front of him, her hands still tied, bare feet now pressed against the glass in the minimal space he's giving her. I don't need to see this. Come on Luca. Fucking think.

"I need to go, Tor. Get rid of him. I'll try to call tonight." As I hang up the phone, I look around for something to use to my advantage. When I see the poor pigeon sitting on the fence, I know it's the only option I have and pray that the universe understands my reasoning and will take my side when I'm standing at the pearly white gates. Eventually. Not yet. Not until Bella is safe.

Quickly, I pull my gun out of the holster and fire, daring only then to make one quick glance up at the window. Tomas scowls at me, before he quickly unties Bella and comes to join the rest of the house to see what the fuck I was shooting at.

Chapter Eleven

Oh, Bella.
ANASTASIA

The past five days have been some of the weirdest I think I'll ever experience, and I'm not sure what to think about any of it. Having Tomas here means a whole host of things for me, including, but not limited to, sleeping in the bathtub with both my bedroom and bathroom door locked and the water running in the sink across the room. It hasn't helped me sleep for any longer than an hour at a time, but at least that is better than nothing.

He isn't here for me, Rurik had stated that very, very clearly. He's here to help Feliks with some more intense jobs they have coming up, but in no way does that mean he isn't going to dip into the years of abuse I suffered at his hands in Moscow.

They say that traumatised kids often black out the worst of the abuse they suffered and, if that is indeed the case, I do not want to know what I'm blacking out, when the shit I remember still features in my nightmares in crystal clear, high definition.

Tomas had come in the day he arrived. Apparently, he needed to make sure I hadn't forgotten my place but before he could do much, Luca started shooting at something outside that turned out to be a bird. They'd been pissed off at first, that everyone had stopped what they were doing, believing someone was breaking in. But after a couple of minutes, Luca managed to sweet talk them into believing it was a good thing that he'd caused a disturbance for nothing. As I watched from the window, he turned them from scowling to laughing, and I simply don't get it.

I don't get why he's here; I don't get what's happening, I don't get why he hasn't tried to sneak me out of here if he knows I'm right here.

There are so many questions in my head that I keep losing count, but I can't even ask them. There are cameras and mics in every room of this house, my own included, so I dare not step out of line or show anyone watching that I have a single clue who Luca is. Truth be told, I know the only reason Tomas hasn't been left alone in a room with me long enough to cause any harm is because Luca keeps causing reasons for him to leave. It's too coincidental for Luca to have nothing to do with it all, and I'm so beyond grateful.

"Anastasia." My blood freezes over as I try to touch up my lipstick in the hallway mirror. Although I'm ready to go out for this date, I'm exhausted and just want to curl up in bed with a book. But I'm dressed and made up, ready to handle a very flirty Lochlan tonight.

I keep my movements slow, standing up and turning to stare at Tomas. His ice-cold navy eyes run up my body. All the way from my chunky black heels to the black bow in my hair. He'll hate that I'm going out, let alone in a dress like this, but it's not him I'm taking orders from when I'm out like I am tonight.

Lochlan likes me in black and after this many dates, a strapless dress is exactly what I need to keep him interested.

Making myself as small as possible and keeping my mouth shut unless I am told to speak is a lesson I'm not dumb enough to be taught again, so I do just that. My submission to these fucked up rules keeps his hands by his sides and my blood inside my body where it belongs.

"Luca is taking you tonight. Alek is… busy. Do not think he will be more lenient with you. I expect you to follow the same rules you do with Alek. Is that understood?"

"Yes, Sir." He hardens his stare on me and I hold it for a few seconds before looking down at the floor, bowing my head the way he expects. He continues watching me for what feels like forever but eventually, he speaks again.

"You'll report to me when you're back. Do not fail me, Anastasia, I am not in the mood tonight." Without giving me a chance to respond, he leaves. His perfectly polished shoes tap against the marble as he disappears into the vast expanse of closed doors. When I hear the door to whatever room close, I finally manage to lift my head to Luca. He's staring at me blankly, not a single emotion written across his face, and I fear that he isn't the Luca I once knew.

"Move then." His eyes move to the door before his glare deepens on me. Any slither of hope I'd been building since Luca's surprising arrival here dies in the blink of a second, instead being replaced with the dreaded weight of confirmation that there is no escape from this without it ending in my death.

I grab my bag from the side behind me and meekly stumble towards the front door, letting the cool air slam into my skin as a painful reminder of why I shouldn't hold onto hope when there isn't any.

The leather of the passenger seat in the awaiting car creaks as I gently settle myself into it and I'm now terrified that I am alone in a car with a man I used to know. Someone I grew up side by side with. I held his hand when he cried over his parents, climbed out of my bedroom window to sit on the roof with him when he was having a rough night. We'd run around the garden in Sicily with water balloons and water guns, and when it seemed like everyone else was against me, it was Luca who would be on my side.

Now he's buckling his belt in the car in silence with a hard glare on his face, and I know that man is long gone if he's here with Petrovich. He's betraying Lorenzo to be here and I am concerned that he's either here because my brother is dead, or worse, that Luca is about to tear the remaining dregs of my family apart piece by flimsy piece.

He pulls out of the drive slowly, eyes fixed on the road ahead, but when we're off the property and a good few metres out of view, he leans over and grabs my hand. I flinch, pulling my hand away from him, but at the same time an instant regret forces me to freeze as my heart races in my chest. When I turn my head to see him he's... smiling?

It's not an evil smile, though. It's not the smile men usually have across their faces as they try to touch me when I'm alone with them. It's big and bright, and I guess a little toothy, and it forces me to take a deep inhale. My body relaxes against my own will as Luca flicks his eyes over to me.

Not a single word is said as he reaches for my hand again. This time I don't instinctively retract. Luca lifts my hand to his lips, pressing a soft, silent kiss on the back before placing it back in my lap delicately, leaving me staring at him like a fairytale creature because I'm so damn confused. I don't know if this is real life, or the start of another really fucked up nightmare.

Luca's smile grows slightly before he winks, presses a finger to his ear then points it at the radio.

They're listening.

★★★

"Are you okay, Anastasia?" Lochlan smirks from across the table. "You haven't rolled your eyes at me since you got here."

I blink slowly, letting him come back into focus. My head has been anywhere but here tonight, specifically on Luca who is sat a few tables away, eyes fixated on me like he has to.

"It's none of your business if I'm okay or not." I throw Lochlan a snide smile. "How was work this week?"

"You have a major interest in my work." He stabs a fork into his dessert. Eyebrows high on his forehead as he tries to not make it obvious that he's taking quick glances at my cleavage.

"Oh, forgive me for making sure my future husband isn't going to land me bankrupt."

"Future husband, eh? Is that what's keeping you up at night? Thinking about me in bed, Ana? You could just call and I'd gladly make your dreams come true." I scoff, not wanting him within fifty feet of my bedroom in any world.

"I'll call you to bed when I know I'm not setting myself up for a life living in poverty. If you can't keep me living comfortably, there are five other guys waiting for me to be free tonight that can." His attitude changes now. A flash of concern flickering across his face, before he smiles gently again and sips on his wine. He swallows, sighs and goes on to tell me the answer to everything I needed tonight, and I do everything in my power to keep my attention on the details of what he's saying.

The rest of dinner goes by quickly, ending with him walking me to Luca's car and pressing a kiss to my cheek. He asks me again if he can just drive me home, but Rurik has heard stories about Lochlan getting handsy in the front seat of his car and for some reason, Lochlan is the line my wonderful Papa is willing to draw. I tell him again how protective my 'father' is and how he can drive me wherever he pleases when it's his name following my own. He tells me to stop teasing before he drops to his knee right there and I roll my eyes, bringing the date to a close before I elegantly slip into my seat and let him close the door.

Luca takes a few seconds, watching Lochlan walk down the street and get into his own car before he gets in beside me and lets out a heavy sigh.

"I honestly thought he'd never get the hint." I stare at him with wide eyes but Luca just smirks. "Oh, right. The bug. Lorenzo and Tori sorted that whilst you were listening to him whitter on about business deals and tax fraud. They can't hear you in here anymore." Not exactly sure how I'm supposed to respond to the sudden change in his attitude, I continue staring at him in silence. Luca just shuffles in his spot and buckles up his seatbelt. "Bella?" I still haven't responded when he turns his head to face me, so he continues, "We're working on getting you out of here, Amore."

"You are?" Luca tips his head at my meek questioning. I'm not sure if I want to hear the answer or not. Three and a half hours ago, this man was barely the shadow of someone I knew when I was a child, and the hope I've had for the weeks he's been here that everything was going to be okay had evaporated into thin air. I don't know if I am ready to hear him laugh at me when he tells me I'm stuck living in constant fear of someone's next move.

"Oh Bella, I really have missed that brain of yours." He chuckles and starts the engine, looking back to me with a smile that's unlike anything I've ever seen before. "Of course we are. You really think we were just going to leave you? With them? No, we just have to tread carefully. There isn't a chance in hell you're staying here."

Chapter Twelve

Si, Amore?
LUCA

Bella lays her head back against the headrest as I set the car in motion. I can see her physically breathe for what I'm guessing is the first time in years, and it feels damn good to have her in a space where I know she is okay. No fucker is laying their hands on her, no one is staring at her in this tight little mini dress, no one can touch her right now, and I am filled with more than a primal instinct of pride. This goes so much further than that.

If Lorenzo hadn't given me strict instructions to just keep her safe whilst he works out a plan to get her out, I'd leave right now. I wouldn't drive us back to that fucking house. Instead, I'd keep going and drive until I couldn't anymore. We'd both be on a plane flying to fucking Antarctica if I knew it was the only place Bella would be safe.

But Lorenzo is still pissed off enough at me as it is, and I know I am walking a very thin line within the family. If I fuck this up, every single person I know could be slaughtered and I know Rurik, he'd make sure I lived to see each of their lives drain from their faces. I couldn't take that. The sight of watching them die before me. The idea of them not living anymore because I couldn't keep it together. That is what is keeping my eyes on the end goal.

Get Bella out and get the Petrovichs wiped from the face of the Earth so they can't ever touch another person again.

It's that simple.

"Luca?"

"Si, Amore?"

"How is everyone?" I give her a quick glance. "Lorenzo and Astoria? And..."

"Pops?" She nods. "They're fine, Bella. Tori and Pops are in Sicily."

"They are?"

"Mhm. Lorenzo shipped them off months ago. Just so they're out of the way and safe. She's – uh – pregnant again. I don't know if I am supposed to tell you that or not. Probably not. Lorenzo probably wants to tell you. But she's like four months gone already so, you know. They're keeping the gender a secret and according to the texts Tor has been sending they can't settle on a name, so if she has the baby over there she's going to sign the birth certificate before he can stop her." Bella smiles. It's not complete though.

It's the kind of smile someone has when they're happy to hear your good news, but their world is burning around them. They're happy for you but don't understand how people can have such great and normal news when everything to them is falling apart at the seams. So I move the conversation on, hoping I can give Bella a small mental break through stupid distractions. "But they're good. How are you?"

She shifts in her seat but doesn't answer and to be honest, I can't blame her. I just needed to confirm she wasn't all right. That what I'd been thinking was going on behind all the closed doors was, and judging by how I'd overheard Tomas talking to Anton last night after she left dinner, I needed to know.

I quickly run a hand through my hair, driving a little slower than I should be, but my time is running out with her in this space. Opting for the most important things she needs to know is my only option right now. There's simply not enough time to tell her everything I want to. I want to update her on everyone in detail. Sit for hours as I recall everything she's missed right up until this very moment. Eventually, I will. But right now I can only tell her what she needs to know.

"I need you to know what goes on in that house, when they're watching, the person I am in there, it's not me, Bella." I spare a quick glance before looking back out at the road. "For this to go the way we need it to, we need them all to believe I want Lorenzo and everyone dead and that I am certain you are. If they for a second-"

"I know."

"You do?"

"Well, I mean, I guessed. I just don't get why you're all risking this much for me. It's not worth it." My heart aches in my chest. She might as well have yanked an organ from my body with the amount it hurts to hear her say she's not worth saving.

"Bella-"

"No Luca, it isn't. I know what they're capable of. I know Rurik and Feliks, and I know first-hand just how far they're willing to go. Pops and the new baby deserve more than watching their family die the way I did. You really should just leave it as it is. Go ba-"

"Isabella." My voice comes out firm and I can feel the way the air changes the second I do. I hate it, but she needs to know it's not happening. I can't have her believing for a single second more that everything we have at risk for this isn't worth it. The truth is that I'd risk so much more for her. Never mind how much Lorenzo would. "Stop. We're not leaving it and that's final. No one's going to touch you, or anyone else in our family for that matter." I look over at her as we reach the road leading to the house. Her skin is a good few shades lighter than it had been when we left the restaurant, her big bright eyes are wide. Her throat bobs slowly as she swallows harshly, and I turn my attention back to the house as it comes into clearer view. Our minimal time together in a safe space is slipping through our fingers, and she is terrified.

"You can't stop them, Luca," Bella whispers, and my grip on the wheel tightens.

"Watch me, Amore."

★★★

It was barely two minutes between when our conversation ended and us pulling into the drive, but those two minutes were filled with such a heavy weight. I'd made her a promise I intend on keeping. It wasn't an official promise. Those words hadn't left my mouth but that's exactly what it is.

The second the car was parked up, Bella was out the door and I pulled my metaphorical mask back on. Astoria had fucked around with the mic they'd installed much the same way she had with the cameras when Lorenzo was first watching her. We didn't want Rurik or Feliks becoming suspicious, so we had spent days recording audio in this car. Somehow she'd wired it so a signal is sent from my car to the device, automatically playing a loop of twenty-three different recordings all ranging in length. We'd been testing it slowly since I knew Feliks put it in a month ago and so far, nothing was suspicious.

The only reason I told Bella to be quiet heading out of here tonight was because I knew they'd be listening more intently than normal, and we weren't risking anything.

I step into the house calmly, closing and locking the door behind me, the way I'd been told. I'm just a handful of seconds behind Bella, but it is enough to only catch a glimpse of her heading off with Tomas. I hate the idea of it but I can't stop it right now. Not with Rurik standing in the centre of the hallway staring at me.

"My office." I nod, following him down the hall and leaving a good few feet of space between us. These visits to his office have become all too common, but I know it's an intimidation tactic.

I sit myself in the chair I guess I have claimed because it's the only one I tend to sit in when I'm in here. I'm trying to maintain my projection of calm and collected but honestly, it's fucking hard. The guy is all out creepy, I'm furious that I'm here in the first place, that Isabella is god knows where having god knows what done to her and I'm kind of petrified that I'm one wrong answer away from putting all of this on display like a goddamn exhibition for exactly the wrong people. There must be something I'm doing right though because Rurik simply peers at me from across the oversized desk as he lights a cheap cigar and takes a long drag before puffing the smoke into the air surrounding us.

"Report." My instincts take over and I don't stutter in handing over every piece of information from tonight. Everything from the wine he ordered to how he sent the bottle back because he thought it made him look impressive. Then I lie and say Bella had played him like a toy all night, when in reality I could see she was mentally somewhere else. I hand over Lochlan's car plate numbers, about the details that Tori had dragged up about him and texted me whilst I was sitting in the restaurant staring at them like some weirdo stalker.

When I am finished, Rurik sits back slightly in his chair, clearly trying to hide the fact he is impressed I had actually done my job. "Is he interested in her?"

"I'd like to think so, but I also know he has the tendency to fuck girls around." Rurik nods slowly and doesn't speak for a long while. So long in fact, I start to doubt myself. Eventually, he breaks though.

"You grew up with the Santonis, correct?" Another questioning session then? Great.

"Yes."

"How was that?" I shrug, sitting back in the chair and looking as relaxed as possible.

"As great as it can be when the people responsible for your parents' deaths are your caregivers." Rurik almost laughs. "You still don't trust me."

"How did you feel when they died?"

"Lorenzo's parents?" He makes a noise, deep in his throat and I take that as an acknowledgement that my question is correct. "I think they deserved a lot worse than burning slowly." He stares at me and I make silent pleas at them, hoping they understand that I don't mean this, that I just want their daughter safe and this is the only way I can do that. "If it was up to me I'd have made them suffer the way they should have."

"What about their daughter? She was only a child."

"Isabella?" He meets my eyes and I snarl. "She deserved it the most. That little brat deserved to rot in hell like her parents." He stares at me for a second and then smirks, nodding his head slowly.

"I'm glad we're on the same page." He pushes a file across the table at me. "I am still trying to locate Alek, so I need you to fill in for him tomorrow again. Anastasia has an event at one of the casinos on the east side of town. You understand I want Anastasia kept safe."

"Of course, she's your daughter after all." I take the folder from the desk and open it, flicking through a couple pages before looking up to see Rurik watching me closely.

"She's more than my daughter, Luca. She's a valuable piece of property to this family. More so than she knows." He looks at me more seriously than he has before, and I'm shocked he manages it. This man constantly looks like he's constipated. "She is worth a lot of money to the right man. Money that could get you a tidy little offshore account if you play your cards right. Understand?"

"Yes, Sir." I say through gritted teeth. Bella is worth so much more than money to be married off for.

"Good man. Now, any more intel on your cousin's jobs for me?"

"Not right now, but I'm working on it. I'm going to drive down tonight to check in." Rurik nods.

"Off you go then, bring me something worthwhile again. I'm thoroughly enjoying watching Santoni's slow collapse."

Chapter Thirteen

Get me out of here.
ANASTASIA

I'm not sure if Rurik knows that I know or not. It's pretty obvious these girls he has forced upon me as my friends are just here as another way for him to watch me closely. I don't know if he thinks it's obvious, or if he thinks I really am stupid enough to believe that these three girls really do give a fuck about me.

They don't.

They're good at playing the part, mind. If I was just a little bit more naïve, I probably would fall for it. Then I'd be dishing out too many details to people who would immediately hand them over to Feliks and Rurik for them to do as they pleased. I know that's what they're doing.

In the five years I've been in Kredrith, not once have I given them any information that doesn't play into the model Rurik wants me to be. Giving them slightly more information than I give Rurik, I play into his plan as much as I can. I tell them about the books I read, tell them I'm planning a future with whichever man he's got me lying to this month, just so that it seems like I'm not onto their conniving smiles. I make believe that these girls are friends and I treat them as such. Within reason.

Tonight is – hell, I don't even know why we're out. All I know is Rurik told me last week that I was going to the casino tonight and to not disappoint him. He'd taught me how to play poker on the flight back from Moscow to Alamea, whilst telling me how important it was to not let anyone know if I was bluffing or not. His lesson must have gone a little too well, because now the man can't tell a lie from the truth when it comes from my mouth.

I keep a straight face as I push a few more chips into the ever-growing pile. There's a solid set of cards in my hands and from watching the rest of the people at this table, I think I have them figured out. My biggest competition is sitting across from me, and I simply don't think they can work out exactly how close they are.

Patience is key when it comes to these things, so I sit there and watch him whilst we wait for his decision on if he's ready to fold, or if he's going to hand over more of his money. He doesn't get a chance to put his cards down when the room erupts into chaos.

My head darts up at the sound of gunshots, and immediately the people surrounding me begin screaming as they attempt to get under the tables for some kind of safety.

A firm hand wraps around my wrist before I can even fully process what is happening, causing pain to radiate through the bruises that are already covering me after last night with Tomas, but I can't focus on that right now.

I'm yanked out of my chair and not given any time to get to my feet properly. My heart races at the thought of being kidnapped again, and it's sickening that I kind of hope whoever it is treats me better than Rurik does. How is it normal that this is where my mind goes now? Not '*Oh fuck I'm getting kidnapped, I'm going to die*', but '*Hm. I hope they treat me better than the monsters I'm with now*'.

The second I stand, though, the strong, rough hand drops my wrist and moves to hold my hand instead. He does so with such precision that it almost feels natural to be held like this, but I can't focus enough on the blur of a man to be able to decipher if I can trust him or not. Everything is moving too quickly for my brain to settle on just one thought. The noise levels in here are something I can barely comprehend. Between the screaming, the gunshots, the shouting of faded demands and the music from all of the machines around me, it's impossible for me to breathe, the least of my worries is my abductor.

He keeps us moving quickly, ducking around the huge attentiongrabbing machines and carefully looks around the corners of each one before he pulls me forward. It's one of those moments, when he yanks me into movement again, that I realise I'm not being abducted by assailants as a way to get money out of Rurik for some useless grand scheme that he'd never give into, it's Luca.

Just Luca.

Doing his job at keeping me safe again, and even though the shots are loud and the screaming in this building is terrifying, I'm not scared like I probably should be.

I squeeze his hand tighter, wanting him to know I know it's him, that I know I'm okay with him, just so he can focus on where he's going rather than worrying about me back here as I try to keep up with his pace.

He stands back against a few of the machines, head tipping backwards so it hits the plastic behind him before he mutters a few words under his breath that I can't fully comprehend. They're Italian, though; I really need to brush up on that.

"I really hope you can run in those fucking boots, Amore."

"I've walked through fire and glass barefoot, I'm pretty sure I can run through a casino in the middle of a shoot-out." He chances a look at me, pulling his gun out of the holster attached to his belt. He's not impressed by my attempt to lighten the situation up a little. "I'm kidding."

"No, you're not."

"No, I'm not, but you look really worried."

"Hm, I wonder if that could be anything to do with the fucking gang of people trying to shoot at us." He smiles quickly before peering back around the machine. The second he does there's a series of shots and he snaps back. "Fuck. Okay, new plan because that exit is a death trap and our cover's blown. Uh-" He looks around quickly.

"The only other way out is at the other end of the room. We've got-" I can't even finish what I'm saying because Luca brings my hand up to his lips, presses a kiss firmly to it, and exhales.

"Stay behind me." Before I can even ask why, Luca decides the exit we were aiming for, the one he'd just said was a death trap, is our only way out. Maybe tonight is the night I die. At least I'm wearing matching underwear and a damn good dress? I'm going to be one well-dressed ghost, that's for sure.

He's gripping onto me so tightly as he ducks around the machines and pulls the trigger what must be a dozen times, and I don't know how he's doing it all at once. The shots across the room stop for a second and he seizes our opportunity.

It takes everything in me to keep up with Luca's long strides as we dash for the fire exit across the room, dodging around machines and the limp, bleeding bodies on the floor in the process.

The second we reach it, Luca pushes the bar down on the door and yanks me outside forcefully before it can slam shut.

The fire alarm begins blaring inside, dampening the still ongoing barrage of gunshots, and I know we only have a matter of seconds before someone follows us.

Luca's head flicks to the left and right, quickly working out our surroundings before he starts around the building, still clinging to my hand like I'll slip from reality if he doesn't use all his force to keep me right here. My lungs are beginning to burn from the lack of oxygen and my head is fuzzy. The fear that I'm going to collapse on the floor right here, not from an injury, but from Rurik's control over my body only spurs me forward. The adrenaline from my anger becomes my only fuel.

We run around the building until we find where the valet parked his car, and I guess I was right about someone following us, because before we can find his car, we're being chased by bullets. They slam into the cars around us, and it becomes a game of who's the fastest, the gunmen or us.

"There!" I see it in the corner of the lot, and Luca squeezes my hand, dragging me between cars. When we reach it, he doesn't hesitate to slam his elbow into the window and open my door before diving over the hood and doing the same to his own. The second he's in the car, he manages to get it started with his key, and we're able to pull out of the spot before the men tailing us can get close enough to finish the job.

When we've cleared the casino, Luca finally lets out a long breath and shifts in his spot before handing me his phone.

"Here."

"What do you want me to do with this? Call the poli-"

"Call your brother and tell him you're okay before word gets out. I really don't want to be dealing with a bitchy Lorenzo tonight." I stare at him for a second. "Bella?"

"Are you okay?" He chuckles and runs his hand over his jaw. "You didn't get -"

"I'm okay, Amore. Pissed I need to get my fucking windows replaced, but I'm not injured." I nod slowly. "Are you? You didn't get hit or anything did you?"

"No." He nods.

"Good. Call Lorenzo, we don't have long until we'll be back at the house."

Chapter Fourteen

Where the hell did that come from?

LUCA

I am trying to keep myself calm. If not for myself, then for the fact that I can see how on edge Bella already is. I'd caught glimpses of the bruises on her wrists that she'd tried to cover with make-up. Just a glimpse in the midst of everything, but I don't have the time to address it with her now. Not that I need to; I know who left them on her, and I know it was whilst I was with fucking Rurik last night.

Befriending Tomas the way I had been was making it easier for me to get him away from her. Asking for advice on how to 'handle Lorenzo' whilst I 'made my plans and weighed up what I wanted to do'. He liked that, us plotting together. Whenever I knew he was intending on going to Bella, I dragged him into a conversation and slipped something into his whiskey, so he passed out in the living room.

I'd spent the night beating myself up in the full knowledge that she'd been subjected to something last night, and I couldn't stop it. If Rurik wouldn't have shot me on the spot for stopping it. If I'd have been able to drag Tomas out of there and put a bullet in his disgusting little brain like I wanted to, without it causing Isabella even a scratch, I would have. It just wouldn't have worked. We'd have both been dead before we got out of her room, and that would have defeated the point.

Permanently ending this, as opposed to the short breaks I've been able to get her, is the goal here, and I'm working as hard and fast as I possibly can to do that. The more distractions I find to keep them all away from her, the more suspicious they are going to start becoming. It's taking too long to get her safe and I'm starting to lose my patience.

I just hope that giving the Murphys that anonymous message this morning about the casino paid off the way I hoped, otherwise Lorenzo will be serving my balls for tomorrow's dinner.

"Lorenzo?" Bella's voice stutters and I instantly reach for her hand, squeezing it tightly as she takes a shaky breath. "No, I'm okay." She goes on to tell him what happened tonight, clinging to my hand so tightly I might've been concerned it was going to cut off my circulation, if I wasn't focused on the fact that she had to be unharmed to be using this much force in her grip.

It wasn't supposed to be that intense. The Murphys had always been a little clumsy, but what happened tonight was next level. They usually have people leaving the buildings they attack with ease. They never usually pay enough attention to shit like that, but tonight they had, and because of them I had to fucking smash my windows. God, she was probably sitting in the glass.

"Bella?" I shuffle in my seat, shrugging my jacket off carefully whilst trying to keep my eyes on the road ahead.

"Mhm?" Bella looks over, her face growing more concerned with every passing second. She's still holding the phone to her ear when I thrust the jacket towards her and she looks at it in confusion.

"You're sitting on glass, Amore. Sit on that instead." Don't want any harm coming to your perfect little ass.

Where the fuck did that come from?!

I clear my throat, focusing back on the road ahead of me as I beat the inappropriate thoughts to a pulp in my head. This is Isabella we're talking about here. We can't be thinking about her or the way her ass looks perfect in everything.

Luca.

"Luca?" I turn my head back to Bella quickly, just enough to acknowledge her. I somehow don't think prolonged eye contact with her is a good idea right now. "Are you okay? You're really red."

"I'm fine."

"Are you sure? Enzo, Luca's really red." Oh God. "Could he have got hit? Well, I don't know! The only time I've seen someone get shot was our parents, and I think this is a little different to that."

The atmosphere takes a deep dive. It's a cannonball hitting a ship that's barely keeping afloat, and I can see the way she immediately regrets mentioning the blue whale in the room. So much bigger than a fucking elephant. "Can we do this another time? Mhm. I swear I'm fine. Okay. I will. Bye."

Wind whips around the car, thankfully filling the slightly awkward silence before Bella clears her throat and holds the phone out to me. I take it, putting it on my lap and keeping my eyes firmly on the road.

"Bel-"

"No." The single word is sharp and so intense it shocks me into an instant silence. "I shouldn't have mentioned it."

"No, Bella, it's-"

"I'm not talking about it, Luca. That's the end of it." I furrow my brow, not a fan of how quickly I'd been dismissed, but know it is probably hard for her to talk about. Especially if she watched it happen.

It might be a little naïve of me to think she'd be able to talk about it by now. To everyone else it is very much something that happened years ago. It fucking sucks, but the world has continued moving and we have all found ways for our lives to carry on.

Isabella hasn't had that and I guess I forgot that. She has been under Rurik's thumb from the moment her parents were murdered in front of her, and from what I've seen (and the conversations I've overheard) since I started here, she's been stuck in hell for every moment since.

I decide to leave the topic. If she doesn't want to talk about it right now, I'm not going to force her to.

Not after last night and now this. She needs to be able to breathe.

Figuring I can tell Rurik I needed to make sure we weren't being tailed, I take the long route back to the house. That should give her enough time to bring herself back to a baseline where her emotions aren't through the roof.

The second we pull back up into the drive and the car comes to a halt, she is out of the car.

"Isabella." My voice is low enough for only her to hear, and I hope she'll slow down for just a second for me to try and reassure her. She doesn't though. She just ignores me, marches up the stairs and through the door without turning back. She's definitely got her brother's stubborn fucking attitude, that's for sure.

I don't bother locking the car door behind me. After all, what exactly am I stopping from happening? She might as well be a convertible right now.

★★★

The morning after the casino is much like any other. I am up at the crack of dawn, ready to do whatever I am told. I'd been texting Lorenzo for most of the night, trying, with help from Tori, to talk him down from the ledge. I know how crazy protective he gets sometimes, and he thinks he's doing the right thing when in reality he just ends up causing more problems. Case in point, drugging and kidnapping a girl because some piece of shit beat her up on a date. Did it work out for the best? Yes, but it also made

Astoria go on a hunger strike, and Isabella is seriously underweight as it is.

"Luca." I freeze, halfway through taking a bite out of my breakfast as Rurik appears in the doorway. It's still early, but as always he is dressed and ready to get on with whatever the fuck he has to.

"Rurik." I carry on eating, staring at him as I do. "To what do I owe the pleasure."

"Last night."

"Ah." I give him a nod. "She's -"

"Fine. I know. I saw the cameras. You didn't call to say something happened."

"Pointless. Nothing happened. Some fuckers decided the casino needed some media attention; I got Anastasia out without a scratch." He watches me as I have another bite of toast. "That was my job, right? Keep her safe. Not a scratch?"

"It was."

"Then I did my job." Aiming to appear as unbothered by the whole thing as possible, I simply shrug nonchalantly. There was absolutely no point in me voluntarily putting our lives on the line, just to make a little headway in this whole thing if he thinks for even a second that I couldn't handle things like this happening. Rurik remains silent as he stands there. Just pushes his hands into his suit pockets.

"Congratulations." Now that catches me off guard. "We found Alek and let's just say he's no longer in the position he needs to be." No shit. Lorenzo had a tonne of fun with him as far as I'm told. I got the lay down of every drop of blood he made that man bleed. Didn't satiate me like I thought it would, though. "You proved you can do what I need you to do last night, so I'm making you Anastasia's permanent guard."

"You want me to do this permanently?" I scoff, rolling my eyes and taking a hard bite out of my food.

"I need her unharmed for what I have planned for her, Luca."

"And what exactly is that, before I sign my name on my own death warrant?" Rurik lets out what I guess he would class as a laugh.

"Lochlan Edwards is surprisingly stupid." He moves into the room, grabbing the overpriced coffee pot and pouring himself a mug. "Getting Anastasia to get information out of him has been a lot easier than I was expecting for the son of the Chief of Police. See, when your cousin set his sights on Astoria, he messed with my plans. Anastasia had been in there gathering information on the Bardots for a reason. My original plan had been for Feliks to marry Astoria. Having a link into the policing of Alamea would be a really good place for us to be. But, since Lorenzo decided to throw that out of the window and ruin my relationship with Russell Bardot by killing him off, my only other option now-"

"Is to marry Anastasia off to his replacement's son?" Rurik smiles over his mug. A disgusting smile that makes my stomach churn with something deeper than hatred. This man is beyond vile. "Where do I come into this, exactly?"

"Well, the key to my plan is Anastasia. If she gets harmed, then my only way in disintegrates instantly. I need her unharmed so I can set this up. If this works, in a few years we will have complete control over not only Kredrith, but the entirety of Alamea." His smile grows. "And every other family who thinks they have any control over anything in this country will be long gone."

Chapter Fifteen

What happens if Earth reverses its spin?
ANASTASIA

Yesterday was ... a lot. A lot to process, a lot to understand, a lot to deal with. It's just a little overwhelming.

Between Tomas and Luca and the casino and then talking to Lorenzo and everything, I just need some time to gather myself back together.

Rurik came into my room first thing this morning just as I was getting out of bed. He quizzed me on exactly what happened at the casino and I gave him a play by play, followed by him checking me over in my pyjamas to make sure we weren't hiding any injuries from him. Thanks to Luca, I was fine.

I'm not taking the fact he got us out of there lightly; I know it's his job. I know that's why he's here in the first place, but it just felt bizarre to me. For someone to put my safety above everything else.

When my parents were alive, I was too young to remember that happening. I was still running around in princess dresses and fairy wings, sprinkling glitter over dad's wounds when he was injured to magically make him better. I didn't doubt that my parents did indeed do everything in their power to keep me safe, though. I figure now, that all of our long trips to Sicily were for the exact same reason Astoria and Penelope are currently over there. They'll be out of the way when everything blows up. They're safe out there.

That constant sense of security isn't something I've had since then. In fact, it has very much been the opposite and I've been the one at the other end of knives and chains. I'm the one that the violence has been aimed at, so for Luca to flip the switch and be the one trying to keep me safe, it had kept me up all night.

I tried reading. Different genres and authors, in the hope one of them could immerse me into their world and I'd be able to not think about how fucked up this all is.

It's not safe to show any kind of emotion here, good or bad, and I've spent the better part of my life locking every single one up in a compact cell in my brain. Banishing them to the deepest, darkest crevice there is in there, just to keep Rurik off my back. But after talking to Lorenzo last night, I am finding it more difficult to keep them back there and out of sight.

So much has happened, and so many years have passed since that fateful night that I know I am fucked, mentally speaking. No one else needs to know the details that will hold me captive forever. I can't fuck everyone else up from knowing just how bad it has been.

Frustration is beginning to build at the surface when I turn the page of my book, and I still can't remember what the paragraph is saying. I'm reading. Actively saying the words in my head, but I just can't attach it all together right now.

There's a quick knock at my door, but I don't have time to do anything other than lift my head before it opens and Luca walks in. He closes the door behind him and drops the stepladder he's carrying by the wall, pulling a screwdriver out of his pocket as he climbs the steps and proceeds to mess about with the camera.

I've learned that asking people what they're doing in my room isn't allowed, so I just sit in my spot under my blanket, watching him work. He finishes on that camera, before doing the same with the other one at the opposite end of my room and then heading into my bathroom. He comes back a few minutes later and stands in the middle of the room with a hard glare on his face.

"So, I've turned the mics off in here now. I can't deactivate the cameras yet without them getting suspicious, but at least you've got a little more privacy. There's a phone in the bathroom with mine, Lorenzo's and Astoria's numbers in, so you can use that. Only in the bathroom until I can get these cameras turned off." He hardens his stare at me, his entire body giving off aggressive energy that makes me so utterly confused.

Luca's jaw tenses, his shoulders carved from concrete as he stands there like a statue warning a country about what will happen if they take a wrong turn and repeat history. And yet, his voice is as calm and gentle as it is when we are alone. They are polar opposites of each other and coming from the same person in the very same moment is sending my brain into a spiral.

"Bella?" I blink, swallowing hard as I focus back on his hazel eyes. Late afternoon sunlight is still streaming in through the window behind him, and I could be convinced he's my saviour. "Did you get all that?"

"Mhm." I shift in my spot slightly. "Mics are off but cameras aren't. Phone in the bathroom."

"Yeah. Lorenzo asked me to tell you to text him but he's sent you a million messages he said you need to read. Pops has sent you a video too because she felt left out. If you need to tell me something, use that phone." I nod. "I'm gonna go, but I'll be in the room next door if you need me for anything."

"Next door? But that –"

"Oh! Alek, yeah. Dead. Very, very, very dead. Lorenzo got a little carried away when I told him that he'd been putting his hands on you. Not going to lie, it's a good job I was here with you, otherwise he'd still be suffering for thinking he could touch you and get away with it." Luca's eyes darken slightly. The shadow of his lowered brow makes him look more dangerous than I've ever seen him, and it has every single hair on my body standing on end. "I'm the replacement, so you don't have to worry about who's coming next." His lips twitch as though he wants to smile but knows he can't. He's halfway out the door when he turns around. "Oh, Tomas is leaving tonight, too. Absolute nightmare of someone planting a bomb in the house back in Moscow." He raises an eyebrow. "I'll change the lock on your door tomorrow, so only we have access."

With the final word out there, he leaves, closing my door gently and I am left, having not moved more than a single inch through the whole interaction and yet, I felt like the world has begun spinning in the opposite direction.

I refuse to think about it too deeply, as I'm not sure if these are good or bad changes, or if they'll eventually come back to bite me in the ass. I'm certainly not about to get my hopes up and put my money on them being the light at the end of my tunnel.

When the appropriate amount of time has finally passed, I close my book and head into the bathroom, locking the door behind me and turning to see the phone Luca has indeed just left on the countertop.

There are over thirty messages on there already from Lorenzo, Luca and Astoria. I open Luca's first, but it is just him giving more detail on everything he'd mentioned before. Astoria's messages are more friendly. Life updates from everyone, pictures of Penelope and family and as much as it feels a little held back, I can tell that she is trying for Lorenzo. I understand her hesitance though, I wouldn't trust me either.

Lorenzo's messages are the hardest. Not having had the chance to speak to him at the wedding really, I guess he is getting all these years' worth of emotion out at once. It brings up an awful lot of feelings and my heart simply can't take it. All I can manage to respond with is a simple 'I've got the phone', I don't know what to else do or say, because as soon as Lorenzo knows the truth about what happened that night, I won't be the person he is trying to protect, I'll be the one he'll be wanting dead.

Chapter Sixteen

You sure got 'little' right.
ANASTASIA

<u>Luca</u>

How are you doing, Amore?

Any problems?

> Everything is fine, Luca. I can keep myself alive, you know.
> I was doing it for years before you showed up.

I never said you couldn't, Bella, I'm just making sure I don't need to come back.

> I'm staying in my room, just like we agreed. I'm fine. Besides, you coming back will just make Rurik suspicious. I'm fine.

Pinky promise?

> Are you 12?

No, but fuck would things be simpler if I was.

Okay, fine. Just promise you'll let me know if you need me to come back. I'm not too far away and this is bullshit.

I roll my eyes at Luca's messages before stepping into the shower.

It's been three weeks since Luca walked in here and disabled the mics in my room, giving me the only sense of normality I've ever had. That little phone has given me so much, I can't quite wrap my head around how it is possible.

I've spent a lot of time trying to find places I can hide with it, behind a book or under my duvet at night. It isn't just being able to talk to Luca freely either. I think I've had more messages from Penelope than I have had from him, and that is saying something. Between her and Astoria, it almost feels like I have friends. Is it creepy to be friends with your four-year-old niece that you've only met once? Probably more than a little.

When she goes to bed, Tori takes over. It's weird, talking to her like this. I've had more than a dozen conversations with her in the past, but that was different. That was Anastasia who was trying to get information for the first time, and it was purely professional. Not now. Now she's my sister-in-law? I guess that's the right phrase.

We've spoken about my time in the office before her dad died, which I now know is her fault. She's told me about all the shit that led to her and Lorenzo getting together, and I guess I like that we have something in common. That we were both raised by shitty men who saw us as property after the people who loved us died. After we made that discovery, things have felt a lot less tense with her and a hell of a lot more relaxed.

But even with the beaming bright light that is the phone, I am still hesitant to allow myself to relax.

In the past, I've had moments where things didn't look so bleak, and they have always been met with a rapid collapse of pure horror. Call it whatever you want, but I tend to go with the fact I am cursed. That, or someone has a voodoo doll of me, and the only person it could be is Veronica from nursery school, because I took the biggest cookie that one time when we were four.

I am terrified to be happy. It isn't like I am a little bit scared of it either. I know in my bones that me being happy just causes pain; I just know it won't end well. My theory has been tried and tested. Completely done expecting things to improve, I have fully accepted my life for what it is, right down to its molecular formula.

A fucking shit show.

Have I told Luca that? Lord no. Luca is the golden retriever of golden retrievers. He genuinely believes the world can be sunshine and rainbows if we make a good enough joke. He won't get it and I don't know if I can handle the way he'll try to convince me I am wrong.

I'm not.

And that's fine.

The noise in the room instantly stops as I shut the water off, dry myself off and take some time to stare at myself in the full-length mirror. Everyone stands in the mirror and sees their flaws rather than their beauty. But all I see when I stand here like this is the battleground that is my skin.

Scars litter me in varying degrees of colour, shape, size, and age. I can look at each one like this and I don't even remember when they all appeared. The bigger ones I can. The burns, the perfectly straight ones across my thighs. His initials carved into my hip so I can never forget everything he 'taught' me in that cell.

My stomach churns and as I look over my shoulder to catch the time on my new phone, I am hit with the realisation that I've had my head buried so far into my book today that I've skipped lunch and it's now eight pm.

I stare at the empty snack box Luca snuck in here for me. He reappears every few days and slides a few more things into it, and I know it is his way of saying I need to eat more, but with Rurik keeping up with his barrage of trainers who love to work me to death, I have to be careful. It is just my luck that today is the day it's completely empty, and he isn't here to demand I eat something.

With an irritated and exhausted sigh, I change into some jogging bottoms and an oversized hoodie to keep my scars covered, so I don't need to put on the usual twelve layers of make-up, just to get something to eat. I make sure to keep quiet, not wanting to disturb the handful of guys that haven't been taken on Rurik's little trip. I have no idea why Luca had to go with them all, but it isn't any of my business anyway.

The plan is to grab some snacks, just enough to see me through the night, and head back up to my room. If I keep my head down and move seamlessly, they won't hear me and it'll be fine. But as we've already covered today, Isabella, the universe doesn't favour you.

As I turn into the kitchen, I am met with Danté. I haven't seen him in a few weeks, and I know it has been pissing him off, considering he immediately smirks.

"Well, well, well." He sips on his beer bottle slowly as I round the counter, grabbing some food out of the fridge. In and out. The quicker the better. "If the princess didn't leave her tower."

"I'm just getting some food, and I'll be back out of your way." I push the food into the pocket of my hoodie, avoiding eye contact as I move back towards the door.

"Oh no. You're not going anywhere, Anastasia." Danté blocks the only exit out of the room with his body. He isn't huge. Not oversized like everyone else, but it's deceptive. He is one of the guys who makes their way into my room when they are bored. I know I'm not getting out of it, and it pisses me off no end.

The only reason I'm down here is to feed myself. I'm not breaking any fucking rules. Not doing something I shouldn't be. I just need to eat to fucking survive, and I can't even do that without some piece of shit thinking he owns my body.

"That new guard of yours has you locked up pretty tight, huh? Are you missing me, Anastasia? That's why you really came down, you missed me and little Danté."

"You sure got 'little' right." I half roll my eyes, looking up at him as his jaw tenses. "Move out of the way, Danté."

"Who the fuck do you think you are speaking to?" He steps forward, crowding over me, and the biggest part of me wants to submit. To bow down and shut my mouth, because it is easier if I do. But there's a slither of me that is just fucking done with this bullshit. I am done taking shit for just trying to keep myself alive. There is not a damn thing I owe anyone and especially not when they think they have a fucking right to it.

"I just –" I'm not even given the chance to finish speaking because Danté wraps his hand around my throat and squeezes. He smirks as I swallow nervously under his hold.

"You need a reminder again, Anastasia? Need me to call Tomas back again? I don't think he'll take too kindly to knowing his little bird is out of her cage again, do you?" His tongue darts across his crusty lips. "God, I love watching that look of fear in your face. It makes it so much more fun when I pin you to the floor and make you take my dick whilst you fight it."

I don't know what it is about him saying that. If it's the building rage, or the reminder of Tomas' vile little nickname for me. Maybe it's feeling the food compress in my pocket and being reminded of exactly why I came down here. Whatever it is, Danté found the final straw. And apparently that's the straw that has been keeping my sanity in place, because in one move I lift my fist and collide it with the underneath of his jaw.

I'm not strong, by any meaning of the word. But I have trained hard enough to be able to put enough force behind me to make him put me down, and that is all I need to grab the dirty kitchen knife from the side behind me.

He cracks his neck sideways, staring me down with the hardest glare he can muster. But I can't back down now. Rurik is going to murder me when he gets back, and if I am going to be punished for punching him, I am sure as hell about to make it worth my time.

"You're pathetic." Danté snarls. "Look at you, thinking you can cause any damage." He moves forwards smoothly, and my heart pounds in my chest with terror. I slice the knife across his forearm as he reaches for me, managing in the panic he experiences from my surprising outburst to get around the far side of the counter.

"WHAT THE- You're going to fucking pay for this, you little bitch." He wraps his forearm around my throat as I try to move past him, but before he has a chance to disarm me, I sink the knife into his thigh and twist, dropping my grip on it as he screams out in pain, and I run, taking the stairs three at a time until I am in my room with the door locked behind me. I close my bathroom door and shakily grab the phone.

> Luca

> I fucked up.

> I really fucked up and they're going to kill me for real this time.

> I'm sorry.

I'm here, Bella.

What happened?

I'm coming.

Answer the phone, Amore.

Chapter Seventeen

Enough is enough, Bella.
LUCA

I've never wanted to be anywhere less in my life. After I tried everything to talk Rurik and Feliks down from dragging me out tonight, they still insisted Bella was fine there and that my presence was needed at this fucking deal.

The safest place for Bella was in her room, so I told her not to leave it tonight just so I could be sure she was fine whilst I was away. The new locks I put on were a hell of a lot better quality than she had in the first place. Lorenzo and Carlos had put the new ones through rigorous testing before Lorenzo was comfortable using them on her door. They are thumb print *and* code activated and with only me and Bella having access, much against Feliks and Rurik's wishes, I knew behind those doors was the best place for her if I wasn't there.

I'd had to make a case about the locks and no one else having access; that the fewer people that could get in, the safer it would be. I'd said that she needed to get in there, especially if her life was on the line, and I, as her personal bodyguard, needed to be able to get into her room too. No one else had any business being in there without my permission. I told them that if they couldn't get in, then neither could any invaders who may attempt to foil their plan by kidnapping Bella. That had been the turning point with Rurik, and within an hour, he had the old locks off and I was putting the new ones on.

And yet, none of that stopped Isabella from texting to say, 'they are going to kill me'. I have no idea who 'they' are or why they were going to kill her, but either way, I abandon my position and get in my car before her fourth text even comes through.

The thirty-minute drive back to the house is too long, so I put my foot down. Every second on the road is a second closer to losing her again, and the first time nearly killed me; this time would bury me too deep to recover.

"Luca?"

"I need you to get on the cameras at the house." Turning the wheel to dodge around cars just trying to get home from work, I spit the words out at Lorenzo. If I say enough prayers, everything will be fine. God, I really hope it'll all be fine.

"Why?" I can hear him fumbling around with the papers on his desk. "Aren't you there?"

"No." I'm met with silence and I can picture it in crystal clear HD. Seriously. I might as well have him sitting on the hood of my car giving me his signature scowl. "That's not the point here, just get on the fucking cameras, and tell me where Bella is."

"Luca-" Lorenzo warns, and my blood boils.

"I don't need a fucking lecture right now, Lorenzo. I'll be there in like three minutes, I just-"

"She's not in her room." My heart stops. Frozen mid-beat. "Her bathroom door is closed, though."

"She always keeps that open unless she's in there." I drag my hand across my five o'clock shadow and let out a breath. At least if she's in her room, no one but me can get to her. That gives me some time. The oversized house comes into view as I reach the top of the road and ready myself for chaos. "Okay, I'm going in. If I don't text you in ten-"

"Send in everyone I have on the sidelines? Have them drag you back here by your stupid fucking head?" He huffs. "I swear, Luca-"

"Ten minutes, Lorenzo." Already knowing how fucking bleak this will be if it doesn't go my way, I hang up the phone before he can torment me with the images more.

I pull up at the front of the house, slam my car door and run into the house without thinking. If it was my life on the line here, I probably would be taking a leisurely stroll, but it's not. This is Bella we're talking about, and as I reach the top of the stairs, I try to not panic. There's blood everywhere, and I'm praying she remembers the first aid basics we were all taught as kids.

"Danté!" I scowl, as his bloody fist print leaves another mark across her perfectly white door. "What the fuck-"

"You!" He turns and storms down the hall at me. "Let me in that fucking room, now."

"Yeah, that's not happening, what the fuck happened?"

"She stabbed me. Ungrateful whore. Gonna get what's coming to her-" I bite down on my tongue, remembering that I cannot leave this guy as a pile of fucking broken bones on the floor for speaking about my Bella like that.

"You need to stop that bleeding."

"Fuck the bleeding. She needs-"

"I'll handle her. If Rurik gets home and sees you bleeding out on his floor, he'll kill the lot of us. Go and sort yourself out and we can talk about what to do with Anastasia once you're not staining his rugs." He stares at me, but I'm not going to back down. He's looking for weakness, and I'm not going to show any of these fuckers even a slither. "What, do you have shit for brains? Fucking move." He flinches slightly, looking back at the door with an intense scowl.

A beat passes before the prick decides he can get his revenge for whatever the fuck happened here later. I'm right in saying Rurik will murder him for getting blood everywhere, I am just glad I have a little time before I need to worry about him.

Punching the code into the pad, I scan my thumb and disappear into Bella's room. The blood droplets inside this room don't exactly ease any of my nerves.

"Bella?" I whisper-shout, reaching up to turn the cameras off. Rurik seeing this if he checks them right now would be a disaster. I'll make up some shit if he queries it but that's a problem to handle later. "Amore, are you in here?"

"Lu-Luca?" The lock on the bathroom door clicks and she hesitantly opens it slightly.

"Just me. Are you okay?" I shove the door open, instantly reaching for her to check where the hell she is bleeding from. A simple move that makes me freeze because never, in all the time I've known Bella, have I ever seen her flinch with a look of utter terror in her eyes. Not like this. "Amore?"

"I'm okay." She nods, wrapping her arms around herself. "I- I messed up. Rurik is going to be so mad -"

"Hey, it's okay. Tell me what happened."

"I just needed some food. That's- that's all but I should have waited for you to get back, because Danté was mad and he-" Bella shakes her head, scowls and takes a slow inhale. "It's my own fault. I shouldn't have punched him."

"You punched him?" She snaps her eyes to mine, and it's clear by the way she furrows her brow that she wasn't expecting to see me smiling. Grinning, really. Like some psychotic weirdo that's proud and maybe a little turned on at the thought of her using physical violence. That's normal. Right? I mean, if it wasn't Bella. Fuck Luca, snap out of it. "Are you gonna tell me why you stabbed him?"

Bella pulls her bottom lip between her teeth. She's standing in the middle of the bathroom, holding her elbows with the saddest, 'puppy dog that's lived in a shelter for eight years' look, and I don't dare push her for an answer because my gut knows it.

I know exactly what was going to happen if she hadn't given him the bare minimum he deserves. I know because it's what they do to her in this house and standing here, looking at her like this, something in me snaps. "Pack your bags."

"What?" I turn and head towards the bedroom door. "Luca."

"Pack your bags, Amore. I've just about had it with these fucking Russians, and there is not a chance in hell I'm letting you stay here another day. Consequences be damned. Pack your bags, I'll be back in five minutes."

Wasting none of the quickly fading time we have, I make sure the door locks behind me as I head into my room to grab my essentials. Most of the crap in here can fucking stay. I have a bag specifically for this moment. For when it was time to get Bella out of this hell hole. It was supposed to be in a few months, when we'd built our team a tonne more, when the family was put into lockdown in anticipation. It was supposed to start in Moscow and slowly we'd break them all down, and Lorenzo was going to have the time of his life seeking vengeance on the people who destroyed his family.

But the plans have changed.

I'm not staying here with her for the next however many months, watching filthy men put their hands on her like she's their property, listening to them talk about her like she's worth less than dog shit on the bottom of their shoe.

Bella is worth her weight in fucking diamonds and platinum and pure sunshine. Not whatever the fuck this bullshit is.

When I come back into her room, she's frozen, just staring at the door. Nothing has moved in here, and I know we're on a ticking clock to get her out of here in one piece.

"Bella," I sigh, "We really need to get you packed. I can't get you out of here without things you want to keep. Can you help me? Tell me what you need." She blinks. "We can replace all your books and everything else. We need clothes and essentials. Yeah?"

"Essentials. Right." She nods and turns on her heel, beginning to move through the room, but it's as though she isn't actually here at all. She throws things onto the bed and I start shoving them all into two bags. Every glance I get of her, her eyes look hazy. I don't have time to try to break her out of it though, so I gather and pack what we can before closing the bags.

When we're done, I pick them up in one hand and extend my free one towards her. Isabella pauses, stares at it and then looks up at me.

"Want to get out of here, Amore?" Her throat works. "Because I promise you, if you do, I will make sure that what happened in these walls never ever happens again. I will keep you safe until my last breath."

"You can't promise that." She says, almost breathless.

"I can, Isabella. If you take my hand right now, I will." She inhales and steps forwards, slides her shaking palm into mine. "Atta girl. Let's get out of here."

I pull her towards the door, throwing it open with a slight struggle considering both my hands are full, but I don't drop her hand. My grip is tight on her as I lead us through the length of the house, noting the fact that Danté is shouting at the TV in his room, with some sports show playing way too loud. He's not going to even realize we're gone until it's too late.

After helping Bella into her side of the newly refurbished car and putting the bags on the backseat, I head around to my side and climb in, pulling off the very second my belt is buckled. As we pull out of the drive, I toss the phone Rurik gave me into the drive, so there is no chance of him using it to track us. At the same time, I hand Bella my burner phone.

"Text your brother the word 'abditory' for me." I spell it out, needing to make sure Lorenzo knows precisely what's happening.

"What does that mean?"

"Hm?"

"Abditory. I haven't heard that word before."

"Oh. It's a word we use for specific scenarios." I shift in my seat. "Abditory is a place where you hide something."

"A hiding spot?"

"Precisely." I nod once. "We have a tonne of different words for different safe houses. They don't make sense unless you know them, so we can tell each other where we are going without disclosing the information."

"And Abditory is one of them?"

"Mhm." Bella pauses for a second, taps on the phone then slides it onto the dashboard carefully. "Don't you want to know where we're going?"

"I didn't think I was allowed to."

"Bella," I smile, shaking my head as I lay it back against the headrest. "Ask whatever the fuck you please around me, Amore. Nothing is off limits." The feeling of her staring at me is almost too powerful to ignore, and I revel in it. In knowing our time isn't limited in this car right now. That we're not going back to that house where I have to hand her off to some piece of scum and stand back while she suffers. I don't think I've ever been happier than I am right here in this moment.

"Nothing?"

"Nothing."

"Luca?"

"Si, Amore?"

"Where are we going?"

"Ah! I'm so glad you asked! We are going to the lake."

"The lake."

"Yes, the lake." I nod, daring a look over at her and it's worth it, even if I only get half a second. She's fucking glowing. "It's a big body of water–"

"I know what a lake is."

"Good, I'm glad I don't need to explain it because I honestly don't know how to give you anything other than it's a big pond."

"It's more than a big pond."

"I mean, is it really? What is a pond? An elaborate puddle."

"No."

"Yes."

"No, it's really not."

"Oh, and what are you, the body of water expert for Alamea?"

"Yes, actually, I am." She lets out the slightest giggle, and I can feel the tension immediately start to ease from my shoulders and chest. She's okay. She's not there. She's unharmed. She's breathing and smiling and laughing, and we're going to the lake. She loves lakes.

I've definitely never been happier.

Chapter Eighteen

Just me.
ISABELLA

It has been one hell of a long drive from Rurik's place to wherever the hell we are now. We'd driven for around twenty minutes before pulling into a garage and moving to another car and from there, I guess I lost count of the hours.

We had grabbed some food from a drive-through an hour after moving into the four-by-four, and I must have fallen asleep to the gentle rumbling of tyres on tarmac because when I wake up, long gone are the city landscapes and power lines. We are officially in a mountainous forest, the winding, forest lined road, only lit by our headlights.

Luca slows the car down as we start to drive past fancy looking cabins. Gone are the views of huge metal fences, bricks and mortar. No, these are much more natural. Or, at least they look it. Every house is natural stone and wood with huge windows. Each one is similar but unique, and as I watch them all pass by through the window, a surreal feeling starts to fill my veins.

I guess I'd never connected the idea of moving away from the Petrovichs to a real thing that could happen. It was always this far-fetched fantasy I thought about during terrible moments of my life. A dream I was building in my head, but never actually believed was possible. But as we pull into the garage of a house that is as much suited to its surroundings as every other one in the area, I'm starting to feel an overwhelming, gut-wrenching mix of panic and calm.

The all-out chaos this is going to cause is terrifying, but at the same time, I feel like this is a dream and I'm going to wake up hungry, naked, and covered in some guy's sweat; with bruises I'll need to hide under layers of special effects make-up.

Luca offers me a gentle smile as we climb out of the car, walking around to meet me as I gently close my door. The garage is nothing to write home about and looks pretty normal. Bare walls, shelves in the far corner holding a range of boxes that are gathering dust. The fluorescent light above us hums in recognition of us being in here.

"Come on then." Luca nods to the door and starts moving towards it. I stay hot on his heels, terrified that the second he's out of sight this dream will become a nightmare, and I really want to make the most of this rest right now. My brain needs sleep to function and if this is the dream before it gets bad, I need as much of it as possible.

Our bags drop to the floor with a soft clunk and Luca uses his free hands to gesture around the space as he flicks the lights on.

"Welcome home, Bella." Luca turns to me, eyes searching mine the same way they have any chance he's had since he got into my room earlier today. "Well, welcome to The Lake House."

"Very imaginative."

"Lorenzo refuses to let us name it officially. Tori and I have fought him on it for years. We were gunning for Oak Haven Lodge, but alas, it's not meant to be." I inhale deeply as Luca guides us down the wide corridor. Each wall is lined with art prints of the lake and woods surrounding us, tables hold plants that either need very minimal care or are plastic. I can't tell. It's homely, but not personal and I guess that's the point if this is supposed to be a safe house. You don't want there to be a tie to who the owners are, but it needs to look normal.

"This is the kitchen, dining area, little lounge space with the fire. There's another living room kind of thing a little down the hall with a tonne of bookshelves. There's nonperishable snacks in the cupboards here, and Carlos is going to bring a food delivery with him tomorrow to stock everything up. In the meantime, we have the basics but no luxuries, unfortunately. Unless you class baked beans and soup as a luxury." Honestly, at this point I'd class any food as a luxury. It's not like I've had free control over it up until now.

"I don't think I've had soup since I was eight." I run my hand over the kitchen island as Luca runs the tap for a few seconds, grabbing glasses and filling them up before turning to me. Every time I mention something like this, about things I've missed out on, just grazing the surface of life under Petrovich's reign, Luca gets this look on his face. It screams sorrow and fury and it makes me feel queasy. "So, is this it?"

"Well, I'd show you outside, but right now all you'd see is the deck and it's almost one am. How about we get you settled, and I can give you the full tour in the morning? I need to call your brother before he sends Tori to castrate me." He quickly gestures back to the hallway, and I take that as my direction to start heading.

"Why would he send Tori for that?"

"Because she would make it so much more painful than he would."

"Really?"

"God, yes," He chuckles quietly, "Getting on the wrong side of Astoria is not something I would recommend to anyone. Especially when it comes to her family." He moves around me as I stop in the middle of the corridor, looking back over his shoulder at me as he stops by another door.

"So, she wouldn't need to come up here, then." Luca raises an eyebrow at me. "What?"

"You're family, Bella." He watches me for a second, inhales softly and smiles again, pushing the door open and knocking the light switch with his elbow as he heads straight in. He sets the glass of water down on one of the bedside tables as I slowly enter the room and take in the vaulted ceilings and oversized windows that I imagine paint the room in stunning sunlight during the day.

It's decorated in the same way the rest of the house is, just a little bit more intricately. In here, there are a few framed pictures on the cabinets that aren't generic. One of Penelope, and one of them all as a family.

I trace my fingers over Lorenzo's face, seeing our father in every inch of his beaming smile. Pops is tiny here. Maybe not even two years old and she's holding a fish in the palm of her hands, supported by her parents, with the most disgusted look on her face and Tori is laughing with her head thrown back. Enzo stares at Tori, one arm wrapped around her back and the other around Penelope's waist. A picture-perfect family. He's got the same look in his eye that Dad had when he looked at Mum.

I'd always caught that look. The way his eyes shone brighter when Mum laughed or made a dirty joke. I remember being young enough to believe in princes and princesses and fairy godmothers and fully believing that mum wished for her prince and had been delivered my dad.

"He looks like your dad, right?" I turn my head to Luca as he re-enters the room, dropping my bags onto the bed carefully. I look back at the frame, carefully setting it back in its place and pulling my hands back into the sleeves of my jumper. Luca observes me for what feels like a lifetime in the silence of the house, whilst I'm stuck staring at everything I've missed out on, a hurricane of emotions wreaking havoc on my insides.

"I know you might not want to talk about everything that has happened in the past fourteen years, Bella. But you need to know that if you ever do, I'm here. No judgement. No questions. No expectations. Until then, you're safe here. The windows are bulletproof, there are perimeter alarms, the doors are all locked like the one I had on your door back there, including this one. No one-"

I crack. Something in my chest fractures and I find myself breaking my own comfort to move across the room and wrap my arms around Luca's waist. He hesitates, his hands moving back as I squeeze him tight, but after a few seconds he's holding me back. Big hands wrap around me so easily as my head lays sideways in the centre of his chest. Luca brings a hand up to the back of my head, pressing me tighter into him, and I am using everything in me to not burst into useless tears right here.

"I've got you, Amore." He speaks just above a whisper, his voice so much gentler than I've ever heard him.

"Thank you." It comes out as a meek whisper, but he pulls me tighter into him before pulling back a handful of seconds later. Luca's finger presses under my chin, tipping my head back slightly so I have to look him in the eye.

"I don't need to be thanked for any of this. I'm just glad you're okay." I press my lips together, but after a few seconds I need to step back because I can't take any more of the physical touching. It might be a hell of a lot easier to be touched by Luca, but it still feels like my brain is on fire. "Okay, bathroom in there. If you need me, for anything, just shout."

I nod at him but he stops in the doorway, turning and waiting for me to verbally acknowledge his statement.

"Shout if I need anything. Got it." Luca's lips twitch and then in the blink of an eye, he's closing my door and I'm left alone, truly alone, for the first time in over fourteen years.

No cameras. No mics. No one is standing by the door. No one is watching or listening or waiting.

Just me.

And I'm terrified.

Chapter Nineteen

The Gilmore Girls fix everything.

ISABELLA

I carefully start to remove the few things Luca had managed to squeeze into the bags he'd given me. Neither me, nor Luca know how long we'll be here, but I unpack anyway, taking out each piece of clothing and filling the drawers before I settle into the bedsheets and stare up at the ceiling that feels a million miles away.

Before I can settle down and force myself to start counting sheep to fall asleep, there are gunshots. Loud and abrupt, and I just know in my gut that this is where I regret ever thinking I could have any peace.

The windows shatter as if they are from a film set, and the room fills with angry looking men I both recognize and don't. It's so loud, with shouting and demands and yet, I'm frozen solid. Unable to move a single muscle from where I am sitting in the bed, clinging to the sheets in desperation. I watch as they try to pull me around. As they scream at me about how I'm going to pay for this, they unbuckle their belts.

Then I focus on the three that leave. The ones that throw open my bedroom door and drag in Luca, Enzo, Tori and Pops. They threaten me again but when I still can't move, I am forced to watch my niece and her mother have bullets carved into their skulls. The life immediately drains from their faces as they remain completely still on their knees.

My heart lurches and I'm screaming internally, trying to pry my skin from the bedsheets and just give myself over to them as I watch the hatred grow in Lorenzo's eyes. I've taken everything from him now. Our parents, his child, his wife.

Desperation to move claws at my skin until I can feel flames burning into my muscles.

I plead with every part of my body, but every time I try to move I am more cemented in place; until I feel like I'm melting into the fabric.

The men push guns into my last remaining family member's heads, and this time, the sob breaks out of my mouth as I beg for them to stop. To let them go if I swear to go back with them and never leave again. I promise this won't happen again and obey their commands to climb out of bed, and this time I can. My feet are barely on the carpet when a gun is being forced into my hand. The barrel pressed against the middle of Luca's forehead, another to the back of mine.

They demand I pull the trigger and I can barely make him out through the tears that are flooding down my face, but I can hear my voice apologising over and over again. Begging for forgiveness as though it will be my salvation. I know how this goes; I know how it plays out. Begging and pleading to some otherworldly being doesn't change anything here.

They push the barrel into the back of my skull and I pull my trigger at the exact same time as I turn to see Lorenzo. Blood pours from his mouth and his eyes turn to the darkest shade of black.

Then it all stops.

I sit bolt upright, eyes bouncing around the room as my heart palpitates in every part of my body that it possibly can, gripping the bed sheets tight enough for my knuckles to crack under the pressure.

The house is silent. Windows intact. And I exhale until my lungs burn and beg for me to breathe in. Closing my eyes for a second before opening them again, just to check everything is still the same.

"Just a dream," I whisper to myself over and over again, leaning over to grab the glass of water, but of course I downed it all before I even settled in for the night.

The air is significantly cooler outside the duvet as I carefully pull it back and swing my legs over the edge. It's only then, whilst wriggling my toes in the air above the bone dry hardwood floor that I remind myself that this house doesn't have carpet. There's a rug, but it's faded white and blue, and the carpet I'd pictured was thick and cream and covered in deep crimson puddles. I squeeze my toes tight, shaking my hands out before I force myself to get up.

There isn't a chance in hell I'll be able to calm my nerves enough to sleep again now. Normally, these nightmares are intense, but that... that was something else. It was on a level I hadn't experienced in a long time, and I hate that my brain makes this shit so vivid that I can wake up and be unable to sleep again because of it.

My bedroom door clicking shut is barely audible as I try to maintain the eerie silence in this place. The last thing I want right now is to wake Luca up and have to explain any of this.

My bare feet pad delicately across the worn wood. I think it's supposed to look like that. It's not unfinished. It's smooth and shiny under me, if a little dusty feeling.

I turn into the kitchen space and freeze when I see Luca stretched out across the long 'L' shaped sofa, laptop sitting firmly on his huge thighs. He lifts his head slowly, brow furrowing before relaxing and offering me a sincere, but sleepy, smile.

"You okay?" He looks at the laptop for a second before his eyes come back to mine. The palpitations are making it hard to speak, so all I can do is give him a soft nod as I fill my glass with water across the room.

"Mhm. Just needed a drink." I take a few more deep and calming breaths before turning back to him. "Shouldn't you be asleep?"

"I could be asking you the same question, Amore." He shifts slightly. "I couldn't sleep, so I'm watching 'Gilmore Girls'." I must look confused because his eyes grow wide. "Please tell me you've seen it."

"I-"

"Oh, my God. You haven't." He gasps and pats the space beside him with a sense of urgency. "We are fixing that, immediately. Come, sit." I'm about to refuse. To go back to my room and replay the nightmare over and over until the sun is up and the clock hanging on the wall tells me it's an acceptable time to leave the room. "Isabella, it's basically illegal for you to never have seen an episode of this. Come sit with me before I have to inform the authorities."

"The authorities of watching TV?"

"Mhm." He pulls the screen back so I can see it as I sit down awkwardly beside him, hitting play on the show when he's confident it's visible to me and not just a dark screen. I can't say I've ever been able to watch TV. What I can say, is this is hilarious. Every time a new character comes on, Luca pauses it and tells me their name and a fun fact about them that leads to him telling me storylines and doing his best to not ruin it. With each passing moment, the reason I'm awake at this time moves further and further to the back of my mind.

We get two or three episodes in when I feel my eyes getting heavy and I guess Luca sees because he slouches down, gently pulls me so my head is on his chest and his hands are gently brushing through my hair as we watch the show. Every time he laughs it ripples through him, and between that and the show playing in the background, I can't keep my eyes open any more.

I allow myself to fall asleep to the sound of his hushed giggles and his pounding heartbeat, in the hope I might not be startled awake again by my own personal recurring hell.

Chapter Twenty

I'm so sorry, Bella.

LUCA

I can't say I had been expecting our first night to go smoothly. The stress of everything today will have been tough for Isabella and I'll do anything to make sure she never feels the way she did back there.

I've spent months watching her from a distance. Watching her be abused and not being able to help. Hearing her panicking in her room in the middle of the night when I was on one of those fucking security walks. But I can't say I'd ever been expecting her to walk into the kitchen looking as torn apart as she did tonight.

I hate it.

Not even in a 'this feels shit' kind of way. I have never hated anything the way I hate knowing what she has been going through for the past fourteen years whilst we've all been moving on with our lives.

It feels as though all my bones are being broken simultaneously. A thousand knives are tearing my skin from my muscles. I'm drowning in boiling oil. And the worst thing? The worst thing is I know, I just know she has felt worse than she does right now. I know the reason she's laying with her head on my chest, quietly breathing, is because those fuckers have put her through so much that even sleep can't be her safe place anymore.

The second I realize Bella is asleep, I turn off the show, not wanting a single thing to wake her up. She needs to rest. Her brain needs time to recover. To rebuild itself in a safe place, and I know she's safest right here, in my arms.

Once I'm settled in my spot more comfortably, I carefully pull her across the sofa until she's squashed up beside me, rather than laying in a position that I know will give her sore muscles if she stays like that for the rest of the night.

Bella's face crumples as I do. The slightest grumble of frustration that ends the second she's back against my chest.

It's only now I have her this close that I can assess her more intensely than I've been able to before. Her skin is still an unwelcome shade of grey. Not completely. Not like she's sick or anything. But I'd seen the miniscule amount of food she was being given there. It's malnourishment. Now she's here, I can start fixing everything they broke. I'll bring Bella back to us, get her fighting fit and healthy, and make sure she never has to experience any of that ever again.

I just wish we'd found her sooner.

That I'd been old enough to realise that something had felt weird about it all.

I wish that I'd never believed what I was told, until I saw her corpse for myself. Because if I had been older and wiser, or if I'd have thought about it hard enough, I'd have found her. I'd have found her sooner and stopped it all, and she'd have been okay.

I never thought I'd be fighting back my own tears as I swipe my thumb over the childhood scar just above her eyebrow. Giving her this scar whilst playing as kids is one of my first memories with her, but the guilt I feel about that is nothing compared to how I'm feeling right now.

"I'm so sorry, Bella." I keep my voice barely audible, not wanting to wake her up, but needing her subconscious to know. "I'm sorry I didn't look harder. I'm sorry I believed them. I shouldn't have given up so easily. I should have been the one that knew you were still alive. I should have made them keep looking. We'd have found you if I had, and none of this would have happened, and you'd have been fine." A rock lodges itself in my throat and I have to sniff to pull back the saltwater desperate to make a stream down my cheeks.

"But I've got you now." I clear my throat slightly, forcing myself to be stronger. She needs me to be stronger and like hell am I going to disappoint her further. "I swear, Bella, I promise I won't let you go again. I won't let anyone hurt you ever again. They will pay for this, as soon as I know you're safe, I'm going to make them pay."

★★★

When the morning finally rolls around, I allow Bella to slide out of my arms and creep back to her room under the impression I'm still asleep. I really don't want her to feel like she needs to talk about it if she doesn't want to, and allowing her to take control over whether she stays there with me or not is the least I can do right now. I wait for a few minutes, until I can hear the water in her bathroom running, to call Lorenzo and unpack last night's events for him.

He chuckles when I tell him his sister stabbed someone, and I can't blame him really. It was seriously out of character for the girl we'd both been experiencing recently. The girl who just took their shit without complaint. But apparently, she hasn't strayed too far from her family bloodline, because that happens to be the most Santoni thing she's done, and she wasn't even raised by them properly. Not for that, anyway.

He then informs me that there are Christmas decorations in the garage, so me and Bella spend the first couple of days unpacking them all. She takes it upon herself to decorate the entire house in a manner I've never seen.

The quality of the decorations here aren't exactly going to win any awards anytime soon, but she makes it look like this place belongs in a holiday movie.

She is still waking up in the middle of the night and after the first one, I make sure I am sitting on the sofa every night, with our show lined up on the next episode, a fresh glass of water on the coffee table for her, and a collection of terrible dad jokes that have been bringing back the light to her eyes just a single drop of sunlight at a time.

Through the day, it's different. She just stays in front of the fire, reading. Barely moving. For hours she sits there, wrapped up in a blanket. Every few minutes she turns the page but otherwise, she could be a statue. She's in her own world when she's like this. There's no worry on her face. No concern. She's not constantly looking around the room or overthinking whatever thought enters her head.

In the four days since we got here, Bella has slowly shown me signs that we're on the right track. She eats the food I cook and put in front of her. Small meals, little and often, until her body adjusts to having it available. She engages with me about our show, we play the dusty board games that sit on the bookshelves, or we sit in a peaceful silence like this as she reads and I do whatever I need to get done.

But I want this to be as normal as possible, and Christmas is right around the corner now. I wait until I see her flip the page again and clear my throat from the kitchen island, slowly stepping closer to the sofa as I do.

Her blue eyes come up to mine and she shoots me a quick smile as I press my hands into the back of the sofa across from her.

"How's the book?"

"It's good." She moves her bookmark between the pages, half closing it as she tugs on her blanket. "This is the last one I brought with us, though." I nod slowly, finding my way in.

"Okay. You should probably put on a jumper and some shoes then."

"Why?" Bella narrows her eyes and I stand up straight, pushing my hands into my pockets as I try to keep this as casual as possible. No pressure. Nice and easy.

"Because we can't have you running out of books, that's essentially illegal. And we should probably start Christmas present shopping, so I can get them back to the main house before Christmas." Bella stares at me and I just allow myself to smile in the hope it will ease the anxiety I can already see starting to bubble inside her. "You want to go into town?"

"I – is it even safe? I mean what if-"

"It's safe, Amore."

"But-"

"Do you really think I'd risk taking you, firstly, somewhere unsafe, but secondly, somewhere that Lorenzo hadn't spent months looking into before even buying? I promise you; no one knows we're here. No one related to them in any way, shape or form has ever even heard of this place. It's practically off the map. It's safe. So, knowing that, do you want to get out of the house and spend your brother's money?" Bella pauses for a second. Just watches me as her brain ticks over. I can imagine she's building a pros and cons list. Trying to decide if what I'm saying is indeed the amount of effort Lorenzo would put into a safe house.

Apparently, it doesn't need much weighing up and after less than a minute, she nods slowly. I'm not entirely sure if it's because she feels safe with me or because she's desperate to have more books.

Who am I kidding? It's the books. It's always going to be the books.

"Good, get ready and we can go when you are. We'll grab some lunch whilst we're out, too. Make a day of it."

Chapter Twenty - One

Come on, Wife.
ISABELLA

It's cold.

Freezing really.

Snow falls from the low-lying cloud, hovering thick and heavy in the sky. It's the kind of snowstorm that isn't heavy but the flakes are big, and despite my hands feeling numb and tinting with a shade of blue I'm one hundred percent sure isn't normal, I haven't felt this alive in forever.

With Petrovich, winter had always been a looming, terrifying presence. It was easy for him to make me suffer when it was freezing out and I didn't have a choice. What had once been one of my favourite seasons had quickly become the period when I feared most for my life. But not now.

Now Luca and I are walking down cobblestone streets, bundled up in coats and carrying hot chocolates from a stall we came across, because this town belongs in a Hallmark movie, and the upcoming Christmas market sprawls across the expanse of streets.

It's not a huge town. Probably no more than seven thousand residents in total, but it's that perfect balance between everyone knowing everyone and still being so small that it's quiet and quaint and … perfect. It's perfect.

We stop to look in another shop window. A dangerous decision with Luca it would seem, because the second I appear to even like something in the smallest degree, he drags me inside.

So far we have made four trips back to the car with bags so we don't have to carry them around, and I'm kind of glad because I really need my hands around this cup to stop my fingers from falling off.

"Come on."

"No, Lu, we really don't need to go inside this one."

"You clearly like that necklace, Amore. Let's get a closer look."

"I don't-" I give up, letting Luca smile brighter than the sun as he gently wraps his hand around my wrist and tugs me into the shop. We end up walking out empty handed, despite Luca's demands that I spend Lorenzo's money on a necklace I would likely never wear.

"You can spend the money, Bella. It's yours too."

"I mean, it's not, but-" Luca scoffs, rolling his eyes at me again. "What?! It isn't! Enzo has been working for it, I haven't." He pulls me to the side of the path, raising an eyebrow at me and cocking his head sideways, until he looks like a puppy not quite understanding what he's hearing.

"It's family money, Bella. Your brother and Tori make the family money by doing something they love, so that those they love don't need to worry about anything. You don't need to work for it, worry about it, wonder where it's coming from. Nothing. You're family, right?"

"Well yeah, I guess."

"Great, then it's your money as much as it's Lorenzo's or Tori's. If you're not spending money on that card, all Lorenzo is going to do is start nagging you about it, because he's already told me eight times that the card is for anything you want."

"I think eight times is a little dramatic."

"A little-" Luca chuckles and tugs his phone out of his pocket where he... nope, yeah Lorenzo definitely told him eight times. "Please, Isabella, spend some money and save me from your brother's abuse." I roll my eyes at him, forcing a chuckle out of his pouting lips before we start walking back down the high street.

The next store we stumble into just so happens to be the happiest place on Earth. The smell hits me the second the door closes behind me and I close my eyes, breathing it in for a second. God, I love bookshops.

Luca chuckles behind me, removing his hand from my hip as he moves around to face me.

"Go wild."

"That's a very, very dangerous thing to say to a bookworm in a bookshop that- oh my god, is that a special edition?" I push past him, no longer caring about what may be deemed polite, because this is much more important.

I take my time wandering down each aisle. The old bookshelves are fully packed with books, and I honestly don't think I'd ever be able to get through every title in the floor to ceiling piles, even if I spent months in here. It's the kind of building that is so much bigger on the inside, and I don't know if it's warping my sense of existence but I feel like this is where I belong. In this specific bookshop, surrounded by old, slightly worn books, new releases and everything in between.

I turn, putting another book into the ever-growing pile in my arms. I'm going to have to whittle this down somehow. As much as I am willing to spend some of the money on the card Lorenzo is demanding I use, I certainly cannot put this many on there. He'd go crazy. I barely take a step before I run into someone I had no idea was standing beside me and we both make that 'caught off guard' kind of 'oop' noise.

"Oh, I'm so sorry." I start instantly. It wasn't a hard bang, but I know how much it can hurt when you get pushed into a load of books unexpectedly.

"No, don't worry, I was reading whilst walking. Big mistake really. But that's on me, not you. Are you okay? That's a big pile of books. Oh! I read that one!"

"You did?" The black-haired girl nods frantically, tipping her head sideways to look at the spines of the other books I have stacked in my arms.

"Mhm. And judging by what else you've picked up; you'll love it like I did. I'm Safiyah, by the way. I haven't seen you around here before. Are you new to town?"

"Uh, yeah." I'm hesitant, looking over my shoulder for Luca. I have no idea what I'm supposed to say here. Are we new in town? Are we passing through? I know I'll say the wrong thing if he's not here, and I desperately don't want to leave the Lake House. Or this town.

"That's cool! People don't move into Swallowbrook too often. Where did you move?"

"Just down Wateridge Lane." My saving grace appears as if by magic behind me. His hand naturally finds my hip as he tugs me in beside him slightly. I can feel my body decompress in his presence in an instant. A sudden feeling of knowing I'm okay floods my veins.

That's what I've worked it out as, anyway. It's taken just over a month and a half of Luca being around constantly for me to be able to pinpoint it, but that's exactly what it is. He makes me feel safe just by being close, and I can allow myself to breathe without worrying about watching my own back, because I know he's got it.

"Really? Whereabouts? We're on there! I didn't realise anywhere was up for sale." She looks over her shoulder. "Conrad, come meet our neighbours." When she looks back to us, her eyes meet me first, obviously noticing my nerves. "What made you buy up here?"

"We were just looking for some peace. Right, honey? It wasn't technically up for sale but a family friend owned it before us, and we kind of mentioned that we were looking to move after the wedding. They wanted rid of it anyway and well, here we are. I'm Theo and this is Zoe." Did he say wedding? Luca takes his hand off my hip and extends it out to her whilst I'm still winding my head around the backstory he's built up.

We're fucking married?!

"Are you okay, Zoe?" I blink, bringing Safiyah, and who I'm guessing is her husband, back into focus. All eyes are on me, and I have to nip my miniature freak out in the bud to act like a normal, perfectly socialised human being.

"Oh, sorry, yeah I was just thinking about getting back home and reading this by the fire. You said you read it, right? Did you read her other series?" Safiyah's smile suddenly changes from concerned to genuine, and I can swallow my nerves.

We talk about books for a solid ten minutes before Conrad interrupts to say they have plans with some other people, but that we should come to the official opening of the town's Christmas market at the weekend. Apparently they're going on Sunday, and it's the perfect time to get to meet all the important people in town which, he explained, is just them and the two other couples that aren't either seventy or battling kids. They both grimace at the thought and I chuckle, knowing I hate it too.

Luca looks down at me for an answer on if I want to do the market or not and, honestly, a Christmas market wasn't something I'd been able to do since I was with my parents and I always loved them back then. I give him the smallest smile and Luca grins, tightening his hold on my hip ever so slightly as he looks back to the couple and makes the plans. Then they're gone.

When they're out of sight, Luca reaches for the books in my arms, not taking his eyes off mine as I raise an eyebrow at him.

"So, we're married now?" He smirks.

"Yeah, it was a beautiful wedding. You should have been there. Big puffy white gown, a thousand people in church pews, everyone cried. Like real tears. Bawling, actually. We had to stop the ceremony when Lorenzo was wailing halfway through." He laughs to himself before nodding towards the front of the store. "Come on wife, let's get moving. We've still got a dozen more shops for you to spend money in."

"I wasn't going to get all of those." I try to pull on Luca's arm, to stop him from getting any closer to the till with the pile, but he doesn't stop. Just takes four giant steps and slides them onto the counter with a gentle smile. "Lu–"

"You're getting the books, Amore." He flicks a look over his shoulder at me. He's so cocky right now. He planned that out. He knew I was going to put some of them back before it came around to paying, and he plotted to take them from me. It's written all over his face. Luca takes a card out of his wallet and pushes it into the reader before the cashier can say the total and when he gets the receipt, it immediately gets crumpled up and pushed into his pocket. "Let's go."

Chapter Twenty - Two

My heart is on fire.
LUCA

I hate the cold, and I've always been the guy that will find any reason not to leave the house once the leaves start falling off the trees. With winter comes bad weather, and I may just despise that more than anything.

But this? Watching Bella this relaxed as we wander around the Christmas market at the slowest pace ever, this is worth bracing the cold for.

Her cheeks are tinted in the slightest pink, the tip of her perfect nose turning her into a Rudolph lookalike, and the golden smile on her face as the steaming hot chocolate slides down her throat with an elegant gulp. It's all worth it.

"What?" Bella's ocean eyes blink up at me. Her thick black lashes dip and rise as a snowflake settles on them, and I can't help but smile, carefully reaching over to dust it off before it has a chance to melt.

"What?"

"You're just staring at me."

"It's my job to watch you."

"But you're not watching. You're staring."

"You're staring back."

"Because you're staring at me."

"Drink your hot chocolate, Bella." Pushing my hands back into my pockets, I'm downright terrified that if I don't have something to occupy them with right now I'll find another excuse to put my skin on hers.

Isabella and I have been alone for ten days. Ten days of watching her every waking second and spending every sleeping one worrying about hers.

It's been ten days of me sleeping on the couch, so I'm there when she wakes up in the middle of the night. Ten days of me reminding myself that Bella is family, and the thoughts that have been circling my head are not appropriate.

Before I got Bella out of Petrovich's place, my mind ventured to places I try my best to not let it go to. To my very uncertain future. It was there that I realised I won't be able to protect Bella forever.

Once this thing with Petrovich is over, once Lorenzo, Tori and I eliminate the threat, Bella and I are going to go home and she'll be free. Free to explore and travel, and see people outside of just me watching her closely. It's this thought that riddles me with anxiety.

I know she's safe with me and selfishly, I want to keep it that way permanently.

I want to wrap her up and keep her in my eyeline forever, so I know that no one can lay a single finger on her in the way they had been. She's had enough pain for a lifetime, and I know that if I'm watching, she won't experience it again.

What about when she starts dating? Because eventually, that's going to happen. I'm just supposed to trust that whoever it is isn't going to put her through the trauma again? They're not going to force her into something she doesn't want? Not going to physically hurt her? Or emotionally destroy her further?

When I got her up here and got to see her in a place where I knew she was okay, where I knew not a single soul could touch her, it stirred something in me.

If I was protective before, I don't know what this is. This is wanting Bella to myself so no one can breathe wrong in her direction. It's my hand on the gun in my pocket, twitching whenever anyone else comes within a foot of her.

I imagine this is the feeling Lorenzo had when he kidnapped Tori after that waste of space put his hands on her. And suddenly, I find myself understanding why he locked her up and went to the extent he did. Because I'd do the same, if not more, for Isabella.

"Zoe!" I drag my eyes from Bella's to the voice from the bookshop earlier this week.

Being hermits up here would draw attention. Rumours would start to stir about the couple up in the house on the outskirts of town, and rumours quickly turn to wildfire in this kind of community. Lorenzo looked into Safiyah and Conrad and thankfully, they were as bland as everyone else in this town. So, it was decided we could allow a minimal friendship to bloom, as long as we held up the façade.

As the couple get closer, I grab for Bella's hand and wrap her fingers between mine, tugging her into my side. She stiffens slightly beside me and it takes her a few seconds to relax. It has to be weird for her to remember that these people think we're married.

I try to pay attention to the conversation, but I honestly don't care. My eyes continuously trail back to my glowing 'wife' and with every glance and every genuine smile she gives me or her new friends, I feel warmer.

She laughs at something Safiyah says and my heart almost jumps out of my chest. It's a real laugh that I haven't heard in forever. It's deeper than it was when we were kids and yet, despite everything, I'm transported back to Sicily. Back to those pastel sundresses and toothless smiles, as Bella tips her head back and lets out my favourite sound.

I'll do anything to hear that sound again. That's my new MO. Hear Bella's genuine laugh at least four times a day. One instant dose and I'm officially addicted to something stronger than heroin.

We end up spending the rest of the afternoon trailing around the town with the couple and another pair we were introduced to. I keep Bella close even when I've not got hold of her hand, pulling her back against my chest so I can feel her breathing steadily.

"So, Zoe, we were thinking," Safiyah starts, "we have a game night at our place on Friday nights. Just us four. You guys should come!"

"Oh, you totally should." The new girl, Farah, agrees as she tugs slightly on the front of her hijab. "We obviously don't drink but Safiyah does, so don't let that stop you." She chuckles. "It makes the games a lot more entertaining when Safiyah is, if anything. She's a lot easier to beat."

"Hey!" Safiyah laughs, resting a hand on her friend's shoulder as she sips from the mulled wine she bought a few moments ago. Bella is sipping on the same kind, and with each sip she melts a little bit deeper into me. "So, what do you think? Friday night?"

Bella tips her head back at me, no doubt waiting for me to decide if it is safe enough for us to do that, but I can see the hope in her eyes. We've spent three hours with these guys, and I can just tell Bella likes them.

As much as I want to wrap Bella up and lock her away in a castle like Rapunzel, I can't. She's been locked away for long enough. I don't want her hurt, but I want her to experience life as much as she can.

"Fine by me, Amore." I swallow the lump in my throat and pull on her hip gently before wrapping my arm around her waist. "I don't think we have any plans."

She beams. The biggest, brightest smile I've ever seen, and my heart sets alight.

Bella looks back to her friends and they start making plans, but I'm too fixated on the girl wrapped up under my arm and how I really shouldn't be getting hard for her. But fuck, if that smile doesn't make me want to give her a reason to smile more often. Preferably on her back with my head between her legs.

Chapter Twenty - Three

Man, I feel like a woman.
ISABELLA

For the first time in almost two weeks, I wake up in my own bed, and it isn't the middle of the night. I am still shaking, still sweating, heart still racing abnormally from the things my brain has been replaying, but if I do my maths correctly, I got six hours of solid sleep, which is more than I've had since I can even recall.

And boy if that hasn't given me a whole new perspective of existence.

Tonight, we're heading across to Safiyah and Conrad's place for a game night and I'm simultaneously terrified and excited. I am worrying about what games are going to be brought out. I'm well aware of the numerous things I've missed, and judging by what seems to be mine and Luca's favourite conversation over the past two weeks, playing poker is likely not a life skill I'll be needing anymore.

But, Luca will be there so I know I'll be okay.

The house is quiet this morning, but I did hear Luca when I first woke up. Quietly moving around the house. I know his footsteps now, know he deliberately misses the creaky floorboards when he thinks I'm asleep.

He isn't working on a night when I go in, I know that, too. That he sleeps on the couch rather than in the other room because he knows I'll need water after a nightmare, even if I bring some to bed with me. He knows, but he doesn't question it. Doesn't ask why I'm up, or if I want to talk about it. He just starts talking about something random and moves up, so I can have my newly claimed spot right beside him.

In the morning, I wake up, well rested but alone in his spot on the couch, covered in a blanket and smelling like him.

But this morning was different. Today I wake up smelling of sweat and salt, and I need to wash it off.

I shower and get dressed in yet another of my comfortable outfits that seem more like a uniform recently.

I was so used to my routine at the other house. Showering and covering the scars in the layers of make-up and SFX clay, because it was expected that my skin should be visible to them, but not the aggressive scars they left covering my body. Nobody wanted to see those.

In the two weeks I've been here, I haven't been able to hide them like I was before. I don't have the materials I need and buying them will just cause Luca to ask questions he doesn't want answers to. So, I've been opting for long length clothes, thankful it's winter and I can get away with it right now. I have no idea what I'm going to do in a few months when it's too warm to wear sweaters and leggings.

I'll have to work out a way to get the make-up I need without Luca or anyone else knowing. But buying it on Lorenzo's card won't be possible, nor will getting it delivered here. Maybe if I'm still friends with Safiyah and Farah, I can ship it to one of their houses and hide it from Luca when we come home. Actually buying it will still be an issue, but at least I'll have somewhere to send it.

My focus is still on the towel I'm using to dry my hair as I enter the open doorway into the kitchen and stop dead in my tracks, because the sight before me is something I will never, ever forget.

I scramble for my phone and instantly hit record as Luca sings along to the music, using a spatula as a microphone. I need this as evidence for when he denies it ever happened. Or as blackmail. Whichever comes first.

I fight my laughter whilst he sways his hips along to the beat but it's the way he adds the country accent onto the words 'Man, I feel like a woman' that has me stopping the recording and bursting into a fit of laughter I can't even control.

The hilarity has me reaching for the kitchen counter to hold myself stable as Luca turns around quickly. His cheeks burn a dark scarlet on his deep olive skin, but it only takes a second before he is beaming again and starts dancing across the room, still singing terribly off-key. He grabs my hands, moving my arms along with his as he pulls me across to the opposite counter, letting me go only to pick me up and sit me on the top.

He doesn't stop there, though. Oh no. I am given a full performance from the man himself. A Broadway worthy show. I'm talking leg kicks, jazz hands and facial expressions to match everything.

By the end of the song, I'm laughing so hard that I'm sure I've pulled a muscle, but Luca just stands with his back to the hob, a gleeful, toothy smile on his face. He waits until I'm able to get my breathing back under control enough to speak, which I'm grateful for, because holding a conversation whilst panting doesn't seem like a fun thing to do.

"Enjoy the show?"

"Oh, definitely." I nod quickly, pulling my feet up so they're crossed, giving him more room to get around the kitchen. It likely wouldn't cause an issue. There's plenty of room between the kitchen island and the other cabinets, but having my legs hanging off the edge feels like I'm intruding on his space somehow. "I might buy a season ticket. As long as I get front row."

"Amore, you will always have front row seats to my shows." He smiles, taking a step forwards to tuck one of my still damp curls behind my ear. "Your curls are coming back now you're not killing them off."

"I know. I forgot how much work they are to look after. My mum used to do it all." He puts his hands on the countertop on either side of me. "I think I need some new products. The ones I have aren't going to cut it."

"You're going to keep them?" Luca tips his head slightly and I feel a little taken aback. "I thought they were just coming back because you didn't bring your straighteners or something."

"I didn't." His eyebrow raises at the exact same time his head tips slightly and I sigh. "Rurik didn't like my curls." I pick at the skin around my fingernails as opposed to looking Luca in the eyes whilst I let him see just a slither into reality. I might not be able to give him everything, but this is hair. It's stupidly unimportant.

"It was one of the first things he… got rid of when I got to Moscow and if he ever saw them he'd – he just shaved my head. So, I just stopped fighting it. If I had to leave my room, I'd straighten it or pull it up in a super tight bun so he couldn't tell, but if I could be alone in my room I'd let it be. I guess that saved them."

I wait a few seconds of silence before allowing myself to lift my head and look Luca head on. When I do he's not looking at me with sad eyes like I was expecting. His brow is pulled tight in the middle in an almost scowl. Then he stands up and gives me a certain nod.

"I'll ask Livia what she uses when she visits. Better yet, I'll get her to send some up from Sicily. Your mum used to sit with her when you were small and Livia would put all this stuff in your hair so you guys have to have the same curl type, and her hair's never crunchy or anything. Leave it with me."

"I can work it out myself, Luca."

"Yeah, I know you can." He shrugs. "But it can take years to find the right products for you. We know Livia's work, so let's start there, and if you don't like them then we can shop around. I'm sure there's gotta be like a curly hair expert somewhere that could help."

"Luca-" He turns around, cracking an egg on the side of the pan.

"You want your curls back, Bella, we'll get them back."

Chapter Twenty - Four

Men are dumb.
LUCA

She's drunk.

Utterly wasted. So much so, she might as well be on a whole other planet. I should be frustrated. Bella being drunk means I have to focus a hell of a lot harder on keeping her safe. It's not a matter of being aware of my surroundings because right now, she's a danger to herself.

Four times since we got ready to leave Safiyah's house. Four times Isabella has tumbled or almost face planted the floor. One of them was her almost falling down the stairs that lead up to her friend's front door, and I'm trying to not even think about the fact that I caught her before she started picking up the pieces of the shattered wine glass with her bare hands.

It's making my job even harder, and I should be frustrated, but I'm not. I'm not the least bit pissed off because this version of her, this Isabella that's sitting on the bathroom counter giggling and swinging her feet as I try to wipe the layers of make-up off her face, the version that sat in the passenger seat of the car arguing with me about the importance of the letter 'Q', she's happier than I've seen her in too long.

I can see it in every single crease by her eyes as she grins. That shimmer is back in her eyes and it's not from her holding back tears, or because she's exhausted.

We spent the night eating and laughing, and with each passing hour I got to watch as she became more and more relaxed. Each glass of wine Safiyah poured them both brought her mind more into the present and further away from the deep-rooted darkness I know she has caged up back there.

"Amore." I laugh as she scrunches her face up tighter. "Darling, I need you to relax your face. You're going to get the soap in your eyes."

"You're getting it in my eyes anyway."

"Only because you're scrunching your face up like I'm trying to feed you raw fish."

"I think I want to dye my hair."

"Dye your hair?"

"Mhm. Blue. NO. PINK!" She beams bright and sunny and all I can do is shake my head at her. I might love drunk Bella more than the sober version. She doesn't have a single care in the world right now.

"Okay." Her face scrunches tighter and I chuckle, trying my best to get the make-up from under her eyes when she finally relaxes. She pauses for a moment before going a little quieter. Bubbles bursting as she seems to mellow out in an instant.

"Luca?"

"Si, Amore."

"Thank you for looking after me tonight." I pause for a second before finishing my work and taking a slight step back. She's stopped swinging her feet now, eyes a little sadder than they have been all night, and I can feel the darkness that seems to fill this house constantly creeping back in. I need to seal this place tight. Stop it from having any chance of sneaking in and taking this version of her from me. "I shouldn't have drunk so much."

Isabella's eyes dip down towards her thighs and I snarl at her self-blaming. No. This isn't how tonight is ending. If it has to end eventually, if she has to sleep, it isn't going to be with her pulling herself apart. Not tonight.

I curl a finger under her chin, lifting her head back to me and giving her a soft smile, hoping to find a way to lighten the situation and bring her happy self back to the forefront.

"I had so much fun with you tonight. I didn't know you were so good at Uno. I'm still a little bitter about the picking up sixteen cards though."

"That wasn't only me! You started it!" *There she is.*

"Yeah, but you didn't need to put another card down too!"

"But then I'd have had to pick them all up! How do I win then?!"

"By making me lose, clearly." She cackles, head falling backwards on her shoulders, long dark curls bouncing as her head shakes. She's beautiful. Mesmerisingly phenomenal, and I am entirely wrapped around her perfect little fingers. "Come on.

Let's get you into bed before I end up losing more of my money to you tonight."

I carefully wrap my hands around her waist, pull her down to the floor from the countertop and entwine our fingers before she can scurry away without me.

I love having my hands on Bella. In whatever form that comes, but holding her hand may just be my favourite. It isn't often I get the chance to, or rather, have the reason to do it without her raising an eyebrow at me. When we're out, I can use the whole 'fake married' excuse, or that I need to know where she is. In the house I have nothing, and I've found myself subconsciously hunting for reasons to have my body touching hers in any way I can. Whether it's holding her mug weirdly when I hand her a drink or sitting as close to her as humanly possible. Any way I can to get that static feeling I get every time, even through my clothes.

Knowing this has to be a tough thing for her, I turn around whilst she changes into her pyjamas, waiting until I hear her final huff.

"I need help." I spin around, keeping my hands over my eyes dramatically. She giggles. "I'm dressed, Luca. I just need help with the buttons."

"Okay," I nod and take my hands away but keep my eyes tightly shut, enticing another laugh from her. I smirk, opening my eyes and finding the button she's struggling to get into the hole in the middle of her shirt. "You managed most of them."

"I know!" Her smile is a little less bright as I struggle as well. I don't think alcohol is the reason she is fighting with this. The hole is too small for the button. Isn't that the whole point behind these? What kind of manufacturer makes the hole too small?

"What's wrong, Bella?"

"Nothing."

"You should tell your face that." I force the button through the hole, sighing as I tuck a few of her curls behind her ear. "You were fine until we got you into your pyjamas. Talk to me, Amore." She sighs.

"I slept through the night last night."

"You did." And I am damn proud of her for it. "Did you feel better this morning?"

"No."

"Why not?"

"Because I woke up here and not on the sofa." She pouts slightly, letting out a huff as she crosses her arms tight across her chest.

"You're upset that you stayed in your comfy bed and not scrunched up on the sofa?"

"No." She sighs. "Forget it. You don't get it." Bella drops her arms dramatically before she turns to look at her bed.

"I didn't realise you like sleeping on the sofa so much."

"I don't. It's uncomfortable and hurts my neck." She's pouting about not waking up on the couch this morning, whilst also complaining about sleeping out there? Bella chuckles at how confused I look, pushing up on her tiptoes to jab a finger at the creases formed between my brows. "You're so cute when you're confused."

"Oh, you think I'm cute, huh?" I instantly raise an eyebrow, and try not to laugh at how quickly her cheeks flush pink.

"Pft. No. You're taking it out of context."

"Nuhuh. I'm not. You said I look cute."

"When you're confused. Because you're dumb." She smiles innocently.

"You're the one who isn't making sense, Amore. *I'm Isabella, I hate sleeping on the sofa but I'm throwing a strop because I didn't wake up there this morning.*" I put on my best impression of her and she snickers, grabbing one of the throw cushions from the bed and hitting me in the chest as she starts to pull back the comforter.

She leans across the bed, pressing her palm into the mattress to grab the other cushions on the far side.

That's when I catch a glimpse of something I don't think I am supposed to. Her top falls forward slightly, uncovering her hips and lower back, covered in scars of varying shapes and sizes. Some are dark and vicious, some a deep red and I know those are fresh. I know they've been healing for the shortest amount of time because there are others that are slightly faded to a pasty white on her pale skin.

Anger bubbles in my chest as reality sinks into my bones. She's not just mentally scarred from her time with those fucking bastards.

I knew they laid their hands on her. I knew she had to have been physically beaten whilst she was with them, based purely on what I'd witnessed Tomas be like with her before I shot an innocent bird to stop him going further. But scars? Some of them are small and round and I just know they're the same size as Rurik's cigar's. Others are straight and I can see the way they raise on her skin, telling me just how deep they cut her in the first place.

"I'm Luca and I'm too dumb to realize Isabella is upset because she didn't wake up smelling of me." I swallow the mountain in my throat as she turns around, smiling slightly, using another pillow to hit me again. "Men are dumb." I scowl, grabbing the pillow as she tries to hit me again, snatching it from her and tossing it across the room. It collides with a photo frame on one of the dressers, causing a bang as it falls over.

The move is much more aggressive than I intended, and I instantly regret it when Bella freezes. But my emotions are too high right now; I'm furious and I feel like my insides are being licked with flames from my stomach. Snarling at the feelings, I take one gargantuan step forwards and scoop Bella into my arms, turning out of the room. "Luca."

"You're sleeping in my room tonight."

"No. That – that's not what I–"

"Don't care." I shrug, holding her a little tighter when she wriggles in my hold. "I'm too tired to set my alarm for two am and pretend I've been awake for hours working. We both need a solid night's sleep and you're only going to get that with me. So, my bed. Not the couch. Okay?"

When I get to the edge of my bed, I immediately lower Bella's feet back to the floor and pull my jumper and tee-shirt off in one swipe. She still hasn't answered as I drop my jeans to the floor, leaving my boxers on for my own sanity and her comfort. Note to self: buy pajamas.

"Isabella," I warn, raising an eyebrow and sighing. "Please, Amore. You want to sleep in here with me tonight?" She nods. "Can you verbally say that for me? I need to be sure you're okay with –"

"Yes." She nods again and lifts her head. "I want to sleep in here." I give her a single nod. Then another as it sets in. She *wants* to be here. She wants to be with me, in my bed.

Fuck.

I step forwards, press a kiss to her forehead before pulling back the bedsheets and carefully helping her in, sliding in myself after. I get comfortable and tug her across so she's tucked into me, my arm slipped neatly through the gap between her shoulder and the pillows she's got her head on. Once we're settled, I pull her as close as I can physically get her and hold her the way I know she likes to be held.

Isabella makes a contented huff and I watch her as she slowly falls asleep to me playing with her curls.

When I'm sure she's out cold, I reach my hand down to her hip, carefully sliding my hand under her pyjama top so I can feel each rise and blemish on her back.

As I trace the ones I can without moving or waking her, before I know it, saltwater begins to puddle on the bridge of my nose.

"I'm so sorry, Amore." I whisper, pulling her closer. "I'll make them pay for what they did to you. I promise. I won't let them live with this."

Chapter Twenty - Five

Dormi, Amore.

ISABELLA

Last night was a mistake.

I knew it the very second I woke up and wasn't in my own room. I felt Luca dip out of the bed when his phone started buzzing on the bedside table, leaving me alone with my own thoughts, in a sleepy haze.

I haven't been able to stop thinking about it all day. No matter how many pages I've tried to read, the shower I took first thing, the fact I tried to put some space between the two of us today. None of it has stopped me going over the fact that it was the best night's sleep I've had in decades.

Since coming up here with Luca just over two weeks ago, I've realised that I am exhausted. A tiredness that I hadn't noticed has been carved into my bones over a series of long and torturous years I never want to relive.

But after last night, my head feels clearer than I can remember it ever being, and yet I am even more exhausted than I was yesterday.

It's to be expected, I guess; that now I'm safe, my body is coming out of freeze mode, and the years of it being abused are starting to catch up on me. I'm putting weight on too, already beginning to outgrow the clothes I brought with us.

My reflection is almost impossible to miss in the huge mirrors dotted across this cabin and each one time I do, it catches me a little off guard.

I can't say I ever recognised myself in the mirror when I lived with Rurik, and it allowed me to separate who he wanted me to be, and who I knew I was. That girl, the one with pale grey skin and too many jagged edges. The girl who nodded meekly and only spoke when she was spoken to. Anastasia. I'm not her. She was a character I was forced to play to survive. But now I don't need her for that. And I'm still not sure exactly how to feel about the loss.

Anastasia was a safety blanket. An armour I could pull on nice and tight, and with her taking the blows, Isabella was safe. She could exist inside me. In her memories and thoughts, she could exist in a world where she was still that nine-year-old girl, before everything went wrong.

But now Anastasia is gone, and all I'm left with is the brutal reality that I can't hide from any of this anymore. What happened, happened. Years have passed since I could allow Isabella to explore life without fear of persecution, and that is both liberating and terrifying.

I no longer have the armour to hide behind, and that means every shot to come, all the trauma, it's mine to deal with and mine alone.

"Bella?" Luca speaks from the other end of the corridor to where I'm standing, completely lost in thought as I stare at myself in the mirror that stretches across this expanse of wall. I blink, turn my head slowly until he comes into view. "You were going to bed, Amore."

"Right." I nod. Bed. Focus, Bella. Luca furrows his brow slightly before relaxing.

The thing about having a clearer mind after such a long time is that everything slams into reality like a freight train. That's how I've spent today. Thinking. Remembering. Fighting myself from crying because I know once I start it will be like opening the floodgates, and I'm terrified I won't be able to stop. That it'll just go on for days, and I don't know if I can handle anyone seeing that right now.

Eventually, I force my feet forwards and wrap my hand around my door handle. Before I can fully open it, Luca clears his throat and it makes me nervous.

"What are you doing?" I turn slowly as the anxiety bubbles in my chest.

"Going to bed?" Luca stares across the hall at me from his open doorway. He hasn't said anything, but I know he can tell I'm barely clinging onto reality right now. He's held himself a little taller all day. Given me space but only for short periods of time before he'd find my hiding spot and do whatever he could to make me eat the snack he brought and talk to him about literally anything. He's kept his voice low and his movements slow and precise and I know he's doing it because he can tell I'm struggling.

"Wrong room, Amore."

"No, it isn't." I glance over my shoulder and then back to him, confirming that I am indeed standing outside my room. Getting this wrong is something I wouldn't put my brain past right now, honestly. "This is my room." Luca's lips lift on one side for a brief second.

"Did you sleep well last night?"

"Huh?" He takes a giant step forwards and I naturally back up to the door. In one swoop, he manages to cover most of the distance between us. Not so he's intimidatingly close, just enough for me to be unable to think about anything else other than his sudden proximity.

"You didn't wake up like you normally do." Luca reaches behind his neck, scratching quickly before letting out a breath. "It's better, right? When you're with me? You can sleep better and the nightmares aren't as bad."

"I-"

"I just figured that's why you wake up every night. You're always shaking and I can see the panic in your eyes, but you didn't wake up last night. I could feel them starting but I think I managed to scare them off." My heart thuds in my chest as I try to work out how the fuck I am supposed to respond to any of this. "It worked, didn't it? You didn't have them last night? Bella?"

"Hm?" He smiles quickly, reaching forward and wrapping my hand in his without me even answering his question. "Wh-what are you doing?"

"Going to bed." Yeah. Great answer genius. Definitely helps me work out what the fuck is happening right now.

"But-"

"You're coming too, don't worry."

"But my room-"

"I don't like knowing they're still haunting you, Amore." Luca uses his free hand to pull back the bedding before turning back to me. "So, if us sleeping in the same bed stops that, then that's what we're going to do. They don't have any effect on you anymore. You're safe here. Until your brain catches up with that, you can stay here with me and I can stop the nightmares disturbing you. How does that sound? Wanna stay here with me?"

Luca watches me closely with hopeful eyes. I'm so tired. And he is right, last night was the best night's sleep I'd had in forever. I know today has been rough, but I also know that I can't avoid this clear head forever. I need to get my mind back to some form of normal before I'm thrown back into reality. Before I have to navigate everything out there alone. I need to force myself through getting back on track, and I simply cannot do that when I'm sleep deprived.

"Okay." I whisper and watch as Luca tries to fight his own beaming smile. He doesn't give me a chance to go back on it because in the blink of an eye, I'm being pulled between the sheets and into his chest, the same way I'd fallen asleep and stayed for the entirety of last night.

Luca tangles his fingers into my hair the very second we're both comfortable, massaging and twirling my free curls around him gently. He's not wearing a top again and it's the calm beats of his heart under my ear that steals my focus. Each one makes my eyes feel heavier than I can fight.

"Dormi, Amore. Si sicuru. Non permetterò che ti facciano più male."

Chapter Twenty - Six

I'm insane.
LUCA

Christmas has never been my favourite time of year. At least not since losing my parents and brother.

It is always this slap to the face reminder of everything everyone else has that I don't. No matter how hard you try to move on from that grief, how fast the years pass or how much more you have in your life, watching everyone else with their families doing the whole thing will always be a stab to the chest.

I wish I could say it got a little bit better after Lorenzo lost his family, because at least someone else got it. But he just stopped coming home for the events.

Deep down, I knew the reason why. He spent Christmases and birthdays and weddings locked up alone in a room staring at screens, so the rest of his team could have time off. In my chest I knew that he felt the agony I did over losing everyone. The difference was that Lorenzo could escape it. He could stay here in Alamea, push it deep into the back of his mind and carry on like it was a normal day.

I couldn't.

Every single event. Every holiday, I sat there and watched Mia be loved by the only family she really knew. She was so young when our parents died that she didn't remember them. For her, this was normal. But I remember waking up with them and heading to the Santoni's house for celebrations. I remember watching the men shoot at glass bottles in the back garden. I remember my parents dancing under the lights and being in their own world. I remember watching their faces light up as we opened our gifts and I remember how they'd try their best to hide how terrible what I'd made them was because, come on, what kid has money to buy their parents something that isn't made in some sweatshop or hand made with playdough?

It's been seventeen years. I don't think I will ever reach a point where Christmas doesn't mean my chest feels like it's filled with concrete, but this year feels different.

It's just me and Bella this morning, sitting on the floor of an otherwise empty cabin, surrounded by everything Lorenzo and Astoria shipped over from Sicily.

He's gone insane on the amount of things he's bought her, but since she was still hesitant to spend on his card, he said he had no choice but to spend it on his sister, like she deserved. He wanted to be here, but Tori is more than halfway through her pregnancy, and moving her and Pops up here for a few days is a little risky.

"Open it, Amore." I clear my throat as she stares at the last box. I'd purposely ignored our 'no gift' rule because I wanted her to have this. She needs to have complete control over her body again and even if it was just an off handed comment while she was wasted, I'd spent an entire day looking into making sure I got the right product to not only show up, but not cause any harm either. It'd cost more than I'd like to admit, but if this gives her even a slither of the joy I think it will, it'll be worth it.

Bella hesitates and slowly begins to pull the paper off the box. She hates this. Being given things. I can see in her eyes just how low Rurik has dragged her self-confidence. I'm determined to remind her she is worth more than the world.

Her eyebrows pull together as she looks at the obscure patterns on the box and carefully looks for the tab to pull it open and when she manages it, her entire body language changes. Her eyes dart up to me quickly, then back to the box.

"You got me hair dye?" Her voice is quiet when she speaks, pulling one of the round plastic tubs out.

"You said you wanted to dye it." Moving across the rug to sit closer to her, I pull one of the tubs out and turn it around for her to see the colour and branding. "I looked it up online to try to find one that wouldn't damage your curls when we do it, because that would be stupid when you worked so hard to keep them healthy. And it's only semi-permanent. Just to try it out. I couldn't get you a hair appointment at this short notice. But if you do like the colour or just the idea, we can have a look around, find one that can work with your curls and get you booked in."

When I look back at her, she's holding the mixing bowl and brush and staring at me with slightly damp, but bright eyes.

"What?" Her grin grows quickly, and I chuckle.

"Can we do it now?"

"Now?" She nods. "I mean, we have plenty of time before we need to head to Safiyah's. So, yeah." Her smile reaches up to her eyes and she quickly shoves everything into the box and stands up excitedly. I'm hot on her heels, following her as she runs down the hall into her bathroom.

I stand in the doorway as she reads the instructions and starts to prepare everything she needs according to them and this, this is exactly what I wanted from her today. I wanted to see her excited to take that control back because she's missing it in so many places.

She can't control that the nightmares are likely never going to stop, nor can she control that we're up here in the first place, away from everything that would give her any sense of normality. We're in this kind of limbo up here where she's no longer in her horrible past, but she's not allowed to live properly. She can't be out making friends, can't be spending time with her brother or niece, or getting comfortable with life outside of captivity.

"Luca?"

"Si, Amore." I blink.

"Can you help me? I can't get the back." I nod, moving closer. I pull on some of the gloves I'd bought and get to work while she starts rambling on more than I've heard in forever. "Lorenzo is going to go crazy." She snickers.

"Nah, I doubt it." I pull the chemicals through her hair carefully. If I'm doing this, I'm going to do it right. She's not going around with patches all over. "Tori once dyed her hair bright purple."

"Purple?"

"Mhm. After her dad and everything. It took a few weeks for reality to kind of set in that it was all over and she didn't need to pretend to be someone she wasn't, ever again. She was so used to having two sides of her that she found it really hard and went through this identity crisis."

"I get that."

"You do?" Bella nods slowly. Maybe me giving her three mimosas with breakfast was making this easier for her to talk about, but either way I was going to try to grab this chance with both hands. "How?" She sighs, eyes catching mine in the mirror, where they stayed.

"Anastasia got me through everything. I guess, like Tori had the side she showed her dad, I had Anastasia. But I had her for so long…"

"You're not sure where she ended and you begin?" Isabella's head bobs slowly as I finish the last strand of hair. I take a moment to take the gloves off and set a timer on my phone so we don't end up over processing it. Only then do I put my hands on her shoulders and turn her around slowly. "No one is expecting you to slide into reality like it's second nature. You know that right? It's okay for you to – to want to try and figure it out. You are in charge now, Bella. I know that sounds scary after spending your whole life with someone taking away your choices and making them for you, but I promise you, the more choices you make, the easier it will become. You've just got to do what everyone else did as teenagers, except you're doing it at twenty-four."

"What, have a rebellious stage?"

"Precisely." I smile. "Though, let's not do the sneaking out of the house thing. I really don't feel like trudging through miles of dense forest would be good for either of our heart rates." She chuckles and I press my hands into the counter on either side of her. "The world is your oyster, Amore. No one else will ever have control over your body or your mind. If you, I don't know, suddenly decided you wanted to tattoo the word 'Ass' on your forehead, I'd use it against you for the rest of our lives, but I wouldn't stop you."

"Lorenzo would murder you."

"He could try but your sister-in-law wouldn't let him get away with it. Besides, Pops would just cross her arms and scowl at him and get her own way. I tried replicating the look but it didn't work for me." Bella cackles as her hands land on my chest and her fingers entwine with the now stained cloth of my white t-shirt. My heart pounds rapidly in my chest.

As good as it is to have her smiling and laughing, I need this burning into her mind. I need Isabella to know how important it is that she takes back the control she's never had. She's so much stronger than she thinks she is.

"But I'm serious, Bella. Your body, your choice, Amore. Don't you ever take anyone else's opinions into consideration. Not Lorenzo, not Tori, not me. You have to do what is best for you and only you know how to do that. You're so strong for getting through everything you did, Bella. Now it's your time to let go a little."

"I don't want to be strong anymore." She looks down to the floor and by the time she looks back, the air between us has changed drastically. Bella's fingers stop twisting in my t-shirt and I swear, the air is slowly being sucked out of the room.

"You don't have to be." I lower my voice slightly. "I can be strong for us both." As I stare into her baby blues, I lose myself in a sea of her. "You don't have to be strong for me."

We stand there for what feels like forever. Barely three inches of space between us and I'm desperate to close it.

My feelings for Bella are growing with every passing second but it's moments like these, when it's just me and the real her. The one she keeps so deeply buried so no one worries about her. I don't just want to protect Bella anymore; I want to give her everything she's missed out on.

I want to watch her flourish into the woman I know she will be when all this pain isn't the focal point of her life. I want to continue being the one who holds her tighter when her breathing picks up and she starts begging for whoever to stop in her dreams. I want to have the rest of our lives with this feeling in my chest that makes me feel like I can't breathe when I'm around her... and not in a bad way.

I swallow, when she still hasn't moved. When she's still looking up at me with those big doe eyes and perfectly plump lips and her freckles just covering her flawless skin. She's too fucking pure for the last man who touched her to have done it so violently.

If I touched Bella, I'd relish the fact she wanted it too. I'd fall begging on my knees to her, and I'd give her everything they never could. I could make her feel like the force to be reckoned with that I know she is.

I could.

I can do it.

I'm going to do it.

Inching my face slightly closer, I still leave enough space so she can make the decision. I'm not going back on my promise that she's in control here. She gets to decide on this.

"You're in control, Amore." I whisper and Bella slowly blinks. "Everything is in your hands."

"My hands." Bella's voice is barely audible. Just words clinging onto her exhale for dear life. Her pupils shift in her eyes as she searches mine. She moves slightly under me, feet edging backwards so she's just a little taller. "I'm in control."

"Only you." I nod once with certainty. Her hands fall flat on my chest before wrapping entirely around the fabric. "You gonna take it back, Bella?"

"Maybe." She's breathless. "Lu-"

She doesn't get a chance to take back control because somehow, fifteen minutes has passed in the blink of an eye and my timer begins blaring on the counter beside us, squashing the moment between two giant boulders as we both jump back.

"I – uh -" I reach over and slam the timer off, shoving my phone into my pocket before scratching the back of my neck.

"I need to wash- need to wash this out."

"Right! Yep. I need to – uhm – clean the – the living room!" I turn on my heel, pulling her bedroom door closed as I leave quickly, not stopping until I'm in my own bathroom with all the doors between us closed. "Get yourself together, Luca." I hit my head against the wall. "She's Enzo's sister. This so can't happen. He'll have your body parts scattered across the world before Astoria even knows what happened."

Chapter Twenty - Seven

Pink.

ISABELLA

"OH MY GOD! YOUR HAIR!" Safiyah screeches when she pulls the door open, and I can't even explain the giddiness that bubbles in my stomach. Luca has done phenomenally on choosing a dye so heavily pigmented. I didn't have high hopes, considering my hair is as dark brown as pure espresso straight from the barista. But this? It's pink. Neon. Fucking. Pink. And I love it more than I ever thought I would. "Farah!" I'm dragged inside and Safiyah only drops me so I can remove my snow-covered boots and coat.

Luca's hand quickly finds its new home on my hip as we venture through the house that I'm beginning to feel more comfortable in. It's a move that makes my stomach churn a little more and not in the prideful way it had a few days ago. This is different.

Things feel a little weird with Luca after the bathroom.

I'm not entirely sure what happened if I'm honest. He was so close and he was saying things that were just… it's like he saw right through my façade and just knew what he needed to say.

I want to unpack it all. To lay out exactly how it felt to have him that close, with my hands feeling his pounding heart, with the smell of his morning coffee filling my nose. I need to. But right now, I have bigger things to focus on.

Maybe there was something in the hair dye that seeped into my fucked-up head and started a chemical reaction, because when I stood in the shower watching the colour flood down my skin, all I could think was how much this would piss Rurik and Tomas off. All I could think about was the punishments I'd suffer for doing something like this. I think it was the stark reminder that I wasn't going to suffer by their hands this time, that had pinned Luca's words to the forefront of my mind.

Because, as usual, he was right.

I am in control now. Not just of my actions and my body, but also of my future and how I respond to this and everything else going forward.

I'd started the morning feeling exponentially guilty that everyone had spent so much time and money on me, and when I was staring at it all on my bed after my shower, I had to chase the guilt away.

I'd spent fourteen years in hell. Fourteen years of abuse, hatred and being despised for just existing, but not being allowed to die. Those fourteen years were over and I was home. Home with the people who wanted me here, who put themselves in harm's way because they wanted me to come home.

They could have left me there to rot. They could have forgotten that I ever showed up to the wedding and continued living as if I had died like they believed. But they didn't.

And I was going to sit here blowing my life away in a pit?

A life I only have back because they all put everything to one side to get me home?

I don't owe my survival to Lorenzo and Luca. Well, I guess I kind of owe it to Luca in some sense after the casino, but that's not the point; I survived by myself.

I'm the one who adapted to handle the shit being thrown at me. I handled it all. I didn't let it kill me. I survived. I will always survive.

But now I have the chance to live.

To breathe freely, to have friends that aren't praying for my downfall, to receive gifts from my brother, niece and sister-in-law who are all alive. I can dye my hair or… get a tattoo or – hell anything. I can do anything now, and I for sure am done letting Rurik and Feliks and Tomas and everyone else still have control over me when I'm not under their hold anymore.

I feel renewed and I think everyone can tell. The girls are watching me with bigger smiles. I am cracking more jokes that have everyone laughing, and I am probably drinking too much, but I don't care. It's Christmas. I am free. I am alive and there is nothing better to celebrate than being alive for the first time in over a decade.

"Zoe, is that your phone?" Farah nods at my phone as it buzzes between Luca and I on the table. Luca flips it over and, seeing Enzo's name across the screen, slides it over to me.

"I'll call him back." I smile, putting my next card down on the pile.

"If you don't pick up, he'll call me."

"And?"

"And if I don't pick up, he'll cause chaos." I turn my head to Luca. "I'll play for you, go talk to him."

"But-"

"Who is it?" Farah takes a sip from her drink, lifting her head to look at the screen.

"My brother. He can-"

"No," Safiyah lays her cards down on the table. "We can pause, you can't not speak to your family at Christmas. Everyone put your cards flat down. Any cheaters have to clean up after tonight. Zoe can take the call and we can all have a break before I beat you all. Again."

"Oh, you are so not winning. I've seen your cards." Conrad smirks.

"CHEATER, YOU'RE ON CLEAN UP DUTY." The pair begin bickering, dragging Farah and her husband into it so easily. A strong hand wraps around my thigh, squeezing once, just to bring my attention back to him.

"Take the call, Amore. I'll be right here. He misses his baby sister." I swallow, nodding anxiously and stand up with my phone in hand. I know healing isn't linear, nor is it something that will be instantaneous, so I know the anxiety that is coming alongside speaking to Lorenzo right now will pass as I get more accustomed to it.

The air is so much colder out on the back deck. Unlike our place, Safiyah's overlooks a small field backing onto the forest. I can imagine it's beautiful in full bloom in the middle of summer, but I can't help but feel a little uncomfortable with the looming darkness hiding god knows what a few dozen feet away. Conrad and Farah both smoke, so the two of them paired up to have a patio heater set up out here and I am so grateful for the extra heat. Safiyah has mentioned how badly she wants Conrad to stop smoking no less than fifty times in the month we've known her and every time she does, he uses her best friend and this heater against her. It's kind of funny.

I sigh, hitting the dial button on Enzo's number since it stopped buzzing before I'd even stood up.

I don't know where this anxiety is coming from, but I am determined to overcome it. I can only do that by tackling the problem head on, and the way my thigh is still burning from Luca's touch is making me need something else to focus on.

"Bella?" There's a click and Enzo's voice takes over my ears, muffling the noise from inside.

"Hey. Sorry I missed your call."

"No- Pops hold on. Yeah I've got her now." Pops' voice is one I'm not unfamiliar with anymore. Almost daily she sends me a video on her mum's phone and they have become a highlight of my week. "Bella, can we switch to FaceTime? Pops wants to say hi."

"Um, sure." I nod, holding the phone back and accepting his request as I try to get closer to the heater for some extra light. The very second that their sweet faces fill my screen, a subconscious smile seems to take over my face. "Hi Pops!"

"Hi Auntie Bel-" She gasps loudly. "Your hair is pink! DADDY, BELLA'S HAIR IS PINK."

"Mhm. I can see that." Lorenzo scowls into the screen and my spine stiffens. Fight through it, Bella. You are in control. No one else.

"You like it?"

"I LOVE IT. MUMMY. MUMMY-" She runs off without even saying goodbye and Lorenzo moves the camera.

"You-"

"I don't care if you don't like it." I say, less than convinced by my own words than I think Lorenzo is, but I power through the self-doubt. "It's my hair, I can do what I want with it. No one else gets to decide that."

"I wasn't going to say anything."

"You don't need to. Your face is telling me you don't approve of it, but I don't care." He stares at me for a second before chuckling and pulling his hand over the start of a beard he definitely doesn't suit.

"Glad to hear it, Bella." He exhales. "Before Pops gets back and shows you all the toys she got today. I just wanted to check in, not through text for once. How are you doing?" There's a clang of something back inside the house, and I look over my shoulder to see Safiyah and Farah staring at a lamp now shattered on the floor. There's a second of them just staring at each other before bursting into laughter. Luca is standing in the corner of the room with the other guys, drinking slowly from a bottle of beer, his eyes stuck to me with the softest smile on his lips and it covers me from head to toe in goosebumps. "Bella? You there? Everything okay?"

"What? Oh, yeah. I just – someone dropped something inside." I look back at the phone and sigh, not entirely sure why I'm slightly disappointed about the distraction Enzo is now causing. "I'm good, Enz."

"Are you sure? Because Luca-"

"I'm sure." I nod frantically, almost laughing because I don't feel like I'm lying right now. It's like I've been walking through the tunnel and I'm finally in the light. Or on the greener side of the fence. Whatever saying you want to use, they're all correct, because this is nothing like I thought it would be. I feel lighter than air and I'm not waiting for the fall either. "I'm – I'm great. I'm really, really great."

"Good." He sighs. "I'm going to try and come up after the new year. If I get the time. It depends on Tor and ever-"

"Oh, no, Enz, don't. You have to be with your wife and kid. That's your priority. I promise I'm so good here. Luca is keeping me busy and I've got the girls and everything. Don't worry about me. I swear, I'm okay."

"Bella. You're a priority too."

"I know, but I'm pretty sure your pregnant wife and daughter should be above me in that food chain. I've been told she can be a handful anyway."

"Who, the wife or kid?"

"I'm afraid answering that might mean I need to go deeper into witness protection." We both laugh.

"Who needs witness protection? Because I might be bigger than an elephant, but I could definitely go for watching another man crumble under my fist right now. Hi Bella, merry Christmas! Oh, your hair! I love it!"

"Auntie Bella, you look like a fairy. Can we play fairies? Mummy says you're coming home soon. Can we play then? Luca can't play because he's away."

"Uncle Luca is with Auntie Bella, Pops." Tori sits down beside Enzo and he instantly pulls Pops onto his lap.

"At least, he best be."

"He is, he's just inside right now. He's watching me though." I can feel him. Even with my back to him, I can feel the warmth of him wrapped around me like a safety blanket, and I don't ever want to take it off.

Chapter Twenty - Eight

Happy New Year, Amore.
LUCA

How exactly am I supposed to react when she's dancing on the sofa, drunk out of her mind? Should I stare at her while my heart pounds in my chest? Probably not. Does that stop me? No. Absolutely not. Her pink curls have faded ever so slightly in the past six days and I am determined to find someone who can make them permanent for her.

It has taken me back slightly, the scale of change I've seen in her since the moment she stepped out with the new look. Her shoulders pulled back a little more, head held just that little bit higher and somehow, I've managed to keep myself from falling to my knees at her feet.

Bella jumps off the sofa, grinning as she comes across to me and forces me to dance along to whatever is playing on the TV. My ears are ringing too loud to be able to notice. She's singing along and it's so off-pitch, but the sound is like having a comforting bowl of soup when you're sick, or have just come inside from the freezing cold.

I like this version of Bella. Where she's happy and free. The longer she's here with me, the more I don't want to let her go. I know things are about to start heating up outside of this house, when in just a matter of weeks, Lorenzo will start to put his plan into action.

I'd talked him out of doing it sooner. Between me and Astoria, we knew we needed to give Bella a break. Just a little chance to even out her stress levels, in the hope that she's reminded of just how strong she can be, when she puts her mind to it. I think it's worked. Given that Lorenzo had called me ranting about her dying her hair and her telling him she didn't care what he thought.

The Bella I had back at the Petrovich house would never have had the courage to do that. I knew it was inside her somewhere. She's a Santoni; it's built into her DNA to be indestructible. She just needed to be reminded of that. To find it inside her and let it out.

"You're thinking too hard." Bella scowls, jabbing a finger into my cheek. "Penny for your thoughts?"

"You don't have a penny."

"Lorenzo does. Many, apparently."

"Have you spoken to him today?"

"Yeah, he told me I'm not spending enough money, which is a weird thing to say. He said it like it's a bad thing."

"If you're holding out on spending because you feel like you shouldn't be, then yeah, it is a bad thing." She rolled her eyes. "Okay, quiz me this, Amore. Why aren't you spending money on his card?"

"Can we not do this right now? You're killing my buzz."

"I don't want to kill anything right now." Except the wastes of oxygen that kept her from me for all these years. "I just want you to stop thinking that you're a nuisance, or that we feel a responsibility to look after you."

"You do."

"Maybe so, but you don't need looking after, Bella." My words clearly catch her off guard, because in an instant her face goes from that pit of sadness to confusion. "You don't. You are more than capable of doing what you need to. You have proved that you're too damn strong. No matter what, you will find a way to survive. You shouldn't have been put in that position in the first place, but you were and you're here because you adapted to survive. You should be damn proud of that."

"I am."

"Good, but you don't need to just survive anymore. You don't need to feel guilty. You deserve to be here; to be living the life you should have been, without punishment. You will not be assaulted or harmed for living, Bella. Not anymore. Not if I can help it." I wrap my arms around her waist, pulling her closer. "I've told you this before."

"You have." Bella nods in agreement. I know she has a looser mouth when she's drunk. If there's ever a time I'm going to get her to open up about anything, it's times like this when the liquor is calming her nerves and she feels calm and confident enough to be herself. "I feel guilty though."

"Why?" She rolls her eyes, twisting her fingers in my cotton t-shirt. The music slows down from the high beat, loud shit to something much slower, so I start us swaying along. Slow, easy and light-hearted.

"Because he'll hate me when he finds out."

"Finds out what? That you spent some money?"

"No." I keep her where she is, swaying carefully and zipping my mouth shut in the hope of cracking another secret out of her. It takes her some time. A few short moments that feel like someone has hit that button on a TV remote to slow it down. "I killed them."

"Killed who, Amore?"

"Our parents." She swallows and looks up at me with damp eyes. "I had to. They - it was either that or they were going to hurt me. Badly." I slide my hand under the hem of her jumper, absentmindedly swiping my thumb over the scars there in the hope of giving her some comfort while she gets this off her chest. "Rurik and Tomas. They – he'll hate me when he finds out I did it to them, Luca."

"No, he won't."

"Yes, he will. He lov-"

"No, Isabella. He will not." I remove one hand from her back, curl one finger under her chin and tilt her perfect head backwards slightly. "Are you listening? Because I'm going to say this once, and you're going to take whatever nonsense you've got in there out. Okay?" She nods hesitantly.

"You had no choice. You might have pulled the trigger, Bella. You might have been the one to do it, but you are not responsible for what happened that night. You were nine. You were a child. A child that they used to get the upper hand. They are vicious, evil men who deserve everything that is coming for them. But you. You are not responsible for anything you had to do to survive. You are not the actions you had to take when your life was in the hands of someone else. Okay? No one, and I mean no one in their right mind, will hold you responsible for anything you had to do to keep your lungs moving and your heart beating."

"But-"

"No buts." I shake my head viciously. "No exceptions. You did what you had to do to survive. And fuck am I glad you did."

"You are?" A smile breaks quickly on my face as her sadness seems to soften.

"More than I'm glad I got you that hair dye." I tuck a stray curl behind her ear, lingering for a second too long. "I'm so grateful for everything you had to do, Amore. I'm grateful you're here with me. I'm grateful you're alive and breathing and that you keep getting up every day to fight the darkness I know is in this pretty little mind of yours, and I'm so grateful that you choose to fight every day."

The universe has a way of things working out. I'm sure. From me happening to open that door in the hotel on the day of Tori and Lorenzo's wedding, to managing to track her down to that godforsaken shithole. To the way that the New Year fireworks go off right on cue as soon as I finish my little speech.

"Happy New Year, Amore." I push my fingers into the hair at the back of Bella's skull, tracing my thumb across her tinted pink cheeks. Then I think I lose my mind. Because before I even know what I am doing, I'm pressing my lips to hers. Bella freezes under me completely as I push my hand into her back a little harder, forcing her against me.

She feels so much better than I'd imagined and it's dangerous, the way I want to slide my tongue into her mouth and claim every inch of it for myself. I want to sit her up on the edge of the sofa and fall to my knees, touch her in the only way she should have been touched, with complete adoration. I want to worship at her altar and give this goddess everything she deserves.

But instead, I pull back. Her softly closed eyes open slowly. I'm not met with a look of horror, just more confusion. The light blush on her cheeks has darkened to a maroon that dances all the way down to her collarbone and disappears under the heavy fabric hiding her skin from me. I take a slow breath and remind myself of every reason why I can't have her. For the fiftieth time today.

"Pops told me a joke today, wanna hear it?" Bella's brows furrow slightly before she stands up straighter and nods. "Why can't a T-Rex clap its hands?"

"Why?"

"Because they're all dead." Bella presses her lips together tight, head falling forward onto my chest as I chuckle and she tries to fight back her own.

Laughing at dumb jokes Penelope told me is such a safer zone than whatever we were in before. Much safer.

Chapter Twenty - Nine

Fuck.
LUCA

It's been two weeks.

Fourteen days, sixteen hours and a little over thirty-seven minutes since I got lost in a moment I certainly shouldn't have and did something completely reckless. I'm not entirely sure if that's what fucked things up, or if Bella is just taking a turn for the worse.

She seems to have pulled in on herself over the past few weeks. She's eating and interacting and talking and reading like normal and honestly, from the outside I don't think you would pick up on it. Not if you hadn't spent the copious amount of time with her that I have.

She started sleeping back in her own room on Christmas Day and while I can still hear her tossing and turning in the night from outside the door, she isn't waking up properly anymore. That I know about, anyway.

I don't want to pin her down and force her into my bed if she doesn't want to be there. The next time Isabella is in my bed, I want her to make that decision herself. I keep my door open every night like it's part of my religion. Just in case.

What her sleeping in a different room means is that I can't judge where her mind is any more.

Up until Christmas, I could kind of work out how her day would go based on how she'd slept.

If she'd struggled through the night, if I'd had to hold her close and keep those nightmares at bay multiple times during the night, I knew we were up for a rough day and I could anticipate it. I could plan something for us to keep her mind off it.

Since she wasn't with me, I was starting everyday walking a thin line and having to watch her closely for any sign. But Bella knows how to lock herself up like her life depends on it. Everything you ever see from her is perfectly calculated to give just enough of an insight that you don't become worried, but not enough that you can see how bad it is. It's like she's a gigantic iceberg and underneath the surface, everything is sharp edges and frozen solid.

And yet, I don't regret kissing her.

If Lorenzo found out, I'd be murdered in cold blood. As shitty as it is, I'd take her building her walls up over it too, but I don't regret it.

I'd spent weeks building it up in my head. How it'd feel to kiss her and leave the feeling of admiration on her lips for the first time, rather than loathing. Every night with her in my arms had been spent with me picturing everything I wanted to do. To eradicate the fucked-up memories in her head and leave her with ones that weren't painful, to replace their vicious marks with my own delicate ones.

Clearly, I'd been the only one building that up in my head.

"Luca," Lorenzo scolds down the phone as I load the bags into the back of the car. "Are you even listening?"

"Yeah, yeah. Need to take your time because they're anticipating a response. Fuckwads are getting away with it until we have everything in place, but it's going to take months. I'm listening to the same shit you've been saying for a month, Lorenzo." My phone automatically connects to the speakers inside the car as I climb in and pull the door shut, allowing Lorenzo's voice to be amplified in a way it definitely never needed to be.

We had been hoping to move this thing along swiftly but, considering the fucking Petrovichs are expecting a response to Bella being alive, security around their whole place has practically quadrupled. And as much as they were, indeed, going to pay for what they did, we are also not prepared to risk everyone's lives over it.

This needs to be planned out in a way that no matter what, nothing could go wrong, and that is taking time. Time Lorenzo isn't comfortable with. Lorenzo has never stood for people hurting his family. He will always take the quickest action possible and this time, it's being dragged out and it's making him moody.

"How's Tori?" I ask, hoping to circle back to something else that doesn't mean I have him screaming down the line at me.

"Pregnant." He sighs. "Stop changing topics."

"I'm not changing them Lorenzo, I'm just reminding you exactly why we need to make sure everything is right this time around. This isn't like how you handled everything with Tori, or anything else, in fact. There isn't just you on the line anymore." There's a silence on the other end of the line, and I picture him giving me that glare. That one that is almost daring me to continue, but I do because no one else is ever going to keep him in place like I will.

"Are your girls safe right now, Lorenzo?"

"Are you fucking stupid?"

"Jury's still out on that one, but I'm gonna plough ahead anyway," I put the car in drive, finally heading back towards the house after running the few errands I couldn't put off any longer. "Isabella is fine here with me. No one knows we're up here, we're good. Tor and Pops are fine down there. I can't see them not being since everyone will be spoiling Pops rotten, and Tor will have Mia and Livia force feeding her pasta and ice cream eight times a day so the baby comes out looking like the Michelin man." He snickers quietly, clearing his throat in an attempt to cover it, but I heard it and knew I was fucking right in my presumptions.

"Everyone is fine as we are right now. We don't need to rush it so that everyone can get back to where they need to be as soon as possible. As long as we finish this before your next child comes along, we're fine." Lorenzo let out a deep breath, and I knew I'd done my job.

As much as Tori was good at keeping Lorenzo locked down and not going insane, there are a lot of things he doesn't tell her about this side of things. Especially when it is as high risk as this. She gets too into it. Starts demanding that she can help and neither of us want to risk her getting hurt again. Not after getting shot the first time around. That was enough nightmare fuel for a lifetime.

"Fine." He huffs. "How's Bella?"

"She's fine. I'm just pulling up now."

"Pulling up? You mean you left her home. Alone?" I roll my eyes, turning into the garage slowly.

"She didn't want to come out. I've had my eyes on my phone the whole time and nothing has passed within eighty feet of the house since I left. Not even a squirrel." There's a long silence. "I'm going inside now."

"Te-"

"Text you once I've seen her. Yep. Got it. Bye." I reach over, hitting the end call button before climbing out of the car.

There's a slight feeling of guilt in my gut for being glad we have more time here than we'd originally been expecting. It is a pit in the bottom of my stomach. A guilty feeling, as though I am keeping something from her but I'm not. I told her we'll go home as soon as we can and right now, it's simply not safe for us to raise our heads above the ground.

Being here with her for longer means more time with her to myself, and that is something I won't be taking lightly.

Time up here at The Lake House is constantly ticking down, and I know eventually it'll be gone and mine and Bella's quiet life will end in an instant.

Lorenzo has put my head in a funk, but I know she is fine. Everything was locked up tight before I left and she was happily reading on the sofa with the fire crackling calmly. My eyes have been closely watching my phone screen for any notifications of movement on the cameras, but there has been nothing. I checked them just before he called and they were all working fine so nothing had been altered; I know she is fine. And yet, I still leave the bags in the car to check the house first.

It is only four pm but sometimes it's this time of day when Bella takes herself for a well needed nap. I don't want to wake her up if she is, so I keep my entrance into the house quiet.

As I enter the kitchen, I immediately see her spot on the sofa is abandoned. She's definitely gone for a nap and I sigh, needing to set my sights on her before I can settle my nerves and confirm with Lorenzo that his sister is indeed fine.

I venture down the creaky hallway as quietly as possible, dodging boards I know for a fact make the loudest noises known to man at three am, but I'm stopped in my tracks when I hear my name.

"Luca..." My temperature instantly skyrockets and I just know that I shouldn't be here. I should have made some noise when I came in, so she knew I was home. I really need to turn around and walk out but when she moans again, all rational thinking goes out the window.

My steps grow faster as I become desperate to hear her better, my cock straining against my jeans as I reach her slightly open bedroom door.

This is a breach of her privacy. It's absolutely insane, and anyone in their right mind would turn around and walk away. Clearly, I am not in my right mind when it comes to Isabella, because the thought of leaving doesn't cross my mind, even when right in my eyeline, through the crack in her bedroom door, Bella has her bare ass up in the air while she goes to town on herself.

She moans again, fingers rubbing fast circles on her clit as she thrusts the fingers of her other hand in and out of her soaking hole.

And fuck, I've never seen anything hotter.

I grab for the door frame just to keep me standing when her moves become more frantic. Her face is pushed into her pillow, each breath she tries to take is a moan that goes directly to my dick, until I feel like I'm going to combust.

"Luca, fuck. More. I need more." Oh god.

I am frozen in complete shock as she squirts, soaking her bed sheets through. She doesn't stop there though. Oh no. Bella keeps going as her moans get louder and her body starts to quake. It's right then, as Isabella comes to her euphoric high, screaming my name, that I do something I haven't done since I was a teenager having a wet dream over some supermodel. I come in my pants without laying a single finger on myself.

The pleasure erupts from the base of my spine, cock twitching in my now sticky pants as I try to keep myself quiet and standing. It's an orgasm that's horrifically useless, because somehow, I need more.

I need to see her like this again. I have to watch her come apart at the seams as I give her everything she desires. It was my name on her lips as she came. Me she was demanding more from. There is not a chance in a thousand timelines where I am not going to fulfil her goddamn dreams.

My head clears quickly as Bella's bed creaks, and I need to move. She can't know I just watched her do this. I don't want to know what would happen if she did.

Without any more hesitation, I backtrack down the hall quickly, heading into the kitchen and this time slamming the garage door loudly. Bella appears a few seconds later with flushed cheeks and wide eyes, and I have to bite my smile.

"Hey, how was town? Did you get what you needed?"

"Mhm. It's in the car, I desperately need the bathroom though."

"Need my help? With the – the shopping. I was just about to shower but–"

"No, you're fine. Go shower." I have no doubt that she needs it after the mess she'd made across her sheets. "Oh, I was thinking it's been a few days since we washed all the bedding, so I'm going to do a load. Want to get yours in first?"

Chapter Thirty

What the fuck just happened?
ISABELLA

Luca stares at me from across the table and I shift uncomfortably. I know things have been a little… weird around here for the past few weeks, but this is on a whole other level and I am not sure how I need to respond.

He was demanding when it came to dinner tonight. Told me that I wasn't allowed to read or eat in front of the TV like we had been doing since New Year's. I'd been avoiding time like this with him for one reason and one reason alone.

This was odd.

My feelings towards Luca had started building weeks ago, and I'd been covering them with a thick coat of 'it's just the situation'. But that kiss? That kiss has ignited something in me I am terrified to admit to.

I have very minimal experience on what it is like to be touched gently in the way Luca had, but even so, the way he'd held me on New Year's wasn't something I'd ever experienced.

His fingers had traced scars on my lower back and I hadn't realised until the next morning when his touch still lingered there. Electricity still danced along the marks as though they were magic, and it had taken days for it to fade.

Instantly, I knew that it was going to be best if I put some space between Luca and I. Things were getting a little too close to a line I don't think it was sensible for us to toe. No matter how much my brain had formed a ridiculous addiction to him, it was insane.

I am too damaged anyway.

Luca is this beaming ray of bright golden sunlight. He's been graced by the universe in a way I can't exactly explain. In the books I read, he'd be the golden retriever character. The one that always has a joke to crack and is there for comedic breaks between heavier content, and he deserves to be with someone that matches that. Someone else golden and unbroken and not covered in scars that will undoubtedly terrify children.

Not only that, but Luca is Luca. We grew up together. He's basically family.

"You're not eating, Amore." Luca chews slowly and the hairs on the back of my neck stand on end at the dark look he's giving me. I push some salad around on the plate, stabbing some dramatically before shoving it into my mouth whilst maintaining as much of my smile as I can manage.

Playing it cool and casual so he doesn't think something is wrong is my only move right now. If he believes everything is fine, I can keep putting space between us and I'll get over this little crush. Problem solved.

I eat as much as my stomach allows without the urge to vomit taking over and look around the room for any other distraction.

"Eat your food, Bella."

"I'm not hungry."

"Really? You worked up an appetite earlier." I narrow my eyes at him as he sits back in his chair slightly, wiping his stubble covered jaw with one of the cloth napkins. "With the laundry and cleaning up."

"Oh. Yeah." I nod quickly. "Had a snack while you were out though, so, you know." Luca bobs his head slowly as I shift uncomfortably in my chair. "I'm gonna have an early night."

I half expect Luca to quiz me about how I've been sleeping, but he just grabs his wine glass and drinks while watching me and that's it, I'm at capacity. My heart is beating too damn fast under his gaze for me to sit here and undo the two weeks' worth of work I've put into shoving these feelings aside.

Knowing I need to rinse my plate and utensils before I can get the hell out of here, I gracefully manage to grab them and head over to the sink.

I'm just about done when I feel swallowed whole by Luca's presence behind me. He's hot and heavy. It feels like I'm suffocating when he reaches around me to carefully run the water over his plate above where my hands are frozen.

"I'm starting to think you're avoiding me, Isabella." My ears start to buzz with anticipation as Luca's fingers brush against mine. He settles his hand softly on my hip and I instantly lose all control over my movements. I can't do anything but watch his hand in the sink. I need to move, I need to put some space between us immediately. But all I can manage is to defrost my tongue.

"Why would I be avoiding you?"

"That's a question I keep asking myself." Luca takes the smallest step forward until he is pressed against me, and I have to actively control my breathing before I suffocate and collapse right here. "Because I've retraced my steps, Isabella, and I can't work out exactly why you'd want to avoid me."

Luca turns his head slightly, hot air covering my cheek and I close my eyes as his fingers disappear under the hem of my jumper.

"Unless of course, something happened that you're avoiding?" His lips brush over my jawline and it's a bolt of lightning directly into my spinal column. The plate clatters in the bottom of the ceramic sink as it slips from my hands in shock and I immediately duck under his arm, out of his grasp. I have to pull the mask back on and regain control over my actions because this cannot happen. This is *exactly* what can't happen.

"There's nothing to avoid." I lie. "I'm just enjoying spending time by myself. Didn't realise I needed a reason to be alone with my own thoughts." Intentional attitude swarms my eye roll before I grab for the fridge door with sweaty palms and retrieve a cold water bottle from inside. When I slam the door shut and turn, he's turned the water off and his stupid smug face is still standing by the sink with his arms crossed over his chest and his hip pressed into the counter. I hate how fucking easy this is for him. "Problem?"

"No, but I think you have one."

"And what exactly would that problem be, Luca?"

"That you want me to kiss you again like I did on New Year's and you don't know how to handle it."

I furrow my brow at him but before I can even defend myself, Luca takes three huge strides across the kitchen and I instinctively back up to the fridge. He only stops when there is just enough room between us for not a single millimetre of him to be touching me. Nonetheless, my heart rate skyrockets as though I've just finished running a damn marathon.

"Tell me I'm wrong, Isabella. Tell me to my face that you're not locking yourself up in your room at night so you don't need to address the fact that you felt something too." I take in a shaky inhale and hold onto my bottle a little tighter as it threatens to slip out of my hands. "Because I think I'm right. I think that for the first time in your life you want someone to touch you again, and you are so used to people making the first move and deciding these things for you, that you think hiding will stop it happening."

"You're insane." I manage to force the words out smooth and steady and Luca just smirks. Our eyes are locked in a battle that neither of us is willing to give up.

"I'm not going to make the first move, Amore." Luca curls a finger under my chin and inches closer, until he's close enough for his oxygen to be the same as mine.

We're sharing each inhale.

Both breathing the same heavy air I want to drown in.

"If you want me to do it again, you'll come to me. And trust me, Bella. When you give in to your stubborn little fight, I'll make it worth your time and wipe every single trace of them from you. But the next time you want to moan my name like you did today, take your fingers out of your sweet little pussy and crawl into my bed so I can have a taste."

My stomach twists on itself and I feel the way colour drains from my skin, leaving only the burning of my cheeks as Luca exhales once more and stands up straight, immediately putting enough space between us and turning his attention to the washing-up.

"I thought you were going for an early night, Amore." Luca's words manage to shake me from the embarrassed shock enough for my feet to carry me down the hall and into my room in utter silence.

What the fuck just happened?

Chapter Thirty - One

Stop fighting against yourself, let go and take control.

LUCA

I shouldn't be enjoying this as much as I am. For the past four days, Isabella has been growing in her frustration, and I can't deny the fact that having her storming around here with a face of fury has made me laugh on more than a few occasions.

It's a nice change of pace. Bella had got so used to being stuck in her head and wallowing in it all, and as much as I had been open to her taking time, I knew she was ready to take that step out of the pit and just needed a push. That, and the fact that seeing her the way I had in her room last week, had truly destroyed any hope I'd had of moving past this.

It was my name on her tongue as she came, me that she had to have been imagining to get her over the edge. I may be a little blind to certain things but that was clear as day. Isabella wants me the way I want her and she can spend as long as she pleases getting mad about it.

I mean what I said though. All that girl has ever had is other people making her choices for her. Especially when it comes to this. Who she dates, how she gets information out of them, who touches her. None of that has ever been in her control, and there isn't a chance in hell I am going to add myself onto that list. If Bella needs to go through the motions, to stomp around and slam cupboards and huff and puff at me while she works this out in her head, I'm going to sit right here and revel in the fact it's such a battle for her.

I've spent time researching how to help people after years of trauma and sexual abuse, and one thing I've learned is how important it is for the victim to have control over things like this.

I can imagine that it's a hard thing to do. To finally have control over your actions after over a decade of not being allowed to have a say, and I know she's had a taste. She controls everything around here but this feels like it's so much deeper. It's not just what we eat or if we go into town for the day. Adjusting to all these changes takes time. And we have as long as she needs.

I look up from the laptop as she shifts on the opposite side of the couch again. Her patience is quickly beginning to run out. She huffs and looks over at me as I force my eyes back to the laptop.

"Stop watching me."

"I wasn't watching you."

"Yes you were. I literally caught you staring."

"You huffed, of course I looked over."

"You're so annoying." Bella huffs again and I smile, tapping a few keys. "And now you're smiling because you get a kick out of this shit. You're so fucking weird, Luca." Isabella slams her book shut, officially giving in. Buckle up Luca, this might be a little bumpy.

"How'd you know I'm not smiling at the laptop?"

"Because you're just clicking around randomly. Do you think I don't know you're just trying to appear busy so you can watch me? I'm not fucking stupid."

"I never said you were." When I look over at her, it takes everything in me to try and contain my smile, even more so when she scowls even harder and stands up abruptly.

"God, you're so self-absorbed!" Bella stomps a few feet across the room and crosses her arms quickly over her chest. Slowly closing the laptop, I sit back in my chair and I watch in amazement as she explodes with countless years' worth of perfectly controlled anger. I don't give two damns if it is coming out at me, as long as she is finally getting it out of her head where it's rotting away at her self-confidence. There's a hell of a lot more I'd take for her than this.

I sit there in silence as she rants at me, hurling insults that are meant to damage my ego in the hope of making herself feel better. In fact, I lose track of the number of times she calls me irritating or stupid. After a few drawn out minutes she scowls harder than I thought was possible. Seriously. I'm concerned she's going to damage something.

"Why the fuck are you just sitting there staring at me like that? Fight back."

"Nah." Bella's eyes darken and I have to bite the inside of my cheek to stop myself from laughing. *She's so fucking cute.* It's like watching a puppy get frustrated when its owner isn't throwing their toy, so obviously, I make it worse. "Keep going. You were telling me about how I see myself as Superman for saving you? I don't by the way, I'm more Batman. Superman's too goody two shoes. But, I mean, I don't want to interrupt your train of thought so..." I gesture at her and Bella shifts her weight onto her other hip.

"You're a dick."

"Mhm." Slowly, I start to stand up, noticing how she calms down slightly and it's then that I decide that this is my chance. "Or, and I'm just shooting in the dark here, are you just trying to convince yourself of all these terrible things about me to try and make you stop wanting me."

"Hmph, yeah, obviously because no one can exist without wanting you, right?"

"You'd know, Amore." Bella maintains her stance as I stand before her. She can deny it as much as she pleases, but I see the way she freezes up. I notice how her breathing changes, and I don't need to touch her to do it. Her forehead just crumples forward, and all I can do is smile at how much this is pushing her buttons. "If you scowl any harder, I'm pretty sure you're going to pull a muscle."

"I am not-"

"I have to admit, you are cute when you're mad, though." I smirk, lifting a finger to push at her furrowed brow gently. "You're getting yourself worked up, Bella. All wound up and tense when really, all you want is to put your tongue in my mouth."

"I do not." She scoffs, reaching up and swatting me away. Before my hand can even fall to my side, she's jabbing a perfectly polished red fingernail into the centre of my chest. Every time she pushes it into me, I have to stop myself from grabbing her face and cutting out all of the bullshit. It would be easier if I did. But I refuse to take this from her. "You need to get a grip on reality. You've built something up in your head that isn't happening. It was one kiss. It meant nothing."

"Meant nothing, huh?" I wrap my hand around Bella's wrist, holding her just tight enough as I fold my arm around her waist and tug her against my chest. "Try saying it again."

"I- It meant-" I move my head down, brushing my nose alongside hers. Bella sucks in a slow gasp of air, ceasing to finish what she is trying to say. It wasn't nothing and she knows it as well as I do.

"Want to know what I think, Amore?" Bella hesitates but gives the smallest nod. "I think you're lying. About everything you've said, about it meaning nothing. You're lying to me and to yourself." Exhaling heavily, I slowly bring my nose across her cheek, up to her ear and she can't hide the way she shivers. "I think you're scared of taking what you want, and you are pushing me right now in the hope I'll make the first move. Right?"

Bella nods so slowly it's barely noticeable as I expand my hand over her back. I carefully trail my tongue up the side of her neck, grasping her earlobe between my teeth and tugging. Just enough for her to strangle a moan in her throat and for my dick to beg me to just give us both what we need so desperately.

"I've told you, Amore. You're making the first move. You want it, stop fighting against yourself, let go and take control."

I stand back and smirk at the flustered mess that is now standing before me. Bella's chest heaves as she searches my face in confusion.

"Now, I'm going for a shower and I'll start dinner after. We need to use up that chicken before it expires, so have a think about what you want." Before Bella can respond, I walk out of the room, dick threatening to combust if I don't resolve it immediately.

Chapter Thirty - Two

Does arguing with yourself make you insane?

ISABELLA

I kick the duvet off my feet, squirming around in the bed as I give up any chance of sleeping tonight. The clock ticks away across the room and every single beat is a condescending reminder of just how utterly fucked I am right now.

I'm pissed off and frustrated and so fucking horny I might actually combust. But Luca is so goddamn sure that I'm desperate for him, and I want nothing more than to prove him wrong right now. Maybe it will knock him off his pedestal a little. Give his head enough of a shake that he leaves me alone.

He's a fucking ass, teasing me the way he has been. Those sly little looks when he thinks I'm not looking. He loves it too much. He's getting a thorough kick out of watching me squirm, and I hate it. I hate it so much and I hate the fact that he's got me laying here, genuinely contemplating if it's worth it.

The sane part of me, the one currently in control, she is firmly keeping me laid here. But it's the primitive side of me, the one with the hormones and the thoughts and wild imagination, that side of me is pushing all the right fucking buttons for me to be so tempted to hand myself over.

I tried to ease it myself. As soon as I heard him head to bed for the night. My hand slipped between my legs with ease and I swear, on every sun in the entire universe, I tried everything to picture anyone that wasn't him. Did it work? Of fucking course it didn't. It always morphed into his hand. It turned into him whispering filthy words in my ear as his perfect lips and rough stubble scratched their way across my skin.

I came so easily to the thought of him, and I was so lost in the haze that I was physically unable to push it out.

It's stupid.

I'm building it up in my head.

I'm trying to get myself on track after a shit tonne of traumatic stuff, and I'd be safe trying this out in Luca's hands. Safer than I would be with anyone else.

No, Bella. We're not even considering it.

But if we were to consider it ... for just a moment. Just a second. Luca knows. There's no awkward need to tell him about what happened, he's never given me a reason to doubt he wouldn't take that into consideration. AND, on top of that and it being good to get the first time over with, he's hot. Like exceptionally hot. He's tall but not like a damn tree, built but not to the point he's more muscle than man. The man's eyes go the most flawless shade of honey and gold when the sunlight hits them just right. His hair starts to curl when it hasn't been trimmed in a while. Not into ringlets, just an adorable wave that I so desperately want to run my hands through.

He's literally everything I'd ever pictured as my future. Luca is my childhood prince charming and the gentle and loving nature I want now, mixed together by some unknown deity and then incarnated into living blood and flesh.

Besides, remember how good it felt when he kissed you?

STOP. Oh my God.

Get up.

No, I really shouldn't. I should stay right here and not be a dictionary definition imbecile.

He's literally right across the hall.

Am I actually arguing with myself? Maybe I've gone insane. Or this is some fucked up dream.

Or it's real life and you're wasting time lying here, alone in bed when you could be there with him.

Covering my face with both hands, I let out a frustrated groan before sitting up and staring at the barely visible clock on the wall.

I'm not going to sleep tonight. Not if I don't find something to ease this tension.

Is it really that bad if I do? I mean, it's just sex, right? Sex is healthy when it's done consensually. It's good for the brain and stress levels and it's natural.

Luca is clearly on the same page; he couldn't have made that more obvious if he'd tried. I can use him to practice. To get used to being like that with someone who I know will understand if I need to stop. He won't ask questions or treat me any differently. And I can always just make it clear that's all this is.

Just practice.

Okay.

Okay.

Before I can talk myself out of it, I swing my legs out of bed, and rush to the door. I just need one night. Just to get it out of my system and balance out my hormones. Only to remember what it's like to have consensual sex again.

My knuckles tap quietly on his door. Two hushed knocks and my stomach twists itself into a suffocating knot.

This is wrong.

I shouldn't do this.

This is Luca we're talking about here.

Luca.

Isabella, what the FUCK?! Are you INSANE?!

I turn, taking three fast steps in the direction of my room, praying he didn't hear me knocking on his slightly open bedroom door. Begging the universe for him to have been passed out asleep.

In a past life, I must have been a royal bitch, because the universe hates me, and I don't even make it to my door before his creaks open. I freeze in my spot, cringing to my very core.

"Where are you going, Bella?" His deep voice echoes through the hallway and I turn slowly, hands instantly tugging on the long sleeves of my pyjamas before I cross them around my waist.

Luca leans against the doorframe with a smug smirk on his lips. Orange lamplight glows behind him, lighting him up like some demonic angel and it's not making me feel any better.

How am I supposed to make up an excuse and cower back to my room when he looks like that?! As though Midas himself has danced his fingers over every sharp line, across his defined chest and down to the waistband of his check pyjama pants, because of course that's the only piece of clothing he's wearing. Of *course* it is.

God this is a nightmare, isn't it?

"I- uh- was just-" Come on Bella, anything. Anything other than the real reason you're knocking on his door. I clear my throat, trying to give myself a little more time to work it out as my face starts to burn from the heat of his observation. "Your light. I can see it under my door."

"You can see my light on." I nod, but Luca's smirk just grows. He's staring at me like he's a predator and I'm his next meal. I roll my lips together, curling my toes as I wait for him to confirm my outright lie has been accepted and I can move on to pretending this never happened. "Funny how that's never been an issue before."

"Well, it's an issue now."

"Is it?"

"Yes." Luca nods, tugs his lips to one side of his face as he stands up straight.

"Well, I'll turn it off then."

"Good." His eyes don't move from mine and it takes me a few seconds of burning under his gaze for me to break it, clear my throat and force myself to move. "Night." I spin on my heel, taking another step forward when Luca speaks.

"Don't knock next time." I turn back around to him, furrowing my brow as he stares.

"What?"

"The door is open for a reason, Amore. You second guessed yourself while you waited, so don't knock."

"I didn't second guess anything."

"Oh, no, I'm sure you didn't." He tips his head slightly. "You know I just turned the lamp on, right?"

"I- yes." I nod, trying to pull this off as if I am not stupidly embarrassed.

"So, you wanna do what you came out here for or what?"

"I didn't come out here for anything."

"Oh, yeah, for sure." Luca almost laughs and he's done it. He's pushed the right buttons to activate the pissed off side of me again. I stomp across the hall and cross my arms over my chest as I glare up at him.

"You think you're so fucking clever, don't you? Think you have me worked out like I'm some fucking experiment? Well, you don't. You don't have a clue."

"I know you're hot when you're angry."

"God, you're such a moron!" I shove his shoulder, making his body shake as it recoils. Luca just rolls his eyes, using the movement to flawlessly grab my hips and pull me against him. "Let me go."

"Kiss me, Isabella."

"Not a chance in hell." I push my hands against his chest, furrowing my brows when his grip tightens, having the opposite effect I am aiming for when I try to get out of his hold.

"Why not, it's why you came out here, isn't it? To kiss me again. Maybe take it a little further. Have me lie you down on my bed and strip your clothes off slowly." Luca's hand gently lifts to my hair, shifting it off my shoulders then gently gathering it in his fist. It's a move that must short circuit my brain because even I feel the way my resistance dies in the blink of an eye. "Where'd that attitude go that you had a second ago, Bella? Hm? Too busy fighting other ambitions?"

"N-no." Luca gently pulls my hair and I allow my head to fall back with it. Heat pools between my legs and I close my eyes for a second as I try to keep hold of the reins that are quickly slipping out of my grasp with every passing breath.

"Then fight it. If you didn't come out here to kiss me, tell me to let you go and I will." Luca brings his eyes down to mine, holding me as his captive. "Or you can do what you wanted to in the first place and stop being stubborn."

I'm frozen. My head is so full of chemicals and thoughts and a full-blown battle that has been ongoing for weeks and I'm fed up. I'm fed up with tossing and turning in bed, fed up with my fingers not being enough, fed up with watching him and desperately wanting to taste him again when my head isn't fuelled by alcohol.

"Fuck it," The words are barely echoed into the universe as I push up on my toes and take back the control that was stolen from me too long ago.

Chapter Thirty - Three

Take your pants off.
ISABELLA

Luca's lips pull up into a knowing smirk, his grasp on my hair tightening as he pulls my head back and kisses me harder. Instantly, I'm dizzy. My stomach somersaults and every single nerve in my body is dancing to an electronic beat I never, ever want to end.

Then he stops.

Takes his hand out of my hair but continues to hold me pressed against him. His eyes piercing into mine as he searches for something inside of mine.

"Troppo." Luca pants. His tongue darts out and slides across his damp lips before he speaks again. "Use it. If you need to stop."

"I don't–"

"It means too much." Luca smiles quickly as he hoists me up and around his waist. "We really need to work on your Italian, Bella."

"Luca, stai zitto e baciami." His head tips back, a booming laugh breaking apart the building tension in the air. He follows through on his instructions though, taking my lips and claiming them for his own.

I can't explain the vast sense of pride that floods me in this moment. Right alongside the anxiety of it all, it's a mix of emotions that is intoxicating and suffocating all the same.

I tangle my fingers into the long hair at the back of his head and the added height he's given me to my advantage. He lets me control it. Allows my tongue to sweep over his lips before he opens and gives me access to explore another inch of him and my soul is set alight.

Luca lowers himself down to the bed, his hands now able to find a way under my clothes and against my skin. I'm overly aware of how it feels to have him like this and I can feel the emotions building in me. This needs to move faster. I need to focus on how this feels right now, rather than how it felt before.

I take my hands out of his hair, reaching down and tugging my top off and tossing it to the floor behind me without a single care.

"Slow down, Bella." I furrow my brow, having zero interest in this moving slow.

"Take your pants off."

"Bella," Luca warns, keeping his eyes fixated on mine as he cradles my face in his oversized hands.

I suddenly feel exposed. Every single wound, every scar and burn and reminder of the past is laid out for him right now. Anxiety knots in my chest and I hate it.

"You're in control here." He states. "You decide how fast or slow this moves. You decide where I'm allowed to touch you. We don't need to rush through it. I don't want you to do this if you're not comfortable with it. If it's too much, we can stop. We can keep it at this, we can stop, we can just lay down and go to sleep if that's what you need. You decide where your limit is. I will not go past that, I swear to you. You are safe in my hands."

They're words I didn't think I needed him to say. I knew I was safe with him, I never even doubted that for a second. But having him say it out loud, stopping when he could see I was panicking and making sure I knew for certain. I nod. Once. Then again with a lot more confidence.

"You're in total control, Bella. Show me how you want me to touch you." Luca moves one of his hands from my face, grasps my own and sets it on the one still resting on my cheek. "You show me, Amore."

I hesitate. Not entirely sure what I want to feel.

Every time I've been like this before, even if it was consensual, it was rushed. I never had a large amount of time where I wasn't being observed like a pet and I didn't want to spend the little time I did on touches and things that would delay the end result.

I start easy though, shakily moving his hand down to my breast. Once it's there, he takes over. Luca's hands massage me slowly. His thumb passes over my nipple and it's a move that forces me to shift my hips in a way that makes him smile quickly.

I bring my lips down to his again, kissing him soft and sweet, slowly building up the pressure and his hand follows suit. Every bit of pressure I press against his lips, he uses against my skin and I feel empowered. Like he's a controller and I'm the only one who knows how to press the right buttons to get it to work.

I move his other hand up my thigh, pushing my hips against him a little more. The thin cotton pants he's wearing do nothing to hide the rock-hard length and it feels right to move against it. To circle my hips and feel the way his breathing deepens against my lips as I do. The friction isn't enough though, and I'm desperate for more.

I pull back from him quickly, grabbing his hand and pulling him to his feet. I am breathing too heavily to speak but when I remove the rest of my clothes, Luca follows suit, dropping his pants to the floor. I don't look. This feels too good right now and I am terrified that I'll look and be hit with a violent flashback. I don't want to ruin this. I don't think I will survive another night pent up this tightly.

"Bella?"

"I'm okay." I nod, stepping closer to him, pushing up on my tiptoes and pressing a series of short but red hot kisses to his lips. "Do you have protection?"

"Yeah." Luca takes a slow step back and I climb onto the bed, sitting on my knees as the echo of him opening the packaging is the only audible sound in the house.

I am safe in his hands.

I decide how fast this goes.

I decide what happens.

The bed creaks, dipping with his weight as he slowly climbs onto the mattress.

"What's the word, Amore?"

"Troppo." Luca nods. "I don't need to stop."

"I know you don't." My heart races in my chest but I move closer. Luca's hands immediately find my hips and he steadies me, stopping me from falling backwards. "But I will never hold it against you if you do need to. You understand that, right?"

"Yes."

"Because if you doubt it just the smallest amount-"

"Oh my god, Luca. Stop."

"I'm just making sure you don't feel like you need to-" I roll my eyes, pushing my hand into his shoulder and forcing him back into the mattress. "I'm usually a big fan of the woman being so desperate to fuck me that she can't wait but-" I cut him off. Not bothering to listen to his anxious rambling for another second.

Luca's head falls back into the pillow, the softest moan I've ever heard escapes his lips as I slide myself slowly down his shaft.

I keep my eyes locked on his as I do. Count the colours in his irises, the freckles on his cheeks. Every inch of this man is something I need to immortalise. I need to remember what it feels like in my chest as he closes his eyes, fingers pushing into my waist with enough pressure to leave dainty bruises on my skin.

"Fuck, Bella." My name slides off his lips with ease and it's the first time I've heard my name like that. Not Anastasia. Me.

"Say it again." Luca slowly opens his eyes, watching me suspiciously. My chest heaves with anticipation. "Please say it again."

"Bella?" I nod and Luca's lips lift into a soft smile. "You feel so good, Isabella." *Fuck.* "Take control, Bella. Show me how good it feels when you take my dick."

My blood fills with the power he's helped me find. Every move I make has him responding in ways I've never seen and I swear, I can physically feel the way it alters my brain chemistry.

My hands press into Luca's shoulders, carrying all of my weight as I take what I need. His hands free roam my skin, electrifying me even further. Every trace of a scar pushes me harder as his hips lift in time with mine. The combination is overwhelming and before I even know what's happening, I'm diving headfirst into the most inconceivable orgasm.

"That's it." Luca lifts his torso as I come down from the high. My whole body tingles with something I've never experienced, and I'm desperate for more. For more of that feeling, for more of him. I need more.

My vision comes back slowly and when it does, I'm still exactly where I was, but the smile across Luca's face makes me feel so much more at ease than I had already felt.

"More." I pant, lifting my hips and moving so we are finally disconnected. "I need more."

"More, I can do, Amore. How you take it is up to you."

"Everything." I lay down into the mattress, kissing Luca's lips as he pushes himself up onto his elbow. "As long as it feels like that, I want to do everything with you."

Chapter Thirty - Four

Don't stop.
LUCA

I don't dare move. If I could help it, I'd stop my chest heaving with each deep breath, just so I could get a little longer with her laying up against me like this.

I know what is coming now. I know she'll pull back as soon as she is left alone with her mind. I know it because that's what she does. She lets herself break free for just a second until the guilt creeps in and she immediately pulls her walls back up.

It is fine. It's okay for her to struggle with what happened last night, it was a huge step and I am just thankful it was in the right direction this time.

I'd seen it on her face more than once, the way she had chased away whatever her mind was throwing at her while we were… busy. She tensed up a few times and I eased off, waiting for her to close off completely, for her to use the safe word and for the whole thing to stop more quickly than it had started.

That word never came, and I won't know until today if that was because she didn't need to use it, or because she didn't feel like she could. I am hoping for the first option. Praying that I made her feel enough in control of the situation, that she'd been able to clearly define that it was me and not the monsters that had touched her before.

One thing I am sure of, no matter what, no one else is touching Isabella like this again.

No one else is going to be able to trace her scars with their fingertips. No one else is going to see the parts of her like I have.

I knew this was going to happen. Isabella is addictive. I've known that for months. But the withdrawals are already setting in and her ass pushing against my dick like this isn't helping the situation at all.

I trace another scar on her shoulder with a featherlight touch. They're all so individual. Some slightly are more faded than the others, but every one is a clear reminder of how much I couldn't protect her from.

I'm captivated by her in a way I didn't even know was possible. She's overcome more than anyone I know, and I'd put my life savings on the fact that she's going to outlive everyone we know.

Bella has a way of surviving that makes me so proud, I can't even put it into words. Her strength is something that would put gods to shame. But I want to be a place where she doesn't *need* to be strong. A home she can build and not worry about being anything but her complete self.

I hope I proved that to her last night. That she can show me exactly what she wants and I will do everything in my power to get it for her.

Beams of sunlight peek through the slight gaps in the curtains, highlighting the curve of Bella's shoulder as she shifts her hips again. She's waking up slowly. Moving more frequently, breathing coming back to its usual pace as though the panic is already setting in.

I shift a little, moving my body closer to her and pressing the softest series of kisses along her shoulder and up her neck. She lets out a slow sigh, decompressing in my arms as she wriggles her hips.

"You really gotta stop moving your hips, Amore." I allow my hand to slide down her body as I try to keep the air around us as calm as possible.

"I'm just getting comfy."

"And I'll be getting my head comfy between your legs if you keep going." She lets out a breath that's somewhere between a gasp and a laugh, and I don't know if she's still half asleep and thinking she's dreaming, or if she's awake and knows exactly what she's doing to me, because the little minx rubs her ass back against me with a lot more pressure and I have to grab onto her hips and plead for my life. "Bella."

"Hm?" Her hand moves to join mine, grasping it tight and moving it so it's flat against her stomach. She's so soft under me and I swear, I'm instantly put into a trance. I keep my touches light as I allow my hand to venture across her skin. Her palm lays gently over the top of my hand, unmoving as I freely roam her thighs and midriff. "That feels good."

"Yeah?" Bella rests her head back into the pillow softly, letting out a hum of approval. "How are you feeling this morning?"

"Good."

"Are you sure?" Bella nods. "Not lying to me?"

"No." Her words rumble in her back, the vibrations tingling along my chest and I pause for a moment to really listen to what she's saying. To listen to the undertones for any sign that something is off with her. I count the seconds that pass on one hand before she huffs and moves my hand herself. "Don't stop."

Isabella moves my hand between her legs, shifting her body slightly as she gives me more space. Her breathing instantly deepens as my fingers slowly move down to where she wants me.

I find her clit with ease, pressing one finger against it with barely any pressure, applying the smallest amount of friction as I move in a gentle circle. I bring my lips to her neck, pressing a gentle kiss just below her ear and letting out a deep breath.

"Is this what you want, Bella? Hm?" I circle her one more time, the blush on her cheeks darkening as she pulls her lip between her bottom teeth, nodding her head just once. "Use your words, Amore. Tell me exactly what you want."

"I want you to make me come again." She's more confident this morning, but something tells me she's still not there completely.

"How?"

"Luca…"

"Tell me how you want me to make you come, Isabella." I move back, removing my hand from between her legs so I can lay her flat on her back. Bella's face is tinted pink, her chest taking in short, shallow breaths. She's already flustered and I've barely touched her. "You want me to make you feel good?"

"Yes."

"Then tell me how, so I can." Bella's throat bobs. "You're safe, Bella. You know you're safe with me, that's why you're lying here wanting me to do this, right?" She nods. "So, tell me what you want me to do. You're still in control."

I stare down at her, keeping my hand on her waist for reassurance. If she thought me giving her control over this ended last night, she's got the wrong end of the stick. I wasn't having it any other way.

"I —" She sighs, closes her eyes and continues, "I want your head between my legs." I smirk, lifting my head to press a kiss to her lips.

"Very well." I slowly leave a trail of kisses down her torso. I get a feeling last night was the first time anyone had done this with her, based solely on how much she tried to tell me I didn't need to. It wasn't the kind of hesitation that told me she didn't want it, it was nerves. Nerves that were silenced as I tasted pure heaven.

I've always got off on watching a woman have a soul shattering orgasm. More so than I really enjoy receiving anything. I'd rather see a woman's cum cover my fingers than my own sit on her tongue.

But with Bella it was another level.

There is a monster inside of me that has taken the reins and all it wants is to watch Isabella Santoni's eyes roll back in her head as she floods my bedsheets.

It wants her panting and screaming my name, and there isn't a chance in hell it is going to stop until either she needs it to, or it is satiated with her flat out exhausted and legs trembling, unable to walk.

When I finally reach her dripping pussy, I am all but ready to devour her entirely. But I want this to last. I want to spend hours with my head here.

"You're so wet for me, Bella." I run a single finger up her slit, relishing in just how desperately she wants this. I clearly left a good first impression last night. "It's like this pretty little pussy knows what's coming. So ready for me to eat, hm?"

I spread her lips, gently rubbing my thumb over the still slightly swollen bundle of nerves that are desperate for some more attention. Leaning forward, I take a slow, leisurely lick from her core to where she loves my tongue. Bella instantly lays her head back, letting out a short sigh.

"I might take my time with you this morning." My fingers carefully trace over her, swiping at the juices sitting at her entrance and moving some up to her clit. "What do you think? Should I take my time with you? Tongue fuck this cunt nice and slow until you're shaking? Hm?"

"*Luca,*" Bella moans. "Please."

"Oh, you're begging, huh?" I slowly slide a finger into her, watching closely for any sign to stop. She pulls her bottom lip between her teeth and I figure you don't bite your lip if you want someone to stop. "This what you're begging for?" I twist my finger, swiping quickly over the spot I know she loves. "Oh! Sorry, you said you wanted my head down here."

In a heartbeat, I change the atmosphere from teasing and gentle to all out chaos. I flick my tongue over her clit and Bella's hand finds its way to my head, becoming tangled in my hair as her body responds to every single move I make to bring her to the edge.

She moans loudly, hips lifting and legs squirming when I hit the perfect combination in the right spot, and I can feel her orgasm building quickly. I sit back as she does, not removing my fingers but moving to a position that would give her more.

"That's it, Bella. You gonna make a mess for me, hm?"

"N-no. Luca. God." Her hand shakily reaches for mine.

"I know you can." I look up at her, using my free hand to circle her clit and add even more friction. "It feels good, right?"

"Lu- I- shit." Bella grabs at the bedsheets as I continue to slide my fingers in and out of her at the perfect pace.

"That's it, baby. Flood these fucking bedsheets. Let me see how wet you can get for me. *Fuck*, I love seeing you like this."

"Oh, God. Luca. I'm so – so – shit."

"Yeah you are. You're so fucking close, Isabella. Are you going to come for me, Amore? Look at you, such a mess for me. Fuck, Bella you're gonna make me come without even touching me."

My own orgasm builds at the base of my spine and I will continue to be shocked at how easy it is for her to get me there without anything. It's just watching her like this.

Watching her hands toy with her nipples, cheeks flushed a dark crimson, eyes shining as her core clamps around me, signalling the peak of her orgasm. But it's the way she moans my name that really does it for me.

"Come on, Isabella. Let me see you squirt, Amore."

Right on cue, Bella stops holding back, making a mess of the bedsheets and forcing my own orgasm to slam into me as she screams my name. I don't stop though. I power through my own pleasure, keeping up my own barrage on her until her legs are quaking and I am sure I've pulled every single drop out of her that she can possibly give me.

I've never seen anything hotter in my entire life, and I have to take a few moments to sit back and let myself exist in this fever dream world while Bella tries to steady her breathing.

She's beautiful. Fully clothed and screaming at me in fury, reading in silence, when she's wrapped in my arms, or just like this.

There's no version of Bella I don't find utterly jaw dropping, but I can't have her sitting here in our mess all day. If I want her back in this bed tonight I need to get these sheets cleaned and dried, and I can't do that until we're out of it.

I slowly climb out of the bed, heading across to the ensuite and turning the shower on before coming back to where Bella is now starting to look a little more present in reality. I scoop her limp body up and hold her tight against me.

"Where are we going?"

"To get you cleaned up. If you're lucky I might make you come again in the shower."

"I don't think I can go again right now." Bella chuckles, burying her head in my neck.

"Oh, I beg to differ, Amore. I think you have so much more locked up waiting for me but you're starting to feel like this is a bad idea." She doesn't respond and I know I've hit the nail on the head. "So, I think we should just fuck that out of you. Thoughts?"

Chapter Thirty - Five

I'm kind of an expert at making sure broken girls are okay.

LUCA

Isabella scowls at the book in her hands. She's been awfully quiet the past week. Not in the way she was before. She isn't actively avoiding me, but I can't get within a few feet of her without another excuse being thrown into the atmosphere most of the time. I have allowed her the space. I've been sitting at the opposite end of the sofa at night, but she still waits for a few minutes before crawling over and putting her head in my lap.

She wants the connection. That is clear. She likes it when I rake my hands through her hair while we watch TV. She's no longer trying to keep me away from her and is instead seeking attention on her own terms, and that is exactly what we're looking for.

I'd been expecting her to pull back like this. The fact that she is still seeking out some form of contact with me tells me she is fighting it hard, and I'm just glad she hasn't completely retreated. She'll come around. It's just going to take some time, reassurance and a whole lot of work. All of those things are okay. She can take however long she needs to adjust. I'm not going anywhere.

My phone buzzes in my pocket and I quickly pull it out, heading out onto the deck to answer so I don't disturb the peace Bella is reading in out of pure fear of what she'd do if I did.

"Menace." I smile, crossing my arms on the railing and looking out at the sunset, that is burning the lake a dark orange.

"Hey."

"Why are you whispering?"

"Because your niece will not leave me alone today, so I'm hiding in a closet."

"You're hiding in a closet from your daughter. What a terrible mother." I chuckle, knowing the distance which separates me and her right now means I am safe from the murderous glare I am currently being shot.

"You really want to mess with a pregnant woman, dickhead?"

"No. No, I do not. You're doing amazing, Tor and you know it." She hums. "Okay, so I'm guessing if you're hiding from the miniature tornado, you need to talk to me and time is ticking."

"Yes, actually. About Bella."

"What about her?"

"Is she okay? I mean, really okay? She just seemed off when I was talking to her yesterday, but Pops came in and took over the call, so I couldn't really tell if it was just a moment or something more, you know?" I stand up, slowly turning my back to the lake to watch Bella through the floor to ceiling windows. She's still curled up under that fluffy blanket with the fire on across the room, looking the epitome of cosy.

"Yeah, I've noticed her being off a little, but she's okay."

"Are you sure?"

"Do you not trust my judgement, Menace?! I am offended."

"No, I trust you. It's just- you know how Enzo gets over people he's worried about and when he's all pent up, it stresses me out and I-"

"You're worried about her too." Tori sighs down the phone and I can't blame her. Lorenzo is a tough nut to crack. He's like a mime sometimes. Putting on a façade for everyone else's sake, and whilst I only know what's going on in his head because of Tori, I know this whole thing with Petrovich has got to be weighing on him.

I watched from the sidelines when Lorenzo destroyed the family we believed to be responsible for his parent's death all those years ago. He's spent all this time grieving the loss of his family, who he loved more than anything. Losing them turned him into the man he is. I can only imagine how hard it is knowing he's been walking around, trying to close that box off while his sister has been suffering through unimaginable things this whole time, and he can't even murder the men responsible because his family won't be safe if he does.

It's a huge imbalance in a world where Lorenzo has always felt like he had control. Everything that's going on right now means he doesn't have that control and I can't picture that being good for him, mentally.

"How's he doing?" I ask.

"Enzo?"

"Yeah." Tori sighs. "That bad?"

"He keeps pulling Pops out of bed in the middle of the night and making her sleep with us. Even then, his nightmares are getting worse. The longer this goes on, Luca, the worse he's worrying about it happening again. He's terrified that if they could do it to Bella then, when no one knew it was them, what could they do now? Especially when it's clear he's out for them. How far would they go? What if they got here? I'm not exactly at my peak. I'm seven months pregnant, Lu, I'm a fucking whale!"

"I doubt you're that big."

"Oh no? My daughter told me she's seen houses smaller than me." I can't help but laugh at that. Pops knows how to insult people in the most creative ways, it's brilliant. "It's not funny, Luca."

"I mean, it is a little, isn't it?"

"No!"

"Just a little." Tori gives out the smallest snicker and I can sigh with relief, knowing I've broken the seal on the stress she's been bottling up. "Everything is gonna be fine, Tor."

"I know," She sighs. "I know it will be. Eventually. I just… I don't know what to do. I can't do anything. I can't get Bella here without opening us all up for shit, can't come over there without Enzo having an aneurysm, can't bring them down until this child is out of me and I can move like I need to."

"I know, and I know you're impatient and just want to get it all sorted now, but this one is just taking some time. Until you're strong enough for Enzo to be away a little, so we can sort this out. Once we can, we'll clear this all up and everything will be sunshine and rainbows and unicorns with glitter coming out of their assholes. I know it's hard, Tor, but everyone is fine right now, you just gotta remind him of that."

"Even Isabella?"

"Yeah." I sigh, watching as she looks around the room. She sits up straighter, turning her head to find me and immediately relaxes when she does. "Isabella is fine with me."

"Promise me, Luca. Her being okay will make this so much easier, and I can't lie to Enzo. He just knows."

"I swear she's fine, Menace. I've got her, haven't I? I'm kind of an expert at making sure broken girls are okay. You know that better than anyone."

"I was not broken. I was fine."

"You didn't eat or speak for almost an entire week."

"I had been kidnapped."

"God, you're so dramatic. It barely classifies as a kidnapping, and you weren't in any danger."

"Oh, just you wait until this child is out of me and we're all back home. I am giving you every single sleepless night and the beating of your life in that fucking gym."

"I'm thinking of getting my own place when this is all over." I mutter, not moving my eyes from Bella's. A blush slowly rising over her cheeks. She doesn't stop staring back though. "I've gotta go, Tor. Bella's looking for me." I don't wait for Astoria to answer me, just pull the phone back and hang up. I don't know what it is about the way Bella is watching me right now, but something tells me I need to be in there with her and not out here bickering with my best friend.

I gently close the glass door behind me, pausing for a moment in the heavy atmosphere to gauge Bella's emotions.

"Everything okay?" She asks.

"Yeah, just Tori wanting to vent a little. Pops called her a house."

"That might be my fault." I slowly round the room to sit down beside her on the sofa. "She was asking me yesterday why the baby isn't here yet and I said that Astoria has built such a nice home for them, they want to stay in there a little longer." I chuckle because Pops one hundred percent took that the wrong way and decided Tori was indeed a house for her unborn sibling. "I didn't mean-"

"No. No, don't be silly. Pops is just a kid trying to work stuff out. You didn't do anything wrong." I settle back into the sofa and open my arms, giving Bella space to climb into my lap. She takes it, lifting one leg over me and sinking herself down until she's straddling me. She instantly lays her head into the crook of my neck, and I hope she just can't feel how hard my heart is pounding at this change in her. She's never wanted to sit like this. I was expecting her to lay down with her head in my lap again. God this is so much better. "How's your book?"

"I've nearly finished it."

"Good?"

"Eh. Maybe a three star."

"Not as bad as the last one then."

"No."

"That's good."

"Mhm." I pull my fingers through the small knots in the back of her hair, feeling her settle into me more with every brush over her head.

"Bella?" She hums quietly. "I've made plans for us tomorrow." Her eyes open instantly, sitting up and looking at me in a state of panic.

"Tomorrow?"

"That's what I said."

"Why?"

"Because I wanted to." Bella stares at me, slowly trying to climb off me but I pull her back down, starting to run my hands up and down her thighs. "I want to take you out, and tomorrow's the perfect day to do it."

"Tomorrow's Valentine's Day."

"Precisely." I give one certain nod. "There is no one else I'd rather spend tomorrow with."

"I mean, there's probably some tourist-"

"Isabella."

"I'm just saying. There's nothing forcing you to take me-" I sigh, leaning forward to press a hard kiss to her lips.

I've spent seven days forcing myself to not do this. To not kiss her if she didn't seem like she was ready, but I'm not letting her think she isn't the only person I want to be around tomorrow. "Luca…"

"I am completely obsessed with you." I mutter, leaning forward for more of my favourite drug. "I don't want anyone else, Bella and just to make it perfectly clear, no one else is allowed to touch you." Bella's hands rest on my shoulders as I trace my kisses along her jaw. "I want you on your back in my bed. You moaning my name. It's you I want to taste on my tongue when I wake up. You, I want to watch as you come undone. No one else."

Bella's breathing hitches as I reach my hand up under her loose-fitting jumper. I know she can feel how fucking hard I am right now. These jogging bottoms aren't exactly thick enough to hide anything and she's sat right on it. I let my hand wander around to her front, swiping a finger under the bottom cup of her bra.

"Do you want me too, Isabella?" She pants. "You want me to be the only one that touches you ever again?" She nods as my hand reaches the waistband of her leggings and dips under the fabric. "Words, Amore. Please use your words."

"Yes." She pants. "I want you, Luca. Just you."

"That's my girl." I nod and pull my hand out of her pants.

"Wha-"

"I can't fuck you in those pants. You want my dick, Amore, you're going to have to take it yourself." I smirk, lifting my hips and freeing myself from my pants. I slowly rub my hand up my length, watching Bella as she stares. It's only a few seconds before she looks back at me, her face twisted in confusion. "If you want a condom, they're in the drawer beside my bed."

"But-"

"You're in control, Isabella. Until you're comfortable enough to not withdraw after we do this, you have full control. You use me like a doll." She scowls again, huffs, and walks off with her arms crossed, only to return a few moments later and throw the foil wrapper at me, and I can only offer her a bright, cheesy smile.

"Put that on."

"Si, Amore."

Chapter Thirty - Six

I'll protect you, Luca
ISABELLA

If you put a gun to my head and demanded that I tell you my favourite animal, I wouldn't go with something like dogs, cats or panda bears. I will always choose jellyfish. I've always had a weird obsession with them. I mean, not weird. Not really. But if I saw one washed up on the beach, I'd spend ages watching it, trying to save it if it was still alive. They rarely were but that never stopped me carefully digging it into a hole and filling the hole with water in the hope it wouldn't die on me.

That continued while I was under Petrovich's control. Because there's no harm in liking one specific animal and he couldn't decide what I drew in the dirt on the floor of my cell in those early years, or what I sketched into my art pads as I moved back to Alamea.

I guess I must have mentioned it at some point, or Luca remembered from when we were kids, because we spent the entire day in the aquarium and not once did he push us to move past the jellyfish tanks. We must have sat there for almost an hour watching them float around.

And that wasn't the only thing that made today feel like a dream. In fact, I wasn't fully convinced I wasn't still wrapped up in bed having something that was about to turn into a nightmare. I've learned that things that feel too good to be true, usually are.

"Bella?" I pull my head around to Luca, a soft smile on his face as he sits beside me. "We should move on a little. We've got dinner reservations in an hour."

"Oh! Right." I stand up, looking around for what is next.

This is a weird first date. Is it even a first date? I guess. Officially speaking it is. But I've been out with Luca dozens of times before. We spend almost every night at the house watching TV or playing board games, and I'm pretty sure ninety percent of our nights can be classed as dates. But this is different. After his insistence at … whatever last night was, this feels more official and with official, comes weight.

I'd dated tonnes. Dating was one of the things I had to do to survive. It was ingrained into me how to behave and what was expected, how men would act. But Luca loves nothing more than to throw all of my prior expectations out of the window.

He grabs my hand as we venture into the next part of the aquarium, something so small that I am still struggling to wrap my head around.

"Relax." Luca leans into me slightly, lowering his head closer to my ear as he rubs his thumb over the back of my hand. "It's just me."

"I know." I sigh and Luca pulls me to a stop, delicately pushing my back up against a wall.

"Talk to me, Amore. What's going through that pretty little head, hm?"

"I don't know." Luca's head tilts slightly. "It just feels weird."

"Weird how?"

"I don't know, awkward?" He continues watching me with soft eyes, pleading with me to explore my emotions in the hope we can crack through something. Then, in a heartbeat, that soft look is gone. Replaced instead with what I can only describe as pure terror. The colour instantly drains from his face, eyes going wider than saucers. "Luca?"

Luca shakes his head, grabbing for my hand and squeezing until I am genuinely convinced my blood circulation is getting cut off. I am too scared to look behind me. He stumbles slightly as the freeze mode in him begins to switch to run. Almost tripping over a small child behind him, Luca tries to slowly back away.

It is then that I manage to gather my own thoughts and turn my head, confusion washing over me when it's just a tank in the wall. I turn back to a still horrified Luca, trying to pull me away from the glass but I don't understand... oh. OH.

I snicker.

"Luca?"

"Can we go now?"

"It's just a crab."

"Just a... nope. Come on. Let's go." I chuckle, trying to pull my hand out of his so I can get a closer look. "Isabella. No."

"It's just a little crab." I yank him forwards, wrapping his arm around my waist and holding him tightly in place. "See?"

"Mhm. I see. Let's go now." I don't have a choice then, Luca pulls me out of the building, not even stopping to look around the gift shop. He only stops once we reach the car where he fumbles for his keys, unlocking the car door with a struggle and ushering me in like we are escaping a shootout again.

I remember Luca being scared of crabs. I remember it being a whole thing when we were kids. Where it stemmed from I have no idea, but it is as funny now as it was then, and I can't help laughing as he climbs into the car and takes off in a hurry without even fastening his seatbelt.

"It's not funny."

"No. No, definitely… definitely isn't. You're right." I roll my lips together, clearing my throat and sitting up straight in the front seat. A few seconds pass before a snicker involuntarily leaves my lips and Luca huffs before pulling the car to a screeching halt at the side of the road and turning to face me.

"It's not funny!"

"It's a little funny." He scowls. "Come on, Lu. They're crabs. Besides a small nip, they're harmless."

"Hmph. Yeah. Sure, they are. I've watched a documentary that proves otherwise."

"Oh yeah, what documentary is that exactly?"

"I don't remember but Nico showed me it." I stare at him. "What? After I got… attacked-"

"It nipped your toe."

"Exactly. I was attacked. Stop interrupting me. I'm telling you all my trauma and you're laughing at me."

"You're right. You're absolutely right. Please, go on."

"After I was attacked, Nico said that they were testing their strengths because they were going to take over the world and he showed me a documentary about it happening in this little seaside town in America and... why are you laughing? It isn't funny, Isabella!"

"Oh my god, you can't really still believe that." I am cackling. Uncontrollable laughter and is it a little shitty that it's over Luca's fear of crabs? Sure, but this twenty-five-year-old man is still convinced the low budget horror film his older brother showed him at nine years old was a documentary. Even I couldn't have been convinced it was real back then and I was six. "I'm- I can't. Fuck." I pant, grabbing my phone from my pocket and quickly wiping the tears of laughter from my cheeks .

"What are you doing?"

"Texting Enzo."

"NO!" Luca reaches for my phone and I manage to keep it out of his hold, stretching as far out of his reach as I can and just managing to send a message to my brother saying Luca and crabs before my phone is snatched out of my hands and tossed into the back seat. "You're being mean."

"I'm sorry Lu, but this – you know that it was a horror film, right? A super low budget one at that?"

"It wasn't. It was so real. There was real life footage and everything."

"Luca." I snicker, resting my hand on his thigh as I try my damn best to fight against my laughter. It's taking everything in me right now, I swear. "Babe. It was a film. Not a documentary. Made up. Have you watched it since?"

"Are you joking?! I had nightmares for a year!" I press my lips tighter together. "I don't like them."

"I can tell."

"They're so gross with their claws and they just shed their shells? What's with that."

"Mhm." My hand makes its way into Luca's hair, hoping to calm him down slightly. "You should watch the film aga-"

"No."

"Oh, come on. We can watch it tonight." He scowls at me but I am determined to show him just how funny this is, because I know for a fact if he watches that film now he'll be laughing just as hard as I am. "I'll protect you from the scary crabs."

"I should be the one protecting you."

"Mhm. But I'm not scared of the crabs and you are, so how about we swap this time. I'll protect you from the crabs on the TV when we rewatch the film and you protect me from everything else. Sound like a compromise?"

Luca huffs; scowl still sitting dramatically on his face like a child not getting the ice cream they had been promised for good behaviour.

"Only if you come and sit on me now."

"I thought we had dinner plans."

"I'll drive with you here."

"Will it make you feel better if I sit on you?"

"I fear I won't be able to move if you're not." I roll my eyes at him, unfasten my belt and carefully climb across into his lap. I settle with my back against the door, making sure he has enough room to drive with me sitting like this.

"Feel safe now?"

"As safe as I can be when there's killer crabs just walking around, preparing for war."

"Well, it's a good job I know some killer crab recipes then, isn't it? Sounds like it's all we're going to be eating for the rest of our existence."

"Oh, ha ha. So funny. You know what? You're going to pay for that. Just wait until we get home, Valentine. Just you wait."

Chapter Thirty - Seven

Scars do not define beauty.
LUCA

"Would you quit fidgeting?"

"I'm trying to get comfortable."

"I don't think you're trying. It doesn't take this long to get settled. I'm literally a big teddy bear." Bella rolls her eyes at me as she sits up, shooting me a glare as she freezes. I'm using her own words against her and she hates it. It had worked in my favour when it was cold. But now the April heat is beginning to kick into gear, the increasing temperature in this lodge is no longer on my side. Who wants to cuddle with a giant teddy bear while the sun is beating down on your skin? Answer? Apparently not Isabella.

"You're not a teddy bear." I pout dramatically as she tries to sit up and move away from me. "You're a slab of concrete. Hard and useless."

"Funny, you don't seem to complain about me being hard when I'm between your legs, and you're not calling me useless when you're begging for me to make you scream, either."

"Of course that's where your mind went."

"You said it, not me." A smile flicks across Bella's face and I steal my chance, grasping for her and shoving a cushion between us so she can still rest her head on me while she reads.

I've run out of things to keep me occupied on my laptop and somehow I have been convinced to pick up a book. I don't know. I'm not completely convinced I haven't been hexed or something. It wouldn't surprise me if witchcraft was one of Bella's secret hobbies as I have never enjoyed reading. Maybe she laced the pages with something that makes it addictive, or maybe I just love how we've been spending most of our days now the weather is nicer.

We lounge out across the various outdoor furniture. Spend as long as possible basking in the spring sun like we're lizards. When we're sitting on the large sofa out here, like today, I get to have her lie on me for most of the day. Other days, she chooses the deckchairs and I have to settle for sitting beside her. Either way, we sit in almost silence. Just the wind and the birds singing in the trees surrounding the lodge prove to us both that we're not frozen in time, no matter how much we wish we were.

It's been two months since Bella took the step to move us forwards and whilst I'd class us as dating now, that's not a topic we have covered officially yet. She's still fragile, and despite the huge changes I have begun to see in her now she is becoming accustomed to making her own choices about herself and her body, she still has a long way to go.

We train together daily. In everything that I can show her so she can protect herself, should the need ever arise. I've taught her how to shoot properly, how to take down men double her size and use their own weight against them. I've taught her just in case there is ever a time when I cannot be here.

When we go back to normal, when this is all over and we move to wherever and we have to leave this bubble I am so beyond happy in, I might not be able to be around her twenty-four hours a day, seven days a week. Lorenzo may need me for jobs and I could be away for a while. If that ever happens, I need to know Bella is okay, and that she can protect herself rather than just survive whatever happens. I need to know no one else is ever going to hurt her the way they already have.

"God, I can see the steam coming out of your ears from thinking too hard. You only have so many thoughts a day Lu, don't use them all at once."

"Oh, you think you're so funny, don't you?" Bella tries to cover her smirking face with her book but I won't stand for the cheek. I grab the book, dropping it to the floor behind the sofa with a thud.

"Luca!"

"Isabella!" She forms a dramatic scowl and I smirk. "Oh no, you'll have to get it."

"You're right. I'll just stand–"

"No, you can just lean over here." I pull on her waist as she tries to stand, and this time she doesn't try to hide her smile as she does, practically shoving her ass in my face as she leans over the back to grab for the book. "Have I ever told you how perfect your ass is?" I move my hand over her slowly, dipping my thumb under the hem of what might as well be underwear but she calls shorts. I don't care. This girl could walk around in her pants and I'd still be amazed every single time I saw her.

"Once or twice."

"You're right." Bella slowly comes back up and I pull her hips until she is straddling me. "Nowhere near enough. Shall we cover it again? Your ass is the best in the universe."

"Oh, you've checked them all, have you?"

"Near enough, yeah." I sigh, allowing my hands to trace over every one of her curves. "You're perfect, Bella. Utterly flawless."

"I think you need your eyes checking. You might be legally blind and need to wear those huge glasses they used to wear in the '70s." Bella jokes, pushing her hand into my chest as she goes to move but I pull to keep her right where she is. "Lu–"

"Nuh-uh, you know the rules." I shift, rolling us so she's laying on her side, wrapped tightly in my arms. I know she's been struggling today. Hiding under blankets when I know for a fact she is too warm, every time my fingers have passed over a scar, her face has shifted. I've just been waiting for her to show me how she is doing, and here it is. "Scars do not define beauty."

"I'm not saying they do. You said that I'm flawless and I'm not. I'm covered in flaws."

"So am I." Bella rolls her eyes, but I continue. "I am. Do my scars make me any less perfect?"

"I never said you were perfect."

"Firstly, I'll come back to the audacity you just had to claim I'm not perfect once we've tackled you. Secondly, answer the question."

"No."

"No, right. All a scar is, is evidence we've gone through some tough shit that could have killed us. I wouldn't have my scars if I didn't have those experiences, and it's those experiences that make me who I am; I wouldn't change that for anything. You survived it all, Bella. You should be a lot more proud of that than you are."

"I am proud of it." Bella interrupts, watching her fingers as they trace over the raised skin on my shoulder. "I know I don't act like it, but I am. It took a lot of strength for me to endure everything I did and I could have given up so many times. Every time I tried, call it fate or God's will or whatever, but I survived and endured more and that's a testament to who I am." My heart swells in my chest as Isabella unlocks things we've been working on for months. "It was hard and I shouldn't have had to do it, but I did; I survived and I'm glad that I did because without all of that, I wouldn't be here."

"And that's a good thing?" Bella scowls and nods ferociously.

"Definitely." I'm floating. Completely weightless as my body takes flight and begins to soar into the atmosphere, leaving all of this behind us both. But then the atmosphere changes. Bella's face turns from looking sure of what we're talking about to a mix of emotions I can't exactly pinpoint. I'm still not sure if I like it or not, though. "What happens next?"

"What do you mean?"

"Well… after here? You, Lorenzo and Tori keep talking about when we're all together again. What happens then?" Her baby blues meet mine for a second before she looks back at my chest with bated breath. "With us."

"With us?" Bella slowly lifts her eyes back to mine, and I can see now that this has been playing on her mind for a little while. "Why does anything have to change?"

"Luca…"

"I'm serious, Bella. Why does going back to normal life need to change anything? Realistically, I know things are going to be a little different, but we don't have to stop anything. Unless you want to stop this?"

"No. That's not what I meant." She answers quickly, and the surety of it settles the anxiety that had bloomed in my chest much too quickly.

The idea of losing what Bella and I have is horrifying to me. I lay awake some nights and watch her breathing slowly, terrified that I'm watching a ticking time bomb, but those are fears I keep firmly buried so she can't see them. Bella doesn't need me making her feel like there's anything to be worried about. She needs me to be clear-headed and confident that everything is working out as it should be, even if I'm not sure I deserve to be the one laying here holding her.

"Then we don't have to. Things will look a little different, but it all depends how long this takes and how you feel when it comes to that-"

"And if Lorenzo knows." Bella's throat bobs.

"Yeah. That's going to be a whole thing, for sure."

"He's going to go ballistic."

"What, that I'm dating his little sister or that I've fucked you on every piece of furniture in his precious lake house?" Bella lets out a loud cackle, and I can't help but feel better now she's less sombre. "Let me worry about him, okay? Don't worry your pretty little mind about it."

"Are you going to bribe him?"

"Me? No, I'll get Pops to do it." She chuckles again. "For what it's worth, Amore, I'm glad you don't want this to end."

"You are?"

"So much it's a little embarrassing." I lift my hand, pushing Bella's curls behind her ears with soft touches. A rock forms in my throat as I gear myself up to say what I've been trying to for the past few weeks. "Bella, I-"

I'm not sure if it's pure coincidence or if the universe is fucking with me, but my phone starts ringing loudly before I can even get the words out, not only burning the moment to the ground but the ringtone is so specific, we both jump out of our skin and quickly reach for it, resulting in banged heads and Bella crashing to the deck floor. I pull the phone up to my ear quickly, grabbing to help Bella back onto the sofa as she laughs, rubbing her head and reaching for the spot on mine that hit hers.

"Hello?"

"Luca." Lorenzo sighs down the phone. "So, I have news."

"News?"

"Mhm. Tor went into labour yesterday evening." My eyes widen and Bella tips her head at me. I flick the phone to loudspeaker, allowing Bella to hear the news we hadn't been expecting for another couple weeks.

"You're on speaker, Bella's here."

"Oh good, are you both sitting down?"

"You're freaking me out, Lorenzo." Panic begins building in my chest. Astoria's first labour hadn't been completely smooth sailing and I can't say that I haven't been terrified of it happening again this time around.

"Yeah, well, welcome on board." He sighs again. "We have twins." Bella and I stare at each other. "I uh – we only had the one scan with everything going on. Everything else has been normal, measurements wise but – yeah. Twins. Two girls. Everyone's healthy, a little small but healthy. Tori's fine, Luca. She's tired but she said she'll text you in a few days." A baby starts to cry in the background and Enzo gives us an exhausted chuckle. "I uh- I gotta go but Tori wanted me to tell you two before anyone else. I'll send you some pictures later. Love you both."

The call ends before either of us can even respond, and we're stuck staring at each other in pure shock.

It's Bella who's the first to break it with a snicker.

"God, he's fucked."

"Oh, completely." I nod, laughing as I reach to pull her back into my arms. "Four girls. Jeez."

"He's still got room to have another wrapped around a finger though."

"No, he's got you, too. Poor guy doesn't stand a chance with the five of you. Anyway, I'd like to circle back to something."

"Mhm?"

"I'm not perfect? Really? Have you seen me?!"

Chapter Thirty - Eight

No objections, your honour.
ISABELLA

I don't mind this kind of weather. Warm but not hot, a slight breeze but not so cold that you need a jacket. It's perfect for the middle of April. We had a few days of non-stop rain, and being cooped up in the house made me feel rough, to say the least.

I hate the feeling of being trapped inside now. After so many years of it being the only option, of only being allowed to exist in designated areas, I love just sitting out here and breathing the fresh air.

It's been a quiet day today. Luca has been on and off calls with too many people for me to keep track of the names, so I've been left to my own devices. Lost between the pages of books and living in worlds that seem so familiar and so different to this one.

It feels like I am living in my own fantasy world sometimes. Especially when I get to sit here like this, cross-legged on the end of the dock as the sun sets on the horizon. Tonight, it's burning the sky a vibrant pink and casting the mountains in the distance in a transcending mix of gold and lilac. I've been staring at it for a while now and I swear, it's perfect. This is what happiness feels like. This is precisely what I survived for.

Luca doesn't say a word as he sits down beside me, just puts his arm around me and into the worn wood beneath us both.

We sit in the silence as the colours slowly fade through indigo and into black, the very hint of colour still peeking over the mountain tops. Yet I can feel Luca watching me.

He smiles when I turn my head to him and brings his hand up to my thigh, pulling me closer.

"How am I only just now realising that you're wearing a dress?" Luca's hand splays itself out across my thigh, slowly venturing across the expanse of skin. Each movement down towards my knee is followed by the hem of my skirt being lifted higher and I don't mind. Something I've found comes hand in hand with anything Luca does.

There have been points in my past where I doubted that I'd ever willingly have sex again but with Luca it's so easy. The sexual chemistry between us is undeniable, and it feels so good that I haven't even thought about denying it since our first night in the hall over two months ago.

In those two months, I've used our safe word once. I'd woken up after a horrific nightmare that morning and by the evening, I wanted to get over it and thought moving through it with Luca would be fine. It wasn't. I used the word and instantly, Luca stopped what he was doing, wrapped me into a hug and assured me it was okay.

He didn't take any time to think, and didn't try to continue a little while later. It was taken completely off the table for two excruciating days. Two days and I cracked. That was it. I couldn't handle it anymore after that. I was so completely desperate to have him again that it was a little embarrassing.

I couldn't help it though. Sex with Luca is like I'm sleeping with a fucking god. Every single time is mind blowing and exciting, and I never want it to end.

I hum as Luca's hand reaches my hip, his fingers twisting around the strap of my new underwear. He lets out a breath that can only be described as a knowing and smug chuckle, slowly bringing his head down to my ear and I instinctively close my eyes, preparing to lose myself in the moment with him.

"I told you when you bought this dress that I was going to fuck you in it, Bella." I smirk, letting him move my legs from being crossed to flat out in front of me. The second he does, the hand on my hip makes its way between my already drenched thighs.

"Maybe that's why I put it on." I move my hand down to his, separating my legs enough so that I can move him exactly where I want him to be right now.

"Oh, you did?" Luca breathes heavily against my neck as he rubs circles across the fabric of my underwear. "Have you been sitting here all day this wet? Waiting for me to be free so you can tell me you need me to make you come again?"

Luca and I work in synchronicity to change our position, I move back a few inches and lay back on the deck to give him the space he needs to get down between my legs.

"Tell me, Bella, what has that glorious mind of yours been thinking about today?"

"You." I lift my hips and Luca smirks, pulling my underwear down and off my legs with ease. "You, with your head between my legs and your fingers inside me, and watching you come when I do."

"When you see yourself like I do when you come, Amore, you'll understand why it's so fucking easy to blow my load just at the thought." And with that, Luca dives in.

He knows now. He knows how to build me up to the precipice he loves bringing me to. He knows the combinations of twists and sucking and the perfect time to slide a finger into me for it to get the biggest effect. He knows exactly where to apply the pressure and what to say and yet even though he knows it all, every single orgasm comes as much of a shock as the first.

Sometimes he draws them out until I'm begging for a release and sometimes, he brings me over the edge and immediately riles me right back up, only to send me back into another pit of ecstasy.

But no matter what, I can always count on the fact that being like this with Luca will always leave my brain a melted puddle of goo, my legs quaking and me desperately wanting him inside of me.

"Is this what you've been wanting?" Luca hovers over me, slowly rubbing the head of his cock over my entrance. His eyes dip from mine, looking down as he slowly slides himself into me with a groan. "Fuck, Bella."

Luca doesn't give me time to respond to him. Just lifts my legs over his shoulders and proceeds to make me see god.

Each thrust forces a moan out of my lungs and each moan makes him fuck me harder.

I'm going to combust.

"Luca." I pant, wrapping my fists tighter around his t-shirt to stabilise us both.

"That's it, Amore. Scream my name. Let the neighbours hear just how good it feels to have me buried inside of you. You look so fucking good taking my cock, Isabella." He grunts, grabs for my hand and moves it between us both. "Rub your clit while I fuck you. Don't stop. Fuck Bella, you look so good playing with yourself."

I follow my orders, applying just the right amount of friction to my clit. My eyes roll and my head falls back to the wood as I lift my hips, allowing Luca to hit deeper into me.

"You gonna come on my cock, Bella? I want to see that perfect pussy give me everything it's got. Don't fucking hold back on me." My orgasm tears through my body and instantly, Luca's moves become staggered as he follows. "Fuck. That's it baby. Come on my cock. Just like that." He groans and I swear, it forces the orgasm to hit me harder.

Static electricity vibrates in every single one of my muscles as Luca slowly pulls out, leaning down to press a quick, sweat covered kiss to my lips, and when I open my eyes, all I can do is giggle at the mess of a man sitting back on his knees staring at me in awe.

"You are fucking phenomenal." He pants. I feel the blush on my cheeks darken, but Luca just keeps watching me with a serious face. Then he smirks, his chest lifting as he lets out a single laugh of air. "I'm not done with you."

"But…"

"But nothing. I want to fuck you on every surface of this house, and I can't do it here." Luca fastens the button on his jeans, leans down and scoops me up bridal style. "Unless you have any objections-"

"Nope. No objections here." I smirk, pushing his damp curls off his forehead. "Not a single one."

Chapter Thirty - Nine

Tutto va beni.

LUCA

I've found that it's good for us both to have a little space for a few hours a week. This is a weird situation to be in really. There's no other world where you're going to be locked up in such an isolated place with no other company but the person you're in a very new relationship with, and we're both very aware of the pressure that can put on it.

I try to step back when I can and give Isabella space a few times a week. Running errands in town, going for a run, dropping her at Safiyah's if she just wants a girls night. I'm not going to say it's easy, but it's healthy for us.

Isabella has grown up constantly being watched, waiting for her to put a hair out of line. That's where she's comfortable. Being observed like a wild animal locked up in the zoo. The good news is, the more we do this, the more space I give her to break free of the chains she's so used to, the more of the old Bella returns.

She's growing more confident in her own abilities on a daily basis. To the point where I walked out of the bedroom after my shower this morning to see her standing in her underwear drawing smiley faces around all of her scars with a biro pen. When I asked her why, she just shrugged and said that if she's going to look at them anyway, she might as well make it fun. I sat with her then, finding shapes in them until she was covered in happier markings. She was still sporting them when I left, though I expect she's had a bath and soaked them off by now.

Getting out of the house also gives me time to think without Bella watching over my shoulder and asking me why I look concerned. I could tell her. Open up about everything that's running through my mind on a daily basis. Every concern. Every possibility I've run over a million times. But I know her mental load is already chaotic. She doesn't need me adding in my worries about having to raise Lorenzo and Astoria's kids if something tragic happens to them, like it happened to our parents. Or any of the other tragic fates I've written for myself that have started haunting my nightmares.

I'm sure once everyone's reunited, when we're all back down in Kredrith living within a few feet of each other, when Pops is banging on my bedroom door at six am and Bella grumbles about it waking her up, and I have to sneak out to get them both food that Lorenzo will no doubt complain at me for feeding them, I'm sure then I'll be able to relax a little. I'm sure the anxiety will settle. When the safety of the people I love isn't in the air like it currently is. I'm sure that's all I need.

I stare at the clock on the dashboard, waiting for it to tick over again and tell me I've spent three hours out of the house. That's all the time I can manage being out here without setting eyes on her right now.

When she goes to Safiyah's I drive home and go for a run, waiting in the tree line like some psychopath from Bella's books. Just stand there watching her laugh with her friends on their deck. And I do that every two and a half hours. Until she texts to say she's ready to come home. Then I bring her home and listen to her tell me about her day with the biggest smile on her face and the life back in her eyes, that I thought was gone for good.

No matter what though, I keep letting her go. I keep taking this step back because I know she needs it. I know she needs to breathe by herself and feel her feet stable on the ground. She needs to know that she can exist without someone else, because I want her to want it. I want her to want me there with her. I don't want her to think she can't survive without me, because if god forbid something happens to me, I know she would be fine; Bella is indestructible. And I think she's finally starting to learn that, thanks to me giving her that space.

The second the clock ticks over, I put the car back in drive and head home with two coffees, and the excitement to see her builds more quickly than I can keep up with. I can't wait to hear about what she did today. Even if she just sat and read, I want to hear her talk about her books and the characters forever. I reckon that's what happiness is. Just me in a room with Bella talking to me for eternity about whatever random thoughts come into her head.

I pull into the garage, hopping out of the car and locking everything up as quickly as I can. I spill the smallest amount of coffee as I open the door, but it's the least of my worries when I turn towards the rest of the house and Bella is standing in the space between the lounge and kitchen, ghost white and covered in red. Blood slowly drips from the point of the kitchen knife she's holding, continuing to form the puddle she's standing barefoot in. Her favourite white sweater is ruined. Her still damp curls a matted mess.

I feel like I've walked onto a movie set. Or maybe it's a prank her and her friends are pulling. But when I put the coffees down on the side and slowly approach her, I can see it's no joke.

Two bloodied corpses lay on the floor. One at the end of the kitchen island by my feet, the other by hers a few feet away. She's not freaking out. I mean, she's frozen but she isn't trying to get out of here, neither are we being swarmed by other men, so I'm guessing it was just these two and we're otherwise alone. I'm not sure if I can take that as a good thing or not.

I step over the first body and have to move faster to catch Bella as her legs give way. She breaks apart the second I touch her. It isn't a slow and tedious descent into it either. It comes out as an instant sob, the knife hitting the floor with a clang before I've even managed to pull her into me completely.

"I've got you, Amore." I pull her in tighter, standing up and needing to get her away from the corpses because they for sure aren't making this easier. Guilt is starting to tear me apart already. This wouldn't have happened if I was here. Petrovich is out here looking to – fuck, who even knows what Petrovich's game currently is – and I just thought leaving her alone was okay? How fucking dumb am I? "I've got you, Bella, everything's okay. I'm here. Tutto va beni."

Part

Two.

Chapter Forty

Pinkie swear?
ISABELLA

I think my body has become accustomed to receiving trauma. Normal people would be a fucking mess after today. They'd be broken and shattered and wouldn't be able to stop thinking about the fact that they walked into their kitchen to find two men creeping around, and then proceeded to kill them.

Me though? I'm thinking about where I put my book. I'm sure I'd left it on the bed when I got out of the bath, but I haven't seen it while I've been back here with Luca. It sucks because I was getting to the good part, too. I was really excited to sit down and hopefully finish it today, but I doubt that's going to happen now.

I can feel it though. The trauma. My heart is beating harder than I'm used to it feeling now. Each thud feels like a huge hollow drum being beaten until it ricochets in my veins. My head is hurting, but I know I didn't hit it. I managed to avoid each of their clumsy punches like Luca showed me. I keep hearing creaks in the hallway and whilst I'm not terrified it's someone else coming to finish their job, I am right back to how I felt when we first got here. I'm counting steps between where I'm standing and the nearest tool I can use to my advantage. I'm retracing all the exit points in my head and trying to work out which is the quickest one in every possible situation I can think of.

I heard Luca on the phone to who I'm guessing was Lorenzo, as I was getting in the shower to wash their blood off my skin. It took me less than ten minutes to gather myself together after breaking down on Luca, and I'm still not entirely sure what caused it.

I lost control of myself when I saw him. It's like the primitive side of me that had been turned on during the fight had finally shut down, and seeing Luca moving towards me, it was as though the nightmare had come to a sudden and abrupt stop, and the devastation just flooded out of me.

I calmed myself down and managed to tell him what happened, and the honest answer was not a lot. I saw them, they saw me, one of them pointed a gun and shot the wall when I ducked and managed to knock it out of their hands. It fell under the sofa and I could see it in their faces, the panic when they realised it wasn't going their way. That was all the warning I got before they both turned manic.

It wasn't a long fight. Maybe ten minutes in total, and I honestly am not sure how long I had been standing in the middle of the room still holding the knife before Luca came in. I can't remember a single thought that went through my head from the second I saw them until I was alone in the bathroom. I don't even remember grabbing the knife out of the holder. I don't remember them putting their hands on me, but I could feel it, and feeling their touch reminded me of Tomas.

I think I've scrubbed multiple layers of skin off in the shower. It's still burning, though.

Overwhelming nausea is stuck in my gut. I know it will eventually fade.

Eventually, I'll pass out from exhaustion and wake up not remembering what it felt like, and it'll be fine. This is temporary.

I still hate it all the same.

That all it takes is one touch and my brain automatically takes me right back there. Back to sitting on the concrete floor staring up at the metal cage wall, as Tomas opens the door and slips inside, slowly removing his suit jacket.

Everything was fine. I haven't had a flashback in months. My brain has been quiet and I've been happy and comfortable. My scars haven't haunted me, and my dreams aren't something from the deepest, darkest crevices of the web. But now I feel like I'm right back to step one on this godforsaken recovery road, and I'm filled with the reminder that this is how it's always going to be, because of them. I'm always going to have joy stolen from me because they had too much power over a girl who couldn't protect herself from their conniving hands.

Is this how I'm supposed to live now?

Am I supposed to sit back and have this constantly in the back of my mind? Forever? Are they going to continue to tear my life apart even though I'm safe? How long does this go on for? Am I going to be flashing back to them when I should be celebrating? Birthdays? Christmas? My wedding?

Why do they get the good life when they're the ones who did these things to me? Why are they up there in their ivory castles and I'm the one suffering? I didn't do anything to deserve this. I don't deserve to have been dealt this hand.

"Bella?" Luca knocks on the door quietly, pushing it open slightly as he inches his head in a few millimetres at a time. "Amore, you've been in here a while, are you okay?"

"Yeah." I sigh, pulling the long-sleeved pyjama top over my head and turning to face him. "Sorry, I got lost in my thoughts."

"Don't apologise, Bella. It's okay, I just wanted to make sure you weren't tearing yourself apart in here."

"I'm not."

"Good." Luca finally lets go of the door and takes a hesitant step deeper into the room. "How are you doing? You look a little pinker than you did before."

"I'm okay." He raises his eyebrow in one perfect arch but I nod my head, closing the space between us because realistically, I am fine. Right now, I am, and I really hate the idea of Rurik or Tomas stealing even a second more of my brain time. They're no longer in control of me. I'm not back there. They're out there doing lord knows what, but it doesn't affect me right now, and that's all that matters. "I promise."

"Would you pinkie swear on it?"

"Mhm." I nod and raise my left hand, pinkie finger extended for him to wrap his around. He stares into my eyes for a few seconds, before a smile spreads delicately across his lips when he's sure I'm not lying, and he gleefully interlocks his finger with mine.

"Carlos and Nicky are cleaning up the mess in the living room, but it's gonna take most of the night, so if you want a drink or some food or something, you'll have to tell me and I can go get it rather than you seeing it all again. I brought some snacks in here though, and figured we could just have a movie night? Might occupy your mind enough to get some sleep?"

"Depends what movie you had in mind." I push up onto my tiptoes, pressing a kiss to Luca's stubble covered jaw. His arm wraps around my waist and the ache in the bottom of my stomach instantly turns to the same butterflies I get whenever I'm this close to him. It's a feeling I've become quickly addicted to. The thought is terrifying to me; that I need to feel the way my body responds to someone's presence on a daily basis. But I tried fighting it for too long, and the fear of this being gone at any second means I'm soaking up the drug while I can.

"Well, I was thinking Home Alone. I know it's not exactly the season, but maybe two guys breaking into a house and failing and it being a comedy might make you feel better about this." I snicker.

"They were a little dumb. Did I tell you they dropped the gun under the sofa?"

"No, but Carlos found it after seeing the hole in the wall." Luca bends slightly, giving me the ability to wrap my legs around his waist so he can carry me back to the bed. "You're getting heavier."

"Oh! Wow! Kick a girl while she's down, why don't you?!"

"No! I didn't mean it like that!"

"Did too."

"Did not, I meant it like you're putting weight on-" I pull away from him as he sits me down on the bed, instantly crawling across to my designated side and getting under the bedsheets.

"Not helping your case here, Bottaro."

"It's not a bad thing, Amore!" Luca kicks off his shoes and pulls the sheet back, quickly trying to find a way to dig himself out of the pit he's jumped into, feet first. "You were too thin when we moved up here. You're at a good, healthy weight now. It might be more than it was six months ago, but it's better."

"Hm."

"It is."

"Yeah, yeah. Give me the remote." Luca watches me as he hands me the remote. I know exactly what he means and I have to agree. I used to look in the mirror and see a girl who was one missed meal away from being six feet under. Now I have curves. I'm stronger than I ever thought was possible. I no longer struggle to hold a full bottle of milk, I'm not dizzy when I stand, I'm not exhausted constantly and I can count on my period to not only arrive but arrive on time, more than I can count on the rise and fall of the tide. I'm still going to milk it though.

I flick through the list, finding the one film I know Luca hates more than anything in the world, and settle on it being his punishment.

"Oh, come on! Have I not suffered enough today?!"

"Clearly not if you're being mean to me when I literally just murdered two men for breaking into our house. Now shut up, I want to watch the killer crabs take over the world."

Chapter Forty – One

I need a connection.
LUCA

Sleep is futile. I'm not even going to waste precious time trying to get some. There is simply too much to do.

I wait until Bella is soundly asleep before slipping out of her room and into the living room where Carlos and Nicky are using a concoction of chemicals to pull the blood out of the hardwood floor. When they're done, I tell them to crash in my room and the spare. They need to be fully rested right now.

I have no doubt the two men that snuck into the house have a link to Petrovich. It just feels weird in my gut. I manage to find an ID on them both. They live relatively close by. Low-life criminals with a history of burglaries, drunk and disorderly arrests, and one of them was arrested last year for trying to rob a petrol station with a toy water gun he'd hand painted. Fucking idiot forgot to cover the logo on the side that said 'Splashtastic'.

They clearly aren't masterminds in any shape or form and after some further investigations, there have been a small string of break-ins over the past month in nearby houses.

I look into everything I can think of over the next six hours while the house is eerily silent. I want to find a connection between them and Petrovich. I'd somehow feel more comfortable in the knowledge that this was planned, rather than it being a coincidence. I still need to work out where they got the real fucking gun.

Lorenzo, Tor and I spent hours looking into this town. The local crime rate is practically non-existent, the house is highly secure but inconspicuous, easy to get to but out of the way, covered enough to hide but not so much that people can hide from us. It's perfect for a safe house. It's supposed to be perfect for keeping Bella safe and if she isn't safe here, in the middle of nowhere where I can control everything, where will she be?

I'd made a promise to her. I swore that she'd be safe with me and now look. I left her for a few short hours. A few hours that slipped by too quickly and look how that ended.

If it is Petrovich, at least I know when we finally have the delight of eradicating his presence from Earth, she'll be okay. If it wasn't him, I don't know where that leaves me. It not being part of Petrovich's plan somehow scares me more, and I hate that. I hate that I'll never be able to leave Bella again, because this space is so good for her. I'll hate that she'll start to feel trapped. I hate that I let her down when I swore she was safe here.

It is seven am when Carlos and Nicky get up, and I am still in the same spot they left me eight hours ago, having made no progress in confirming it was Petrovich.

I just need one coincidental run in. One single sighting of either of them with anyone in Petrovich's clan. Just one. That's all I need to pin this on him and I can take action. I can... hell, I don't even know what I can do, but I can do something.

"Luca?" I lift my head quickly at the soft, sad voice that manages to break me from my thoughts. Bella tugs on her sleeves, pulling one hem and twisting it as she shifts in her spot. Looking around to make sure we're alone, I double check the time before responding.

"You should be sleeping, Amore."

"I woke up and you weren't there." She sniffs slightly.

"Bad dream?" She nods and I pull the laptop off my lap, moving it to make room for her. I raise my arm and she quickly comes to settle into her favourite spot. "I'm sorry. I should have been there." Bella nuzzles her head into my chest as I slouch down, kicking my feet up onto the coffee table. I'm not sure if I'm talking about not being there for her nightmare, or for yesterday evening. Both, I guess. Every time I leave her side right now, something happens.

"I'm okay. Any idea who it was?"

"No. Well, yeah. I guess. Just some common burglars from what all the evidence says. No link I can find to anyone." Bella reaches for my hand as it tries to untangle a knot in her hair, pulls it around to her face where she places a handful of kisses across my palm.

"It wasn't your fault, Luca."

"I didn't say-"

"I know you're tearing yourself apart up there. You always are." She turns now, laying her head back so she's staring up at me with the most all-knowing look I've ever seen, and it's like she can see right into my brain. Every thought, every reason, everything that could happen. She sees it, and in a single heartbeat she takes it into the palm of her hand and squashes it to dust. "You're not responsible for any of this, just like I'm not responsible for my parents. Understand?" I sigh, closing my eyes and nodding as she cups my cheek.

This girl.

How on earth was I ever lucky enough to end up with this girl?

"Nicky and Carlos are out checking all the cameras."

"I wondered why it was so quiet." Bella smiles quickly, raising her head and pressing a slow, calming kiss to my lips. "I'm going to go brush my teeth and change before they come back. We can have breakfast; I'm thinking pancakes, and then you can have a nap."

"I'm not-"

"It wasn't a question." Bella smiles, standing up and giving me another kiss before disappearing down the hall. A few seconds pass before she turns on the speaker in her bathroom and some of her favourite songs start to muffle through the walls.

I wait a few moments, just listening to how things sound some kind of normal, before standing up and getting started on her favourite pancakes. I'll be damned if I'm disobeying her, and the last time she tried to make pancakes she set the fire alarm off and smoked out the whole house.

I'm barely halfway through weighing out all the ingredients when my phone flashes on the countertop with movement at the front of the house. Considering the guys said they'd come back through the glass doors behind me and they definitely haven't been gone long enough to finish the job, there isn't a chance in hell it can be them.

I don't have time to check the cameras, though. In fact, I barely have a few seconds between the notification and the garage door creaking open a mere two feet away.

I instinctively grab my gun from the kitchen island, swiftly taking a handful of steps forwards and pressing the gun to the intruder's forehead as they enter the kitchen.

"Luca, what the fuck?!" *Mia?* "Put the gun away before-"

"GOTTA PEE. GOTTA PEE. GOTTA PEE!" I'm pushed out of the way by a thundering five-year-old who seems to remember her trip here a lot better than any of us were expecting.

Penelope tears into the kitchen, around the corner and down the hall to the spare bathroom, the door slamming behind her, and I find myself quickly shoving my gun onto the countertop as far out of reach as possible. This house is not suitable for a five-year-old right now.

Wait.

WHY IS THE FIVE-YEAR-OLD HERE?!

"Oooh! Are you making pancakes?! I am starving."

"Mia, what the hel-" The garage door slams and suddenly the air is sucked out of the building. Oh no. I hadn't called him yet, how the fuck did he- "Lorenzo!" I turn around, forcing a bright smile onto my face. He looks exhausted and a brand of furious I haven't seen on him since Astoria was refusing to tell him about Rowan. Those were dark days. "Hey. Hi. What's up?! What-"

"Start explaining why the fuck I had Nicky calling me at five last night saying he was being brought up here to clean up two dead bodies instead of doing his fucking job, and start explaining now. Before I fill your pockets with cement and drown you in the fucking lake."

Chapter Forty – Two

Is that weird?

ISABELLA

I feel ready to take on the world today. I don't know why. I just feel like all these problems I am having are absolutely tiny. I am in such a good mood and honestly, I think murdering two men in cold blood helped. Is that weird? That watching two men bleed to death on the kitchen floor actually made me feel more excited about existing?

It's definitely weird.

As I finish getting ready for the day, I know there is likely a tonne to work out before the day is done. I know Luca is going to put up a fight about napping today, but I'll wear him down. Even if I have to take one for the team and physically exhaust him. What a shame that would be.

But before I can tie him to the bed and watch him beg to touch me, I need fuel, and pancakes sound so good right now.

I step out into the hall and barely make it five steps towards the kitchen when something runs into my legs with just enough force to almost knock me over. I take a few steps back, naturally grabbing the running object and freeze when I see my niece grinning up at me. Perfect blue eyes. Her dark curly hair is a chaotic mess across her head, flyaways sticking out in every possible direction.

"Auntie Bella! You're here too?!"

"Pops?" Maybe I'm still asleep. I mean, it would make sense as to why I'm having a good day, I guess. I bend my knees, bringing myself down to her height. "What are you doing here?"

"Daddy brought me. He said Uncle Luca was going to be in lots of pain over the next few days."

"Your dad's here?"

"Yes. And Auntie Mia! Come!" Pops grabs my hand, yanking me towards the bottom of the hall before I can even stand up completely. She doesn't stop pulling on my hand until we're in the kitchen, very clearly having interrupted something. Lorenzo's face is a shade of maroon I didn't think it was even possible to turn, Luca looks like he's about to literally shit himself and Mia is eating a pancake, watching the pair of them like it's her favourite TV drama show. "Daddy! Daddy, I found Auntie Bella. I didn't know she was here, too!" Lorenzo tears his eyes from Luca to me.

"Good job, Pops. How about you go with Mia and find your toys in storage, huh? It looks like a nice day out on the deck."

"But I'm eating my pancakes."

"I'll cook you some more and bring them out." Luca drags a hand down his exhausted face. "Probably best to help her and keep her busy." Mia sighs dramatically but stands up from her seat.

"Right, Princess Penelope. Where are these so-called 'toys' your father mentioned?" The pair disappear down the hall and with it leaves any kind of calm. Lorenzo strides across the room and wraps me up in the tightest hug that is possible before a human being physically bursts.

This is the first time in almost a year I've seen my brother, and after spending the majority of my life believing he was dead like the rest of my family, I think I need the hug the same amount that he does. As much as I speak to Lorenzo almost daily, I've only seen him in person once since we were kids, and that time, we were kind of running on a clock.

He pulls back after a good few minutes, holding my head in his hands, and the man standing before me now isn't the one that was here when I walked into the room. He's paler, breathing deeper. Fuck, I forgot how much he looks like dad.

"Are you okay? Did they hurt you? I knew you should have been in Sicily. You look a little pale."

"Enzo." I chuckle, wrapping my arms around his waist and pulling myself back in for another hug before I start to cry again. "I'm okay."

"Are you sure?"

"Yes, I'm positive. I'm fine. Absolutely fine." He exhales against me and I manage to lift my head, taking a step back. "Now, why the hell are you here and where the fuck is Tori with my new nieces?"

"She's at home. I wanted to come alone, but leaving her to handle Pops and the girls is too much." I nod slowly.

"I mean, you could have just stayed down there with them both. I have this under control." Luca pushes a plate across the counter and points between it and me. Despite his efforts to maintain his cool and casual façade, Luca's voice is weaker right now than it has been in the entire time we've been up here. "Eat."

I lift my head hardly an inch and I'm caught looking between the pair of them. Both giving me the same stare, both of them waiting for me to sit and eat some food, both of them looking equally stressed out.

"You two need to take a chill pill each." I roll my eyes but sink down onto the same stool Mia had been sitting on and cut a piece of the pancake off. "I'm absolutely fine."

"Yeah, no thanks to Johnny English over here." Lorenzo huffs. "Apparently, he can't be trusted to keep you safe, so I'm here."

"Excuse me?" I swallow the food, and reach for a glass of water that is sitting on the side. "Luca's the reason I'm here in the first place. Do you know how many times he's stopped something horrific happening?"

"That doesn't matter. Yesterday-"

"Was purely coincidental. Right, Lu?" Luca lifts his head from where he's almost cowering in the corner.

"Hm?" I'm worried about him. I hate the way I can see him pulling himself apart over something he has no control over. "Oh. Right. Yeah. No links to Petrovich or anyone. Just a standard break-in gone wrong."

"Still. It wouldn't have happened if he'd have been-"

"I told him to go." Lorenzo snaps his head to me. "We needed to do the food shopping, but I wasn't feeling up to going outside. We could have ordered it but I really wanted Luca's pasta and we didn't have what we needed. I told him it'd be fine. I'm a big girl, Lorenzo. I can handle myself."

"But-"

"No buts about it. Had I been here or not, they would have still broken in. Had Luca been here or not, they'd have still broken in. It's just one of those things. Stop blaming Luca for something that isn't on him. How do you think it feels to constantly be told something uncontrollable is your fault? I can tell you because I was told it for years, and the answer is it fucking hurts and tears you apart inside. Luca deserves more than you shitting on him for trying his best." I slowly take a drink of the water, staring at my brother head on, daring him to try and blame Luca again. "You gonna apologise then, or just stand there staring at me?"

Lorenzo sighs, looks over at Luca and says: "I'm sorry. It's not your fault someone broke in. I'm just pissed that this happened and I was too far away to do anything."

"No, I get it, Lorenzo." Luca seems to settle. His shoulders drop just a little as he exhales. "You're just looking out for your family."

"Good. Communication is good. Well done. I'll get you both some gold star stickers." The guys both turn to look at me with unimpressed glares and I simply smile. "You're both giant drama queens."

"Please, he's so much more dramatic than me." Luca finally smiles softly, moving to make more pancakes.

"Oh yeah?" I stab another piece of pancake with my fork, and Luca raises an eyebrow at me. "Enzo, you know how I texted you on Valentine's Day the word crabs?"

"Isabella." Luca warns but I turn to my brother with a smirk. What's he gonna do? Punish me? Spank me? Oh no. I'd *hate* that.

"Luca's terrified of crabs and thinks they're gonna take over the world." Lorenzo bursts into a loud cackle, and Luca scowls at the fact that I've put his biggest fear out into the world.

"Oh my god! I forgot about you hating crabs! Tor is going to have a fucking field day with this. She is going to love getting revenge on you for the whole chicken thing."

"Wait, chicken thing?"

"Oh, there's a whole story about it." Lorenzo drags out the chair beside me and sits down. "But first, here, I took some photos of the twins for you."

Chapter Forty – Three

Nothing quite like a sibling heart to heart.

ISABELLA

"But I'm not tired." Pops is throwing what may be considered the biggest tantrum known to man over the fact that she'd been told it was bedtime. She is beginning to run out of excuses and I swear, Enzo is so damn close to letting her run riot. I know she has everyone wrapped around her tiny little fingers, but this is on another level. It is kind of funny to watch.

"Pop-"

"I'm not, daddy! I'm wide awake!" Lorenzo closes his eyes, taking a steadying breath.

"Come on Poppy, I'll read you one of those books you found with Auntie Mia." Pops instantly snaps her head to Luca who pushes himself up from where he was sitting beside me. He extends his hand but she still doesn't move. "Fine. I'm going to go and put on all of your princess dresses." Luca turns on his heel, walking off quickly and apparently her uncle wearing her dress-up outfits are where Penelope draws a line because this time she jumps over the back of the sofa, running down the deck to catch up with him while she begs him to not ruin them. Luca picks her up, tosses her over his shoulder and holds her ankles tight as her whole body stretches out behind him. She cackles, laughing loud enough that it echoes across the deck and out onto the lake, disappearing into the house with them both.

Mia has taken an early night. She's taking the spare room; Enzo is having Luca's room and Luca said he'd stay on the couch while they're here. I'd rather he stay with me, but Lorenzo is under enough stress right now. Telling my brother I am sleeping with Luca might be the final straw that knocks him out with a heart attack. If we can avoid that when everything else feels like it's going to shit, that'd be great.

That leaves just me and Lorenzo sitting in silence on the couches on the deck. The fire pit crackles quietly, the only other noise besides us both breathing steadily from separate ends of the seating area. Lorenzo shifts in his seat, having not properly settled back since he sat down once Pops had left with Luca.

It has been weird having this house filled with people for the past two days. I'm not used to there being other people around and grasping time alone with Luca isn't possible. The most we've managed is the brushing of fingertips as we pass each other.

I can see in his face how weary he is right now. As much as Luca thinks he hides it well, after this long alone with him, I can see right through his mask. I know he's tearing himself apart. It's like I can see him overthinking everything. I can see the way he watches Penelope and Mia like he's terrified someone is going to tear them from him in the next passing second.

As much as Luca likes to say his biggest fear is crabs taking over the human race, it isn't. It's losing the people he loves.

I watched Luca have his parents torn from him. I didn't fully understand what exactly had happened at the time. I'd just turned seven, and whilst our parents had never truly hidden death from us, I'd never properly experienced it like I did then.

Luca had always been this beaming light. Irritating and annoying but, no matter what, he found a way to make you laugh when things were tough. When I broke my arm at six while climbing a tree at the bottom of his parent's place, he was the one who put me on his bike and pushed me back to the house to get help. He spent the whole five-minute walk telling me the most ridiculous stories I'd ever heard, just to keep my mind occupied on something other than the pain.

But when he lost his parents, it just vanished for a little while. He tried. When he was around people, you could see the way he'd do stupid shit to try to get people to stop thinking about it. I remember three days after it happened, sitting at the table for dinner and it was so awkwardly quiet. Until Luca excused himself and came back to the table with a pair of scissors and started cutting his spaghetti with them. It caused an outrage. Everyone started bickering and I swear I saw him relax when they did.

I heard him that night. On the porch roof outside of our bedroom windows. He'd snuck out of his window when everyone had gone to bed and was just sitting there with his knees pulled to his chest.

You could see his house in the distance, lit up on the hill. I climbed out beside him, but it didn't feel like a moment where we needed to talk. So, I just sat there with him.

Six-year-old me had no idea what he was going through back then but I knew he had to have been hurting.

He was quiet for a little while before wrapping his arm over my shoulder and pulling me into his side.

"Tutto va beni," he'd said. *Everything is going to be okay*. It's a phrase he still says to me regularly and the more I think about it, the more I'm not sure if he's trying to convince me, or himself.

"Bella?" I blink, the fire coming back into focus before I lift my head towards Lorenzo. He's sitting forward, elbows pressing into his knees with his hands interlocked under his chin. He sighs and lowers them. "I want you to come home with me."

"Why? I'm fine here."

"Because it'd be easier to keep my eyes on all of you when you're in one place. There's too much at stake right now." I stare at him. This is a topic that I can tell is playing on Lorenzo's mind, but I'd already made it clear that I'm fine here.

Going back to Sicily would mean me and Luca would be under constant watch and right now, I don't want that. I am happy here with him, living in our own bubble where nothing else exists. I like waking up with him, and the past two days where I haven't have left me feeling more than a little heartbroken. I like sitting on the sofa with him and having his hands in my hair, I love our pillow fights while we get ready for bed, I love the way he kisses me when I lose. I love being able to be us. We can't do that with people around. Especially not Enzo.

"Do you remember when Dad used to take us both down to his gym?" Lorenzo's face softens and finally he seems to settle in his seat, pushing himself backwards but keeping his eyes fixed on me. "I remember asking why the guys were covered in scars and Dad used to say that each one was from a time when someone hurt them so badly that the only way they could survive was by remembering everything they have to live for."

"I remember that."

"I'm covered in scars, Enz. So many in fact, that I could spend a couple hours telling you the story behind some in grave detail because I remember most of them like it happened five minutes ago." I swallow, clenching my teeth at the threat of them all coming hounding in at once. The cigar burns start to tingle, the cuts start to feel like they're once again oozing red.

"But I didn't have anything to live for. As far as I knew, you were dead like everyone else. I was trapped, with nowhere to go, and no way out. No one was coming to get me, I had no idea how to get from where I was to where I'd be safe, even if I did get out, and I didn't have anything to survive for. I did it because I had no other choice than to do as I was told, take their shit, and behave under their constant watch; twenty-four hours a day, seven days a week.

"I know it's not the same. I know coming back there with you wouldn't be the same as it was there, but you need to understand that I've spent fourteen years having every single one of my moves punished if it wasn't correct. Being surrounded by people who only cared that I was alive because I was giving them something they could benefit from. Coming back with you, even though I know it's different, is going to feel the same.

"You're going to be watching me constantly. Everyone's going to ask questions I don't know if I'm ready to answer yet. I know externally I look like I'm handling this well, Enzo, but it's fucking hard. I'm trying to process and work through fourteen years of abuse that I hope you never know the extent of, knowing that they're still out there living like kings. I have days where I can't stop crying. I wake up in the night sometimes so paralysed by fear that I end up punching Luca as he tries to calm me down, because I'm convinced he's them. The smallest things sometimes bring back the worst memories, and I can't fucking control how my body responds."

I take a breath, letting the confirmation that I'm not actually okay hang in the air between us. None of what I said was a lie. I do still have days where surviving is extra hard. Where Luca touches me and it takes everything in me to not recoil and vomit up my entire stomach contents right there on the floor.

All of these things are normal. They're a normal way to respond to the things that happened to me and all things considered, I'm doing so fucking well. But things like this take time. I need time to fully adjust to being okay. I need time to allow my brain to process that it's over, and I don't need to be on edge now.

"Me coming back with you right now isn't a good idea, Enz. Not when you've got the girls. Here, it's just me and Luca. I know that. I know it's just Luca and I, and when the flashback starts I can slowly bring myself out of that because I know it's just us two out here. I know if someone's touching me that it's him and he can take the punches, and he knows how to bring me down from that high before I hurt myself."

"I'd be able to help if you came home."

"Do you really want Pops seeing that though?" He lets out a slow sigh. "She doesn't need to see the side effects of what happened. She doesn't need to see me so out of it that I can't control myself. I'm terrified she'll touch me when I'm like that and I'll hit her without realizing it." Lorenzo stares at me and I take a slow breath.

"I'm okay here. I can look after myself and you said it yourself, this break-in was purely coincidental. It could have happened anyway, it could happen in Sicily, in Kredrith, anywhere. It just happened while I was home alone. Once we finish this with Petrovich, are you never going to let me be alone? What about if I decide to move into my own place? Am I going to have men sitting in the corner of every room then? Like I had back there?"

"Of course not. That's insane."

"Exactly. I've got to learn to exist outside of the constant surveillance, Enzo. If I come home with you now and we eventually get to the point where

318

we can finally sort Rurik and Feliks and everything, I'm going to move out alone, eventually. And I'm always going to live in danger because I'm a Santoni. No matter what, there's always going to be something looming." He scrunches his nose up at me, but I know I have him. I'm not backing down from this.

"I'm a big girl, Lorenzo. I'm a big girl who has already lived through fucking hell on Earth and survived. And that was before I had something to live for. If something ever was to happen again, I have things to do it for. I have somewhere to go, I have you and Astoria and Luca and Penelope and the twins. There isn't a chance in hell I'd back down the way I had to before."

Lorenzo tips his head back slightly, pulling a hand down his face before he stands up, takes a handful of steps across to me and sinks down onto the sofa beside me. I lay my head on his shoulder and he matches the move, resting his head on top of mine.

"Luca told me about what happened on the night they died." Lorenzo lifts his head slightly, pressing a fast, soft kiss to the top of my head before he lays his back down. "He said you were worried that I'd hate you for it."

There's long silence. One where I don't want to speak. I'd spent years tearing myself apart for it. Constantly see-sawing between me doing the right thing and wishing I'd have just shot myself instead. Since moving up here, since talking to Luca and hanging their photos up around the house so I could see them constantly, I think I've come to terms with the decisions I made that night in some way.

"I don't hate you, Isabella." Lorenzo finally speaks. "If it was me. If it was kill them or kill myself, I'd have made the same decision. You killing them means you're still alive and if you hadn't killed them, they'd still have been killed and you might have been alongside them." He pauses, breathes deeply before continuing. "They'd be so fucking proud of you for getting through everything you have. I can't put into words how proud I am of you. I know you can look after yourself, Bella. You just shouldn't need to. I'm your big brother. It's my job to keep you safe. If I'd have known, I'd have been there and I wouldn't have stopped until you were back with me."

"But you didn't know and that's neither of our faults." Another beat of silence passes between us as a single tear escapes and slides down my cheek. I'm quick to wipe it away, not wanting to move too much right now. I like being this close to Lorenzo. "We'll make them pay for what they did."

"The very second Tori is able." Lorenzo nods, squeezing my hand as he sits up straight. "The very second everyone is safe, Bella. I swear. They are not getting away with everything they put us both through."

Chapter Forty – Four

Just a blip.

ISABELLA

"My favourite is Jupiter." Pops smiles brightly as she continues trying to colour inside the lines of whatever colouring book she'd brought with her. I have no idea how we got onto the topic of our favourite planets, but neither me, nor Mia had been given a choice when she'd sunk herself down here after lunch, and I was happy to grab any second with my niece before she's halfway across the globe again.

Penelope desperately wanted to swim in the lake like we had been doing all morning, but Lorenzo is a little too strict on the no swimming after dinner rule. As if he didn't used to scoff his dinner so quickly all I could see were blurs and then jump into our pool before he'd even finished chewing. We were likely well over the time she needed but we all seem to be happy right here.

"Now that's an opinion I can get behind." Mia raises her eyebrows, her eyes focused dead on the paper in front of them both. I'd thankfully escaped being forced to colour with them because I have my book. I haven't made much headway with it since Pops came running down and shattered the peace like a wrecking ball, though. "I feel bad for Pluto."

"Why?"

"Because it's not really a planet." Pops looks up at me and I swear, I may have just destroyed this girl's entire sense of existence by the look on her face. "I mean, not technically."

"But why? Daddy and Mummy say it is."

"It used to be. When I was little it was. But scientists decided it wasn't anymore."

"They can just do that?!" Pops drops her crayon and sits up until she is on her knees. "So, is it or isn't it a planet? How does it stop? Did it die?"

"Planets aren't really living things, Pops." I chuckle as Penelope looks between Mia and me. According to Lorenzo, one of his favourite things about having kids is forming them into people. Watching them develop their own thoughts and feelings and beliefs that will help them navigate their own world in years to come. From the look on her face, this is one of those moments.

I used to be obsessed with stars and planets and the universe as a kid. It was wild to me then and I guess it still is, just how astronomically huge it all is and how in reality, we're just a speck in the nothing. Barely a blip in time that doesn't really change anything. The world will keep turning, the universe will keep expanding, stars will be born and die and what I had for breakfast or where I spent the past fourteen years doesn't change any of that. I'm not sure if that's a horrible way to think, or if it's weirdly freeing.

In times like this, we get so focused on what's going to happen in the future. Is the decision I'm making right now the right one? Am I going to regret it ten or twenty years down the line? Am I going to wake up one day and regret not going home with Enzo tomorrow? Am I making the right decision in staying here with Luca? Did I make the right choice in sleeping with him and continuing to do so? Despite everything that could go wrong?

These are all things that rack my brain more times a day than I care to admit, but in the reality of things, when you look at it on the bigger, universal scale, does anything really matter?

"Auntie Bella?" Pops jabs me with the crayon and I smile, blinking to bring her back into focus. "Where have you been?"

"Hm?"

"Well, Daddy said that you've always been my auntie, just like Mia and Uncle Luca, but I didn't know you and no one talked about you like they do now. Mummy pointed you out in pictures in Sicily, but there's not many and Daddy got sad when I asked him where the rest were and said you were away for a long time. So where did you go? Have you been on holiday?"

Fuck.

I knew this was likely going to come up eventually, but honestly I was expecting her to ask her parents or Luca and then for me to hear about it through the grapevine a few days later.

"Pops…" Mia shifts slightly in her space beside me.

"No, it's – uh – it's okay." I shuffle slightly, pulling my shoulders back as I try to work out a safe way to tell Pops where I've been without scarring her freshly five-year-old brain. "Well, I guess I've been all over."

"All over the world?"

"Kind of."

"Well, if it isn't my three favourite girls." Saved by the bell. Luca collapses to the deck beside me, crossing his legs and getting comfortable like it's exactly where he belongs. His knee brushes against my bare feet and I relish in the most physical contact we've had today. My heart flips in my chest. Somersaulting rapidly and I roll my lips together to stop myself grinning like a Cheshire cat. "What are we talking about?"

"Auntie Bella's holiday. She's been all over the world!"

"Holiday?" Luca looks over at me, smiling with that perfect shine in his eyes and I don't know what it is about this moment, but I feel like time itself slows down more than I've ever known. He laughs, sun glowing behind him like his own personal halo. "Bella!"

"Hm? Yeah?" The group laughs at how I completely zoned out, and I feel the blush rise up my cheeks. *Get yourself together, Bella.*

"Oh good, I was worried I was gonna have to push you in to wake you up then."

"Push me in and I swear you'll regret it."

"Oh yeah?"

"Yes." I roll my eyes at him, looking back down at my book.

"You couldn't push me in if you tried." Luca states, his tone teasing and I swear, if we were alone, I'd flash him and lock myself in the bathroom while making the loudest moans I possibly could, just to get him back. But we're not alone. So, I sit and wait. "In fact, I could stand here, on the edge with my feet barely on it and I bet you three girls couldn't push me in."

"Yes we could."

"Nuhuh." Pops huffs at her uncle. "You'd all be too worried about me getting hurt. Mia wouldn't want to break a nail, you're not even big enough to-"

I don't let Luca continue to barrage us with soft insults. All it takes is one hefty push with my foot against his knee and the idiot falls backwards into the water below with a loud splash.

He wanted me to retaliate. To fight back with him until our verbal sparring match turned to me storming off and he'd be able to get me alone for just a few minutes under the guise of 'apologising'. I just don't think he had been expecting *that*.

Mia, Pops and I all move to the edge of the deck, peering over as Luca breaks the surface, shaking his head quickly. His sodden waves flop across his face and when he turns to face us, confirming he is alright, we can no longer contain the laughter that has been bubbling under the surface.

"Oh, so you think you're funny, Isabella?"

"Dunno. I definitely saw crabs in there the other day, though." His face flicks to pure terror, switching back to calm when I laugh harder at him. Luca scrunches his face up, swimming towards the ladder a few feet away.

Pops and Mia are clinging to each other, barely breathing from laughing so hard, but as Luca pulls himself up onto the deck, water droplets sliding down his face, dark t-shirt clinging to every curve of his skin, I know I am in trouble.

"You're going to pay for that, Amore." My heart stammers. Those words are ones I've heard dozens of times. Usually followed by horrible actions and pure agony but right now, my adrenaline is pumping and I can't help but grin as I jump to my feet, running down the deck and back towards the house.

I put everything into moving as fast as I can but I can feel him hot on my heels, chuckling as he wraps his arms around my waist and lifts my feet off the ground abruptly.

I let out a scream that turns to laughter as he throws me over his shoulder.

"I am so throwing you around like this when everyone's gone." Luca's arm presses firmly across the backs of my thighs as I continue to wriggle around on him. I could get out of this if I wanted. I know if I wasn't laughing, or if I called out our safe word, Luca would put me down but I don't want him to.

All of this, the running, the words he's used, the throwing me over his shoulder. Every action is something I have experienced before so differently and yet, not a single ounce of terror or anxiety swims in my veins.

I'm not struggling to breathe. Not about to be beaten or raped or stripped bare and left to starve in a cage. Those thoughts don't even raise their vicious little heads in the corner of my subconscious.

Because I am with the one person I never have to worry about those things with.

"Maybe I'll let you." Luca chuckles, slowly pulling me down from his shoulder and placing my feet on his.

"Watching you wander around in this skimpy little bikini is torture." Luca keeps his face casual, hands wrapped tight around my wrists as he edges us closer to the drop. "Do you know how many times I've thought about pulling it to the side and slipping into you right here?"

"What if I wanted you to?" I smirk and Luca's eyes narrow. "What if I had a long shower this morning and spent the whole time fucking my fingers? Or, and this is purely hypothetical, what if I took one of the toys hidden in my bathroom and slid myself up and down it until my legs were shaking."

"Keep going." His tongue darts out, swiping across his lips. "Tell me all the dirty things you have been thinking about me doing to you, Amore."

"Oh, I never said I was thinking about you. My book boyfriend–" Luca arches a brow at me, his lips twitching into a devilish smirk and I know I am pushing his buttons. I just want to see how far I can go. Will he crack? Toss me back over his shoulder and pull me inside? Lock my bedroom door and not give a fuck about Lorenzo figuring out what is going on? God, is it wrong of me to kind of wish he would?

"Oh yeah?" Luca's eyes darken. "I've been reading all the dirty shit on those pages and trust me when I tell you, if you think the idea of being fucked into oblivion is good on paper, wait until it's my dick you're suffocating on. The only 'boyfriend' you'll be thinking about then, Isabella, is me."

Before I could even let his confirmation of the title sink into my head, he steps forwards, taking us away from the deck and falling into the water below and for the first time in my life, I know I won't survive if I don't have someone by my side.

Chapter Forty – Five

I want to.

LUCA

"Do not make me regret leaving you here alone with her." Lorenzo glares at me, lowering his voice to an almost whisper, so Pops and Mia don't hear his threats from inside the car. It's fine. I've been counting on him being like this when he leaves to go back to Sicily. It's honestly going a lot tamer than I'd been expecting. "If one more thing goes wrong, Luca, I don't give a shit if you're family, if Pops adores you, if Tori will murder me herself, if one more thing goes wrong on your watch, I will hold you responsible and you will pay for it. Do you understand?"

"No." I smile at him. Big and bright because he needs this. He needs someone to keep his goddamn ego grounded somehow, and I know I'm the only person who does that without it being tied to sex, and that is one battle I'm not willing to take for the team. Besides, nothing else is going to go wrong. This one was too fucked up for me to even doubt for a second. Nothing else is going to go wrong. It is that simple. I'm not going to allow it to. "Of course I do. I'm not fucking dumb."

"Hm." Lorenzo raises an eyebrow, still staring at me. "That's my sister in there. When all this is over, I want her back in Kredrith, unharmed, untouched and safe. If anyone else lays a single finger on her between now and Petrovich's family being slaughtered, I will be adding you to their tallies. Do not think I'll go easy on you. I will pull you limb from limb and watch you bleed out on your childhood bed."

"Oh, what a lovely picture you're painting me." I roll my eyes at Lorenzo and his drama, pulling open the driver's side door for him and taking a slight step back. "She's fine. Have a little faith that I can look after Bella the same way I have faith that you can look after Mia. Now stop being a dick and go home to your wife and your newborn twins." I leave him at that, turning on my feet in the gravel and waving as I walk back into the house.

It's moments like that with Lorenzo that make me so hesitant to tell him, or anyone, about me and Bella. As much as I know he means he doesn't want anyone touching Bella and hurting her, I'm very aware that his words don't exclude the kind of touching we do, and I somehow just don't think he'd be okay with me fucking his sister multiple times a day until she can't breathe.

It's been five days since this house had just me and Bella inside. Five nights of not sleeping beside her, and I'm not sure if I'm going insane from the lack of sleep, or the fact that I'm desperate to just be around her. Not just for the sex either. I just want to wrap her up in my arms and cuddle on the sofa. I miss sitting her on the counter while I cook. I miss being able to be close to her, to touch her and feel her breathing. I've missed it just being us.

As soon as Lorenzo and the girls have pulled out of the drive, I get back into the house and lock the door. It's when I turn around that I almost have a heart attack.

Bella is standing in the middle of the hall in black lace lingerie, stockings and matching heels, with the most innocently mischievous look on her face and I almost, *almost*, collapse to my knees at the sight.

"Are they gone?" Bella takes a hesitant step forwards, and I don't know if I left my brain on the roof of Lorenzo's car, but I can't speak. All I can do is nod as Bella reaches me. My hands find a place on her hips as she drapes her arms sensually around my shoulders. "I have been really mean this week." She drags her hands around my t-shirt in such a smooth and confident manner that I get lost. "Teasing you in the skirts and thongs and the bikinis. You've been so good though, and I thought I should pay you back for it."

Bella takes the smallest step back and lowers herself down to her knees. She looks up at me with the biggest innocent eyes as she tugs on my belt.

"Can I show you how good you've been, Luca?" I nod and as she lowers my jeans to the floor, she's met with exactly how fucking turned on she's got me.

"You-" I croak, forcing me to clear my throat and try again. "You don't need to do this, Bella."

Oral is a hard one for her. She mentioned it once, after our first night. I'd sat her down at breakfast and made sure we had an honest and open conversation about what she was and wasn't comfortable with.

Hair pulling, choking and her giving oral were the only three things we pinned down, and I haven't even attempted any of them because of that. Even though Bella is initiating this, I don't want her to feel like she has to. As much as I want this, she doesn't need to do it if she doesn't want to.

"I know." Bella's hand wraps around my length, pumping once or twice as she looks up at me from her knees. "But I want to."

With that, Bella uses her tongue to mop up the pre-cum seeping out of my tip before taking me in her mouth, and I can't take my eyes off her for even a second.

The way I can just see her ass, pushed up against the back of her heels, the huge doe eyes she is giving me as she takes more of my length, swirling her tongue around me. I need to focus because if I don't, if I just let this moment go without control, I am afraid I'll cut it short, and I need this to last. I need to burn this into my memory permanently.

I try to steady my heart rate. To breathe deeper as I watch her and I almost succeed, until she goes so deep that her eyes start streaming, and the noise that leaves her mouth as she gags on me almost finishes me off right there. I push her curls behind her ears as she pulls back, disconnecting the string of saliva from us both before using her hand whilst she regains her breath, going right back after a couple of seconds.

"Fuck," I pant, making Bella hum against me. I am desperate to take control of this. To wrap her hair around my fist and watch her take it from me but I can't. "You look so good with my dick in your mouth." Bright blue eyes look back at me, lips twitching as she reaches for my hand, putting it on the back of her head. "Bella."

"I want more." She pulls back, moving her hand over my length slowly. She's so fucking precious. I curl a finger under her chin, pulling my thumb across her slightly puffy lips. "I want you to take control."

"You want me to take control?" Bella nods, slowly moving her free hand between her legs. "How wet are you for me, Amore?"

"Dripping." She says, bringing her fingers up and holding them in the air as she peers up at me. I lean down and put them in my mouth, swirling my tongue around them both with a groan. "I love having your cock in my mouth." *How is it even possible for me to get any harder?!* "I've been thinking about this for days."

"Yeah?"

"Yeah." Bella nods against me, opening her mouth and taking my thumb in between her lips. She sucks slowly and as she reaches her hand back between her legs, I swear, she's chipping away at my ability to stay in control.

"You're going to kill me." I sigh under my breath, tugging my thumb from her mouth and cupping her face in both of my hands, bringing my face down to hers. "Can I be rough with you now, Amore? Can I fuck that pretty little mouth and fill it with my cum?"

"Yes, God. Please." I stand up abruptly and watch Bella for a second. For any sign of doubt or concern or worry. There's none of it. Her face is filled with excitement and mischief, the sound of her fingers pumping in and out of her soaking wet cunt confirms it, and I'm so turned on it fucking hurts.

"Open your mouth then." Bella smiles bright, opening her jaw the perfect amount and laying her tongue flat for me. "Tap my leg twice if you need me to stop." She nods, eyes widening. "Don't you dare stop fingering yourself. You stop, I stop."

Before Bella can respond, I sink myself into her mouth, wrapping my fist around her faded pink curls and pulling tight as I take control of her mouth.

Each thrust into her is pure ecstasy. I don't know how I am ever going to live without this again. It feels too fucking good to have her like this, and I know it is going to be a memory that repeats itself in my dreams. I am going to have showers alone with this memory for the rest of my life.

Bella moans as I increase my pace, her fingers working quickly below us and I can hear exactly how much she loves it. Sloppy slaps of her fingers into herself match the perfect time of me in her mouth.

I push myself deeper into her, watching as her eyes darken and tears leak out the sides, feeling the back of her throat twitch against my tip as she gags. I pull out quickly, giving her a second before continuing my barrage on the goddess that's on her knees just for me.

Her moans become faster paced and when the drops onto the hardwood floor turn into a splatter as she comes, my spine tingles. I'm not going to be far behind her.

"Fuck, Bella." I pant. "I'm gonna come, Amore." Bella hums, eyes rolling back in her head. "I'll pull out." Bella scowls, putting her hands around the back of my thighs and pulling me closer. "Oh, you want to taste me? God, you're so fucking good to me."

Bella pushes her tongue up to the underneath of me, bringing her hand back around to my length and regaining control as I lose the ability to do it myself.

"Make me come, Amore. Make me come and then let me see that shit on your tongue before you swallow it all. Don't you dare let a drop go to fucking waste."

My orgasm hits me like a truck, and I have to reach the door frame beside me to keep myself stable. But even as I unleash five days' worth of cum, Bella continues to suck me dry and waits until I can open my eyes, then shows me the load with a big smile. She swallows, opening her mouth again to confirm she'd done as she was told.

"You taste better than I expected." Bella chuckles, grabbing my shaking hand, standing herself up and dusting herself off. "I need to mop the floor now." I scowl, still not able to find my tongue and I decide to let my actions speak for myself. I toss Bella over my shoulder, slapping her ass hard before running my hand up her slit and pushing a finger into her as I walk us back to my room.

"Non ho ancora finito con questa figa."

Chapter Forty – Six

French toast on the deck? Yes, I am in heaven.

ISABELLA

I wonder if the saying 'waking up on the wrong side of the bed' is correct sometimes. It hits me at weird points in the day, and I can never remember if I got out on the left or right side and how that affected my day. I'd say I've spent probably a month or two in total thinking about this specific topic without getting an answer.

Today, I woke up on the left side. Luca's side, more specifically. It was one of those sleeps where you aren't entirely sure what's going on when you wake up. When you're confused and rested but sleepy and content.

It had been five days since I'd slept in the same bed as him and honestly, I'm glad things are going back to normal now.

I love my family. I loved having Penelope and Mia and Enzo here. I loved having their laughter and pranks fill the house. I loved sitting down to dinner with them on an evening and feeling somewhat like a normal family. Like we've been doing this all along because nothing weird ever happened – there was never a point where we all thought everyone else was dead – it is completely normal.

But I am ready to go back to me and Luca. I'm ready to crawl back up the bed and rest my head on his chest, ready for our two pm naps when things feel a little heavy.

I am ready to go back to not talking about what's going to happen when Tori is back up to strength.

Because of course, Petrovich is a looming cloud over every single positive thing I'm turning my life into. I wish it wasn't. I wish I was normal and none of this had ever happened. I wish Pops had her grandparents, I wish Lorenzo wasn't having to teach her how to run and hide in case something happens. I wish I wasn't covered in scars, and I wish that Luca was here right now.

I sigh, laying the note he left on his bedside table in my lap.

He's got up early and gone to get breakfast for us both. Breakfast and coffee from our favourite coffee place five minutes away, just because.

I don't remember feeling him move out of the bed, so I figure it must have been a little while ago and that he'll be back soon with pastries and French toast and oh, god I'm hungry.

I stretch my arms above my head, helping my back to extend fully before carefully climbing out of bed and changing into some designated training gear.

I'd like to think that me being dressed for it when Luca comes back means we'll actually be able to work a little more today, as opposed to spending the next seventy-two hours with his head between my legs. Don't get me wrong, in theory that sounds... perfect. Extraordinary, really. But I'm starting to feel like there's a deadline to this peace, and I'd rather be in a position to fight and get back to this peace than lose it forever, and I can't do that if I'm unable to defend myself.

I drag one of Luca's jumpers over the top of the sports bra and gym shorts, putting on the shoes I've found it easier to train in. They're good for running and fighting, and have a good grip for slippery surfaces, all things Luca told me to be careful of.

He said that Tori has fought in heels before and the more I train with Luca, the more confident I become in my ability to physically take down whatever a man throws at me, but the more I question the reality of this story, because I mean come on… six-inch heels?! I can only just do it in Converse!

I'll get there though, I guess. Tori has a hell of a lot more experience with fighting back than I do. Maybe when she's back in Alamea, I can train with her. That'd be a fun sister bonding activity, right?

I tie my laces, tucking the excess into the shoe to stop them falling out and becoming a trip hazard. Again.

The house is a little cooler this morning than it has been in a month. The deck looks damp from the rain we must have had overnight, but the views out the windows are as perfect as ever.

It's an instant decision to eat out there this morning and my nerves start dancing at the prospect of it. The sun on my skin, breakfast on the deck, the perfect hot coffee, the perfect man.

I really did luck out on him. Luca is the epitome of perfection and the fact that I get to be the one he's here with blows my mind constantly.

If you'd have told me this time last year that this is how my life was going to look, I'd have walked away. I'd have thoroughly believed you were luring me into some sort of trick under Petrovich's demands. Anastasia wouldn't have allowed me to believe it for a second.

But Anastasia is dead now.

I left her back at that godforsaken house and as much as it hurts to be without someone who kept me safe all those years, she also held me in the worst of it. Leaving Anastasia means leaving the worst part of my existence.

I'm able to draw a clear line in the sand between what happened as her, and what is going to happen now I'm me again, and that brings me more comfort than I think I realise.

I don't feel guilty about it, either. Not really. She was the broken pieces of a puzzle that they'd jammed together to look like a person they wanted. The pieces never quite fit, there were always cracks and slithers missing. They thought they'd erased every memory of my life prior to them. That Anastasia was a perfectly polished doll that they'd taken out of the box and put to use.

But what they didn't take into account was that I was their Russian doll. They could keep chipping away at me, stripping me of my heritage, of my hair and my name and my accent and my languages. But at my very core I was a Santoni, and that was never going to vanish.

I remembered my parents and Lorenzo. I remembered running through gardens and vineyards in Sicily. I remembered huge family dinners and cooking pasta, and I remembered the sun setting on my skin at the beach.

No one was ever going to take any of that from me.

No one was going to completely erase who I am.

No matter how hard they tried, how much they damaged my will to exist, how much they pushed me to the edge.

I swipe the cloth across the table, removing the puddles of water before standing up, closing my eyes and smiling as a gentle breeze reminds me just how free I am here. The deck creaks behind me and my smile grows infinitely bigger as my stomach demands the food Luca is holding hostage.

"I know your note said to stay in bed but–" I turn around and the world falls from under me.

"Nice to see you again, Anastasia."

Chapter Forty – Seven

'She's ours.'

LUCA

There comes a point in your life where you are perfectly content with everything exactly as it is. There's nothing you want to change, nothing that sticks out as a problem. You're just happy existing exactly as life is right in that very moment, and last night laying in bed with Bella after our shower, that was the moment.

Things had been a little weird with Lorenzo and everyone here. It was bizarre for me to be in the room with her and not be able to touch her. Somehow, being unable to pull her across into my lap had been a hell of a lot more challenging than I had ever expected.

I guess I knew in some deep crevice of my brain that it would feel a little abnormal when we were eventually around her brother, but I had also been expecting us to have a few more months behind us before that happened.

I hate hiding this from him.

Lorenzo has just got his sister back after years of her being missing. He grieved a whole life for her to just turn up, and for it to come out that she's been through everything she has. It isn't insane to think he's going to be excessively overprotective when it comes to something like this.

But telling him and everyone else that I'm dating Isabella feels like a really intense step.

I can hear the way he's going to respond, constantly cycling around my head on repeat. I might need Penelope, the twins and both Astoria and Bella wrapped around me as some kind of protective shield. Lord knows that man is going to explode in some kind of cataclysmic nuclear explosion that changes Earth's orbit.

Maybe I should tell him whilst he's in Sicily.

Or I can put me and Bella on a rocket to the International Space Station. Six months should be enough for him to calm down, right?

That's something for us to think about eventually, though. Maybe not right now. Or, at least when I'm back home.

Lorenzo and the girls left after dinner yesterday evening and Bella and I spent the rest of the night doing unspeakable things I was certainly keeping locked in my brain for the rest of eternity. I want to keep us on the right track today, so got up early to get her favourite breakfast. The place is five minutes away and 'does the best French toast on the planet'. Supposedly. I personally don't get it but whatever floats Bella's boat, floats mine.

I'd managed to slip out of bed without waking her, calling in the order for collection and changing before driving down to pick it up.

Part of me is still excessively stressed when it comes to leaving her alone, despite the protests she'd given Lorenzo and I whenever it was brought up.

Neither of us wants to take away Bella's independence now she has it and considering all the security systems had an update and upgrade while everyone was here, five minutes is fine.

We can work on longer time frames when it isn't so fresh. Maybe start with her being at Safiyah's and build up from there.

She can protect herself, I know that much. She's starting to give me a run for my money when we're training and I know once Tori's fit enough to start working with her, I'll be fighting off them both which isn't exactly fair. Tori is a fucking challenge as it is.

I don't want Bella to ever feel like she needs me to keep her safe.

I don't want her to need me like that. The idea of her becoming dependent on me being around her to feel safe fills me with dread, because I know there will be times where it simply isn't possible. I don't know much of what the future holds, but I know me being around Isabella twenty-four hours a day, seven days a week is as likely to happen as donkeys flying.

I feel more confident now in her ability to protect herself should she need to than I think I ever have, and I know that as we work more and as she spends time with Tori in the gym, I know that's going to grow. I'm always going to worry about her getting harmed, though.

The thought of her getting hurt curdles my blood as I pull up to the garage, and I instantly feel like I need her in my arms again. Just one thought that sends my brain to picturing things I never want to again.

I try to picture her face when I bring her breakfast in bed instead. Her sleepy smile when I set the tray down and press a kiss to her forehead, brush her crazy curls out of her face and get ready to listen to every random thing her brain dreamt up last night.

The second I get out of the car though, the energy in the house feels off.

It's not something I can pinpoint and looking around the garage, nothing is out of place. I shove it down, figuring it's the first time I've come home since walking in to Bella covered in blood, and it's evoking something in me.

They say you should always trust your gut, though.

That even if you don't think something is wrong, your body can pick up on things you cannot, and my gut has been blaring from the second I pulled into the drive.

Walking into the kitchen is where things go drastically wrong.

And not in the sense they had the last time I came home.

No, this time the big glass doors to the patio are wide open. My eyes are drawn to a shattered plate on the decking and I immediately go into panic mode.

"Bella?!"

My first move is down to her room. I throw the door open and find it empty. Bed made, no sign of her where I left her.

I check the bathroom, the spare room, my room. Every room in this house in the hope she's thought of some project that needs her immediate attention. That she dropped the plate and figured she could fix it if she had the right craft products and maybe, just maybe, Pops had what she needed in her huge box.

But she isn't there.

And the blood splatters I find on the pieces of the plate, along with the state of the house proves to me that I failed her, yet again.

I grab my phone out of my pocket to start pulling anything I can find. Someone on the property, a car, her. Anything. But the cameras are all dead. Just blank screens with a single message across each one.

'She's ours.'

I can't even begin to think when the last person I want to hear from right now splashes across my phone screen. I swipe at the answer button and shakily pull the phone up to my ear.

"Tori, I-" Shit. How do I even tell her Petrovich has Isabella again because I turned my back for five minutes? I shouldn't have been trusted. She trusted me with this. They both did. I swore she was safe. I promised everyone, and all that has happened under my watch is issue after issue.

"Hey Lu, are Enz and the girls with you?" The front door slams across the building as Tori speaks and I'm so shaken I can't even grab my gun from my holster. I just turn to face the assailant, ready to hand myself over. I honestly can't live with myself after this anyway. Them murdering me here will just save myself from doing it later.

The second they come into view; I wish it was Petrovich himself. It'd probably be a better outcome. But right now, I am going to die and it's by my own hand. My own fault for turning my back and thinking I could protect her and keep her safe. It's my own fault that Bella isn't here, and I wouldn't blame Lorenzo if he put me out of my misery right here.

"That Tori?" Lorenzo strides across the room smoothly, nodding at my phone with a face like fury. All I can manage is a nod as he reaches me and snatches the phone out of my hand. "Astoria. No, no we're not fine. Some fucker pumped the plane full of something before we took off, and I woke up to find the girls gone."

Chapter Forty – Eight

One person's ice cream is another's Colin Farrell.

ISABELLA

They say that trauma survivors have an inbuilt instinct to take in a situation without realising it.

For some, it's working out a person's mood based on their footsteps or how they breathe or close a door.

For me, it's knowing to assess a situation before I open my eyes.

I start with the most immediate concerns, am I alone, am I dressed, is it light or dark where I am, am I inside or outside?

I'm definitely inside. It's chilly but not freezing. There's no breeze on my skin, I'm not covered in goosebumps, the floor feels too hard below my feet so I figure I'm likely inside. I can still feel my clothes against my skin, so that's a huge plus.

What I can also feel is the immense amount of pain I'm starting to be riddled with, as whatever I was dosed with starts to wear off properly.

I have to push through it, though. I keep myself completely still, having not moved a muscle as I woke up, just in case. I turn my attention to the room, listening for the slightest sound that will tell me if I'm alone or not. It's silent. Then a sniff. Short and meek and soft. Nothing like a sniff I'd be expecting from whatever guard Rurik has watching me. A tiny whimper follows immediately and when there's no response, I know I'm alone with whoever is sniffing and it is for certain no one posing a risk.

I'm slow as I open my eyes, letting them adjust to the light level gradually before I dare to sit up.

My lungs scream as I do. Ribs crying out for rest. It's a pain I've experienced more than I'd like to admit. I hope they're just bruised. Bruised ribs are easier to deal with. They take longer to heal but the chances of them piercing my lungs and making me drown in my own blood is significantly lower.

I take in a long slow breath as I straighten. It hurts but not enough for the bones to be broken, and I guess I'm thankful for that in some fucked up way. At least they didn't break any bones this time. At least I'm alive. At least I can find a way out of this.

But the thankful feeling fades when my eyes become fully adjusted to the dimly lit room. The single lightbulb above us sways as my niece wriggles in the chair opposite me. Her arms are tied like mine and she's still in the same dress she was wearing when she left the lake house. She's trying to get out of whatever they've used to keep her restrained there. Her hair is a mess as she tries to pull her feet free.

"Pops?" She instantly looks up and I can see it. The way she isn't sure what's going on. Her eyes are bloodshot red, tear stains down her plump little cheeks and it makes me irrevocably angry in a way I don't think I have ever felt before.

I understand why Petrovich wants me back in this very moment.

I know he sees me as an accomplishment. As someone he can abuse and force into a mould to use as he pleases. I know that having me gives him a sense of power. I know he put years of work and time and people into getting me where he wanted me, and I know that man better than he knows himself.

I know me leaving means he wants me dead. That he brought me here to put me through one final round of hell before he uses me to teach his next prodigy a lesson.

And I'll be damned if he puts Pops through even a fraction of what he put me through.

It is not happening on my watch.

"Hey, Princess."

"Auntie Bella?" I force a bright smile onto my face as Penelope whimpers. "What- where- where's daddy?" I turn my head slightly as another chair creaks and I don't know if I should be glad or feel worse that it's Mia sitting beside me, starting to stir as she begins to wake up.

"I don't know babe, but we're okay. Okay? I'm here and auntie Mia is here, so everything is going to be okay."

"But-"

"Hey, I know!" I shuffle. "Do you remember when you came into the living room the other day after you went to bed? You needed a drink and there was a movie on the TV? The one with all the shooting and stuff?" Pops nods, sniffing as her eyes fill with tears again. "That's gotta be what this is."

"A movie?"

"Mhm. But we have to be surprised so we make it look real."

"It's not real?"

"This? Nah! No way! Your dad wouldn't let this really happen, would he?"

"No." I pull my fingers along the material keeping my hands tied tight around the back of the chair, turning it until I can get the knot into the perfect position. Luca showed me how to do this. It was one of the first things we worked on months ago. The rope burns my skin and I twist it with all my might but I push through it. I can do this. I *have* to do this.

"Exactly." Mia groans beside me and I am thankful to have someone else who can help me convince Pops that this is all a fucked-up game. "It's just a — uh — a big game of pretend. But you have to do what auntie Mia and I say while we do this, or the film people will get mad and we'll have to redo it. I don't know about you but I'm thinking once we're done, we go get the biggest ice cream sundae we can find and have twelve of them."

"With sprinkles?!" Pops sits bolt upright, any sign of distress instantly melting away into nothing. This will be so much easier if she thinks it's fake. Maybe, just maybe I can shield just a slither of her innocence if she believes it's special make-up and sound effects.

"Did someone say ice cream?"

"Of course that's what wakes you up." I roll my eyes, managing to make enough space in the restraints to pull my hands out. "Welcome to the party, Mia. We're filming a movie but we've got to pretend we don't know, right Pops?"

"Right, or we have to do it again and we can't get ice cream." I stare at Mia with a fake smile, waiting for her to acknowledge that this is the story we're running with. Mia rolls her lips together, lowers her eyebrows just the right amount that I catch it, but Pops wouldn't and smiles brightly.

"Oh my god, does that mean I'm going to meet Colin Farrell on the red carpet? Can we take a limo?!"

Chapter Forty – Nine

We will find them
LUCA

Lorenzo hasn't said much since ending the phone call with Astoria back at the lake house yesterday. He instantly started making phone calls to the rest of the guys still down in Kredrith, confirming that we are no longer waiting for Astoria to be fighting fit again. Petrovich is sitting on a ticking time bomb now he's touched his girls again, and there isn't a person on Earth or in hell that can stop him from waging the war path he is setting us all on.

I don't blame him.

Every passing second is a second that not only my sister, but his sister and eldest daughter are out of our hands. It's another second of them being dished what can only be assumed is torture.

The seconds had passed too quickly and the hours too slowly while we'd been on that plane. The two of us sitting on opposite sides of the table watching every second of footage from every camera in town until, right before we landed in sunny Sicily, we found the one car that confirmed our suspicions.

It isn't hard to track Petrovich and his cars. He always uses the same pattern of letters and numbers. It's a trick we found years ago and use to detect people linked to them. When I was working for them, Feliks said it was so we knew who was trusted. If they had the right number plate, they were part of the Petrovichs and were easy to identify.

What it meant was that the car that pulled into town at eight pm last night was where we needed to be looking. The problem was that every camera within the four miles surrounding the town had been shut down with absolutely no record of anything being wrong. No alerts, nothing.

When we got off the plane, Carlos called to inform us it was a bug that'd got into the network. He'd managed to track it back to last week. That the blip had been hiding in all the code when he updated things and it'd somehow made it past the firewall. Lorenzo simply grunted and hung up the phone.

It is weird being back here. In a house where I grew up, but never felt happy. Not like I did with Bella. It had always felt like there was a gaping hole where she was supposed to be, and now I'm back here, without her again, I know that's what it is.

She'd kill me herself if she knew how I was beating myself up. She'd tip her head slightly and sigh before pushing her hand into my hair and telling me that it's okay. She'd tell me I was being ridiculous for blaming myself when I didn't do it, then she'd remind me how I've kept her safe all this time. That getting her out of their hands in the first place was my doing. That she is alive and healthy and happy because I managed to do that. That she can keep herself safe because I taught her everything I could in the time I had, and that she's going to be okay. That her and Mia and Pops are going to be fine because she will make sure they are, thanks to what I taught her.

I know those are the exact words that would leave her mouth and yet I can't stop it.

I can't stop the amount of hatred I have boiling over in my chest for not knowing better. I can't stop thinking about the things I watched her go through in that house, and how I know what I did see was merely the tip of an iceberg reaching down to the centre of the Earth. And then I remember that she's not alone.

I remember that Mia is with her. The one piece of my family I have left. My own blood. I feel my parents turning in their graves. Nico is screaming about how it's my job to keep her safe. My job is to make sure she's not buried next to them until she's over a hundred and has lived a full life. It's my job to make sure that I survived for a reason.

I can't even bring myself to think about Penelope. She's younger than Bella was when they got their grubby hands on her. They can do so much more damage to her. She's a literal child and I have no doubt that they won't bat a single eyelash at harming her the way they did Isabella.

"You're going to work yourself to death." The chair beside me scrapes on the polished floor as Tori sinks herself down next to me at the dining table. I don't move, though. I keep my eyes fixed on the screen. On the list of properties we know Petrovich has any link to. On the half of my screen that shows every inbound and outbound call from every device we've hacked into from that family, as we wait for someone to slip.

Just one mention. One comment about something. That's all we need to find them.

"Luca?" Tori sighs beside me, grabbing my hand as it continues to tap morse code into my thigh. She holds it tight, squeezing my fingers until I let out a slow breath and sit back in the chair. "They're gonna be okay."

"You don't know that." I pull my hand from hers, rolling my shoulders back and shifting in my seat. "You and I both know you don't know that, Tor." She sighs.

"No, but I know they're resilient. More so than I think we give any of them credit for. I also know that Bella knows these guys. She knows how to play them to survive, and that's all we need them to do while we find them, and we *will* find them. There's no other choice." I turn my head to her. She's exhausted. It's written into every single inch of her skin. I had been excited to be near Tori again. I couldn't wait for us to be bickering, or for her to be screaming at me when I gave her kids something after she said no. But this isn't how I wanted it to go.

"Do you feel like you're dying?" Tori continues watching me as I sit back, tipping my head back on my shoulders and staring at the ceiling. She doesn't say anything. Just sits quietly right there and the silence is making me feel heavy, so I continue. "She'd be so mad that I'm working on this and not resting right now. I was just thinking about how she'd stand there with her arms crossed and raise an eyebrow at me. She wouldn't even need to say anything, either. She would in the morning though, because of course I'd give in and head to bed just so I didn't have to have her watching me with that... that disappointment on her face." Bella's face flashes in my mind, and I scrunch my face up as my stomach ties itself into a tighter knot and I start to feel nauseous again.

"What would she say? In the morning?"

"What wouldn't she say?" I almost laugh. "It'd be the rant of a century, that's for sure. She'd tell me about how important sleep is to our health and how getting the right amount of sleep helps our brain process things and work out puzzles, which is exactly what this is, right? A big puzzle I need to work out. Then she'd start telling me to relax because she's got it under control and I know... I know she does but I feel like it's my fault. They shouldn't have even got to her, because I should have been there. That's my job. That's why we were out there in the first place.

"We were out there because Petrovich wants her. Because I took her before we should have. Because I went against the plan. My one job was to keep her safe and out of his hands and what did I do? I went to get breakfast. I went to get her French toast just because she loves that fucking French toast. I just went to get her breakfast and I came back and she was gone, and all I could think was how badly I've let her down over and over and over again."

"Luca..."

"No, I have, Tor." I'm more definitive as I sit up straight, blinking hard enough to chase the tears away. "I let her down with Tomas because I couldn't break cover. I heard what happened in that room, and he's still walking around having touched her the way he did. I let men walk into her room and beat her because I was so worried about screwing up. When I did get her out of there, I took her to the place I knew she'd like the most rather than getting her out of the country immediately so she would be fine.

"She'd have been fine here; we'd have all been fine here. But no. I wanted to stay there where we could stay in our own little bubble and pretend Petrovich wasn't after her. I wanted to keep us both there so we didn't have to talk about the fact that I'm so fucking in love with her that I didn't want to ever exist without her beside me again, and that's what coming home meant. Coming back here meant I couldn't have her, and instead of putting her first and keeping her safe like I should have been doing, I was too fucking selfish and wanted to keep her for myself."

The words fall off my tongue before I can stop them and I wait. For a response. For Lorenzo to appear and murder me right here. For something to make this pain ease.

I wait and I wait but it never comes.

After what had to have only been a few seconds of silence, I take a deep breath and sit straight, pulling a hand down my face as I try to gather my brain back together. I pull the laptop back across the table, going back to hunting for my girls.

"You're not selfish, Luca." Astoria speaks with calm confidence. My face twitches, not believing her for a second. Then she moves me. Pulls on the chair so it moves away from the table and turns me so I'm facing her, and I hate that she's strong enough to do that. "Listen to me."

"Go to bed, Tori."

"No. I won't go to fucking bed. Not when you're being so fucking stupid." She rolls her eyes and shakes her head at me. "No one blames you for this. No one blames you for the fucking burglars getting in, or for anything that has happened because none of it is your goddamn fault. You did what you thought was best for Isabella in the moment. That's all that matters."

"But-"

"But nothing." Astoria stares at me. The kind of stare she gives you when you need to pay attention. The kind of stare that would scare me if I didn't know her like I do. "She survived them once, Luca. And you know as well as I do that you've made sure she has more skills this time around. She's not the pushover she was before. She's not going to let them get away with this, and I know that from just talking to her on text, so I know you know that too. Mia can handle herself and hell if it came to it and the two girls couldn't help her, I know for a fact Pops will just scream until they leave her alone. We will find them. Nothing is going to happen. They're going to be fine. Okay?"

"I feel like we've been here before." Tori cracks the quickest smile as I let out a breath, leaning over to wrap her into a hug. "Thank you."

"I'd say anytime but if it could not be when our three girls are out in god knows where next time, that'd be great," Tor pulls back and smiles. "So, you and Bella, huh?"

"I have no clue what you mean."

"Oh, come off it. Me and Mia were placing bets on how long it'd take. When did it happen? I really want to win."

"You were so not betting on me."

"I so was. Are you kidding? You're all protective, she's all broken, you have a thing for broken girls and fixing them up all nice, you had the history. Plus, I mean, you're literally obsessed with her. It was a matter of time." I smirk, turning back to my laptop as Tori starts laughing. "See! SEE! I KNEW IT!"

"Shh. You're going to wake the twins."

"No, I won't, Enzo's got the white noise machine on. Stop trying to change the topic. We're talking about you being in love with my husband's sister right now."

359

Chapter Fifty

I am not ready to die.

ISABELLA

We have to get this right.

I'm not stupid. I know that there isn't a chance in hell Petrovich wants to keep us here for long. I know us being in one place right now isn't a smart idea, and wherever we currently are is temporary while they throw Lorenzo and Luca off track, so we can completely disappear.

I also know that if we have any chance of getting out of their grasp alive, it's here. As soon as they're ready to move, they aren't going to want dead weight and that is exactly what me and Mia are. We're too risky now. There's too much of a chance that we'll fight back. No. They'll use us to set an example and send a message to Lorenzo not to fuck with them, or Pops will be next.

The clock is ticking down and whilst I don't know very much about what their plan is, where we are or who else is in this building, I know one thing for sure. I am not ready to die.

Not yet.

I am not going to be the story they laugh about in their old age. I refuse to have escaped their torture and finally started living, just for them to steal it from me at the first chance they get. Mia and I are not going out by their hands and neither is Penelope. They are not hurting her the way they hurt me. They are not getting the pride that would come with succeeding this time.

I was just about done with the power Petrovich still had over me before this fucking kidnapping. The deep-rooted sadness has been slowly turning to rage, and I think it's safe to say that being locked in here with the girls has changed my brain structure.

Because now, I am done.

I'm done pandering. I'm done tiptoeing around to hide. I'm done feeling sorry for myself.

It's taken time for this to happen. For the shock of my freedom to settle in and right when it did, it was stolen from me again.

Not only that, but these vile creatures don't deserve to live knowing what they put me through. They don't deserve the power trip they'll get from remembering it all. They stole everything from me that they could. And I am done allowing them to get away with it.

This ends now. Their control over me and my family ends today.

Once I untie my arms and legs, it takes me a few minutes to get the girls out of their restraints. I start with Mia so she can help Pops, while I try to find something in the room that can help us.

I come up with nothing. The room is completely bare. It's going to make things even more difficult, but we'll work it out. I will get us out of this alive. There is no other option.

"I'm hungry." Penelope whines from the chair she is now sitting on more comfortably.

"I know, babe. As soon as we're out of here we'll get you the best dinner ever, but you need to-" A door slams down the hallway and Mia instantly stops talking. Her eyes dart over to mine, going as wide as saucers.

Okay.

Okay. This is our chance. This is it, Bella. No more hesitating. No more waiting. We're taking it back now. Right now.

I point at the chair, ordering her to sit down.

"Pops, remember what we said. Pretend to be sleeping." I place my hand gently on her shoulder as I move against the wall the door is on. I am glad the room is mostly dark. It gives me enough shadow to keep out of sight just long enough.

I listen carefully, praying to every god I've ever read about that there is just one of them right now. If there are more, there's too much of a risk that doing this unarmed ends in one of us getting hurt.

The footsteps draw closer and stop just outside the door. A set of keys jangle and as they unlock the door, I'm still not convinced whoever it is, is alone. But I'm ready anyway.

The door opens with a creak and he steps in. I recognise his face from somewhere in my past. The scar down his left cheek is marked on my mental list of guards in Moscow, and I'm glad I have more of an indication of where we are.

He looks at the two girls with a blank face. Before he can notice the lack of a third girl sitting in the chairs, I clear my throat.

His head snaps to me and I smile brightly.

"Hi." I sweeten my voice before hitting him with every drop of force I can muster, straight into his chin. His head recoils backwards instantly, knees giving way under him as he drops to the filthy floor with a loud thud.

I shake my hand once, noting how it hurts more than I had been expecting, but it was a nice distraction from the pain currently raging across the rest of my body.

I quickly poke my head out into the corridor, confirming he was alone before pulling him in completely.

That punch can have one of two outcomes. The first, he comes around in a few seconds and causes a rampage. Or the second, we're currently in a room with a corpse.

But now is not the time to start thinking about that in too much detail. This isn't the first guy I've killed, if that is the case.

"What now?" Mia stands up, pushing the chairs out of the way as I search the guy for weapons or anything of any use. I'm lucky when I find a fully loaded gun with an extra case and a small pocket knife. I take his wallet too. Figuring that he wouldn't need it as a dead man and if we can get out of here, we're going to need a way to pay for things until I can get a message to Luca.

"Now, we work out where the hell we are." I take the cash out, handing it to Mia and tossing the rest to the side as waste. "Here, keep this safe. We might need it once we're done here." She nods, takes the cash and pushes it into the pocket of her jeans.

Once I've scavenged what I can, it's time to move. I open the door slowly, checking if the corridor is safe before opening it completely and stepping out. I'm not shot down immediately, and I take that as a good sign.

"Okay, we're good. Let's go." I hold out a hand for the girls, allowing them both to join me. I wait until they're out before heading back into the cell. I am not taking any chances. I run my knife along his throat, deep enough that his blood splatters across my bent knees and white Converse before beginning to pool around me.

There's no going back now.

I am not stopping until I've got Rurik, Feliks and Tomas' blood on my skin and their corpses at my feet.

Chapter Fifty - One

A foolish decision.
ISABELLA

"Are you sure you're going to be okay?" Mia looks over her shoulder to the corner where Pops is trying to get comfortable. We found an office with a few beds made up for the guards. It is super basic, but there are some provisions. Snacks and drinks on a desk where the CCTV has been set up.

Finding this room has been a saviour, it's allowed us to make sure we have indeed eliminated all the current security. I counted on the feeds how many lives I've slaughtered in the process of getting us up here.

Twenty-three men I've made my way through, and while I could sit here and grieve for the lives I've stolen today, I'm not sure if I'm numb or if I just don't feel anything about it.

Mia managed to shield Pops from most of it. Gunshots excluded. But the actual viewing of the mess I am leaving in our wake, she is none the wiser to.

"Yeah." I nod. "I just need to check the places the cameras don't touch. I wouldn't put it past Petrovich to have been keeping other people too and if they're here, I can't leave them." Mia presses her lips tightly together. "I'll come back as soon as I can, but if I'm not back by morning, you and Pops-"

"I'm not leaving you here, Bella."

"It wasn't a question." I stand up straighter, pushing the spare gun into the back of my gym shorts. If I'd known I wasn't staying at home, I'd have worn something much more appropriate for the situation, but I was stuck with what I had.

"Bell-"

"I get it Mia. I swear I do. But these guys don't fuck around. If I'm not back by the time Pops wakes up, take the money we found and leave out the back exit. Get as far as you can, find people, call Luca. I'll be fine. I can handle them. She can't." I tip my head back towards Pops. "Promise me you'll get her out of here." Mia stares at me with the saddest eyes I've ever seen, but nods.

"Okay." I walk over to Pops, bending down beside her bed and pressing a long, hard kiss to her forehead.

"You behave for auntie Mia, Pops. I'll be back soon."

"Don't go on holiday again." She pulls the blanket up under her chin. "Like before. We can't get ice cream if you go away." My heart tugs at her innocence, and all I can do in response is kiss her cheek.

I stand up before I get stuck in the moment, leaving with nothing else other than raising my eyebrows at Mia in a mutual agreement to keep our niece safe.

The building, as we managed to work out through our little adventures, must have been an old factory. The machines have all but been removed, leaving some huge open spaces that feel more than a little intimidating.

The walls are covered in mould. Their paints peeling and chipping around cracks that make me concerned the whole building is one heavy breeze away from collapsing under its own weight.

I turn another corner and it confirms my theory. A few of the walls have indeed come down. Broken bricks scatter across the floor, but that's not what stops me in my tracks.

"Anastasia," Anton smirks. "Just the person I was hoping to see today, although I must admit I was expecting you a little more… unconscious."

"It's Isabella, actually." He freezes for a second, just long enough for me to point my gun directly at him without hesitation. "Least you could do is get the name of your murderer correct."

"Feliks is right through that door, Anastasia. You don't want to-" The bullet floats through the air, before piercing the centre of his throat. He drops to the floor and I swear, some of the pain stops. I can breathe clearly without wanting to sob, and I take the chance to take in the most amount of oxygen possible.

He wouldn't be lying about Feliks being here. Wherever Anton is, Feliks is never far behind and considering I haven't caught them on the cameras, I know they haven't been here long. They probably don't have a clue what has gone down here yet.

I mean, didn't know.

Likelihood is the gunshot has given him a warning.

Still, I go to step right over Anton as he bleeds out on the floor. As expected, he's not going to go down without a fight, so when he grabs for my shin, I kick him in the face with everything I have in me and he instantly stops moving. His arms collapse down to the floor. I don't stick around to see what happens next. He isn't getting out of here alive when he's in that shape anyway, so it doesn't matter to me how long it takes for his pain to stop. In fact, the longer, the better.

The door creaks as I shove it open, walking into what I'm guessing was a delivery warehouse at some point. At the furthest end, the shutters are wide open, giving just enough of the morning sunrise for me to be able to focus on Feliks as he pushes himself up off the front of his perfectly polished car. It feels obnoxiously out of place considering the rest of the room looks like something from after the apocalypse.

"Ah! The woman of the hour!" Feliks nods his head once and I'm suddenly aware of how I entered the room and didn't bother to check for anyone else. A foolish decision to have made, because it lands me with a man pinning my arms to my side. *Fuck.* "You know, I did think that after spending four months hiding, you'd look a little better, but I guess it's understandable considering you've been on a rampage for the past twelve hours."

He approaches slowly, snatching the gun from my hand with a sly smirk.

"I'm still toying with how you're going to be punished for your disobedience, Anastasia." My heart pounds in my chest as he presses a finger under my chin and tips it back. "What a shame that you couldn't just behave as you were taught. I told my father he should have been more forceful. It's not a mistake we will make twice."

"Yeah, because of course I'm coming back to that hell hole." I scrunch my face up at the prospect. There isn't a chance in hell that is happening.

"Oh, no, not with you." He chuckles as I move in the grasp of the guard. "With Santoni's daughter. Penelope? Is it? You were the perfect test run, honestly. But she's younger than you were when you joined our family. It's a lot easier to get a younger mind to comply. Memories are easily forgotten about and they learn a lot quicker too. A few weeks in what was your cell and I'm sure she'll be the perfect daughter I need her to be. Not that she'll have a choice in the matter."

"Touch her and I swear, Feliks, you'll regret crossing me."

"Hm. Not much you can do when you're dead." Feliks shrugs, lifts the gun he stole from me and points it at my head. His lips lift in a psychotic smile as he pulls the trigger, but I'm not the timid girl he was expecting.

In one swift move, right as his finger retracts, I use my captor's strength against him and turn, using his spine as a shield. He collapses as it hits, and I know that time is of the essence. I manage to get myself out of his grasp as he slumps to the floor. I grasp for the spare gun I have in the back of my shorts, using it to put him out of his misery before he can get me first. I look around the room, quickly stopping another man as he runs towards me.

Then I turn to Feliks. He is trying to get back to his car, clearly realising this isn't the easy win he had been expecting. I manage to stop him in his tracks before he gets too far, putting a bullet through the back of one of his kneecaps.

He falls to the floor, dropping the gun from his hand. He reaches for it as his last line of defence against me, but it's just far enough out of his reach that I make it first, kicking it as far away as I can and holding the gun aimed at his head. He stops trying to get away.

Instead, he slowly turns over onto his back. He's a little paler, a lot less smug and as my chest heaves, I realise a shot to the brain isn't harsh enough for him. It's not enough for any of them. They deserve so much fucking more than being put out of their misery like that. They deserve the agony I was put through. They deserve to smell their skin burning, feel their wounds bleeding out, to know the torment of choking on their own blood. And I deserve to know that karma served them their dues.

"What are you waiting for, Anastasia?" I clench my teeth, stepping forwards and stomping my foot down on his throat with enough pressure to make his eyes bulge.

"Where is Rurik?"

"You think you're going to get to him? Alone?" He chuckles, doing everything in him to act like his face isn't covered in panic. "The chances of you getting out of Moscow are slim to none once he knows you're out of here. Let alone getting close to the house."

"That's for me to work out." I push harder, revelling in how he reacts this time. He grabs at my ankle, doing his very best to ease the force I'm using. "You're going to die anyway, Feliks. How slowly I make it happen depends on how well you can do as you're told. Now be a good boy and tell me where the fuck your father and Tomas are, and I might just take pity on you and let you die next to your precious Porsche rather than in a dingy cell in six months' time."

Chapter Fifty - Two

Do fingers stop being fingers once removed from the body?
LUCA

Danté screams as the electricity pumps through his body. Just enough to leave him in agonising pain. The same amount he gave me while I was under their fucking tests. Seems like each time we're in a room alone with each other, we're trying to get some kind of secret out of the other. This is the last time we'll be in this situation though, and I hate how sealed this prick's mouth is.

I turn the machine off and give him a few moments to start breathing again as I tap the burning cigar in the holder.

"I'll ask you again, Danté. And let me just be clear that each time I have to ask, you wear my patience that much thinner. I'm almost entirely out." I lift the cigar and stare at the smouldering end, turning it ever so slightly. "Where are the three girls?"

He doesn't answer. The only noise he lets out is yet another muffled groan of pain as he tries to act like this isn't affecting him.

But he's put the nail in the coffin, and now I am done playing kids' games. He wants to keep this to himself, but I am going to find a way to get it out of him, or at least cause the most amount of pain in the meantime.

I wonder how fond he is of his digits.

Just over four years ago, blood made me want to vomit. I could barely watch a horror film without instantly wanting to spill my guts onto the floor.

But the world keeps turning, and my desperation to make Lorenzo and the rest of the Santoni's proud of me forced me to get used to it. That, and Tori straight up bullied it out of me. I'll never give her the benefit of knowing that, though.

If you'd have told me four years ago I'd be here, doing this, I'd have had you declared criminally insane.

Danté screams as I toss the first of his fingers to the floor. Crimson pools on the table around where his hands are fastened down. I don't want him dead. Not yet, anyway. But I need answers, and finding him landing at the local Sicilian airport just outside of town was the perfect insight into the plan the Petrovichs don't have a clue we're already aware of.

"You won't stop them." He groans. "Tomas will make sure of it." I continue staring at him from my spot on the chair beside him. "You'll never see them again."

"Are you sure about that?" Danté pants, doing everything he can to keep his secrets just that. I've lost track of tactics I've used on him now. I tried to keep it tidy. Using methods that have left him soaked, and ones that have left a vile burning smell in the air I am worried will be clinging to me permanently.

Every time I second guess my choices, I remember the nights Bella woke up screaming. I feel the way she froze when I first touched her scars. I picture the look on her face every time she comes to from a nightmare and the anger burns shades of scarlet I didn't know were possible.

It bubbles in me again and this time, I let it out, raising the cleaver and slamming it down against his wrist. Dante's scream echoes around the room as I stand up, no longer in the mood to watch this piece of shit bleed out. I need more ideas to get this out of him and considering Bella already stabbed him once, I want to put his life in her hands. She can decide what happens to the people who harmed her. Not me.

I slam the door behind me, walking into the dusty, damp main room.

"Patch him up. I don't want him bleeding to death until Bella is back." I speak to the two young men sitting on the worn sofa. Lorenzo brought them on not long ago, knowing we were going to need all the hands we could get. I don't even know their names, but they can't even be twenty yet. I don't care enough to hear their back stories right now. "Hang him from the rafters too. I want to hear his scream when his shoulders dislocate."

They stand up in unison, walking into the room with a first aid kit and smirks that tell me I'm right in thinking they're not going to be gentle.

I collapse onto a sofa, tipping my head back and letting out a long, slow exhale.

"You aren't hiding very well, Menace."

"Who said I was hiding?"

"The fact that you were standing in the darkest corner of the room staring at me." The sofa compresses beside me and I slowly lift my head up to her. She rolls her eyes at me, sitting back with a huff. "Have a nice nap?"

"No. I'm somehow more tired after it than I was before. But your godparents are watching the twins, so hopefully, I might actually be able to get sorted before we leave."

"Leave?" Tori's smile grows. "Menace."

"So, while you were playing at physical therapy and Lorenzo was dropping the girls off, I got to work and just so happened to find a thread I could pull and well… I found Feliks."

"You found him?" I turn to face her so quickly that I almost fall off the sofa.

"Mhm, and he called for their jet to be sorted back in Kredrith. Anyway, I managed to tap into his spare phone from there and would you know, there's an anniversary dinner tomorrow he's heading up to Moscow for and, shock horror, he also said he'd drop by and check on the 'newest additions'." Tori's smile is so forced I don't know if I can even feel excited about this news. As much as I want to get them back, one of the people out there is her daughter. Her baby is in danger and I know it's taking every ounce of self-control to not tear this world apart to get to her.

"So," I stand up, clap my hands together and smile. "I guess I'm off to Moscow. What do you want bringing home? You can drink again, so vodka?"

"Oh, you think I'm letting you go alone? Why do you think the girls are with Livia?" She grins, standing slowly to her feet. "I'm done letting you two handle this. Clearly you need an expert."

"Please, you've been out of the game so long I bet you can't even pull a trigger."

"Wanna test that theory, dickhead?" Tori shoves my shoulder. "Come on, we've got some blood to spill and our girls to bring home."

Chapter Fifty - Three

Reinforcements.

ISABELLA

How do you get revenge on one of the worst people you've ever met? How do you make them feel just a slither of the agony they put you through? Is it even possible to make them regret the role they had in your pain?

I don't know, but watching Feliks's terror as the fire begins to lick up the length of his already massacred legs isn't having the effect I was expecting. I stuffed his mouth with whatever cloth I could find. Whilst I could keep her out of view of this, the screaming would for sure traumatise Pops if she could hear it.

The fire starts to dance over his gasoline-soaked skin and I can't take my eyes off him as he burns alive across the room. The air grows thick with a smell I wish I could say I don't recognise.

He's not the only one I want to watch suffer. Compared to Rurik and Tomas, Feliks' crimes are minimal. He never laid his hands on me. Not in the ways or as harshly as his cousin and father had.

Knowing they were *just* dead wouldn't cover it anymore for me. I needed more.

The past forty-eight hours has awoken something inside of me I didn't know existed, and watching Feliks burn like this is feeding it.

I've discovered that there is a hidden monster in me that I guess runs in the Santoni blood.

I am no longer content with the idea of living peacefully. Not when they are alive and enjoying their days.

I want their blood on my hands, their agonising screams in my daydreams for the rest of eternity and their corpses laid at my feet after I destroy them all one by fucking one. I want to sleep at night fantasising about the looks on their faces when it clicks that they fucked with the wrong girl.

It may have taken me too long to get here. I may have accepted Anastasia's fate, but Anastasia is dead and she is not being resurrected.

It is Santoni blood running in my veins. Strong and vengeful and determined to destroy our enemies. I may have killed my parents, but they did not die for me to lay down and become someone else's doll.

"Bella?" I turn my head as Mia approaches. We'd pulled Feliks' car out of the building before I started the fire, deciding that we need a sure-fire way to get out of here, I just need to see this through first. "We should get going before Rurik works out something is wrong. Last thing we need right now is them tracking the car while we get as far away as possible."

"Right." I nod. I have no intention of going with them. The two of them need to get out of here, but from the texts Feliks had sent to Rurik before he pulled up here, I know now is my chance.

We are in Moscow. A handful of miles away from the house they held me captive in, and they just so happen to all be celebrating something tonight. Meaning Rurik and Tomas, as well as every other significant piece of shit, are within my grasp.

I'm not taking the girls into that.

It's going to be chaos, and they need to be as far away as possible in case it all goes tits up.

"I don't like it when you have that look on your face, you know. You look like you're planning something and I just know it's never good." Mia tips her head sideways.

"You can drive, right?"

"Yeah…"

"Okay, good. I need you to drive as far away from Moscow as you can get with Pops. I can disarm the tracker so you should be fine on that ground. If you pull over in the town I can get-"

"You're insane if you think I'm leaving you to go take them down alone."

"Mia."

"No. Absolutely not. You can get in that car and we can get out of here. You can wait until we're back with everyone, and then we will plan what to do next. You are not just storming in there alone, Isabella. It's a goddamn suicide mission, and I am not going to just stand here and let you walk into it!"

Mia scowls, crossing her arms as she straightens her back, so she's a good few inches taller. "I know you want this over, Bella, but you can't just abandon us to finish it. You're trying to keep me and Pops safe; I get it, but what about you? Do you not think we want you to be safe too? What... what am I supposed to tell Lorenzo? Or my brother? 'Oh, hey Luca. The girl you're in love with wanted to walk into a Mafia party and open fire, and I just let her go because she said I had to?'"

"He is not in love with me." I screw my face up at her, turning to walk back towards the car. I am trying to not think about Luca right now. It complicates things.

Thinking about Luca right now means thinking about how he'd feel about this. He's always been a rational thinker and I know, I know this is insanity. I know he'd be right in telling me to wait and make a plan and act when the time is right, but I've been waiting for the time to be right since he pulled me out of that house. All it's caused is sleepless nights, break-ins, a kidnapping and me ending up covered in blood, watching men die at my hands.

Thinking about Luca means I have to think about how he'd feel if it went wrong. It means thinking about leaving him without me telling him everything that has been on the tip of my tongue for fucking months. It means us never living the life we've been talking about. Never growing old with him in a big house with our nieces and nephews running around. No holidays where we stuff our faces with ice cream and pasta. None of the things he'd been so excited about. And it breaks my heart to think of us not jumper. He loves this outfit but he's also mentioned how the idea of any other guys seeing me in it makes him excessively jealous. If the situation wasn't so heavy, I'd probably laugh at the fact he's jealous of the men I've been around and not even considering the fact I'm covered in their blood.

"A little bruised but nothing serious." I force a smile and Luca matches it. It's short and sweet and so soft my heart manages to settle.

"I'm fine, by the way. So glad you're concerned for my safety too." I chuckle at Mia's drama and pull myself out of Luca's hold. His face is written in concern, and I know he needs to check his sister over with the same care he's just given me.

I give them both some space, heading over to Lorenzo, who has pulled a passed-out Pops from Feliks' car and put her in his own. I catch the smallest glimpse of Tori in the midst of the chaos and I have no doubt that she is in that back seat right now cradling her daughter for dear life.

He closes the car door and pauses with his hand on the vehicle before slowly turning around to me.

Every time I've seen Lorenzo, he's had a solid face. The kind of emotionlessness that has made me think he is part robot, at times. But right now, it's different. Right now, his brow is furrowed and he's clearly distraught.

"We told her it was a film." I nod over at the car where his girls are. "Promised her the biggest ice cream sundae in the world too, so-" Before I can finish telling him about how Pops was likely not going to stop until he got her the sundae, Enzo has me engulfed in a suffocating hug that I melt into. It's stronger than any of the hugs he's given me since my reappearance, and despite the fact that my ribs feel like they're being torn from my body, I let him hold me how he needs to.

"Thank you." Enzo speaks into my ear. "For keeping her and Mia safe, for making sure she was okay, for being alive when I got here." He sucks in a long breath and I swear, I feel it shake as he lets it go. When he pulls back, he lets out the softest laugh as he rubs his thumb over something on my cheek. Could be mud, could be blood. Who knows at this point. There are tears in his eyes. No matter how much he would try to deny it. I see them. "There's a shower on the plane and a dressing gown, but I didn't have a chance to bring any spare clothes. I'll get someone to bring them when they meet you girls at the airport."

"Airport?" I pull back slowly. "I'm not going back to Sicily yet."

"Sorry, did you miss the part where you were just kidnapped and we almost lost you again?" Lorenzo's face suddenly changes and it pisses me off no end. "You're going home, Bella."

"No, I'm not." I take a step back and steady myself in my stance. "Not until this is over."

"Isabella." Lorenzo warns.

"Don't 'Isabella' me. This is my fight, Lorenzo. I get you want to protect me from it all but guess what, there's nothing more to protect me from that I haven't already been through. You want to stop them hurting me? Too fucking late. I am covered in the proof that it's too damn late for that."

"You're going home. That's the end of the discussion. It's not safe."

"I don't give a shit!" I raise my voice and the air around me seems to stop moving as the rage builds in my chest. "I don't give a fuck if you deem it not safe, Lorenzo. I am not leaving this country until Tomas and Rurik's lives are under my control. That is not a question, it is not up for debate and it's certainly not a fucking discussion. I am telling you that you do not get a say in it. You might be my brother, but you don't get to control how I get closure on my abuse.

"I spent the past fourteen years with these guys beating me, breaking my bones, starving me, punishing me, raping me. From the moment they put a gun in my hand and a knife to my throat and forced me to kill our parents, I have felt more blades, more bullets, more whips and chains and burns than you could ever imagine. I was a fucking toy to them, to pass around among whoever was able for the sake of controlling me, and when I didn't comply, I was punished beyond the realms of what you think could even be possible for a thirteen-year-old girl to survive.

"Do you really think it's fair that I stand back and let you handle this? I want to know they will suffer like I did. I want to watch them bleed slowly, and I want to know it was me that took their lives. You do not get to decide if I get that or not. You do not get to decide how my rapists and abusers die. That's mine. I deserve that."

When I finish, he's staring at me with a slack jaw, and I try to ignore the amount of information I just unloaded onto him and everyone around us. I fight back against the embarrassment that, for the first time, I just spoke into the world exactly what happened while I was there.

People knew. Luca and whoever else had cared to look hard enough. If they didn't know, I guess they would just have presumed that was what happened, but this was me saying it. This was confirmation that what they thought had been happening, had been and yet it was so much worse than they thought. I can see it written all over Lorenzo's face.

I don't think I'd ever totally added up all of the torture I'd experienced. Not really. I knew it happened and I pictured it on a case-by-case basis. But those things had been happening practically daily for over a decade. It ran so much deeper than I'd been allowing myself to think about.

The atmosphere compresses down on me and I almost crumble as my knees threaten to break under me. I almost let the realisation of just how bad it really was destroy me, but I don't.

Because they are still alive.

They're still alive and if it's not me they're doing it to, if I've stolen their next option in breaking me, Mia and Pops out of here, they are just going to find someone else.

They're not going to call it a night and figure out something else. No. They're just going to find another girl to harm. Until this family is wiped from the planet, there is always going to be another girl they use.

"I have to make sure that I'm the last, Lorenzo." My voice is weaker than I want it to be. A single tear streaks down my cheek and it makes me furious. "They can't hurt anyone else if they're dead, and I need to be the one to make that call. I need to prove to them they got nothing from it. I need them to spend eternity in hell knowing they created a monster who took back everything she gained for them for her own. I did the work. I took their shit and I deserve to be recompensed for everything I had to do."

Lorenzo's shoulders stiffen and he holds my stare. I know he's waiting for me to back down, and I understand why. I understand he wants to keep me safe. I understand that he loves me and that he wants his sister to be alive and healthy and not shot and bleeding out somewhere. I get it.

But I'm not backing down on this. I'm not going to take a step back and let him handle it. I'm not going to give up my chance at closure just because it's dangerous.

"I survived them before." I harden my stare and straighten my back. I raise my head as I steel myself in my stance. "They didn't kill me then and they won't kill me now. I'm not dying yet. I've got too much to live for."

Chapter Fifty - Five

Anastasia deserved better.
LUCA

I don't know exactly what to do right now. In general, I do. I know the plan was pretty haphazardly thrown together over the space of eight hours. I know we are going in, guns blazing, and I have to do everything in my power to make sure Bella comes out of this unharmed.

But when it comes to Isabella, I am stuck.

I want to protect her, but she doesn't need me to do that. I want to hold her hand through this, but she is strong enough to not need it. I want to lift this weight from her shoulders, but I know that weight isn't mine to carry, and she needs to release it in the way she needs to.

Lorenzo talked Tori into staying with Mia and Pops and had put them on a plane, not leaving until it had taken off twenty minutes ago. He'd put enough precautions in place to keep the three of them safe this time, from their route, to the airport they departed from being the last one anyone would have expected.

He also managed to have the rest of the Petrovich family disassembled at the same time. This job went worldwide and luckily, we have been preparing for long enough that none of us are concerned we can't pull it off and eradicate this family from existence.

That means that his entire attention is here, and he is focused and enraged.

Fourteen years ago, I watched from a distance as Lorenzo turned from my happy-go-lucky cousin, into the grumpy, bitch-faced man I know now. The death of his entire family changed him beyond comprehension, and the only solace he found in that was the knowledge that the people who caused it had been brutally murdered by his own hands.

I think Bella's speech got to him on a level he hadn't been expecting. He realised that she too wanted them to suffer. That the agony he has in his chest has been eating her alive too, and he understands it; he understands Isabella's pain and her need to have the control back as much as he does.

He was never going to let her take the lead on this, even if he does understand it. Centre stage draws too many eyes and I could see in the way he was thinking too hard that he wanted her to feel like she was playing an important role, while putting her in the safest place. Which has landed us here.

In the basement.

Of Petrovich's Moscow mansion.

A building that has left Bella all too quiet as we make our way cautiously through it.

It's musty and damp down here. Lorenzo and the team's gunshots upstairs are muffled and echoing around between the giant stack of crates that I guess contain weapons, drugs and pieces to everything that Petrovich has a deal in.

At least, that's all it is until we reach the corner closest to the stairs up to the rest of the house, and my stomach becomes instantly uneasy.

Bella's, not so much.

She stalks forwards slowly, pulling open the heavy metal gate and creeps inside. I am right behind her, standing in the doorway of what can only be described as an animal's cage.

It's two walls of bare brick, holding back the ground. The damp patches of discoloration don't need me to touch it to confirm it is wet from the soil behind. The other two walls are thick metal bars forming what has to be a seven feet square. In the middle of the space sits a shallow puddle, a heavy rust covered chain draped right through the middle of it.

Yet Bella is looking around the space like it's an old TV show she's seen a dozen times.

She lifts the chain and drops it with a clunk before she slowly rises from her bent knees and walks to the wall, traces her fingers over the lines that have been carved into it and it's that move that causes my breathing to cease and reality to come crumbling down.

It's not a cage.

It's a cell.

No. No, this is so much more than that.

It's *her* cell.

"They loved this fucking thing. I think I lost count of how many times I was told I should be grateful for them building it '*just for me*'." Bella shakes her head as she slowly looks around. "I made a mark for every person who came down here. I couldn't work out what time it was and sometimes they just wouldn't bring food, so I figured it was a way to track how time was moving. That I was being checked on, I guess?" I bring my eyes to the wall. The tallies only go up so high. As high as she could reach when she would have been in here. They cover the floor too and it's then, in the dim light that I can see the outline of dark brown stains on the floor beside them.

"I think the last time I was in here it was the winter before they moved me to Alamea, so I'd have been seventeen." She kicks the chain. "It was Tomas' big farewell. I was stripped of everything and locked in here. I remember being so fucking cold I could barely think. The- uh- the walls were leaking so the puddle just covered the entire cell and I was sitting in it. I was in here for two weeks that time, before I got so sick I ended up on an IV. Tomas was pissed. That's when he sat by the bed and used the cigar the most. Kept saying that if I didn't like the cold then I'd handle the heat. That I deserved to be punished for miscarrying his child and not doing the only thing I was supposed to do here."

She turns to face me slowly. Her face is completely void of emotion while I feel like I'm burning in her past.

Bella never went into details about what happened. I never expected her to. But this? I wouldn't treat our worst enemies the way she'd been treated and I understand it now. I understand why she ran at the wedding, why she was terrified when Tomas showed up, why she never talked about him or ever existing in Moscow.

"That wasn't even the worst I had, either. I spent the first few years in here. There was a bed at one point but I was let out for … hell I can't even remember what, but I managed to lock myself in the bathroom and took a tonne of whatever pills I could find. When I woke up and the doctor said I was fine a few days later, I was dropped back in here and it was like this. Tomas was away and when he came back…" Bella stops talking, shaking her head as she relives the memory.

I watch in silence as she clenches her eyes shut and slows her breathing.

"Anastasia deserved better." She says, waiting a few seconds before opening her eyes. "*We* deserved better."

"You deserve the world, Amore." Bella walks over slowly and I allow my arm to gently wrap around her waist. "But you deserve to have closure too. You deserve to know that this is done, and that you'll never have to be in any situation like this ever again. You can move on." I swallow the lump in my throat, gently tucking a stray curl back behind her ear. "You can move on if and when you're ready to."

Bella looks behind her into the cell and then back to me slowly, then nods her head.

"I'm ready." I smile, press a kiss to her head and carefully guide her out of the cell, closing the door behind me.

This is the start of a new book for us. I can feel it in my bones.

A book in which Anastasia and what happened to her ceases to exist. Where Bella lives the life she deserves and fuck me if I'm allowing anyone else to give her that.

A book where Bella doesn't think about how much pain is locked in this basement a whole world away.

"When we're done here," I let Bella go, keeping my eyes stuck on her. "I'm gonna be out of the house a lot."

"That's a weird thing to say."

"Well damn, Bella, I can't just say 'Amore, I'm going to be looking for an engagement ring to give you so I'll be busy.' Can I? It'd ruin the surprise." I smirk but Bella stares at me in horror.

"You're not even making it out of this basement, Bottaro." Metal clicks behind me before I feel the burn of a gun barrel being pressed into my temple as an arm wraps around my neck and squeezes. "You did always love your cage, Ptitsa. Think I'm gonna need to find another one for you to use after I've finished getting rid of your pathetic family. How about we start with this one?"

Chapter Fifty - Six

If you do as you're told, I'll suck your dick.

ISABELLA

I've had moments where time has frozen. Where the world has stopped completely and everything just stops.

But this feels like the opposite, and I feel myself react in a way I never thought I would around Tomas. I pounce.

They're standing at the perfect angle for me to knock Tomas away from Luca and send the gun flying into the cell. I try to remove my own but clearly Tomas has caught up to my speedrun because in one move, he slams his fist into the side of my face and grabs my arm. He spins me around against his chest, pushes the arm up my back and tugs my gun out of the back of my shorts, tossing it on top of one of the boxes before dragging me into the cage and shoving me to the ground with all his force. "You are my fucking property, Anastasia. I taught you to kneel when I enter this cell so do it."

"I'd rather die."

"Oh, Ptitsa, no." An evil smirk takes over his face as he bends down to where I am still reeling from the force of his punch. "You're too precious to die. I've told you this. You'll die by my hands when I'm done with you, and I'm nowhere near finished." Tomas wraps his hand around my throat, squeezing until it starts to burn like my ribs and face. "I never should have let you out of my sight. I should have had you tied up in here like the animal you are. You could have played along, Anastasia. Could have been the good wife you were trained to be. But you fucked up in killing our child."

"You killed it." I gasp, clawing my fingers into his hands until I can feel his blood leak onto my hands. He still doesn't release me. "You drugged me and threw me down the stairs. *You* did that. Not me."

"You should have been strong enough." His grip tightens until I'm suffocating, but I fight back the panic. "It will not be a mistake you make twice. This time you will carry our child and you will not lose it. And we're going to start right now."

Tomas drops his hold on my throat, pushing my upper body towards the floor.

"I'm going to get you pregnant, Anastasia, right here while your brother bleeds out above you and your little boyfriend dies right there with a bullet in his skull. And this time I'm not taking the risk." Tomas grabs my wrists, pinning them above my head as he tries to remove my shorts. "You'll do as you're told this time, or I'll keep you comatose and tied to my bed. Understand?"

"Fuck you." I spit at him and the glare in his eyes is a promise. A promise that he's not kidding about keeping me drugged up and tied to a bed to do as he pleases. It's something he's done before. The way that first pregnancy had come to happen. I wasn't doing it. He wasn't winning.

I lift my knee into his diaphragm, winding him with enough pressure that he releases his grip momentarily. That's all I need. A second. Just a second to regain control again. Just a second to flip us both so he is laying in the puddle and I can pin his arms under my legs. Just a second to slam my fist into his face before he can recover. But it isn't enough.

The chance of me ever getting enough power behind my fist to kill him is slim to none and if I move right now, he'll overpower me again.

So, I grab the only thing within my grasp. The rusty chain he'd used to keep me here all those years. I wrap it around my fist quickly, having imagined the amount of damage it would do to his precious face more than a million times.

With each punch, Tomas becomes unrecognisable and stops fighting. His body goes limp as I break through skin, muscle and bone and my own skin becomes tainted with his blood. I am not done until I feel his breathing cease under me.

With my chest heaving, I sit back and stare at the mangled mess of shattered bone and blood that would no longer be recognised as a human. I let the image of this burn into my brain, so I'll never forget it. It is a moment that doesn't last long because the groan of a man behind me reminds me of exactly what led us here.

I scramble to my feet and out of the cage, collapsing down beside Luca and pulling his head into my lap. There is so much blood covering his upper body that I can't find the source.

"Amore?"

"I- I can't find where you're bleeding." I whimper, pulling his t-shirt to rip it open. "I need to stop the bleeding."

"I love you, Bella."

"Stop. Stop talking. You need to... to lower your heart rate."

"Bella." Luca's hand lifts to my cheek, swiping away tears I don't know I am shedding. "Stop. Just for a second."

"I- I can't. I- I need to-"

"I'm not getting out of here, Amore. Please just talk to me. Stop stressing right now and listen to me."

"No." I scowl. "No, you are not dying in here, Luca. You're not. You're not allowed to." He smiles, trying to hide the way he winces when I finally find the wound on his shoulder and manage to apply the pressure needed.

"Amore."

"No, you listen to me, Luca Bottaro. You are not dying here. Not here out of everywhere and not until we're old and decrepit. You promised me an engagement ring and that you'd look after me. You promised me the house on the lake, and the ice cream, and your pasta, until we can't walk anymore.

You make me happy, and it's not fair that I just got through all of this for them to take you from me too. I am not losing someone else I love because of them."

"Aww, you love me?"

"Yes, you idiot, of course I fucking love you. I love you and I want to hear you teasing me for it for the rest of our lives." He lays his head back in my lap, the biggest smile splayed across his paling face.

"You love me too." I look around the room for something to help. Anything I can use to stop the bleeding and stabilise him. I manage to get his phone out of Luca's pocket, texting Enzo our code for needing help before tearing more of his filthy shirt. "I was going to marry you."

"You will. Stop being stupid. You're not dying."

"*Amore.*"

"I've told you you're not dying, and that's an order. You love it when I tell you what to do."

"It makes me hard." If he wasn't in such bad shape I'd laugh. "Like really, really hard."

"Are you hard right now?"

"A little."

"Good. Because if you do as you're told, I'll suck your dick to make it worth it." Luca groans, tipping his head back as his smile somehow grows bigger. "But you have to live because sucking a dead guy's dick is fucked."

"It'd bring me back. I'd come back to life. Kill me and make me live all at once. Maybe that's the secret to immortality. A blow job by the *legendary* Isabella Santoni." I tighten the wrapping above his wound, going as hard as I can until blood is no longer pouring out of his arm and into the puddle around us both. I don't know if I managed it in time. He's lost a lot of colour and he's gasping for air with every word he says.

I'm doing my best to not think about it. To not take note of how fast his heartbeat is against the palm of my hand, how weak he sounds, or how cold and sweaty he feels.

"I'm so proud of you, Bella. For everything. You always handle everything life throws at you and if I die, I know you'll be fine."

"But you're not dying."

"No. No. I'm not. But if I do. You'll be fine." He blinks slowly and I can see it starting to take over him, no matter how hard he fights it. "Whoever you end up with is going to be the luckiest guy."

"Don't... don't say that."

"The luckiest guy, and he'd better treat you right. He'd better bring you flowers, and your favourite French toast, and listen to you talk about your books, and he'd better know how special you are." Luca brings his hand back to my face. "Don't cry, Amore. Please don't cry. God, I hate seeing you cry." I blub, sucking my bottom lip in between my teeth. "It's okay. You're gonna be okay. You're going to be okay without me, Bella. Tutto va beni. *Tutto va beni.*"

Chapter Fifty - Seven

Goodbye.

ISABELLA

The flames dance in every single visible window, and I just sit there on the hood of the car watching intently as the air fills with smoke and the screams of all the men that touched me whilst I was held here.

Saying it was a rough fight is an understatement, really. When we came out and things had calmed a little, Carlos called Lorenzo and confirmed he'd cleared up his half of the job back in Alamea. Apparently there was a shit tonne of paperwork in a few of the places they checked, and there were a few captives that they'd released but other than that, everything had gone to plan and the Petrovich hold on the world had been completely extinguished.

Watching this house burn felt like vindication. Hearing the screams slowly die out as the flames got hotter made me feel lighter than air and I could almost float away.

We'd torn that place to shreds. Every crevice and cupboard had been torn down in the past twelve hours. I'd relived some of the worst moments of my life while wandering through the halls that were now coated in a fine sheen of blood and bullet holes and for the first time thinking about the past fourteen years of my life didn't hurt.

It doesn't hurt to think about, I don't feel haunted. I don't want to break down.

I feel kind of separate from it all.

As though me handling this myself, in deciding how those men met their fate, in knowing Tomas suffered, it's as though Anastasia is no longer haunting me. She's had her closure now. The ghost that has been holding me hostage has moved on to the bright light and this is her funeral.

It's apt that I'm wearing her family's blood in the same ways they wore mine. That the last thing they ever saw was me taking back the power they stole from me over and over again. I know she would be proud of that. I know that Anastasia was one of the best things that happened to me in the way she kept me safe and took that weight, but it's time she got to let go. Properly, this time. Instead of just shoving her in the closet.

The car bonnet creaks beside me as I am joined in my peace. Nothing is said. They just settle in beside me and watch as the flames begin to meet with the night sky.

"Isabella?" I blink, tipping my head to the two men standing in front of me with a beaten and tied up Rurik by their feet. He's barely recognisable after whatever Lorenzo has just finished putting him through. Dark red splatters cover the scraps of his white shirt that is hardly covering any part of him. Blood leaks from his series of injuries, but there isn't a single atom in me that feels any kind of sympathy. "Sorry, Lorenzo said to ask you what you wanted to do with him."

"Oh." I look at the man who was in charge of all of Anastasia's torment. "I haven't really thought about it, to be honest. I need some time to work out how he's going to pay for what he did. Can you get him back to Kredrith?" The two men nod, yanking Rurik up and dragging him across the pebbled drive. His bare feet quickly become damaged as they scrape the rocks but Rurik has given up entirely; not even showing the slightest sign of a struggle.

If things hadn't been so urgent with Feliks and Tomas, I'd have spent time planning their demise, like I intend on doing with Rurik. I'd have had them waiting and pondering if today was the day I end their misery, and I'd keep it going for as long as I could. I'd make them suffer and beg for me to end them and when they tried to kill themselves, I'd make sure they were fighting fit again before tormenting them further.

But I guess one out of three is better than none, and knowing the others are dead by my hands is good enough for me.

"Kredrith, huh?" Luca lays his head down on my shoulder. "No more Swallowbrook?"

"I don't know." I shrug and tip my head so it's on top of his. "Just feels like a bad omen. The only reason we were there is because of all this. And then we kind of lied to Safiyah and Farah and the guys. They don't need dragging into all of this. Probably best if we just drop them a letter and they never see us again."

"I'm sure they'll understand if we explain. You were in witness protection."

"Oh, is that what we're calling it? I was *abducted*."

"Abducted." Luca scoffs and sits up. "Amore, the only reason I abducted you is because you stabbed someone."

"He deserved it."

"I'm not saying he didn't. I'm just saying if anything is a bad omen, it's your fault."

"You're annoying. Go back to being dead now, please."

"Oh no, you're stuck with me." He beams, throwing his good arm over my shoulder and pulling me into him. "You would miss me too much anyway. I wasn't even going to die, and you were blubbering like a baby."

"Okay, you know what, you're only alive because I stopped the bleeding and he missed your head. I can always shoot you myself and finish the job. I've got a good aim, and I'm sure it won't take much anyway since you're weak as shit." Luca laughs, loud and hard and all I can do is close my eyes and soak it in. That's my favourite sound. Luca. Alive. Laughing. Nothing will ever top it.

For a minute there, I wasn't going to hear it again. Holding him there in the basement was going to be the last time Luca's voice pierced my ears, and the thought of doing anything without him by my side terrifies me.

He kept saying I'd be okay without him and maybe I would be, but I don't want to do it without him. I want him here with me, and I want everything he promised me. I don't want anyone else.

"I love you." I speak against him and wrap my arms around his waist. "Thank you for not dying."

"Pft. Like I was ever gonna let some other guy have you." He nuzzles his head into my hair. "I promised you no one else is going to touch you like I have, Amore. I don't break my promises." There's a loud crash in the building and I sigh, making him chuckle. "So, we need to find a house in Kredrith then? Or we could look for a lake town closer than Swallowbrook? Might be easier for seeing Pops and the girls and everyone."

"A lake town sounds good." Luca hums against me.

"What about the wedding?"

"What wedding?"

"Ours." I lift my head to look at Luca with a raised eyebrow. "Home or in Sicily?"

"You haven't even proposed yet."

"Am I supposed to just pull a ring out of thin air? I need time."

"You don't need a ring to propose, but whatever." I roll my eyes at him and turn my face back to the house as it begins to crumble. "My book boyfriends would have made one out of a blade of grass or some scrap paper."

"Oh, my go- okay fine. Isabella-" I laugh when a throat clears beside us and Luca's face grows instantly pissed off.

"Sorry to interrupt, but I've got Tori on the line and she's demanding to talk to you." Lorenzo holds the phone out at Luca who rolls his eyes. "He's rolling his eyes, Tor."

"Don- you're not supposed to tell her that!" He slides off the car, taking Lorenzo's phone and pulling it to his ear. "Menace! How's the sun- okay don't shout at me! I did not nearly die, he's being dramatic…. well yeah, but that's beside the point." Luca tips his head back on his shoulders and groans before walking away to take the call. I had no doubt Astoria was about to verbally murder him for almost dying.

There's a long silence when he leaves. A good few moments of Enzo just silently watching me as I watch the fire.

"So. You and Luca?" He finally speaks. "Want to tell me about that?" I press my lips together and turn my head to face him. I can't tell how he's feeling about it and it gives me no help at working out how to handle this. "Of all of my guys you could end up with it's him? He's fucking stupid." He points his thumb over his shoulder to where Luca is standing at the other end of the courtyard, holding the phone back from his ear as Tori screams at him.

"You're so harsh! He's not just some guy, it's Luca."

"Yeah, exactly, it's Luca." Lorenzo rolls his eyes. "I'm going to be supportive, but only because Tori threatened to hang me by my ankles in the shed if I wasn't, but you should know if he fucks up, I'll have his balls in a jar and his head mounted as a warning to anyone else who tries to touch you."

I roll my eyes at him and climb down off the car, walking into his arms for another crushing hug.

"How long has it been going on?" Lorenzo hesitates before hugging me back.

"Since New Year's, I guess?"

"New ye- NEW YEAR'S?! HE SAID A FEW WEEKS. LUCA! YOU'VE BEEN DATING MY SISTER FOR ALMOST FIVE MONTHS?! YOU'RE FUCKING DEAD."

Epilogue
LUCA

I have never been more glad that Bella and I decided against having kids, because if this is what we would be signing up for… I am more than good.

It is alright when it's just the three girls alone. I can hand them back when they are screaming uncontrollably, or they're fighting over a toy we bought them three identical copies of.

But a garden full of kids aged between one and eight is too much.

And one of the kids has a gluten and dairy allergy so we can't even have cake until later? I'm in one mind to sue Astoria for forcing me to come to this thing.

"Oh, you look so moody." Bella laughs, slumping down beside me on the long sofa overlooking the rest of the garden. "You know, if you keep your face like that I might have to edit someone else's over our wedding pictures, because you'll get stuck looking miserable forever. I reckon I can get them to put Tom Hiddleston over your face."

"Try it. I dare you." I throw my arm over my fiancée's shoulder, pulling her down against me. "I'm more handsome than Tom Hiddleston anyway."

"Mhm. Keep telling yourself that and I might believe you. At least you have a fighting chance when you don't look like someone told you that you've got to spend eternity married to me."

"Excuse me? Being married to you is going to be the best adventure of my entire life."

"Tell your face that." She prods her finger into the centre of my forehead. "What's got you so grumpy?"

"Tori won't let me have cake until all the stupid kids have gone." She laughs as I pout dramatically and cross my arms over my chest. "Not even a little bit."

"Aww, my poor baby." Bella snickers, running a hand through my hair. "Just wants his cake."

"You tease, but all these screaming kids are a punishment. She made me come because I'm making her wear a suit next week."

"I mean yeah, she could have worn a dress as best woman, Lu."

"Yeah, she could have, but where's the fun in that?" I smile at her and this time she shakes her head, knowing it is easier if she doesn't get involved with mine and Tori's teasing. It only means her being thrown over my shoulder and my attention being turned to her anyway.

"I have a ques-" Bella is cut off when Pops runs in front of us and trips over her feet, collapsing to the grass with a thud. I instantly start laughing, not even trying to hide it.

"Luca." Bella slaps me hard in the chest with the back of her hand and stands up, walking quickly over to our niece and helping her stand up, sorting out her dress and checking out the grass stains on her knees.

I'm so fucking lucky that this is how life panned out for me. A few years ago, I was being shipped out here because of a mistake. I was furious at everyone for dragging me away from Mia and my home, but now I can't imagine being anywhere else. Being right here beside Bella is exactly where I am supposed to be, and seeing that smile on her face every day makes everything worth it.

Pops scowls at me and runs off, clearly not learning her lesson about running around. Bella approaches slowly and holds a hand out at me, opening and closing it as a gesture for me to take it.

"What?"

"Wanna go hide in one of the guest bedroom bathrooms for a little bit? Lock all the doors we can?" I narrow my eyes at her, knowing exactly what she's hinting at but not wanting to make it easy. "Lu…"

"I don't know what you mean, Amore." She huffs and takes a few steps forwards. Bella's hands press into the back of the bench as she brings her mouth down to my ear. She exhales and I instantly harden for her.

"Please come upstairs with me. I want you to bend me over the counter and fuck me until my make-up is ruined and my legs are shaking." She presses a kiss below my ear and moans. "Then I want to get on my knees and suck your dick dry."

"Yep." I nod, standing up abruptly and wrapping my fingers between hers. "Mhm. We can definitely do that." She laughs but there's no chance I'm not doing that with her right now. Fuck it being at a party. I'll lock the doors; she can be quiet. It's fine.

I push the kitchen door open and realise my mistake instantly.

Of course I was being lured into this. I should have known better when she came over and was so adamant right after I'd teased Pops. God I hate that those two are besties now. It used to be me; you know?! I used to be the best. But no. Not now Bella's here.

I try to back up but Bella pushes me back into the house, closing the door behind us.

"Look Uncle Luca!" Pops holds up the plastic crab.

"I thought Ruby went missing?" I scowl and Pops steps closer. I knew I got rid of that fucking crab. I tucked it into my jeans when she wasn't looking and threw it out the car window going ninety down a country lane on the other side of town. There's no way she found it.

"He did, but mummy bought me another and then daddy got me more in case he went missing again!" She smiles and holds it up at me. "Auntie Bella said you don't like crabs."

"I don't." I grit my teeth.

"But this crab is okay, right?! And you'll come play tea party with me and Ruby and my other dolls."

"Uhh… but it's your birthday party, Pops. Don't you want-"

"Auntie Bella said you wanted to play." Pops instantly puts on her sad puppy dog eyes, pouting at me as hard as she can. I swear, the fact that her favourite animal became a crab is definitely no coincidence. I'd put money on Astoria and Lorenzo bribing her into it with a real life unicorn. "Do you not love me anymore?"

"What? No! Of cour–"

"So, you'll come play!" Pops grabs my hand and slams the toy crab into it. "You can play with Poopie and I'll play with Herb." I look up at the counter where Bella is sinking her fork into a slice of cake beside Tori. The two of them beam as they try to fight their laughs from breaking out.

This is so unfair.

HOW COME SHE GETS CAKE BUT I DON'T!?

Oh, you are so paying for this. I mouth the words to Bella as I'm pulled out of the room. The second Pops and I are out of view, I can hear them both break into laughter. I am sooo glad they both find this funny.

"OH!" Pops gasps. "I forgot to show you what Auntie Mia got me for my birthday! You were on holiday and I forgot!" Pops changes her direction, dragging me into the living room and right up to a –

"NOPE." I fight to pull my hand out of her vice-like grasp, but she's clinging on for dear life.

"This is Snappy and Squirt! Aren't they cute?!"

"Ha. Uh. No. Let me go, Pops."

"BUT LOOK AT THEIR CLAWS!"

Translation Glossary

<u>Russian</u>

Ptitsa – Little Bird

<u>Italian</u>

Amore – Love

Si – Yes

Troppo – Too much

Stai zitto e Baciami – Shut up and kiss me

Tutto va beni – Everything is fine

Dormi – Sleep

Non permetterò che ti facciano più male – I won't let them to hurt you anymore

Ti ho trovato – I found you

Ti troverò sempre – I will always find you

Non hu ancora finito con questa figa – I'm not done with this pussy yet

Coming Soon….

Santoni Book Three.

Name to be announced.

Prologue

The featherlight snow that had settled on my lashes begins to melt the very second I am safely back inside. I can't say I ever really minded winter, but this year has been a gross mixture of excessively heavy wind and ice-cold rain. This snowfall would likely not even settle and we'd all still be expected to head out into the world, as if it isn't unbearably horrible to get from A to B.

The good news is that tonight, I don't have to. I've run my errands, finished my shifts for the week and now, there's a bottle of wine, some left over trial bakes, and a Thai food take out menu with my name on it screaming for some of my cash while I wallow. That's what anniversaries like this are for.

This week has been long, busy and overwhelming. I want nothing more than to safely make it into my apartment without seeing a single other soul.

But it's like she can sense my presence.

That or she's somehow talked our landlord into having access to the security cameras and sits there watching and waiting for me to come home.

I hardly get the key in the door when Betsy pulls her door open, and I just know that my plans for tonight are about to be left deserted.

"Ah! You're home!" I close my eyes, giving myself all of two seconds before I turn around and force a calm smile onto my face.

"Hi Ms. Green." Betsy rolls her eyes at me.

"Girl, you've known me for six months. I see you more than I see my own children. I think it's time you stopped with the formalities." She shoots me a glare that dares me to continue, but she knows as well as I do that it simply isn't happening. We don't address it though. Instead, she moves the conversation on smoothly. "I need your help reaching that damn flour off the top shelf again."

Betsy turns back into her apartment, leaving the door wide open for me to follow her in, and I do. She's right in saying she sees me more than her own kids. They're both busy with their own lives, and Betsy hates calling them to help with anything. Marcus is the closest and even then, he still lives an hour away.

It's not that I mind helping her. We have a lot more in common than would appear on the surface. And that's beside the fact that we're both out here alone.

"I've told you, we can just move the things off those shelves to somewhere more accessible for you. You've got plenty of space to get one of those moveable cart shelf things, and it would be great for your baking bits. Plus, you wouldn't need to wait for me to get home to get your flour, and I'm guessing you're going to need the caster sugar while I'm in here?" I look over my shoulder as I climb up onto her worktop.

"Well, since you're up there." I can't help but chuckle at her, carefully ducking as I pull the dark stained wooden door open and grab what she needs from the cupboard. "How was your day at work? It looked busy when I passed earlier."

"It was hectic. Those new offices around the corner opened up and Eden went around to offer them a free cookie with any coffee to celebrate. Must have gone through five or six batches today." I sigh, finally putting my feet back on solid ground and dusting my hands off. "I did manage to run those testers through though. You were right. The lemon zest really worked with the white chocolate filling. Eden wants to get them in the unit on Monday."

"Of course I was right, dear. I always am." Betsy smiles, now sitting happily at her round dining table, her frail hands wrapped around a mug of tea.

"You were wrong about the tea not helping with your arthritis, though." I lean back slightly against the countertop as Betsy laughs, shaking her head.

"Yes, well, maybe I should give you more credit."

"Yes, you definitely should, which is why we're going to look into moving the things from these top shelves so it's easier. You're not going to get rid of the pain when you're constantly overextending yourself."

"Yeah, yeah. Enough of the lectures." Betsy laughs to herself. "Anyway, I'll let you go. I need to get ready. It's going to take longer to walk down to the library in this weather, and I don't want to fall and break a hip." Betsy stands up, trying her best to hide the aches I know she's not treating properly.

I'll wear her down eventually. I'm getting there. A little at a time. The rosehip tea was a fight as it was, so seeing her drinking it without me forcing it into her fills me with more pride than I think it probably should.

"You're walking to the library?"

"Well, unfortunately, my wings are at the dry cleaner so flying isn't an option this week." She laughs like it's a joke. "Go on now, I'm sure your TV is desperate to be running that rubbish you call a show."

"It's not rubbish, it's entertainment." I follow closely behind Betsy as she heads to her doorway, pulling on her thick winter boots with a huff. "It's really icy outside Betsy, can't one of the girls pick you up? You've mentioned … is it, Harriet? Her son brings her in, right?"

"Harriet is in the Bahamas sipping on piña coladas brought to her by her new boy toy. No one else passes this way. It's only a short walk. I'll be fine. Now go on. Get." Betsy tugs at her coat, pulling a bright red knitted beanie over her head.

I can't let her walk herself down there. She'll fall in this weather and then what? I'll forever know I had the chance to make sure this didn't happen and I just let her go out there.

"Give me two minutes to put these in my fridge and I'll walk you down."

"Oh, no, you don't need to."

"No, it's fine. I don't really have anything going on tonight anyway. I'm sure the Thai restaurant will still deliver tomorrow." I offer her a tight smile before heading out of her place and to my own, where I put the snacks into the fridge and get back to her before she can manage to lock her apartment up.

I can't say I've ever really asked Betsy much about what these weekly meetings are for. She talks about them a lot. The women she met there that have become friends, the food table that apparently can be very hit and miss but recently one of the girls has been bringing some cookies that are almost as good as mine.

That's what Betsy says anyway.

What I can say is that walking into the library, I'm not met with a book club like I was expecting, nor is it a knitting club or… I don't know. I don't know what I was expecting Betsy to be doing on her Friday evenings. But I certainly didn't think she'd be coming down here every week for group grief counselling.

I'm stuck looking around a room filled with small groups chatting and laughing and smiling and for a second, I think the sign on the door is wrong. That they haven't taken it down from another meeting yesterday or earlier today, because these do not look like grieving people.

These look like happy and content people that don't feel like their heart is being ripped out of their chest with every passing second.

They look like they've spent their entire lives floating on a cloud, whereas I'm stuck underneath it soaked to my bones in tears that never seem to stop the hurting.

"Oh, since you're here, I want to introduce you to the girl who bakes those cookies I keep telling you about." Betsy unbuttons her snow covered coat and proceeds to scan the room like a robot. "Mia!"

Out of nowhere, a stunning brunette appears in my vision with a beaming smile.

Golden brown eyes, perfectly hand curled hair, with just the right amount of make-up to seem put together but not showing off. The brightest aura surrounds her, and I can't work it out. She's too bright.

"Hey Betsy, what horrific weather, right? Did you get down here okay, I could have dropped by and got-"

"Yeah, we got here fine! Mia, this is the girl I was telling you about." I look between them both, suddenly realising I walked myself right into her bear trap. God, she's so fucking sly… "Laura! Right on time. I need to talk to you about –" Betsy doesn't even finish her sentence, just grabs a woman passing by at the top of her arm and walks off. Leaving me alone with the stranger.

"She's such a character, right?" Mia starts, smiling and pointing her thumb in Betsy's general direction. "I bet living opposite her is a whole thing."

"Oh, like you wouldn't believe." The woman Betsy left with stands at the front of the group, announcing they're going to get started if everyone could take a seat and I sigh. "I… uh… I should probably go."

"What's your name?" I look back at Mia and clearly my face confirms that I'm not sure if I can answer that or not, because she just softens her smile slightly and watches me with slightly more intense eyes. As though she's trying to work me out and I don't like that. I don't like having her look too closely.

"Hana."

"Well, Hana," she sighs, "I know it looks dumb as fuck, but... look you're here anyway. Might as well give it a shot. It might help."

"Oh. No. I haven't-"

"I know that look in your eye." She states. "No one has that look in their eye if they haven't already lost too many people to count." Mia's smile fades quickly before she regains control and it's back to soft and calming. "Come on, we'll sit in the back, and I can tell you all the gossip about everyone, I promise you won't even realise it's not just us two having a good bitch for an hour. And as a bonus, you get a friend out of it. Whatcha say?"

Mia stares at me like a kid waiting to hear if they can have their favourite meal for dinner. The rest of the group are seated and talking amongst themselves but they're clearly waiting for us and I nod in agreement, hating the thought of having everyone in here waiting for me.

Mia's smile expands before she turns and heads to the back row, sinking herself down into one of the two plastic chairs that are still empty. My chair creaks as I settle down into it and my chest tightens despite me taking off my coat.

"Okay, so that's Laura. She runs the group. Lost her husband in a plane crash. That was five years ago. But if you ask me, he faked his death and has been hiding in Canada since, with a new identity and a new life. I mean, she's clearly milking how depressed she is though, because she's sleeping with Mark, Ben and Christopher, and that's just the three from this group."

"Oh my god, do they know? About each other?"

"No." Mia snickers. "They're best friends too."

Mia goes on to tell me every bit of gossip about the group and honestly, she was right. It doesn't feel like I'm in a group therapy session, and for the first time in years, I am reminded how it feels to have a friend.

God how I've missed this.

Survival by Summer Paige.

Santoni Series book two

Copyright © 2025

All rights reserved. No part of this book may be copied, reproduced or distributed without prior written confirmation directly from the author; Summer Paige. Unauthorised sales, production, sales or distribution is illegal.

It is not authorised to use any part of this book to create, feed or refine AI models, for any purpose, without prior written confirmations from the author; Summer Paige. The uploading of this book without said permission is theft of the author's intellectual property and the correct actions will be taken against perpetrators.

All characters, scenarios, settings and events featured in this book a purely fictional and a product of the author's own imagination. Any resemblance to real persons, alive or deceased, actual events or locations are purely coincidental.

Independently published June 2025

1st edition

Cover designed by Millie Speakman

Edited by Claire Hill and Summer Paige

Printed in Great Britain
by Amazon

669e13ce-c551-4878-84a5-4a4766b4bc5cR01